Yesterday

Books by Fern Michaels

Books by Fern Michaels (Continued)

Hokus Pokus
Hide and Seek
Free Fall
Lethal Justice
Sweet Revenge
The Jury
Vendetta
Payback
Weekend Warriors

Captive Passions
Captive Secrets
Captive Splendors
Cinders to Satin
For All Their Lives
Texas Heat
Texas Rich
Texas Fury
Texas Sunrise

The Men of the Sisterhood Novels:

Hot Shot
Truth or Dare
High Stakes
Fast and Loose
Double Down

The Godmothers Series:

Far and Away
Classified
Breaking News
Deadline
Late Edition
Exclusive
The Scoop

E-Book Exclusives:

Desperate Measures
Seasons of Her Life
To Have and To Hold
Serendipity
Captive Innocence
Captive Embraces

Anthologies:

Home Sweet Home
A Snowy Little Christmas
Coming Home for Christmas
A Season to Celebrate
Mistletoe Magic
Winter Wishes
The Most Wonderful Time
When the Snow Falls
Secret Santa
A Winter Wonderland
I'll Be Home for Christmas
Making Spirits Bright
Holiday Magic
Snow Angels
Silver Bells
Comfort and Joy
Sugar and Spice
Let it Snow
A Gift of Joy
Five Golden Rings
Deck the Halls
Jingle All the Way

FERN
MICHAELS

Yesterday

KENSINGTON
PUBLISHING CORP.

www.kensingtonbooks.com

KENSINGTON BOOKS are published by

Kensington Publishing Corp.
119 West 40th Street
New York, NY 10018

All Kensington titles, imprints, and distributed lines are available at special quantity discounts for bulk purchases for sales promotion, premiums, fund-raising, educational, or institutional use.

This book is a work of fiction. Names, characters, businesses, organizations, places, events, and incidents either are the product of the author's imagination or are used fictitiously. Any resemblance to actual persons, living or dead, events, or locales is entirely coincidental.

To the extent that the image or images on the cover of this book depict a person or persons, such person or persons are merely models, and are not intended to portray any character or characters featured in the book.

Special book excerpts or customized printings can also be created to fit specific needs. For details, write or phone the office of the Kensington Sales Manager: Kensington Publishing Corp., 119 West 40th Street, New York, NY 10018. Attn. Sales Department. Phone: 1-800-221-2647.

The K logo is a trademark of Kensington Publishing Corp.

ISBN-13: 978-1-4201-2309-8 (ebook)
ISBN-10: 1-4201-2309-2 (ebook)

ISBN-13: 978-1-4967-3447-1
ISBN-10: 1-4967-3447-5
First Kensington Trade Paperback Printing: August 2021

10 9 8 7 6 5 4 3 2 1

Printed in the United States of America

Dear Readers,

I'd like to start this letter by saying that I hope you like *Yesterday.* Many years ago, I saw a television interview with the famous movie star Natalie Wood. The interviewer asked her a question that stayed with me all those years until the day I sat down to write this book. "You're rich, you're famous, you're beautiful, you're married to a rich, famous man, and you have beautiful children," the interviewer said. "What more could you possibly want?" Natalie Wood responded, "I want yesterday."

I started to think about my own yesterdays and the yesterdays of many of my friends. I thought, What a wonderful idea for a book. But it wasn't enough just to think about yesterday. I needed to know what happened to yesterday, so I centered my story around a house—a house I almost bought, in South Carolina. It was a big plantation, but so in need of repair that I backed away from it; it was more than I could handle at the time. Like Natalie Wood's interview, the picture of that house stayed with me for years. It still wasn't enough for a book—until I created a family of children and the wonderful Mama Pearl who tends to them. *Yesterday* is the story of four children who grow to adulthood and who have never forgotten their childhood or that wonderful plantation house and Mama Pearl. It's the story of one particular homecoming for Brie, Callie, Sela, Bode, and Mama Pearl—and what that special homecoming means to each of them.

I hope you all enjoy reading Yesterday as much as I enjoyed writing it.

Fern Michaels

Prologue

The night was dark, warm and secretive, Brie Canfield thought as she opened the casement windows. She took great, heaving gulps of the honeysuckle-scented air, but it didn't help to alleviate the terrible nightmare she'd just experienced.

Behind her, the air conditioner whirred and wheezed, a sign the filter needed to be changed. The room was dark, too, because she hadn't changed the lightbulb. She hadn't done the dishes either or her laundry. For weeks. Maybe it was months. She simply could not remember.

Brie strained to see something in the darkness, something that would reassure her that things were right, normal—and that life was going to be the way it was before. Cars passed, like ghostly blue shadows. Why did they look like that? She should know. Maybe it was important. She swayed, and her grip on the windowsill tightened so that her knuckles snapped and crackled.

Maybe she needed to eat something—something more substantial than broth and a slice of bread. But the cupboard was bare, the refrigerator empty.

She panicked then. That meant she would have to get

dressed and go out to the store. She also had to keep her appointment with the department psychiatrist. Maybe she could do both things on the same day. She took in more deep breaths.

She started to cry, knowing full well that tears wouldn't help. Unless . . . She backed away from the open window and sat down on her bed.

Unless . . . she gave in and called Bode Jessup. Bode would know what to say to her to make things right. She should have called him sooner. Why hadn't she? *Because I love him, and he doesn't love me, that's why. Because he loves Callie Parker, one of my oldest and dearest friends.*

She tried to pep-talk herself, but it wasn't going to work because her stomach was tied in knots, and she was sweating profusely, even though the thermostat said it was only sixty-two degrees in the apartment. She began to weep again because there was nothing else for her to do. She couldn't call now—Bode would hear the tears in her voice. So, what was wrong with his knowing she was upset? Why else would she call him in the middle of the night? Although he might think she had called to talk about Callie Parker's wedding . . . to someone other than himself. So, who cared about that either?

Brie's hand stretched out. She didn't need to look up Bode's home phone number, even though she carried it on a slip of paper in her wallet. It was the first name in her address book under the A's. She didn't want his name in the middle of the book. Callie's number was right under Bode's, and so was Sela's. Her three best friends in the whole entire world. And she hadn't called any of them.

Brie snatched her hand back from the phone, howling her despair. Then the phone was suddenly back in her hand. She punched out the area code, followed by Bode's number. While the phone rang, she blew her nose. Five, six, seven rings . . .

She was about to hang up when she heard Bode's voice say: "This better be good, whoever you are, because it's three o'clock in the morning."

"Bode, it's Brie," she said, her voice hoarse with all the crying she'd done.

"Brie Canfield, the Brie who's supposed to be my best friend in all the world, the same Brie who says she'll call and write, but doesn't. That Brie?"

"Bode . . ."

His voice was alert now, all trace of sleep and mockery gone. "What's wrong, Brie?"

"Bode . . ." She was whimpering and hated herself for it.

"We've established the fact that I'm Bode, and I'm here on the other end of the phone. Do you want to hang up and call me back, Brie?"

"Bode . . . I . . . Bode, I killed someone. I'm having a real hard time with it."

"*Whoa* . . . don't spring a hit on me like that. Start at the beginning—the very beginning, Brie. We'll talk. It'll be like old times. Two heads are better than one. Come on now, share. I'm listening."

"It wasn't just someone. It was a boy. He was sixteen. He had a gun, and he was going to shoot my partner. I told him to put down his gun, but he didn't. I don't know who was more scared—me or him. We both fired. He . . . missed. I didn't."

"And you decided that you're going to take the rap for this, right? Were there any witnesses?"

"Stop talking to me like the lawyer you are and talk to me like my friend. We are still friends, aren't we? Of course there were witnesses. The Board cleared me. There was a real big stink about it from the boy's parents and friends. They want to transfer me to another precinct. I have to see a shrink once a week, and I do, but I can't get a handle on it. I can't sleep, and I can't eat. All I do is cry. Do you think I'm having a nervous breakdown? I'm afraid to ask the shrink. That's the shape I'm in."

"No, you are not having a nervous breakdown. Trust me, Brie. What you need is a good dose of Mama Pearl. You're coming home for the wedding, right?"

"Oh, God. Probably not."

"You mean yes, you are. I'll pick you up at the airport. Did they give you a leave of absence? What do you mean, you can't eat or sleep?"

"Just what I said. Don't pep-talk me, Bode."

"Do you want me to come out there and bring you back, Brie?"

God, yes, she did, but she'd never admit it. "No, of course not. Bode, I took a life. Kids shouldn't have guns. You should have heard this boy's mother. The kid was a saint, an altar boy, tops in his class, a loving son. The truth is the kid was a gang member, so high on crack his brain should have exploded. He didn't go to school, probably never saw the inside of a church, and beat his mother, who worked two jobs to support herself and five other kids. I killed him. Me."

"And the alternative? You said he would have killed your partner."

"Shot him in the back. He's got twenty years in. He was handcuffing another kid and didn't see what was going down. We had two witnesses who saw the whole thing. How can I make this right, Bode? You always had the answers. I need an answer now."

"You just *thought* I had the answers. You always did give me too much credit. You go on, Brie, because life goes on. You have to put it behind you. That's a goddamn order, Brie."

"You aren't God, you know." Brie hiccupped.

"When did this take place?"

"Six weeks ago tomorrow."

"And you're just calling me NOW! Are you telling me you tried to ride this out by yourself? Did you call Callie or Sela?"

"No. Just you, Bode."

"I bet you're the best cop San Diego has," Bode said.

"One of the guys brought over my gun and shield yesterday. They told me to take as much time off as I want. I said I'd let them know. By the way, I've been accepted into the FBI Academy."

"Then there's nothing to stop you from getting on a plane and heading for South Carolina. Congratulations! Are you on disability or what?"

"Nope. Full pay. It's not the money, Bode."

"You know what they say, kiddo—the past is prologue. Now, are you going to pack up and do what you have to do to get here?"

"I need some time . . ."

"You had enough time. Why didn't you call Mama Pearl?"

"Because hearing her voice would have done me in. I didn't want to cry again. I wanted to work it out by myself."

"Is the shrink helping?"

Brie laughed ruefully. "We're up to the part where you're teaching us our numbers under the angel oak. It's very hard, Bode."

"Life is hard, Brie."

"Are you referring to—"

"Life. Don't try putting words in my mouth. Now, can I call Callie and Mama Pearl and tell them you'll be coming to South Carolina?"

"Yes, but I don't know when. Thanks for listening, Bode."

"You should have called me on day one."

"On day one I didn't even know my own name," she said.

"See? You should have called me, and I would have told you. Sleep well, Brie. Today is a whole new day, and it's going to be whatever you make of it."

Brie looked at the pinging receiver in her hand. A smile tugged at the corners of her mouth as she curled up in the big double bed. Now she knew she would sleep. Bode always made things right.

In Summerville, South Carolina, Bode Jessup pulled on his jeans and sneakers. A hooded sweatshirt was next. A headache hammered behind his eyes as he wheeled his bike out of the apartment and into the alley. He climbed on, switched on his night-light, and pedaled away. He had a lot of thinking to do.

1

Brie Canfield removed her dark glasses at the same time as she turned off the engine of her rental car. She sat for a moment savoring this time, this place, her mind a crazy quilt of emotions. She climbed from the car, aware of her thin legs when her skirt hiked up to mid-thigh. She tugged at the elbow-length sleeves, trying to cover her equally skinny arms. She wondered if she looked as bad as she thought she did. How would the others view her? Would they comment on her appearance, or would they pretend she looked healthy and robust? Had Bode called them? Had he alerted them to her arrival? Were they even expecting her today? Hardly, since she hadn't called anyone to tell them what time she was getting in.

Perspiration beaded on her forehead and dripped down her cheeks. She'd forgotten how hot and humid it was in South Carolina in August. It felt good, the warmth seeping into her bones. She hadn't forgotten how beautiful Parker Manor was, though. A feeling of peace settled over her as she walked up to the split-rail fence that defined the perimeters of the Parker place. She could see now that the wood was old and rotted, the paint peeling. When she was younger she'd helped Bode whitewash it every summer.

Overhead, the sun beat down on her head and back. In the distance the main house beckoned her. She looked at it now with adult eyes. It wasn't just beautiful, it was magnificent. Despite the flaking paint, the soaring white columns stood sentinel to another time. The old brick, softened over the years to a warm, petal pink, brought tears to her eyes. She swallowed, a lump in her throat, as she stared at the banks of flowers in bloom, the emerald grass, greener than any jewel, where she'd romped and played as a child.

Yesterday.

Yesterday was gone, tomorrow wasn't here yet. All she had was today. Today and a lifetime of memories. Bode, Callie, Sela and, of course, Pearl, were such a part of her life it felt like they were all attached by some invisible umbilical cord.

Brie dug her feet into the sandy earth as she propped her elbows on the rotted fence. This was home—maybe not in the legal sense of the word, but it was the only place where she had felt she truly belonged. And all because of Pearl and her childhood friends. She sank down on the turf and closed her eyes. When she opened them again she was a child, driving up the long brick-lined drive surrounded by the glorious angel oaks she was staring at now, twenty-five years later.

"Will I like coming here to play, Mama?" Brie had asked fearfully.

"You'd better like it, as I'm not coming to fetch you till six-thirty. Now, remember, if they ask you to stay for supper, you say yes, it's okay for you to eat with them."

"What if you forget to come and pick me up? Will I have to sleep here, too?" Brie whimpered.

"If they ask you to sleep over, you can say yes. When Mr. Parker came into the cafe to ask if you could come out here to play with Miss Callie, he said there would be times when you would eat with Miss Callie and maybe sleep over. You mind your manners, missy, and don't be giving them any problems. You can get out now and walk up to the house."

"By myself?"

"You're five years old, Brie. Act like it," her mother said. "I have to get back to work."

Brie slid from the car. She poked her head in the open window, and cried, "What if they don't like me, Mama? If they don't like me, should I come out here to the fence and wait for you?"

Mrs. Canfield worked her face into something that resembled a smile and a frown. "It's up to you to make them like you. I don't have the money to pay someone to watch you during the summer, Brie. You'll have to stay by yourself at the apartment, the way you did this last year. You need to be responsible. You went to kindergarten. You were supposed to learn how to get along with other kids. You did, didn't you?" She sounded like she didn't care one way or the other.

"Yes, Mama."

"Go along now, I have to get back to the café."

"Good-bye, Mama." She stretched her head as far into the car as she could, hoping her mother would give her a kiss or a pat on the head, but she didn't. Brie backed away until her little body was pressed against the fence. Tears streamed down her cheeks. She wiped at them with the sleeve of her dress. She just wanted to cry and cry until she fell asleep in the bright sunshine with the umbrella of trees that dripped Spanish moss.

She looked down the drive then, at the big white house with its stately columns. It hurt her eyes to stare at it, pretty as it was. It was Callie Parker's home. She must be a princess, Brie decided. And her father, the king, asked Brie's mother if she could come here and play. She wondered if Callie Parker, the princess, had a magic wand that she waved around. Maybe she wasn't a plain princess, but a fairy princess. Miss Roland read stories about fairy princesses in school. Or maybe Callie Parker was like Cinderella.

Brie started to weep again as she allowed herself to crumple to the ground alongside the fence. What was she going to do if the princess didn't like her, or want to play with her? "I'm going to stay right here and wait for my mama to come and get me," she said defiantly. Eventually she dozed off, the sun warming her trembling body. She didn't wake until she felt herself being picked up and cradled in strong arms.

"Chile, are you all right? How did you get here? Who are you?"

"My name is Briana Canfield. My mama brought me here to play with Miss Callie. Is she a princess? Are you her mama? My mama said I had to make you like me so I could stay. I don't know how to play with a princess. I was waiting for my mama to come back for me. How long is it till six-thirty?"

"Lord, chile, that's a *long* time. That's suppertime here at Parker Manor. We don't have any princesses here or even a prince. We have a little girl and a little boy. My name is Pearl and I take care of things here. I'm going to take care of you, too."

"Truly you will?" Brie said, her eyes round with awe.

"Truly I will," Pearl declared, hugging her so tight Brie found herself gasping, but she didn't loosen the hold she had on Pearl's neck.

"Does that mean you will love me? What do you want me to do, Miss Pearl? I can fold towels and dry the dishes. I know how to make my bed, and I carry the trash outside to the can."

She got a second hug, this one even better than the first. "It feels good when you do that," she whispered.

"Doesn't your mother hug you, chile?" Pearl asked in surprise, as she rocked the small body in her arms.

"Hardly ever. She's too busy making a living and going to town with people she says are my uncles. I don't think I have any uncles. Miss Roland at school said I didn't have any uncles. Am I too heavy for you, Miss Pearl?"

"Honey, you're lighter than a feather. You look tuckered out, so I have a mind to carry you all the way up this long drive, around the back, and into the house where you can have breakfast with Bode and Miss Callie. That's if you haven't eaten yet. Have you?"

"No, Miss Pearl. Mama gave me a donut. She had to drive me here and then go to work. She didn't have time to make me breakfast," Brie said as she tried to mash herself closer to the large black woman holding her. She felt so good, so snug and secure, and the kisses Pearl was giving her felt better than anything she'd ever experienced in her young life.

The closer they got to the main house, the wider Brie's eyes became. "Is this a palace, Miss Pearl? It looks like a picture in my storybooks."

"It's just a house, chile. It looks big because it's white, and the sun shines on it. I think you're going to like coming here to play."

"Will the children like me?" Brie asked, her face puckered in worry.

"Of course. Another little girl is coming out today, too. Mr. Parker made the arrangements. I thought you were both coming together. If I had known you'd be here this early and alone, I would have walked out to meet you. It's not nice to leave guests alone at the gates."

"I don't mind, Miss Pearl. Did my mama make a mistake? I can tell her if she did."

"No, chile. I'm the one who's at fault. I guess I didn't understand Mr. Parker's instructions. It looks like we have a welcoming committee." Pearl set Brie down on her feet.

Brie hung on to Pearl's skirt, her face flushed, as she stared at the two children on the back porch. She felt tears well in her eyes at the sight of Callie Parker in her pink, ruffled dress with the matching hair ribbon. Her gold hair hung in ringlets about her ears, but it was the heart-shaped locket around her neck that drew Brie's eye. She *had* to be a princess: only princesses wore gold around their necks. With five-year-old wisdom, she knew she was dressed all wrong. Her frock was old and faded, her shoes scuffed and unpolished, her socks a grayish color. She didn't have a hair ribbon in her own dark hair; she didn't even have a barrette. Her hair was pulled back with a rubber band. Brie wanted to cry again until she felt Pearl's hand in her own. The woman gave it a reassuring squeeze.

"Miss Callie, Bode, this is Briana Canfield. I think she likes to be called Brie. Her mother brought her out here to play with you. There's going to be another little girl coming at lunchtime. I want you all to be friends, but first I'm going to make breakfast. You can all sit here on the back swing and get acquainted. Briana, this is Callie Parker and Bode Jessup."

Brie's eyes followed Pearl as she walked through the kitchen door. The urge to cry again was so strong she pinched herself. This hurt so bad her eyes started to smart. She blinked hard and fast so the children wouldn't think she was crying. "I like Miss Pearl. A lot," she said.

"You should like her a lot," the boy named Bode said. "She's the nicest person in the world."

"I love her," Callie said. "Loving is better than liking, isn't it, Bode?"

Bode pondered the question. Because he was seven years

old, Callie thought he knew everything. He always tried to come up with a response that made sense. He knew he could fib to Callie and she wouldn't know the difference because she was only four and believed everything she was told, but he didn't like to lie. "Today Brie likes her," he said. "Tomorrow she can love her like we do. Today is the first day. Will you love her tomorrow, Brie?"

"Oh yes. Maybe by tonight even."

"Push us, Bode," Callie said. "Hold my hand, Brie. Then you move your legs in and out when Bode pushes us. He hops on after we get going good."

Brie did as instructed, squealing with delight.

"Bode pushes better than Pearl. He does everything the best. I love Bode. Do you love Bode, Brie? Pearl says everyone loves Bode. If Pearl says it, then it's true words," four-year-old Callie said importantly. "Do you love him?"

"Yes," Brie mumbled as she worked her legs under the swing to pick up momentum.

"Tell Brie about your name, Bode. She needs to know that. Pearl said we have to 'splain things."

Bode walked around to the front of the swing. He grinned at Brie. "You spell my name B-o-w-d-e-y Jessup. But," he said, holding up his hand, "you pronounce it Bo-dee and you spell it B-o-d-e. My teacher figured it out for me. Mama Pearl said it was right, so it's right. Mama Pearl never tells a lie. Never!" he repeated solemnly.

"You have to love Pearl, too, but you can't love her as much as we do," Callie piped up. "We were here first, and Pearl loves us first, too. That means she loves us more—isn't that right, Bode?"

"No, that's not right. Don't you be saying things like that to hurt Brie's feelings. Pearl has lots and lots of love."

"She loves me most, she truly does. You came after me,

Bode, and now Brie is here. She has to love me more. Pe-e-e-arll!" she wailed.

The housekeeper was out on the porch in the time it took Brie to take a breath. "What's wrong, honey?"

Bode shuffled his feet and Brie hung her head. Pearl repeated the question, her voice stern once she was satisfied that Callie was all right and hadn't fallen off the swing.

Hands on hips, head tilted to the side, Pearl said, "I'm waiting to see what that caterwauling was all about. Some chile on this porch better speak to me quick."

"You love me best—that's true words, right, Pearl? I love you best, then I love Bode, and then I love Brie. Tell them the true words, Pearl."

Brie stared at her new friend and saw how anxious the little girl was. Instinct told her it was very important for her new friend to be loved best. She looked at Bode, saw his miserable eyes. He wanted to be loved best, too—she could tell. So did she. She remembered how wonderful it had felt when Pearl picked her up and cuddled her. Childishly, she crossed her fingers and said under her breath: "*Let her pick me. Just for today. Please let it be me.*"

Pearl's hands moved. Bode hopped on the swing, his eyes glued to Pearl as he waited.

"Love is a wonderful thing," the housekeeper told them gently. "It's not something to fun with or talk about in a mean way. God says we should all love one another. There's different kinds of love, but you children are too young to be knowing about that. I love each of you, not one more than the other. My heart is near to bursting knowing you all love old Pearl. Now, come to Pearl so she can give you each a kiss and a hug before she serves you your breakfast."

Callie scrambled off the swing first to run to Pearl. She wrapped her arms around the woman's heavy thighs, blubbering, "I love you the mostest, Pearl. Bushels and bushels."

Bode was on his feet, his arms around Pearl's waist. Brie heard him whisper, "It's okay to love her the best, Mama Pearl."

Brie held back, uncertain if she belonged in the tight little circle. Tears burned her eyes. She wanted to be there, wanted the kiss and the hug, wanted the warmth and the smile from the housekeeper. The moment she saw her hold out her arms she moved like lightning. The kiss and hug were everything, almost better than Christmas morning. She grinned at Bode who poked her lightly in the arm.

So loved . . .

Brie sighed mightily. She should get back in the car and drive up the road between the arc of angel oaks. Memories hurt too much. Better not to call them up—but then, how did one do that?

She shielded her eyes from the bright sun as she stared around at the place she loved more than anything on earth. In so many ways it was home. A home she hadn't visited in years and years. *And why is that, Brie Canfield?*

Because, she said, answering herself, *I couldn't bear to see Bode, and I couldn't fool myself any longer about the fact that Pearl loved Callie and Bode best.* She dropped to her haunches alongside a thick row of daisies that Pearl had planted. Daisies were Brie's favorite flower because you could play "he loves me, he loves me not" with the petals.

So many memories, so many years. Another time, another life. And now she was back for Callie's wedding. Not to Bode Jessup but to Wynfield Archer. She picked a daisy, started to pluck the petals—"he loves me, he loves me not" . . . and wiped at a tear sliding down her cheek. Then she saw him. The same old Bode, riding his bike. He was wearing jeans and an open-necked white shirt and on his feet were scuffed,

$10.98 high-top Keds sneakers. He was an attorney now in Summerville. Family law, Callie had written in one of her letters. She'd gone on to say that the Judge, meaning Judge Avery Summers, had said Bode was the best lawyer to come out of the state of South Carolina. Brie had been so pleased to hear that—but then she'd always known Bode would be successful. Bode was a kind, generous, compassionate man. If he wasn't all those things, she wouldn't love him. God, it still hurt.

He saw her then, his face lighting in a smile that was so warm it rivaled the sun. "I see it, but I don't believe it," he said, sliding off the bike and leaning it against the fence. "I called you a hundred times, Brie, but you didn't return a single one of them."

"I know. I didn't want to . . . impose." She was mangling the daisy in her hand.

"*Impose?* You wake me up in the middle of the night to talk, and I oblige. You promise to call—you don't. I goddamn worried about you, Brie! That was a damn selfish thing you did."

"I'm sorry, Bode. I needed to talk that night, that's all. I had to get a grip on things on my own. It was something I had to do alone."

Bode squatted down and picked a daisy. "And did you?"

"I'm here, aren't I?"

"You look like a skeleton," Bode snapped.

Brie smiled wryly. "I just put on five pounds."

"Jesus. Well, Mama Pearl will have you ten pounds heavier by this time tomorrow—count on it. I forgive you," Bode said, putting his arm around her shoulder.

"Who asked you to forgive me?" She bridled. "Stuff it, Bode."

"Testy, aren't we?" He grinned.

Brie didn't rise to the bait. When Bode made her smile, that meant things were all right between them—and things *weren't* all right.

"What are you doing here at this time of the day?" she asked. "Why aren't you out there doing whatever it is you legal types do? Did Callie and Sela get here yet?"

"I have court this afternoon. I'm on my way to the store now because Mama Pearl wanted me to pick up a few things for her. I try to get out here at least three times a week. To answer your other question, Sela is due sometime today and Callie is driving down from Columbia this evening. You didn't tell them, did you?"

"No. Does that mean you did?"

"No. They're your friends. I thought women tended to cluster up and talk things to death when one of them was in difficulty."

"That just goes to show you don't know diddly about women."

Bode shrugged. "Are you okay—that's all I want to know."

Brie stared at her childhood friend who had taken his place in the world, ever so successfully. He wasn't handsome, and he wasn't ugly; he was somewhere in between, with dark eyes, curly black hair and skin so blemish-free she wanted to swat him. He had dimples that he hated, a cleft in his chin that she adored, and a rangy body that rivaled Clint Eastwood in his younger days. His smile was special. It was like Pearl's: it welcomed and warmed you at the same time; and when he held out his hand to take yours, you knew you were one of the chosen few he allowed inside his private world. *And he loved someone else.*

"I'm okay," she said slowly. "If I wasn't, I wouldn't be here. Yes, I've lost too much weight, but I was getting a little thick in all the wrong places. It's going back on slowly. I can't truthfully say I'm the old me yet, but I am okay. You can stop worrying, Bode."

"What happened to us, Brie?"

She wanted to say: "You jerk, you know damn well what happened! I threw myself at you at my graduation, and what did you do? You told me 'thanks, but no thanks.' Things were different. We weren't kids anymore. I suppose it was the moment, graduating and being scared of going out into the world. When you showed up at my graduation, I mistakenly thought that you and I . . ." Brie struggled to her feet, a handful of daisies in her clenched fist. She opened it and let the blooms fall to the ground.

"Brie . . ."

"What?" she snapped, her eyes beginning to water. Without waiting for an answer, she trudged down the road, leaving her car at the gates and Bode staring after her. This was like that first time, a lifetime ago. It seemed to her, through her tear-filled gaze, that the oaks swayed, their branches bending to create a haven, an umbrella, to shield her from all her troubles. When she was almost to the end of the tunnel the oaks created, her feet started to move faster, as if they had a will of their own.

"*Pe-e-e-arll!*" she wailed, the sound carrying across the acreage. When she saw her, she dropped to her knees, her arms stretched out in front of her. Within seconds, Pearl had her in her arms, was stroking her hair, raining kisses over her face.

"Sweet chile, tell Pearl what's wrong."

"Oh Pearl, it's so good to see you. Just hug me for a minute. You smell so good. You feel even better, just the way I remember," Brie mumbled, closing her eyes. She could have drifted off to sleep, that's how safe and secure she felt.

"Now, now, Miz Brie, old Pearl's here. I'm not going anywhere." To prove her point, big as she was, Pearl gracefully lowered herself to the ground from her kneeling position, without loosening her hold on the young woman in her capacious lap. She crooned old lullabies from the past, Brie singing along with her in a whisper.

A while later, Pearl raised her eyes to see Bode standing at the end of the tunnel. She knew he had been there for as long as she'd been sitting on the ground. Her head dipped slightly. Bode turned around. She watched until he was out of sight. Tears burned the old woman's eyes. Only the Lord knew how much she loved that boy and this girl in her arms, although Bode was a man now and this feather-light bundle a woman. To Pearl they would always be children—*her* children, because no one else had the time to give them the love they needed and deserved.

Brie stirred. "Oh Pearl, I fell asleep. I'm sorry. How long have we been sitting here in the middle of the path? It's so good to be back. I never know how much I miss you and this place until I come back."

"Now, you tell me what's wrong. We aren't moving from this spot until Pearl knows why you look like you do. You tell me and don't leave out even one word."

Safe in Pearl's arms, Brie bared her soul. "I'm okay now," she finished. "Talking to Bode about it helped a lot. I should have come back here sooner, but I wanted to work it out on my own. I nearly called you so many times, Pearl, but I knew I'd cry and that would set me back so I . . . I have it under control now. I've made decisions, I've followed through, and my life is going to take another course. In a way, I'll still be in law enforcement. I guess none of this makes sense to you, but that's okay. No man is an island . . . that kind of thing. God, I am so glad to be here! I've missed you, Pearl. There are no words to tell you how much. And Bode, he made it right. How *does* he do that, Pearl?"

"My boy, he just knows how to do that. He's a fine man, Miz Brie."

"Yes he is, Pearl. He's so caring and unselfish. I don't know many people like that. Well, maybe one other person."

"And who might that be?" Pearl bridled.

"You, Pearl. Bode is like he is because of you. If I searched my soul from now till the end of time, I couldn't give you a better answer. All of us—Callie, Sela, me, Bode—are what and who we are because of you. Did I ever thank you, Pearl, for all you did for me over the years?"

"Every single day, Miz Brie. It was easy because I love you all so much my heart wants to burst sometimes. Don't you be thinking you can slack off now because you're all growed up, mind. Pearl won't stand for that."

Brie chuckled. "Come on, Pearl, I'm going to walk us *home.*" God, how wonderful that one little word sounded.

When Brie was on her feet, Pearl's large hands cupped her face. "You listen to me now. What you did, you did because you didn't have any other choice. Lots and lots of times I make mistakes that bother my soul. I pray to my Maker and explain things and He lifts the burden off my shoulders because He knows my soul is pure. He knows you did what you had to do. He's not punishing you, Miz Brie, you're punishing yourself. You can't be doing that anymore. You have to get on with your life and trust the Lord knew what He was doing when He took that boy into His arms. He did, you know. He's probably an angel now, watching us and listening to us talk. The Lord acts in mysterious ways. The preacher says that most every day."

"I didn't know you made mistakes, Pearl," Brie teased.

"One or two that was important. Maybe a few others that aren't too important. The Lord didn't strike me dead so I guess He's working on making my mistakes right. Leastways, I hope He is. We're done with our serious talking now, Miz

Brie. I'm going to make you some griddle cakes and you're going to pick some flowers for the kitchen table. Don't be picking them so short I can't put them in the milk bottle."

"Do you want me to pick some for you to put on Lazarus's grave?"

"I done that this morning, early."

"Are you ever sorry you didn't marry Lazarus, Pearl?" ' 'You're minding my business now, Miz Brie."

"I'm sorry, Pearl. You're right, it's none of my business."

"That's what I said," Pearl snapped. "You run along now and pick those flowers."

"Yes, ma'am," Brie said, moving off to the left where the garden was in full bloom.

Brie looked around at the wild array of flowers, all planted by Pearl. She knew a handful wouldn't be missed if she picked them, yet still she hated to break off the stems. Maybe she'd pick just one flower and make the bouquet full of green leaves and grasses. She smiled, remembering the old glass milk bottle with the narrow neck; as children they'd all picked huge bouquets and then watched while Pearl tried to fit them into the bottle. In the end she'd groused and grumbled and stuck them in an old lard can she stored under the sink right next to the jar where Bode kept his money.

Brie whirled around. "Thank You, God—for Pearl, for Bode, for Callie and Sela. Thank You for this place, thank You for *everything*. I swear to You, I'll always try to be as good as Pearl and Bode because I know they're two of Your favorite people. I'm going to go back to church again, too. I don't know when that will be, exactly, but You know I never break a promise." She ended her little talk with the Lord the way Pearl had taught her. "This is Brie Canfield at Parker Manor." She skipped her way back to the house, a single white daisy and a clump of greenery in her hand.

Home.

Brie watched Pearl as she worked at the kitchen sink. "I think I'll go up to the gate and wait for Sela, unless you have something you want me to do? I always loved it when you came up the tunnel, as we called it, to greet us. I'll take your place and greet Sela. I miss her. I bet you do, too."

Ever the diplomat, Pearl said, "I surely do, just the way I missed you, Miz Brie, and my own baby chile. Miz Callie would come down once a month from Columbia, but she called me most every day. It's right, you young people have to live your lives. This house belongs to another time. You run along now, and I'll have some breakfast waiting for Miz Sela when you bring her down."

As she made her way down the dappled tunnel, the moss on the ground was springy under Brie's sneaker-clad feet. She stopped for a moment and bounced on it. Then she laughed and started to run, zigzagging to the left then to the right the way she'd done thousands of times when she was a child. When she came to her car and the split-rail fence, she was breathless, and there was a smile on her face as she dropped to the ground, her back against a gnarled oak.

Brie lost all sense of time as she roll-called her memories. Arms locked around her knees, she only looked up when she heard a car slow down and come to a halt next to her own rental car.

"Brie! What are you doing sitting up here?" Sela called as she fought with the door to get to her friend. "God, it's good to see you. Let me look at you! Uh-oh—what have we here? You're way too thin, and are those bags I see beneath your eyes? Yes, they are. Well, I have just the thing for those in my cosmetic case. And why are you sitting up here all by yourself? Is something wrong? Where's the mistress of the manor?"

Brie was on her feet in a second and in Sela's arms.

"One question at a time." She giggled. "I came up here to wait for you. I got here earlier. Yes, I'm too thin, and thanks for the offer of the cosmetics. The mistress of the manor is due this evening. She's driving down from Columbia and should get here around nine or ten, or so Pearl said. Bode was here earlier. Pearl's in the kitchen where she always is. In fact, she sent me out to pick some flowers, and she's making breakfast for us. God, it's good to see you, Sela. You look great, but then you always do. And beautiful."

"Beautiful my ass." Sela grinned. "I was the plain one, remember? I was also the wild one, the mouthy one, the one who was always in some kind of trouble. I was the first one to have sex, too. But I shared all my knowledge! And no, I don't regret anything. I've learned not to look back. Yesterday is gone, Brie."

"Yeah, I know. Sad, huh?"

Sela lit a cigarette and offered one to Brie. They leaned against the split-rail fence and smoked, each trying to outdo the other with perfect smoke rings. "I wanted to come back more often, I really did," Sela confessed. "You have no idea how much I miss Pearl. All those memories . . . sometimes I can't handle it. When I did come it was so bittersweet it took me weeks to get back into the swing of my life. When you grow up and move on with your life you're supposed to be able to leave your childhood and the memories behind, but I've never been able to do that. It hurts too much. It even hurts to stay in touch, to call and write. Everything stirs up. Guess I'm all messed up—how about you, Brie?"

"I pretty much feel the same way. Just out of curiosity, how many pounds of makeup are you wearing?"

Sela didn't take offense at the question. Sela rarely took offense at any remark when it came from one of her friends. "A pound and a half. Takes me a long time till I'm ready to go out into the world." She sighed dreamily. "You know, Brie, I think this is one of the prettiest places on earth. I haven't been around the world, and I don't care if I never do—I just *know* there is no place like this. Damn, now my eyes are all watery and my makeup is going to smear . . ."

Brie saw her friend turn away as though in slow motion, and knew she was doing the same thing she'd done herself, when she'd gotten here earlier. Sela was remembering yesterday . . .

"What if they don't like me, Mom? What if they don't want to play with me? Will you come and get me?"

"I'll come and get you at six o'clock."

"I'm hungry, Mom. You didn't give me lunch."

"That's because you were invited for lunch. Walk down that road to the house."

"I'm afraid."

"Get out of the car, Sela. I told Mr. Parker you'd come out here to play with his daughter. That other girl is here, too. You behave yourself, or I'll lock you in the closet. You mind me now! You need to be more like your mama, Sela. You must learn how to have fun and how to laugh. Someday you might be pretty like me, but I think you're going to look like that no-account daddy of yours."

"Am I ugly, Mom?"

"You aren't ugly, honey; you just aren't pretty. When you grow up and put on lipstick and rouge, you will be. Do you want to look like me when you grow up?"

Sela stuck her thumb in her mouth and she shook her head. Tears dripped down her cheeks.

"Ungrateful little snot. Go on now and mind your manners. Mr. Parker leaves me good tips, so don't make things bad for me. You hear me, Sela? Stand up straight, girl, stop slouching. And pull up your goddamned socks."

Sela took her thumb out of her mouth long enough to say, "They won't stay up because they're dirty. Three days dirty

just like my underwear." Whatever her mother responded was lost in the sound of the car's engine. Sela's thumb went back into her mouth as she trudged down the mossy road to the house. Through her tears she could see a giant of a woman advancing on her. She froze, ready to flee, when she saw two girls and a boy run ahead of the giant. Suddenly she was in the giant's arms, and she was being kissed. She wasn't afraid anymore when the woman holding her carried her into the kitchen that smelled like Christmas day. Later, she was being led down the hall to the bathroom, the other little girl alongside her.

"This is how we do things here," the giant said comfortably. "First you take a bath and have your hair washed. That's so you won't smell like cigarette smoke and . . . other things. Then Pearl is going to dress you up in clean clothes and wash your other clothes. Then you're going to have lunch and play all afternoon. You can stay to supper if your mamas say it's all right. Now, let's scrub-a-dub-dub."

Sela hung her head as she slipped down into the soapy water that was so warm and sweet-smelling she never wanted to get out. The other little girl, Brie was her name, was hanging her head, too. She knew she was ashamed as she was.

"Lordy, Lordy, you children smell prettier than the gardenias by the verandah. *Hmmmm!*" Pearl sang out as she nuzzled each little girl behind the ears. "My own special flowers. Now, we'll just fluff up those curls and then you can sit down and eat Pearl's special chicken pie. And if you're real good, there will be a chocolate ice-cream cone for dessert."

Her heart in her eyes, Sela held out her plate the moment she finished. Even at the age of four and a half she knew she wasn't holding it out for the ice-cream cone; she was holding it out so Pearl would smile, kiss her, and say something nice. One of Pearl's warm smiles was better than a cold ice-cream

cone. Lots better. She did her best to remember the last time her mother had hugged her and kissed her. When she couldn't remember, she looked up at the motherly woman, and asked, "Is it all right to love you?"

"Chile, this old woman would be pleased to have you love her. I love all of you," she said, pointing one fat finger at each of the children. "In this house we're a family. Don't you be forgetting that."

Sela tossed her cigarette in the general direction of the road, and turned to Brie. "My mom was drunk, that first day when she brought me out here to the Parker place. Jesus, I was scared out of my dirty panties. Pearl washed them—do you remember how she used to do that every day? My socks were curled down around the heels of my shoes. Brie, how could my mother not notice that I was cleaner when she picked me up than when she dropped me off? I guess she was drunk all the time," she said, answering herself.

"I think Pearl was the only one who ever washed my hair. I loved the way I smelled after she got done with us. I killed a kid, Sela."

Sela blinked. She fumbled in her pocket for another cigarette she didn't want. It explained the troubled eyes, Brie's thinness. All she could think of to say was, "Why didn't you call me? I would have packed up and gone to California. I don't know what good I would have been, but I would have tried to comfort you. I know you, Brie, you went through it alone, didn't you? Oh, damn you, Brie—why? You don't have to prove anything to anybody. I'm not even going to ask for details. I know you did what you had to do. I also know you were cleared. Am I right?"

Brie nodded. "At the time it seemed . . . I was outside of it for a while. Yes, I was cleared. I wanted to call. God, you

have no idea how bad I wanted to call, but you all had your own problems. I did call Bode one night. His threat to come and get me was all I needed. Don't take it personally, Sela. It was something I had to work through on my own. I'm okay, I really am. I'll never forget it as long as I live, but I *can* live with it. I told Pearl when I got here. Telling Pearl something is like getting instant absolution. You know what I'm talking about."

"Do I ever. C'mere," Sela said, opening her arms to her friend.

"You aren't half as good as Pearl, but you sure smell nice." Brie giggled. "Sela, do you ever . . . what's the word I'm looking for here? Do you ever *marvel* at the fact that our friendship has withstood the test of time? Twenty-five . . . or is it twenty-six years? That's a quarter of a century. Is it because we shared so many yesterdays? Was it Pearl, or Callie and Bode? Was it because we were white trash and all the kids called us that so we couldn't deny it? Callie certainly thought so. Said it in a lot of little ways without actually coming out with the words."

"All of the above," Sela said softly. "Things like that stick forever. I bet you right now, this very minute, if you and I walked down Main Street there would be someone who would remember us, and say, 'There go those two girls—what's their names?—oh yes, Sela and Brie. *White trash.*' Then they'd cluck their tongues and shake their heads."

"I'd never take that bet," Brie vowed. "Bode rose above it. They don't say those sorts of things about him."

"They might not say anything, but they sure as hell think it—and you damn well know it. Oh, who gives a good rat's ass." Sela grinned.

"Now, that's the Sela I know and love. Hey, look!"

Sela turned to stare in the direction Brie was pointing,

down the long mossy drive under the oaks. A quarter of the way up she could see a large figure trundling slowly along. *"Pearl!"* she screamed. Her spike-heeled shoes flew in two different directions; her cigarette and purse were also discarded in haste. Brie watched as Sela's dress hiked up to mid-thigh as she ran to meet Pearl.

"Welcome home, Sela," the old housekeeper said, her eyes misty with tears.

2

It was like a thousand other mornings, this special breakfast time in Pearl's kitchen. The daisy and assorted greenery Brie had picked earlier stood in the old milk bottle in the center of the table. For just a moment Brie felt overwhelmed by the warm, fragrant kitchen. Her eyes, full of adoration, traveled across to where Pearl was standing. If Pearl walked out the door, the square yellow-and-white room ceased to be anything but a room containing old, outdated appliances and shabby cabinets. When Pearl was in the kitchen, the plants seemed greener, healthier, the pots and pans glistened more, and one no longer saw the cracked, peeling paint. Everything Pearl touched took on a life of its own.

Pearl's kitchen.

"Is Bode coming back for breakfast, Pearl?" Brie asked, sitting down across from Sela. She continued her scrutiny of the kitchen. The room of uncountable memories—the room where tears had been shed and solutions found to hundreds of childhood problems. A happy room of good smells and wonderful food. Pearl's kitchen, with the green plants and herbs on the windowsill. Pearl's rocking chair, Pearl's knitting, Pearl's scent. Pearl.

"Yes'm. Now, you sit there while I fix you breakfast like I used to. My boy will be chewing on the doorknob when he gets here. That boy does have an appetite. A good strong wind would blow you over, Miz Brie. You too, Miz Sela."

"I'm in your hands, Pearl. You have four days to fatten me up. I was under the weather for a while."

"I saved all your postcards, chile. I have them in my room. Does California really smell like orange blossoms?"

"Sometimes when you're downwind. It's heavenly."

"I like lemon verbena myself," Pearl said smartly as she prepared bowls and frying pans. She turned. "And what do you have to say for yourself, Mr. Bode Jessup?" She surrendered herself to Bode's embrace the moment he walked through the door.

"I say I got here just in time. Your good food, and friends to share breakfast with. We are friends, aren't we, girls?"

As children, the response to this ritual question had always been: "Forever and ever!" He was waiting, not with bated breath, but waiting nonetheless. Brie worked a smile onto her face for Pearl's benefit. "If you say so, Bode," she responded. She was aware of the strange look on Pearl's face and the pink flush that warmed Bode's neck. Sela remained quiet, her eyes puzzled.

"Flapjacks, scrambled eggs, and waffles," Pearl announced, bustling over, "with my special syrup. And just because you're here, Miz Brie, I'll melt the butter."

"What about me, Mama Pearl?" Bode asked lightly.

"Yeah, Pearl, what about him?" Brie asked tightly, but she relaxed immediately. This wasn't going to get her anywhere. If there was one thing she'd learned, it was to leave the past behind. Baggage was not something she carried these days. "I'll share," she offered.

"Now that sounds like the old Brie," the housekeeper said.

Old Brie, young Brie, new Brie—what did it matter? "Tell

me, Pearl, how are the wedding plans going? Is everything taken care of? Callie must be delirious. How about you, Bode? Is the game plan still the same, that Callie is going to work with you after her honeymoon? Now I find that *very* interesting."

"Everything is just fine. Miz Callie will be home tonight. Her wedding dress is hanging in her room if you want to sneak a peek at it. All the presents are at Mr. Wyn's house in Beaufort," Pearl muttered as she expertly flipped a flapjack.

"As kids you found everything interesting. It didn't matter what it was, that was your standard comment," Bode said coolly.

"That was because you made me feel stupid, and I didn't know what else to say," Brie explained. He hadn't answered her question about Callie's job, and she wondered why.

"Miz Sela asked me to fix cornpone and black-eyed peas. I said I would."

"Ooohhh, I love that." Brie smiled. "I can feel the weight going on just thinking about it. What's for dinner, Pearl?"

"Ham, hickory-smoked, did it myself in the spring. New peas, those little ones you girls always said looked like emeralds, sweet potatoes, my special coleslaw, homemade bread with blackberry jam. I just made the jam two days ago for y'all. Pecan pie with homemade ice cream. Bode churned it last night."

"Are you going to put all that sticky good stuff on the ham?"

Pearl turned to open the oven door. "It's baking right now."

"Will you be here, Bode?" Brie asked nonchalantly.

"No. Tonight's my night to work late. I'll get a burger someplace," he said wistfully, his eyes on the ham in the oven.

Breakfast was pleasant enough, Brie thought as she wolfed down the massive meal Pearl set in front of her. She offered to do the dishes, but Sela said she'd help Pearl, so she opted to walk Bode out to the gates.

"I see something in your eyes that puzzles me, Bode. Something's going on. You're about to make some kind of decision, aren't you?" Brie asked.

"You watch too many movies, Detective Canfield. I'm glad you're okay, Brie. A day didn't go by that I didn't worry about you. I tried calling you, hundreds of times. I want to make sure you know that. I'll see you around. How long are you staying?"

"A few days. Thanks for worrying. We can't get it back, can we? I'm talking about that wonderful time in our lives when we were kids. So often I want yesterday. Is that wrong, Bode?"

"You can't live in the past, Brie. It's what's ahead that's important—today and tomorrow. Life. Memories are what they are, and are best left alone until there's nothing else to occupy our minds. That's my advice for the day."

"I'm sorry about Callie, Bode. I know—"

"You *think* you know. It was great seeing you again, Brie. I really miss all of you. Whatever else you may believe, believe this: you're part of my life, and I don't want to see it fade away until we only communicate with Christmas cards."

Brie whooped in horror. "Who is it that never calls, never writes and only shows up when there's a crisis of some kind?"

"The fact that I show up is proof enough that I care."

"Like my graduation?"

"Yes. My advice to you now is go take a nap—you look like you could stand some rest. If you don't like that idea, pick some flowers for Mama Pearl and walk around the grounds. Get a feel for it all over again."

"Yes, sir," Brie said, ripping off a smart salute.

Bode's shoulders shook with laughter as he pedaled out to

the main road, but the moment he was out of sight of Parker land he sobered.

Forty-five minutes later Bode Jessup was back in his storefront law office on Main Street. He wheeled his bike through the back door and parked it in a storage room. It was his one treasure left over from childhood, and he wouldn't part with it for a pot of gold. Satisfied that his treasure was secure, he headed to a tiny, sparkling washroom, where he washed his face and brushed his hair. He yanked at his string tie—his concession to a real tie—and pulled it over his head. He shed his jeans and stepped into a pair of khaki-colored twill trousers. The Keds stayed on his feet. A new business day.

Bode Jessup's office was normally neat, everything in its place. Today, because of his work yesterday and into the night, it was cluttered with boxes and barrels. He was packing up shop and moving on. He hadn't lied when he said he had to go to court later in the day. He had one last motion to plead, and until then he'd be here to supervise the labeling and transfer of the boxes and barrels to UPS. He could feel his shoulders start to slump when he sat down in his chair, a gift from Judge Avery Summers when he opened his family law practice. It was worn in now. UPS had promised an oversize packing crate so it could be shipped with his other things.

Bode sat down and closed his eyes. He heard his sixty-year-old secretary, to whom he paid only a pittance, set down a cup of coffee on his desk. She always knew just the right spot to place it. His eyes still closed, he reached for the brew. It wasn't half as good as Mama Pearl's, but he needed it.

Jesus, how had he gotten to this place in time where he was giving up everything he loved and cared about? He could feel his body start to tremble as he sipped at the coffee. He had to get himself together, or he was going to blow everything. His head felt like a home for nesting bumblebees, buzzing with fierce intensity. He was leaving the only mother he'd ever known, leaving Callie to another man, and running out on Brie and Sela, the people he loved as much as he loved life. Did that mean he was a coward? He didn't know anymore.

He wished now he'd had the guts to tell Callie weeks ago that he was quitting, that they weren't going to work together when she returned from her honeymoon. Callie an attorney . . . it still boggled his mind when he thought about it. Brie was a detective these days, and a damn good one, according to her. A smile tugged at the corners of his mouth. Brie was special . . . Another time, another place . . .

It was the summer Brie turned six and Bode himself turned nine, when a catastrophe of sorts happened that set the tone for their relationship in the years to follow.

It was a bright, sunshiny day without a cloud in the sky when Sela and Brie arrived with Mrs. Canfield, who all but pushed the girls from the car in her hurry to get back to town. Brie dawdled, her sandal-shod feet digging in the sandy ground. Holding hands with Callie, Bode had run to the gate to meet them. Callie tugged at Brie's arm as Bode stood to the side listening to Sela. As young as he was, he could see that both Brie and Sela needed a bath and to have their hair brushed. They were both wearing the same dresses they'd worn the day before and the day before that. Breakfast was ready—golden scrambled eggs, extra crisp bacon, and a mountain of toast spread with butter and jam. Pearl rang the breakfast bell. As one, the children looked in the direction of the back porch, then at Bode, who dropped to a crouch so Brie could get on his back. He counted to three, and they all galloped toward the house. Pearl was mixing Hershey's chocolate into big glasses of milk when the children sat down at the table and unfolded their napkins.

"It's not 'portant," Callie pouted.

"Is so," Sela insisted.

"It makes you special," Bode said.

Brie cried quiet tears as she munched on her toast.

"Tonight when you go to sleep the Tooth Fairy will leave you a present. She left me one when my front teeth fell out," Bode lied with a straight face.

"Will she leave me one, too?" Callie demanded.

"Probably so," Bode said, "but not till your teeth fall out."

"My mama said I look ugly with no teeth and all the freckles on my face. Mamas don't lie. I don't want to be ugly; I want to be pretty like my mama," Brie said.

"You are pretty. Look at us, we don't have freckles so that makes you special. Isn't that true, Mama Pearl?" Bode turned to her for help.

Pearl's eyes rolled back in her head as she slapped the dishrag against the hot frying pan. "That's right, Miz Brie. The Lord gave you freckles so's other people can see them. They match your curls. That makes it real special. When your new teeth come in they're going to look like *real* pearls. You listen to me now and don't you be crying."

"Yes'm," Brie said, choking off her tears.

"You finish up now and scamper into that bathroom and turn on the water. Bode, you carry the dishes to the sink. Miz Callie, you fetch me two dresses and some hair ribbons. Don't forget to bring the underwear, too." The children separated and met later on the back porch.

There Bode set up shop and outlined the day's agenda. "Today is going to be Brie's day. We're going to do whatever she wants. Tomorrow is Callie's day and the next day is Sela's day. It's fair," he said sternly.

"Am I really special, Bode?" Brie asked.

"Yes. First we're all going out to the angel oak and sit down. We're going to take turns counting your freckles. You have to sit still and hold your face like this." He demonstrated a stretched-out look. "No laughing."

"Will we win a prize?" Sela asked. She had all the prizes she'd won in a paper sack in her dresser drawer.

"Nope. Brie gets the prize because she has the freckles."

"I wish I had freckles," Callie said wistfully.

"Me, too," Sela said.

Brie preened as Bode started to count.

When the freckle-counting came to an end, Brie threw her arms around Bode and said, "I love you, Bode."

"I love you, too," Callie said.

"I do, too," Sela chimed in. "Do you love us even if we're girls?"

"Yeah," Bode said gruffly.

"We're sisters," Callie said happily. "What are you, Bode?"

"He's our brother. Isn't that right, Bode?" Brie demanded.

"It's pretend. You need to know the difference," Bode said.

"Is that the same as belonging together? I want to belong," Sela said stubbornly, tears sparkling in her eyes.

Callie jumped up, and shouted, "Bode is mine—I saw him first. He lives here. He's mine! He belongs to me." Sela and Brie started to cry. Bode flapped his arms in dismay.

"A long time ago people owned people. They don't do that anymore. I can't belong to you, Callie—it's the law. We go together, but nobody owns anybody else. The only way you can belong to someone is to your mama and your papa. Maybe when I get married I will belong to someone. I have to ask the preacher. I don't want to be telling you wrong," he said solemnly.

"Will you marry us?" Brie demanded.

Out of his depth, Bode said, "Sure."

"Oh boy, oh boy, oh boy," Brie chortled. "We're getting married. When?"

When? "When we get old and go to college and make something out of ourselves."

Brie started to cry again. "What if Pearl says we can't get married? What will we do? We have to mind Pearl, or she won't love us."

Bode thought about his response. Finally, he said, "I don't know what we'll do. We'll get smart when we go to college and maybe we can do it then."

Callie hated to be put off. "What if we can't? Will you marry some other girl?"

"I don't know, Callie," Bode said fretfully.

"You can lie and say you don't want to," Sela said.

"It's a sin to tell a lie," Brie said.

"I don't want to think about it today," Bode said. "We said we're going to do whatever Brie wants to do. We promised, and you aren't supposed to break a promise."

"Let's go cat fishing. Whoever catches the biggest fish gets a prize."

"What's the prize, Bode?" Sela asked, her eyes shining with happiness.

"If I tell you it won't be a surprise. Get the fishing poles and I'll meet you by the pond." Now he had to come up with two prizes, one to put under Brie's pillow and one for whoever caught the biggest catfish. His shoulders slumped with the weight of his dilemma.

Bode hopped from one foot to the other, his face a mask of misery. He was waiting for Pearl to finish picking up the picnic basket. "Mama Pearl, I think maybe I told a lie. I told the girls I would marry them. They pester me. I don't know what to say to them. Is it a bad lie?"

"Not for now. When you start to grow it will be a bad lie. You can't marry three girls. You get that notion right out of your head, Bowdey Jessup. Someday when you is growed like a man, you're going to meet a girl who will love you like Pearl does. She'll give you fine children that you will love and squeeze, but it can't be them girls down at the pond. You hear me now, Bode?"

"I hear you, Mama Pearl."

Bode finished the coffee, his eyes damp with his memories. Seeing Brie yesterday and again this morning had been such a shock. She looked so fragile, so vulnerable. Her tart tongue, her "tell-it-like-it-is" persona was still the same, though. Coming back here for Callie's wedding would heal her, even everything out for her. It wasn't that Bode was a mind reader, it was just that he'd been so close to all of them, that he knew instinctively when things were right and when they were wrong. It was almost as though all four were extensions of one another.

They were grown now, living hundreds of miles apart, but it didn't matter. They stayed in touch with letters and phone calls, but he only called and wrote on birthdays and Christmases. He didn't know which he hated more, writing letters or talking on the phone. He did his best to avoid both whenever he could.

Bode wished for yesterday the way he always did when his memories took him back to his childhood. So many years ago. He could remember the day Clemson Parker had come to fetch him from the preacher's house to take him to Parker Manor. It was still as fresh in his mind as though it were yesterday.

Yesterday. . . .

"Do you have everything, Bowdey?"

"Yes, sir. This is all I have," the six-year-old said, pointing to the paper sack at his feet.

"Pearl will take care of that. We'll get you some new

clothes and some shoes and maybe a pair of sneakers. Would you like that?"

"Yes, sir, I would. Who's Pearl?"

Clemson Parker dropped to his knees. "Pearl is a wonderful woman who is going to love you so much you will be smiling all day long. My little girl will be your sister. I want you always to be kind to her and to love and respect Pearl. Do you think you can promise me to do that?"

"Yes, sir, I can make that promise to you. I'll never break it either," Bode said solemnly.

"I believe you, Bode. I guess you're wondering why I'm taking you away from here. A friend of mine, Judge Avery Summers, told me the Reverend had too many mouths to feed. The Judge and I, we decided to see if we could find good homes for you and three of the other children to help out the Reverend. I'm going to adopt you, Bode. Later I'll explain what that means. For now I don't want you to worry about anything. I'm going to give you a good life where you'll be loved and happy. You'll have your own bedroom, your own things, good clothes, and good food. We'll be a family. Family is the most important thing in the world, Bode. I don't ever want you to forget that."

"I won't, sir."

The man got to his feet, and with a hand that was as big as a ham hock, he tousled Bode's hair. It felt good, wonderful really. What felt even better was when Clemson Parker shook his hand and called him young man. "I don't want you to be scared, now. You just be yourself and grow up to be a fine, upstanding young man Pearl and I will be proud of."

Bode wanted to ask about Mrs. Parker, the little girl's mother, but stopped himself. It didn't sound like Pearl was the mother, just someone who maybe was a pretend mother.

The little girl who was his new sister and who he was supposed to be kind to was sitting on the porch when Clemson

Parker ushered him up the back steps. A big black woman with a thick braid in her hair was standing in the doorway, her arms outstretched. Bode knew instinctively that he was supposed to walk into those comforting arms. "Are you Mama Pearl?" he whispered.

"Yes, chile, I am," Pearl said, hugging him. She tousled his dark curls the way Clemson Parker had done, but when Pearl did it, it was so soothing he wanted to close his eyes and drift off to sleep. "Did you have any lunch, Bode?" she asked, never loosening her hold on the boy.

"No, ma'am."

"Well then, you just climb up on that swing with Miz Callie and wait for me to fix you something. Miz Callie, mind your manners and say hello to this young man. His name is Bowdey Jessup. Your papa is going to adopt him, so then his new name will be Bowdey Jessup Parker. He will be your brother. Your papa said he's going to bring some children from town to play with you both. In a while. I don't know when that will be. Soon, I expect."

Bode sat down on the swing. He hopped off almost immediately when he remembered Mr. Parker saying he was supposed to be kind to Callie.

"I can push you if you want me to," he offered.

"Yes, push me, Bode. You can stop when Pearl brings your lunch. I like to swing, don't you?"

"Sure," Bode said, and Callie smiled up at him. He saw the golden curls, the smile, the pretty hair ribbon and ruffled dress. Her shoes were black and shiny, and her socks were so white they looked like snow. It wasn't going to be hard to be kind to this little girl. He was never, ever, going to break that promise to Mr. Parker.

"Where did Mr. Parker go?"

"Up to see Mama. My mama doesn't come downstairs. She stays in her room and takes medicine. I see her every afternoon. That's why I have on this dress and hair ribbon. After I see her I change my clothes and shoes. I can play with you then. We can have a tea party. Pearl will give us cookies and soda pop."

Bode groaned. "If I have a tea party with you, will you help me catch some frogs? We can have a contest if we catch some. You know, to see whose frog can jump the best. We can have a prize for the winner."

"Oh, my goodness. What will be the prize?" Callie cried excitedly. "I don't have prizes for tea parties."

Bode stopped pushing the swing. "Then why do you have a tea party?"

"For the cookies and soda pop. What's the prize?"

"It's a secret. I'll make it. I like to make things. Maybe we can have the cookies and soda pop at our frog contest."

"Should I bring my tea set?"

Bode remembered his promise. "Okay."

Pearl stepped onto the back porch, a tray in her hand that she carried over to a child's table and chairs in the corner of the porch. Bode watched as she spread a white napkin on the little table and removed the plate that held a thick ham sandwich onto another napkin. There was also an apple and a slice of peach pie and a huge glass of milk. He never had this much food at the preacher's house. He'd never been *really* hungry, but he always left the table wanting more. He understood, though, that the preacher had many mouths to feed, and the food had to be portioned out so everyone got some. Orphans had to be content with what the Lord provided. The preacher's words were always kind, but it didn't help the rumbling in his stomach.

"While you eat your lunch, Bode, Callie is going upstairs to see her mama. She can play when she comes down."

"Thank you, ma'am," Bode said, sitting down on the child's chair, only to find that his legs were too long to fit under the table. He felt agonizingly self-conscious, felt his neck grow red. In a second Pearl had the food transferred to the tray again and was on her way to the kitchen, where she placed everything on the big table just the way she'd done at the little table. "You sit here, Bode." Her smile warmed him all over. And that warm, wonderful, loving smile stayed with him until it was time to leave Parker Manor and go away to school.

Yesterday. Family. Bode's chair thumped to the floor. He blinked, coming back to reality. He was leaving his family, leaving yesterday behind. He could do it now with a clear conscience. He'd kept his promise to Clemson Parker. Callie was getting married and didn't need him anymore. Mama Pearl was going to live with Callie in Beaufort with Callie's new husband, Wynfield Archer.

Bode eyed the boxes and barrels again, and then he looked at the stack of labels on his desk. UPS had said they'd be here at noon to pick up his belongings and crate the chair.

"More coffee, Bode?" the grandmotherly secretary asked, poking her head in the door.

"One more cup and that's it for the day. I have to write out these labels."

"I already did them, Bode. The labels on your desk are extras in case you have some last-minute things you want to ship. I have some cartons in the outer office. You still haven't told anyone, have you?"

"No. I don't know why I'm being such a coward about it. I did tell the Judge. He's going to give Callie a job for a year or until he retires—whichever comes first. I'm going to miss you, Mavis."

"It's just as well. It's time for me to retire, too. I want to work in my garden and spend time with my grandchildren. Family is very important to me. People tend to lose sight of that in their quest to make money and be successful. I hope you're doing the right thing, Bode. I'm going to worry about you just the way I did when I taught you in the third grade."

"You shouldn't have worried," Bode said softly.

"I had to, Bode. You carried the weight of the world on your little shoulders. I knew way back then that you would be successful someday. Whoever would have thought that I would be working for you! I'll never forget the day I walked into this ramshackle office and you took one look at me, and said, 'You're hired, Mrs. Mason.' You didn't care that I'm crippled up with arthritis and that it takes me twice as long to do the things a young person could do in half the time. You also pay me too much money."

"Watch it or I'll take it all back," Bode threatened with a smile. "I can never repay you for all the extra time you gave me back in the old days, all those evenings you spent tutoring me, asking for nothing in return except that I give it my best. I really am going to miss you, Mavis. I want you to keep all the plants and the furniture. Sell it, if you like. And please, promise to write to me. I'll answer, but not quickly. More than likely I'll call."

"How are the girls, Bode? The whole town is talking about Callie's wedding. I expect Sela and Brie will be here."

"Yes, they've already arrived, and Callie is driving down from Columbia this evening. I'll see them all together. It's been years since the four of us were all together at the same time."

"When are you going to tell Callie, Bode?"

"I don't know, Mavis. Soon. When I walk out of here today I won't be coming back. Now, you're sure you can handle closing up and turning my cases over to Chase Montgomery."

"Bode, I'm sixty years old. I think I can handle it," Mavis

drawled. "I don't have a good feeling about this at all. I don't think you do either." She stalked from the room, her arms full of folders. At the door she turned and offered a parting shot. "She's not married yet, Bode. Until the eleventh hour you can still—Never mind, you always were stubborn. There's no reason for me to think you're about to change now. Damn, I'm going to miss you. Give my regards to Pearl and the girls."

Bode's fingers drummed on the desk. He should be doing something constructive, like . . . what? His eye started to twitch, and then his nose began to itch, a sure sign that he was under stress. And why the hell shouldn't he be? Callie, in his opinion, was marrying the wrong man. If no one else knew it, he did. And there wasn't anything he could do about it. Callie was old enough to make her own decisions. She was an attorney and had been working in Columbia these past years. A good attorney, she said, to anyone interested in listening. Brie was settled more or less. She was back in the saddle, as the saying went. She might have a few rough spots, but she'd make it. She didn't need him. Callie might think she did, but she didn't. Sela would always be okay; she was a born survivor and would always land on her feet. Not needed. Maybe he wasn't even wanted at this point in time. Mama Pearl . . . Jesus, it was going to be so hard to say good-bye to her. She'd say she understood because she loved him, but she'd get that look of disappointment in her eyes and he'd be a six-year-old boy again.

Bode knuckled his eyes. The filter must need to be changed on the air conditioner. "Yeah, sure," he muttered.

What you're doing sucks, Bode Jessup, and you know it. You aren't even being a man about it. You're leaving at the eleventh hour, sneaking out the back door. What kind of a person are you, that you won't attend a best friend's wedding? You made a promise to Clemson Parker. You made a promise to Mama Pearl, too, and don't forget Judge Summers. Bode argued with himself. "I kept my promises," he muttered aloud. "I honored the commitment I made. Callie's getting married. I'm not needed any longer, haven't been needed for a long time. Everyone is going to be just fine. *Except me.* Once I'm away from here I'll be fine."

He'd had to take responsibility from the time he was a kid. When Clemson Parker died he'd taken on Parker Manor, Callie, and Mama Pearl. He'd worked like a damn dog. He'd never complained, never whimpered. He'd done all that was required of him. He remembered it like it had just happened—Clemson Parker's funeral and his fear that he'd be sent back to the preacher because he hadn't been adopted the way Mr. Parker had promised. That fear hadn't been there when Mrs. Parker died, but then he'd never actually *seen* Mrs. Parker. Once or twice he thought he saw her by the window, but Callie said she didn't get off her chair at all. Maybe the sun played tricks on the window glass, and he just thought he saw her.

Mama Pearl's face was worried the day of the funeral, and she looked so tired. That scared him, too. Callie fretted all day. They were on the swing, Callie complaining about her shoes. He'd tried to be helpful. They were sitting on the swing . . .

Bode held her hand and wiped Callie's tears with a snowy white handkerchief Pearl made sure he carried in his pocket. He sat with her all evening on the swing on the back porch making her repeat over and over a prayer he said she needed to say at the cemetery.

The hour was late, the air warm even though it was October. Pearl sat down on the swing next to the children and told them quietly, "The Judge said right now there are no problems. Maybe sometime there will be a problem."

Bode's heart started to pound. "Do I have to go away, back to the preacher's house?"

"No, chile. You'll be staying here with Miz Callie and me. You belong here. Mr. Parker brought you here and here you stay. I asked the Judge, and he said that's right. He's your guardian. Things will be a mite different for a while, I expect."

"Will Sela and Brie still come out here?" Bode asked.

"Yes. That isn't about to change unless their mamas don't want them coming here, and I don't think that will happen."

"Can we have some soda pop, Pearl?"

"I'll fetch it if you say yes, Mama Pearl," Callie offered.

"Bless you, chile, yes, you bring it. Pearl's feet are tired tonight. Bring some cookies, too." Pearl dabbed at her eyes.

"Today is a day of great sorrow," she told Callie when the little girl returned. "Your papa was a fine man, honest and fair. He was always doing kind things for people in secret. The Judge told me that today."

"Was my mama a fine lady, too, Pearl?"

"Yes, she was, chile. She was sickly all her life, felt like she had failed your papa. She wanted to do so many things for that man, but she didn't have the strength."

"Was she a drunk lady like Sela's mama?"

Pearl spluttered. "Now where did you hear such a thing?"

"Sela told me."

"Well . . . I don't know about Miz Sela's mama, but I know about your mama, and she didn't—"

"It's all right, Pearl. I don't want you to have to tell me a lie," Callie said. "Let's pretend I didn't say anything. I remembered the whole prayer today, the one Bode taught me. I should go to church, Pearl. I don't want to grow to be a heathen. Can I go with you?"

"I asked the Judge, and he said if I want to take you, I can. You'll be the only white girl in my church, mind."

"Will the Lord care, Pearl? Won't He be happy that I go to church?"

"I expect so, honey."

"You look tired, Pearl," Callie said softly.

Bode held out the tray with three glasses and three bottles of soda pop on it. A plate with six sugar cookies sat in the center, along with paper napkins. "If you want to go to sleep, Mama Pearl, it's okay. I'll take care of Callie now. I'll be the man of the house unless the Judge says it isn't fitting. Will he say that, Mama Pearl?" Bode sounded anxious.

"No, the Judge said that same thing to me himself today. You be the man here now. I think I will be going to bed. You children don't stay up too late."

Bode's chest puffed out. He poured the soda pop and handed Callie a cookie.

"Pearl must be tired. She never lets us stay up this late, and she always makes us go to bed first." Callie yawned.

"She knows I'm in charge now," Bode said importantly. "It's a sacred trust."

"What's that?"

"That's when someone trusts you enough to put all their faith in you. Mama Pearl and the Judge know I will always do the best thing, the right thing."

"How do they know that?" Callie demanded.

"They just know. You ask too many questions sometimes."

"Did you mean what you said—that you are going to look out for me and take care of me? I don't feel so bad knowing that, Bode."

"Of course I mean it. That's what trust and faith is all about."

"Oh Bode, I just knew you were going to make everything feel right. I miss Papa and Mama, but I 'spect I'll get over that soon."

"No. You aren't supposed to forget about people when

they die. They were part of your life, and you always want to remember them."

"Okay, Bode. I'm getting sleepy, and I don't like wearing these shoes. They pinch my toes."

"I'm sleepy, too. Make sure you brush your teeth and wash your face and don't forget to do your ears. Be sure to say your prayers. You can leave the light on until you fall asleep. I'll turn it off before I go to bed. I'm going to tidy up the kitchen for Mama Pearl and set the table for breakfast so she doesn't have to do it."

"Good night, Bode. I'm always going to love you, Bode. Are you always going to love me?"

"Well, sure. I promised to take care of you, and I never break a promise. Never," he said vehemently. "Go on now and mind what I said."

Bode sat on the swing for a long time. The moon was high in the sky when he finally stirred himself. His stomach felt fine now that he knew he wasn't going to have to leave Parker Manor. He loved it here. He loved Mama Pearl, Callie, Brie, and Sela with all his heart. He swore to himself that he would never let any of them down. Never, ever.

He'd applied for a job delivering newspapers and would start on Monday. He had a large delivery route that would net him around fourteen dollars a week. He'd give it all to Mama Pearl for his keep.

He had a bicycle now, a rusty affair for which he gathered parts at the junkyard. It was good enough for now, even though the tires had been patched and repatched. Tomorrow he was going to paint it, with the girls' help. The big decision was the choice of color, since everyone had a different opinion.

Bode smiled as he tidied up the kitchen and set the table. When he was finished he went to his room, knelt beside his bed, and said his prayers.

* * *

Bode accepted his new responsibility with gusto. He had a morning paper route and one in the afternoon after school. On Mondays he worked two hours in the supermarket bagging groceries. On Tuesdays he worked an hour at the drugstore delivering prescriptions on his bike. On Wednesdays he worked an hour and a half at the library shelving books. On Thursdays he worked at the hardware store till closing. On Fridays he washed cars at the Texaco station. Saturdays he worked half a day at the supermarket if they called him in. Sunday was for church, catching up on homework and playing with the girls. He still did his chores and carried an A-B average at school. His work pattern was set up by the Judge, who monitored it carefully. If Bode started to look "peaked" the Judge called his employer and arranged for him to have time off.

The Judge and Bode were the only ones who knew that he couldn't have kept up his work schedule and still go to school if it hadn't been for Brie. She got up every morning at five o'clock, sneaked out of the house, and pedaled her bike to the drop-off point, where she cut the heavy twine that bundled the papers, and then folded them neatly in a stack. She then fit the huge canvas bag into a rickety wagon hitched to her bike and pedaled it to Sumter Avenue, where she waited for Bode.

Like Bode, she took her job seriously. She never missed a day, even when she had a cold or it was raining or the temperature was in the low thirties. When the need arose, she also delivered the papers. She did the same thing after school because she got out a half hour earlier than Bode.

Bode knew Briana Canfield would have walked through fire for him. The day he kissed her on the cheek right in front of Adeline Brown's house was the happiest day of her young life. She told him later that for days she washed around what she called the kissing spot. She never told a soul, except him. She said she wrote about it in her diary, the one with the bright blue cover that he'd given her for her birthday.

All the monies Bode earned went into a large Mason jar in Pearl's cupboard. He told Pearl he would only take what he needed. Most times he didn't need much, except at Christmas or if his bike needed repair.

Judge Avery Summers told everyone in town that Bowdey Malcolm Jessup worked like a tireless old dog.

Bode perched on the edge of his chair, the glass of lemonade Miss Nela, the Judge's wife, handed him trembling in his hand. He knew that whatever the Judge was going to tell him, was going to be bad. He could feel the bad news rumbling in his stomach. He waited, hardly daring to breathe, afraid to sip the tart lemonade in case he dribbled it down his chin.

"Bode, I think it's time for you to know the true state of affairs at Parker Manor. I want you to look at this ledger and tell me if you can figure it out. If you can't, then I'll explain it. Take your time," the Judge said kindly.

Bode set the lemonade on the desk and opened the ledger. His hands, he noticed, were still trembling and were covered with news ink. He tried not to smudge the pages. He was aware of the Judge's keen gaze, the scent of his cigar, the smell of old leather and good whiskey.

Bode knew exactly what a ledger was and how to follow it because the Judge had given him one for his own small business. He needed to look at the expenditures and then the bottom line. His tongue felt thick, like he'd swallowed molasses and peanut butter all at the same time. It took him a full thirty minutes before he understood that the money Clemson Parker had left was all gone. There appeared to be a sizable debt. He closed the ledger and wondered if Brie was delivering his papers.

"Judge, I don't have any more hours to work. What should I do?"

"Son, Clemson Parker was one of my best friends. Unfortunately, he was not a good businessman, and his wife's . . . illness cost him dearly. I have a plan I'd like to propose. You tell me if you think it will work. You don't have to go along with it, but it's all I can come up with so other people don't know our business."

"I'd like to hear your plan, sir," Bode said.

"I'll carry the bills and pay the taxes because Clemson appointed me as your guardian. I want you to go to college and then law school. I expect you to work some, but don't want your studies to suffer. You'll always be able to count on me. If you feel absolutely that you have to tell someone, that someone should be Briana. No one else. When you finish your schooling you can start to pay me back—whatever you can afford. I'll never hound you for the money. It's going to be a huge debt, Bode, but I just don't see any other way. Well, there *is* a way, and that's to sell off the land and Parker Manor, but I don't think we want to do that. Take all the time you need to think about this."

The Judge paused. "You're a fine boy, Bode. I don't know another youngster in this town who could have buckled down the way you did. I'm very proud of you. Another time we'll talk about Callie and her future. Now, you best be drinking that lemonade, or Miss Nela is going to think you don't like it. I think it tastes like horse piss myself, but I drink it to keep her happy."

Bode gulped the lemonade and privately concurred with the Judge's opinion of it. He offered his hand manfully, thanked his benefactor, and left.

Brie was waiting outside, the wagon empty.

"Leave the wagon on the Judge's lawn, Brie, and let's me and you go down to the Azalea Park and sit on the bench."

"If we do that, you'll be late for supper, Bode."

"I know, but I need to talk to you about something. It has to be a secret, okay? A cross-your-heart-and-hope-to-die secret." Brie nodded solemnly as she climbed on her bike.

They sat on the grass in the park, legs crossed Indian fashion, and Bode told her everything the Judge had said. "I don't know what to do," he concluded. "It will take me all my life to pay off the debt, but that's not what's really bothering me. How can I tell Mama Pearl she has to be careful how much money she spends? How can I tell her she can't be buying Callie fancy dresses and shoes? How can I tell Callie her father didn't provide for them? The Judge said it was just between him and me, but he said I could confide in you. He likes you a lot, Brie. He said you're like me, a hard worker. You won't tell, will you?"

"No, I won't tell. I can get a job, Bode. The Judge can help me like he helped you. My mother is never home; she doesn't care what I do after school. I can give you all the money. I won't keep any. It will help a little, won't it?"

Bode's slumped shoulders straightened. "It will help a lot, Brie, if you're sure you want to do it. You're only thirteen, though. What can you do?"

"I can baby-sit; I can rake leaves and mow grass. I can make deliveries. I can do lots of things. I'm not afraid to work, Bode. Is it a deal?"

"It's a deal," Bode said, his face flushed with relief. He told her about Miss Nela's lemonade and the Judge's comment. They both doubled over laughing.

"I have some Kool-Aid in my bag. Want some?"

"Sure."

And so a conspiracy was born. Brie thought she was contributing to what she considered to be Bode's financial debt. Bode's shoulders lightened with the twenty-five dollars or so that Brie handed over to the Judge at the end of each week. Judge Summers banked Brie's money and marked it for college use with his wife's full knowledge. In a ledger he carefully noted the monies that went out to Parker Manor from his own account. He told himself he was investing in the futures of two fine people and after all, he was a Judge and who would dare to question him? Except maybe Bode Jessup . . . someday.

3

Bode Jessup sat at his desk, his head full of memories, for another hour. How bare his office looked with all the plants gone. He'd told Mavis to take them all, along with the draperies. She was coming back tomorrow for his desk that she promised to store in her garage in case he ever decided to come back and start up his practice. He wanted to tell her he was never coming back, except maybe to visit, but he couldn't get the words out. So, he'd hugged her one last time and helped her carry the last of the things out to her car. Back inside, he'd closed the blinds and locked the front door. When it was time to leave, he'd put his bike in his car and drive away for his last appearance in court, and then he was a free agent. Free of the past, free of memories, free of . . . everything.

Bode looked at his watch. He had just enough time to drive to his apartment, change into his suit for court, plead his last motion, then come back and get stinking drunk—a drunk that was ten years overdue, maybe fifteen.

Bode closed and locked the door behind him and wheeled his bike over to his car. He was aware of everything, the awful humidity, the bright sun, his ancient Volvo parked in the shade under a massive oak, the waves of heat shimmering upward from the asphalt parking lot, the long clumps of Spanish moss hanging from the oak and actually touching the hood of his car. He wondered why he'd never pulled it off. He wasn't going to do it now either.

He saw her then from the far end of the parking lot. Suddenly he wanted to run, to hide, to pretend he didn't see her. How could he, a grown man—not to mention a practicing attorney—be so cowardly?

He could tell her now, get it over with . . . but he knew he wouldn't. Telling her was something he had to do at Parker Manor. That's where it had begun, and that's where it was going to end. He felt dizzy with the thought.

"Bode! Wait!" Her voice was low, drawling and yet musical somehow.

Bode opened the trunk of his car. He needed a few extra seconds to square his shoulders, to shift his thoughts into a neutral zone, an extra second to compose his features. He turned.

"Didn't you see me, Bode?" Callie said, throwing her arms about him.

"Guess my mind was somewhere else. I have to change for court." Jesus, she was prettier than the first day of summer, the stars at night, prettier than the perfect azaleas that surrounded Parker Manor.

Her voice was playful, teasing. "I see you haven't changed a bit. You cut it right down to the last second. If you'd dress in the morning, you wouldn't have to rush home to change. You could even keep a suit and clean shirt in the office. I do that, but then I guess we do things differently in Columbia. Why haven't you called me, Bode? You didn't write either." Her voice stopped just short of being accusing. "You aren't going to talk to me now either, are you? Did I do something to make you angry? It's Pearl, isn't it? I told her she could stay here, but she wants to come with me. It was her decision, Bode, truly it was."

"I know that. Mama Pearl belongs with you. What brings you down today? I thought you weren't coming till this evening." He closed the trunk of the car as far as it would go, looped a section of rope around the hitch on the back. His treasured bike was secure.

"I came to see you." She moved closer, the scent of her perfume in his nostrils. Her hands were on his shoulders, her face just inches from his.

She looked ethereal, somehow translucent. Maybe there was something wrong with his eyes, maybe he needed to wear his glasses more or maybe he was having one of those anxiety attacks people talked about so much. He stepped back, but there was nowhere to go; his spine was pressed up against the rear wheel of his bike protruding from the trunk.

"You act like you're afraid of me, Bode," she teased. Her hands were still on his shoulders, her face an inch closer than before.

"That will be the day," he croaked. "You didn't answer my question, Callie. How come you came down early?"

"I'm going to be a bride, remember? I have things to do, places to go, and I do have my priorities. I came to see you. I called, and Mavis said you'd be here till one-thirty. It's only twelve o'clock. We have a lot of things to talk about. I have lots to share. You were the one who taught us to share, Bode. Brie, Sela, me. We always shared. *Everything*. You never really did, though. It took the three of us a long time before we figured that out. Sometimes, Bode, I don't think I know you at all. I don't think any of us really knows you, except Mama Pearl. Is it us or is it you?"

"You're being silly, Callie. I shared as much as you did, you just don't remember." He was sweating. Damn, now he was going to have to take a shower before he changed for court.

"I remember everything, Bode, from the first day you arrived at Parker Manor. Every single thing. I wrote it all down in my diary. I have sixty of them, do you believe that? Girls do that, you know, write down things—their secret thoughts, their dreams, their desires. The only thing is, I didn't know what desires were until Sela told me. I don't think Brie knew either."

His sneakered foot scuffed at the asphalt. "Brie's here. She arrived early this morning. I went out to the house and she was sitting by the wall. She's had a bad time lately and needs her friends and Mama Pearl."

Callie tweaked Bode's cheek. "That's almost funny, Bode. Brie is as tough as buffalo hide. I don't think she has any feelings, and I know she doesn't have a nerve in her body. I guess that's why she became a cop. I'll never figure that one out." Her voice was so airy, so breezy-sounding, that Bode reached up and removed Callie's hands from his shoulders. She was forced to step back and allow him room to move to the driver's side of the car.

"What's the matter—don't you like Brie, Callie? What you said isn't very complimentary. I thought you were best friends." How angry and defensive he sounded. Why was that?

"What an awful thing to say, Bode Jessup. Brie is my best friend just the way Sela is my best friend. Facts are facts: Brie is tough. I didn't mean it to sound the way you took it. We're squabbling, Bode. Pearl would smack our rumps if she heard us. Something's wrong, I can sense it. Talk to me, Bode."

Damn, he had to get in the car, away from her, and put some distance between them. Now. Her hand was on his arm; he thought he felt a jolt of electricity.

Her voice when she spoke was soft and intimate. "Bode, I really came back early to . . . to see you. I want—oh, so many things. Lately, this past week especially, I started . . . I'm not sure . . . I always wanted you—us—but you shut me out. In my diaries, the early ones, you were the prince and I was the princess. Why didn't it work out that way, Bode? I want to know. I *need* to know. Is it that you don't find me attractive? Is it that orphan thing with you? Do you think of us as brother and sister? I never did. Brie and Sela never did either. Think about us like *that,* is what I mean. I want to go back to your apartment with you and I want us to—I want us to do what each of us has thought about for years and years. I want to do it now, before I get married. I need to know if I'm making a mistake."

Bode closed his eyes to shield them from the bright sun. It didn't matter—he could still see her behind his closed lids, her pleading expression, her quivering lips, the tremor in her hands. He opened his eyes and for a minute thought he was seeing Brie Canfield, but it was a trick of the sun. He wasn't sure if he should laugh or cry. All three girls had propositioned him. Sela a hundred times at least. Brie once and now Callie. He'd said no to Brie and Sela and everyone had their dignity intact when they walked away. Now, he had to do it again. His arm went out, stiff with resolution. He hoped the anger he was feeling wasn't showing in his eyes. The other two times he'd been flattered; never angry. "No."

"No?"

"No."

She reached up to pluck the clump of Spanish moss touching the hood of Bode's car. She held it for a moment before tossing it to the ground. "I forgot, it's full of birdlice. Yuck. So, you're turning me down. I rather thought you would. I've always loved you, Bode," she said, backing away from him. "Each of us loved you in her own way. I thought . . . hoped . . . that someday, when we had our schooling done, our debts paid off, and we held steady jobs, you would . . . but you didn't. Now I've made a fool of myself by asking you to go to bed with me. Do you love any of us? I don't mean that family love we all feel for one another. Why did you offer me the job? Why did you do that, Bode? How am I supposed to work with you in the same office knowing . . . How? Why? I don't understand." She dabbed at her eyes.

She really was prettier than the first day of summer with her yellow dress the exact same color as Pearl's marigolds by the back porch and her straw hat with the band of daisies. Her eyes were cobalt blue with her tears, and wisps of pale blond hair were sticking to her cheeks. If he needed to carry a memory of her to Santa Fe this would be it: his good-bye to Callie Parker. But then that wasn't true either. He hadn't told her yet, which meant he had to go out to Parker Manor and explain that he was going away, that he wasn't going to attend her wedding, that there was no job with him. He had to tell her all those things, and of course he had to say good-bye to Mama Pearl, Brie, and Sela. He was about to respond when Callie spoke.

"Do you remember, Bode, when I had my first date with Steven Bryers? Pearl was worried sick. We went to the movie, and you followed us on your bike. I swear I didn't realize he was taking the wrong way home, and when he parked and wanted to . . . get to know me better you jumped out from behind the bushes and whipped him silly. You made me get on the back of your bike and brought me home. You broke Steven's tooth, and it was the only time I ever heard you swear. Pearl was like one of her wet chickens that night. I'd never seen you so angry. I thought we had an understanding from then on. I assumed you felt . . . more than protective. I know we didn't speak about it, and I know how hard you had to work to pay off Steven's dental bill. What I'm trying to say to save face is I thought we . . . that we were . . . I hate you, Bode Jessup! I hate you for doing this to me. Now you've spoiled everything."

He watched her run from him, but made no move to go

after her. Like Callie, he remembered *everything*. Remembered working from early morning until late at night so Pearl wouldn't have to take in extra work to buy Callie new shoes and dresses. He'd honored his commitment longer than was necessary. He remembered his promise to Clemson Parker always to be kind to Callie. Well, he'd honored that promise, too.

The Volvo turned over with the first tap to the gas pedal. His old car was as faithful as his old bike, as faithful as he was. They endured just the way he'd endured. He backed up the Volvo, saw the clump of Spanish moss. "I guess I was waiting for Callie to pull it off the tree because I couldn't bear to do it," he muttered. As he drove away he wondered if there was something symbolic in what she'd done.

It was midnight when Bode staggered from the bathroom to the living room to pick up the phone. He dialed a number in Santa Fe, New Mexico, and waited for the phone on the other end to be picked up. He blinked, trying to focus on the shabby furniture in the apartment, none of which was his. The moment the phone was picked up, Bode said, "Hatch, this is Bode. Yep, everything is right as rain. Speaking of rain, we could use some. Tell me one more time that this is the right thing for me to be doing. Of course I know what time it is. What kind of a drunk do you think I am? I realize I'm drunk, why else would I be calling you? I could see right through her. It was the craziest thing. I know that means something. It didn't have anything to do with the sun, even though it was bright and strong. It's something else."

"Is there a reality check to back this up or are you speaking figuratively? Or are you saying something else entirely? Do you by any chance mean you saw through her as in you saw through her, which is to say she isn't what she appears, that she's some kind of phony who has deluded you all your life? Just how drunk are you, Bode? You never get drunk, you're worse than a teetotaler," Hatch Littletree muttered.

"I don't know," Bode muttered in return, his words barely distinguishable over the long-distance wire. "You always had all the answers, that's why I called you."

The voice on the other end of the phone scoffed. "You said you called to ask me if you were doing the right thing. The answer is yes—in my opinion. It's *your* opinion that counts, Bode."

"She didn't go back to the manor house. I called Mama Pearl. I don't know where she went. She might be there now. It's too late to call again."

"She's almost thirty years old, buddy. She was probably out there doing girl things. Go to bed, Bode. Call me in the morning. If I don't hear anything from you, I'll pick you up at the airport as scheduled."

"Yeah, but I told her Brie was there. She should have been anxious to see one of her best friends." When there was no response, Bode reared back, a look of mystification on his face. "He hung up," he muttered to no one in particular. He flopped back on the bed, the receiver hanging loosely over the side. He heard an operator squawk her disapproval. He pushed the offending instrument onto the floor and rolled over, his fists beating the scrunched-up pillows.

One of the pillows ripped at the seams, feathers spiraling upward. The curtains at the windows billowed inward, creating a breeze that sent the feathers in every direction. Bode thought it was the funniest thing he'd ever seen. He slapped at his knees, laughing until tears streamed down his cheeks. He was still laughing when he fumbled his way out to the kitchen to make himself some coffee.

His memories attacked him again as he waited for the coffee to drip into the pot. Who should he think about? Mama Pearl who loved him with all her heart? He loved her with all his heart, too. Of the four of them he was the only one allowed to call her Mama Pearl. That was because he didn't have a mother and the others did. Not that the girls' mothers were any great shakes in the maternal department. Still, blood was blood.

Tomboy Brie whose mother didn't give a hoot what she did or when she did it. Brie with the bruises and welts she sloughed off and never complained about. She'd even got into a girls' cat fight over him one day. Well, by God, he wasn't going to think about *that*.

He'd given Brie a bracelet when she was fifteen. He didn't know her wrist turned green until Sela told him. It was Sela who also told him how Brie had put nail polish on it and when it fell apart, had Scotch-taped it to the back of her blue diary—another present from Bode.

Bode's thoughts homed back to Brie's fight in the schoolyard. Things changed among the girls after that. Callie and Sela banded together, but they didn't exclude Brie. Again, it was Sela who told him Callie was jealous of all the time Brie spent with him. He'd tried to explain that they had jobs, but both Callie and Sela pooh-poohed that aside as if it was nothing.

Brie with the skinned elbows and knees. Brie with the freckles and patched coveralls and scruffy sneakers. Brie was his friend. Brie was that one true person in the whole of the world who would always be there for him. If he needed her, he knew she'd drop everything and ask questions later. If. And he would do the same thing for her. How ironic that neither of them ever asked the other.

Callie and Sela were a different story. Oh yeah, they'd be there for him, too, but only after they had asked for a million details. He finished his coffee and poured out more. He stared at the cup. He didn't even remember the coffee dripping, much less pouring himself the first cup.

It was time to put all his memories away and get on with his life. That meant leaving those nearest and dearest behind him—something he should have done years ago. To this day he didn't know why he hadn't set up shop somewhere else. Was it Mama Pearl or the girls? Both.

Who was he—really? Maybe it was time for him to find out. Maybe it was time for him to do a lot of things he'd shelved so he could take responsibility for what he considered to be his family. And they were his family: Mama Pearl, Brie, Callie, and Sela.

Each of them had her own life now, and he no longer had to be in the background waiting. If that was what he'd been doing these past years, then he had wasted those years because the four women hadn't needed him at all. Maybe he needed them. Maybe that was why he hadn't left. He needed to be needed.

If a person didn't know his beginnings, how could he know where he was going in life? He now had the wherewithal to make that search, if he wanted to. Hatch would help him. Jesus, what if he needed a bone-marrow transplant someday and he couldn't tell the doctors anything about his parents? Hell, he'd just up and die if they couldn't find a match or whatever it was they did in such situations.

What was it Judge Summers, his mentor, had said? "Leave it alone, Bode. You can't undo the past. You might stir up something you aren't prepared to deal with." So, he'd listened and hadn't done anything. But not doing anything had held him back from forming relationships, because he didn't have a background before the age of six. Girls, women in particular, always wanted to know about parents, bank accounts, and things like that. Grandparents always came into play when the word *marriage* entered the conversation.

He wished now, as he had wished millions of other times, that Clemson Parker had adopted him the way he planned to. At the time he'd just been so grateful to be allowed to stay at Parker Manor he didn't consider the adoption important. Nor did it become really important until he went away to college. Or maybe it became important the day Callie said, "The Judge told me that there's barely enough money for me to go to college so you can't expect me to share my fund with you." Then she'd gone on to say she didn't mean that the way it sounded—but she *had* meant it. He'd wanted to hit her that day, to tell her it was he who had paid for her brand-new bicycle, all those pretty dresses and fancy shoes. He'd even paid for her first car, a shiny little Triumph, and all those dancing lessons, riding lessons, piano lessons. He'd honored his commitment, paid his dues, earned his keep, and been kind to Callie Parker. The Judge said it would build his character, make him a better person. He was right, it had—but at what cost to him personally?

For a time he was in love with Callie Parker, or as much in love as a schoolboy can be. He'd never acted on those feelings in any way. Mama Pearl reminded him, gently, for she always did things gently, that he had to stay in his place, and because he loved her and respected her, he'd done what she said.

Then he'd fallen in love with Sela, and Pearl had taken him out to the barn and laced into him with a vengeance. She said she couldn't control what Sela did away from Parker Manor, but she wasn't going to allow such goings-on at home. Instead she'd instructed him how to tactfully, and in a gentlemanly way, tell Sela that her behavior was unladylike. When he'd tried, Sela had laughed wickedly, and said, "Want to experiment?" He'd taken off like a scalded cat. He'd gotten so many hard-ons that year he thought his penis was going to fall off.

Then came the fights. The boys at school learned early on not to tangle with Bode Jessup, so if they had sex with Sela they didn't brag about it. It was the best he could do. Then, as if by magic, Sela settled down and really listened to him during her last year in high school. In college she had several affairs that she said were meaningful, but the men weren't marriage material. Then she'd paid him the supreme compliment by saying, "I'm looking for another Bode Jessup."

"Briana Canfield." Bode watched as his childhood friend reached out to shake the dean's hand. He brought his own hand to his mouth and let loose with a long, sharp whistle, the same kind of whistle he'd practiced when they were children and it was time to go fishing and the girls lagged behind. He watched as Brie turned and almost tripped, a stunned look on her face. She knew it was him; he could see her eyes search the crowd.

Bode interrupted his roll call to rub the grit from his eyes. He felt sober once more, and wondered if he really was. He must be; otherwise, why was he dwelling so much on the past? *Because I feel goddamn guilty, that's why,* he told himself. *I was always here, there, whatever, never more than a phone call away.* He wasn't just leaving Mama Pearl, Callie, and Sela; he was leaving Brie, too.

He was in love with Brie. Somehow, the freckle-faced girl had sneaked into his heart, carved out a niche, and refused to budge. He'd tried so many times, but just when he thought he was succeeding by loading down his days with studies, other activities and then his law practice, he'd tire out and then he'd dream about her. All night long.

He'd let her go, because Mama Pearl said he wasn't to mess with the girls. He'd let her go off to college to become a woman to be reckoned with. The only thing was, he hadn't reckoned with her. He'd let it all go by him because he was gutless. He just knew she was a hell of a cop. Detective, actually. But she hadn't called him when she was in trouble—not until she really had it pretty much under control and needed to hear him say so. That was Brie. Brie could do anything, be anything, because she was Brie.

Bode let his mind go back in time once more, to Brie's graduation. He'd hitchhiked from Washington and got there just in time to let loose with his famous whistle when she accepted her diploma. The look on her face had been worth all the time he had spent on the road.

She spotted him as the new graduates filed out. He was grinning from ear to ear, a single red rose in his hand and a bag of boiled peanuts in the other. She stepped aside, right into his outstretched arms, crying words of joy he would always remember. He was hugging her, squeezing her and then he kissed her—not one of those friendly, fraternal kisses either. He was light-headed, his knees weak.

"You kissed me!" Brie said.

"Yep."

"I *liked* it. Do it again."

He did.

"God," was all she could say.

"Let's go celebrate. I have six dollars and fifty cents."

"I have a hundred. The Judge sent it to me. We can go out on the town if you want. Do you want to? I do. I'm so happy. I don't think I've ever been so happy. Are you happy, Bode? I couldn't believe it when I heard you whistle. I knew it was you, I just knew it," she babbled. "How'd you get here?"

"I hitchhiked, and I have to hitchhike back so we're just going to have time for me to spend the six-fifty on some hot dogs and a couple of beers. I wish I could stay longer, but I can't."

"Listen, I have an idea. I'll give you the hundred dollars the Judge sent me, and you can take the train back. Then we'll have more time to spend together. I want to go to bed with you," she said happily. "A friend of mine is letting me use her apartment tonight because she's spending this last

night with her boyfriend. Did you hear me, Bode? I'm propo-
sitioning you."

"And I'm turning you down. Not because I want to—I just
couldn't bear for you to have regrets later. Right now you're
happy I'm here and—"

"And you love Callie Parker, and I'm a poor replacement.
It's okay, Bode. You're right, I got carried away. Don't give it
another thought." She smiled. "Someday you're going to regret this."

"I already do." Bode laughed.

"How's law school?"

"Tough."

"I bet," Brie said. "Is there going to be a strain between
us now?"

"No. There are no words to tell you how . . . flattered I am
that you would even consider . . . Come on, I'm hungry."

"Me too. Just remember, Bode Jessup, it's your loss."

"I'll always remember that, Brie."

"Let me make sure I have this all straight so I don't make a
fool out of myself again where you're concerned. You came a
long distance, and hitchhiked to boot. You're treating me to
dinner and then you are going to get on your stick and hitchhike back, the same long distance. I want to thank you for
that. For being my friend all these years. You have no idea
what our friendship means to me. Well, maybe you do." She
grinned wryly. "As corny as this may sound, when I offered
myself to you, I wasn't being grateful or anything like that. It
was something I have wanted to do for a very long time. I
wasn't asking for commitment, a relationship. I simply wanted
it to happen. I need to know, am I repulsive, am I funny-
looking, am I too skinny or is it this pimple on my chin? I
guess you don't find me attractive. It's a little hard to swallow all that since I've been attracted to you since we were
kids. Why did you turn me down? I have to know, Bode. I

don't want one of those 'because I said so' answers either. It's Callie, isn't it?"

"There you go, answering for me," Bode said quietly. "Look, I'm illegitimate. I have no idea who my parents were. A person needs to know that or come to terms with it. I haven't done that yet. I understand why Mama Pearl wouldn't marry Lazarus because she didn't have a last name. I gave myself my name. I don't think the man has been born yet who wouldn't find you attractive. As for the pimple on your chin, it's . . . endearing. We were always such good friends and don't think, even for a second, that I will ever forget how you busted your butt with me to help Mama Pearl."

"Don't you mean Callie?" Brie asked tightly.

"Callie, too," Bode said soberly.

"Do you know what I remember the most? Both of us busting our humps so Callie could get that fancy dress and shoes to go to the prom. Four boys asked me to go, but I didn't have enough money for the prom gown. Sela didn't have a dress either, but Callie was decked out to the nines. I remember the day you handed Pearl the money. She all but swooned. Her baby was going to the prom and be outfitted like a queen. Do you remember what we did that night, Bode? We played records under the angel oak and you danced with me and Sela. Even Pearl came out to dance with us. And Callie didn't even say thank you. She expected it, and we made it happen."

"Didn't it make us better people, Brie?"

"Look, I didn't do it for Callie. Get that straight right now. I did it to ease the pain in Pearl's eyes and to take some of the load off your shoulders. You were too damn skinny to carry so much weight around. Damn you, Bode, you aren't Callie's savior. When is she going to wake up and see the world the way it is?"

"Are you sorry, Brie?" Bode asked quietly.

"Sometimes," Brie said honestly. "Like right now. I threw myself at you and you turned me down. I guess I thought you'd remember the old days and . . . you know. We aren't kids anymore. Both of us are old enough to take responsibility for our actions. You didn't answer my last question," she said with a bite in her voice.

"Brie, I love you. I love Callie, and I love Sela. When we were younger and I couldn't sleep because I was bone tired I would lie in bed and fantasize about all three of you. One night it would be you, one night Callie, and one night Sela. Hell, there was one night we had an orgy. In glorious Technicolor. I won't muck up the friendship we all have."

He could see her anger building. "Is that how you look at it—mucking up a friendship? Do you know what I think, Bode? I think you need to do some more fantasizing about Callie and then go to her and make it happen. The golden girl is going to hang over your head for the rest of your days if you don't. I like Callie and yeah, I'm jealous. I work on that all the time. It's clear to me you need to do the same thing. Thanks for showing up. I'll try and do the same when you graduate from law school. The hot dogs were great. I'll have heartburn all night." She bolted from the students' beer cellar, but stopped in the doorway long enough to shout, "I hate you, Bode Jessup!" Then she ran across the campus.

A kindly grandmother picked up Bode for the first leg of his journey back to Washington. They talked for a bit and then Bode fell silent. He had a lot of thinking to do, but the lady was so nice he didn't want to offend her.

"You look tired, young man. Did you graduate today?"

"No. I came to see a friend of mine graduate. I hitchhiked from Washington. It was a nice graduation."

"Are you just tired or are you unhappy?" the grandmother asked shrewdly.

"A little of both I guess. I don't think I'll ever understand the female psyche."

"You and half the men in the world. Don't fret, young man. I always say if something is meant to be, it will be. Remember one thing—a smile is universal. People respond to a smile. It takes fewer muscles to smile than it does to frown. I am a retired librarian and I know these things. If you'd like to talk, I'm a good listener. My husband was a professor at Boston College, and he would talk my ear off for hours on end when he was alive. I like to think I gave him a lot of input in those days. When you hold things inside too long they have a tendency to fester. Now, if you'd rather sit there and stare out the window I won't say another word."

After that invitation, the words tumbled out so fast Bode had a hard time catching his breath. When he finally wound down and repeated Brie's last words he choked up.

"Life is never easy, son. My husband would say it's time you either fished or cut bait, but I sense you aren't ready to do that yet. When do you think you will be ready?"

"I don't know," Bode said miserably.

"Have you given any thought to the fact that perhaps you don't want to relinquish your—for want of a better word—*hold* over all four women? You need to ask yourself if you really are trying to pay back for being allowed to move into the Parker family, or have you been helping and doing without so you'll have some kind of hold over them? Now, I know that sounds callous, but it is a possibility. I hope you'll forgive me for saying this, but your friend Callie sounds to me like a very selfish young woman. Your friend Brie, on the other hand, sounds like a bit of a martyr. From what you said, all her sacrifices were for you. For you to smile at her, to say, good girl, give her a pat on the head. That's love, young man. As to your friend Sela, I see she doesn't involve herself—and maybe that's good and maybe it isn't. I guess it's who she is."

"I always say I'm going to sit down and think things through, but when that time comes I find something else to do," Bode confessed. "I know I have a mental block. It's just easier not to think about it. I guess when I finish law school and go it alone I'll be able to sort it all out."

"Are you in love with any of those women?" the grandmother asked. "Now, I'm not talking about puppy-love feelings, I'm talking about adult feelings and where those feelings lead."

"I'm illegitimate, ma'am."

"Oh, pish and tosh," the grandmother snorted. "This is almost the millennium—and things like that don't mean anything anymore. I'll be dropping you off soon. You can hitch on Interstate 90. I don't think you'll have a bit of trouble. Lots of people are heading to Washington at this hour."

"I appreciate the ride and your advice. By the way, my name is Bode Jessup."

"I'm Lillian Ingersol. I'm in the phone book if you ever feel the need to talk. You can call me any time of the day or night. I miss that, you know. Students used to call Henry at all hours and then we'd discuss their plight and try to help. I know how to keep my lip zipped, too," she said, gurgling with laughter.

Lillian slowed and pulled over to the curb. "You be careful whose car you get into, Bode. There are some mighty weird people out there."

"But you picked me up," Bode said, puzzled.

"That's because I'm a keen judge of character. You looked so forlorn and miserable I just knew you needed a kind word and a hug." She leaned over and put her arms around him. "Henry would say you were worth taking the time to get to know. Try and be happy and only do what you can. Other people need to take responsibility for themselves, and I'm not talking about your Mama Pearl here."

"Thanks, Mrs. Ingersol. I appreciate you listening. I'll call."

"You be a good boy now. I'm sorry, I'm so used to saying that I find it hard to stop. Get on with you now." She waved as she looked behind her before pulling back onto the road. Bode watched the car until it was out of sight.

What was it Sela always said? "Life's a bitch, and then you die."

Bode raised his eyes. "Help me," he whispered.

The kitchen chair Bode was sitting on thumped to the floor. Two down and one to go. Brie offered herself to him and then said she hated him. Callie had done the same thing today—or was it yesterday? He squinted at the clock. Yesterday. Everything in his life could now be relegated to yesterday. There was a time in his life when he loved all his yesterdays, but not anymore.

4

They were giddy young girls again, cuddling under the lacy canopy of the high four-poster. Only this time they weren't whispering about what it would be like to "do it." Now they were all grown-up and could talk openly.

Calliope Parker, Callie to her friends Sela and Briana, picked at a frayed thread on the spread, her eyes starry and a bit misty. "I told both of you all good things come to those who wait," she said happily.

"I hate that sappy look on your face," Sela grated as she, too, picked at a loose thread on Callie's bedspread. "I can't believe you waited all this time to get married. You're going to be thirty at the end of the year." She made the word *thirty* sound obscene.

"And end up like you," Brie said quietly.

"What's that supposed to mean?" Sela demanded.

"It means you were so damn hot to get in the sack with that Neanderthal you married, you didn't take the time to get to know him the way Callie has gotten to know Wyn Archer. You saw all his money, and that's all you saw. Now that he wants some nubile eighteen-year-old, you're out in the proverbial cold. You'll be lucky if you get the clothes on your back. As smart as you say you are, I'm surprised you didn't sock away a few 'jools,' " Brie said, not unkindly.

"Is that another way of saying I shouldn't hit you up for a loan? Don't worry, either one of you. I can handle this—and so what if I run up a few thousand dollars in legal bills? I can get a job. You got one, so there's hope for me," Sela sniped.

"I thought weddings, mine in particular, would bring out the good things in both of you. What's wrong, what's happening here that I'm missing?" Callie asked as she ripped a huge thread from the spread. She tied it in a double knot as she stared at her two best friends.

Sela's face crumpled, "It's me, and I apologize, Callie. I hate what's happening to me, and I'm taking it out on you and Brie. I'm feeling sorry for myself, that's all."

"I accept your apology," Brie said, crunching the pillow against her stomach. "I wish there was a man who loved me the way Wyn loves Callie."

"Does that mean you haven't met any eligible men in California?" Callie asked. "As a detective on the police force, I would think you'd meet a lot of men."

Brie's freckles danced across the bridge of her nose when she wrinkled it to show what she thought of Callie's remark. "Oh, I meet a lot of men all right—criminals, and detectives who never get to see their wives and children except on weekends. Who wants someone like that? On a more serious note, I don't want what happened to Sela to happen to me. When I get married, *if* I get married, I want it to be forever."

"That's how I feel, too. Why do you think I waited so long to say yes to Wyn?" Callie said softly. But her starry eyes were now full of shadows. Brie wondered why.

"I think you waited this long because you wanted to see if Bode Jessup would finally wake up and notice you," Sela said.

"So, okay, that goes under the heading of being sure," Callie said, a flush mounting to her high cheekbones. "Let's not get started on Bode." She was never *ever* going to think about yesterday afternoon.

"You're the one who said you'd like to drag Bode to bed, just once. Those are your exact words, Miss Calliope Parker," Sela said.

How was it possible that Sela Carron Bronson was her best friend, Callie wondered. She was mean-spirited, selfish, arrogant, and had a mouth like a longshoreman. Maybe she needed a little of Sela's confidence, a little . . . *something*. Sela was beautiful too, these days, with hair the color of honey and large dark eyes that looked like huge chocolate drops. Wyn said Sela had bedroom eyes—eyes that enticed and beckoned and promised.

Sela was an interior decorator, a profession she'd worked on for exactly ninety minutes or, as Sela said, until she set eyes on Dylan Bronson.

"I was a child then—it was nothing more than girlish chatter," Callie said defensively. "Furthermore, Miss Know It All, Bode is like a brother to me." Part of it was true, Callie thought, her neck growing warm. Her eyes filled with more shadows.

"My ass it was girlish chatter! You were twenty, for Christ's sake. Don't go switching up on me now just because you're getting married. If there's one thing I don't need to do right now, it's question my own sanity. You were twenty goddamn years old when you said you wanted to go to bed with Bode. Furthermore, you said—and this is a direct quote: 'I want to rip off his clothes and drag him onto this very bed we're all sitting on.' End of quote. Go ahead and deny, Mrs. Soon To Be Archer."

"So what?" Brie snapped, joining in. "I thought about dragging Bode to bed myself, many, many times. Admit it, Sela, you would have given up your false eyelashes for Bode to even wink at you. You goddamn lusted after him. Why are we even talking about Bode Jessup today? Callie is getting married tomorrow, and we should be talking about her honeymoon, the presents she's going to get, and how happy she's going to be, being Mrs. Wynfield Archer." Brie's own eyes were full of pain.

"Fine, fine, let's talk about all the tacky gifts she's going to get—silver, crystal, satin sheets, more silver, more crystal, china, and a few ugly things she'll hide in the attic. She's going on a honeymoon to Hong Kong and other places where she will screw her brains out for ten straight days, come home, put the satin sheets on her bed and screw some more. She'll plan on having three children, two boys and one girl. That's it," Sela said, flouncing off the bed.

She is my friend, my best friend, Callie thought in dismay. "Is it possible, Sela, that you missed it all by getting married by the justice of the peace? Please, listen up. I don't want to worry about you today. Be happy for me. Am I asking too much of you?"

"Well, now that you mention it, yes. Those stupid antebellum gowns cost a fortune, not to mention the shoes. Then there was my airfare. And the gift," Sela said, going into the bathroom and slamming the door behind her.

"Whoa." Brie let out a long breath, rolling her eyes at Callie. "Sela's going through a bad time. I guess it's hard for her to see how happy you are. You are happy, aren't you? I see something in your eyes that doesn't compute."

"You were always the one who made the most sense," Callie said, rolling the thread that was now a triple-tight knot between her fingers. "I'm going to miss this house. By the way, I see something in your eyes, too, that I've never seen before. Explain, please."

"Allergies. Are you selling it?"

"Who would buy this ramshackle white elephant? No, I

deeded it to Wyn. This afternoon at the cocktail party I'm going to give it to him. It's all I have—not that it's worth anything," Callie said ruefully. "It's called a deed of trust. Bode did it for me."

A frown built above Brie's eyes. "The land, too?"

"The whole thing, all five hundred acres. Hey, he's not getting a prize here. Half the land is wetlands and they have to be preserved and the other half, or at least most of it, is fallow. It will still be mine in a way, don't you think?"

The frown cut deeper into Brie's forehead. "This is a wedding gift, right?" Callie nodded. "What's Wyn giving you?" She held her breath waiting for her friend's reply.

"First off, he doesn't know I'm giving him the deed of trust. I want it to be a surprise. But, to answer your question, he's giving me his grandmother's pearls. Brie, they are to die for. And he couldn't wait to put my name on all his holdings. I think I'm supposed to sign all those papers this afternoon. There was one small hitch so maybe the papers won't be ready till we get back from our honeymoon. Everything, Brie, has my name on it. He is so generous. Everyone today wants prenuptial agreements. Not Wyn. What's his is mine and what's mine is his. That's the way it should be. I'm sorry Sela's husband didn't feel that way. What is she going to do?"

"She told me last night, the only thing of value she has is the Rolex watch Dylan gave her. She's selling it and taking a real-estate course. She wants to be a real-estate mogul or maven or something like that. With the balance of the money she can live cheaply until she sells some property. She admitted she stole a Chinese vase and sold it right under Dylan's nose. I think she got eighteen thousand dollars for it. She'll be okay, but she'll have to watch her money."

"She actually *stole* it?" Callie whispered, her dark eyes unbelieving.

"Yep. The lady has balls, but then we both know that. You are happy, aren't you, Callie?"

"Lord yes. We're going to try for a baby right away. Wyn is wonderful, and he loves me as much as I love him. If I told him I wanted a star, he'd try to get it for me."

"Trying and getting are two different things," Brie said quietly.

"You don't like Wyn much, do you? It's okay if you don't. I can handle that. Do you want to talk about Bode?"

No. "I like Wyn just fine. What I don't like is he races greyhounds. I just hate it. I know you don't like it either, but you put up with it. Why is that, Callie?"

"What do you expect me to do? His father did it, his grandfather and his great-grandfather did it. I made my views known. It is a sore point between us," she admitted miserably.

"I thought Bode was the only sore point," Brie said sourly.

"You like him better, don't you?"

"I can't forget how wonderful he was to all of us. He's a good, kind, gentle human being."

"If you have something to say, maybe you should say it now," Callie said tightly.

"What is there to say? Wyn hates him. Hates the relationship you have with him. You never told me why that is. I think we should talk about this. Bode doesn't know who his parents are. You were the one who said he just appeared one day. Pearl said she didn't know anything, said your father brought him home one day, and that was that."

Callie hated arguing and defending Bode. She always defended Bode because she loved him. A vision of Bode in the parking lot *respecting her* flashed in front of Callie's eyes.

Bowdey Malcolm Jessup, Attorney at Law. It was Bode who had encouraged her to attend law school in the north. It was Bode who promised her a job in his one-man office when she finished law school and her internship. It was Bode she called in the middle of the night when something was bothering her. He was supersmart, devilishly handsome, a kind, gentle, good man, just the way Brie said he was. Bode was perfect. Yesterday, he finally, with words and his eyes, let her know where she stood in his life.

"What does Wyn have to say about you working with Bode?"

Callie's lips tightened. "He doesn't like it, but he's leaving it up to me. It's what I went to school for. I want to practice family law. My two and a half years working in Columbia has really helped. I'll be an asset to Bode."

"Okay—don't get your panties in a wad." Brie grinned. "I say go for it. Do you think I'll ever get married, Callie?"

"Absolutely. Stop being picky and give those guys in San Diego a chance. What's it feel like to pack a gun?"

"Awesome. I'm a good cop, Callie—detective, I mean. I've been accepted to the FBI Academy."

"Congratulations! Honest, Brie? A female FBI agent! I'm so impressed. Sela will be rich and famous and I'll be . . . happy working for Bode and having Wyn's children. We've come a long way," Callie said.

She sounds defensive, Brie thought. She revised the thought almost immediately. *Frightened* was probably a better word. Damn, she liked Bode Jessup more than she liked Wynfield Archer. But if a contest were in the making, her vote would have to go to Wyn because he loved Callie heart and soul, and whatever made Callie happy made Brie happy. But then Bode loved her, too. She knew it as sure as she knew the sun would set later in the day.

Poor Bode.

"A penny for your thoughts," Callie said.

"I don't know if they're worth that much," Brie said ruefully. "How's it going to work if you take Pearl with you? Wyn has his old nanny. Won't they clash? That's what I was thinking," she lied.

"Wyn is pensioning off his nanny; she's going to live in the guest cottage on the property. Pearl said she wanted to come with me. Thank God. She's . . . I can barely remember my mother. She's all I have except Bode, and he isn't a blood relation. Trust me when I tell you, the only way I would give up Pearl is if Bode wanted her to make a home for him. He wanted her, I know he did. But in true Bode fashion he agreed to let her come with me. I don't want her to work so hard. She'd be picking up after Bode all day long and cooking and cleaning seven days a week. She wouldn't even have time for church."

"Bode would drive her to church. He used to do it all the time," Brie grumbled. "You owe him now for Pearl. He has as much right to her as you do."

"I don't owe Bode anything. The decision was Pearl's. She loves Bode, and he knows that. It's fine—really it is, Brie. What *is* that girl doing in the bathroom?"

"Putting on two pounds of makeup. It takes a lot of time to cover up unhappiness. You, on the other hand, sparkle, almost. I'm so happy for you, Callie. I wouldn't have missed this wedding for anything in the world even though those bridesmaid dresses are shitful. Sela is right about that. Whatever were you thinking when you picked them out?" Better to move on to other things. Talking about Bode was too painful.

Callie flushed. "Actually, Wyn kind of . . . more or less . . . he gave me . . . input."

"And lavender! I hate to say this, but I feel like I'm laid out, you know, as in dead, in that color. It washes me out. If I had your nice tan, I could see it, but I'm too fair; Sela, too."

"Oh God, I can't do anything right. I wanted to please Wyn so I agreed. Bode said the same thing. Maybe if we take the crinolines and hoops out, the dresses won't be so—"

"—Shitful?"

"I was going to say 'awful,' but yes, 'shitful' pretty much sums it up. They are the exact same color as the wisteria that covers Wyn's garden—I think that's why he picked the color he did. Do you have any suggestions?" Callie asked.

"Well, I do," Sela said, emerging from the bathroom perfectly made-up. She wore a daffodil yellow dress that was so plain and so severely cut, Callie knew it had to be an original of some kind and outrageously expensive. Sela made a face as much as to say, "I had to get what I could while the getting was good." She said, "We could take down your drapes and curtains, and swag them across our bodies in a toga effect. *Anything,* Callie, would be better than those awful gowns. Brie?"

Brie looked at Callie, who winced and shook her head. "Taking out the hoops and crinolines will help. It's too late to make other changes. God, you don't think this is an omen of some kind, do you?" she asked. "When things go wrong at the onset it pretty much goes downhill after that."

Brie hitched up the baggy pajamas that were so glorious in color Sela said she needed sunglasses to look at them. "I see that your fashion sense hasn't improved, Brie," she said bitingly. "When was the last time you wore a dress? Are you sure you aren't a dyke? God, you *are* skinny!"

"Up yours, Sela," Brie said, heading for the bathroom. She slammed the door so hard the windows rattled.

"Testy, isn't she?" Sela drawled.

"You bring out the worst in her, Sela. Why do you keep doing it?"

"Because I'm jealous of her just the way I'm jealous of you," Sela said honestly.

"For God's sake, why? I have less than you have. Brie is doing what she loves. She always wanted to be a cop, and I bet she's the best San Diego has to offer. And now the FBI Academy. That's not shabby. She went after what she wanted, and she is not a dyke. I hate that word, Sela. Please don't call her that again. Look around—this house is so rotten it's falling apart. This room and the kitchen are the only rooms that are livable. Pearl's room is okay, too, but that's it. I have no money. I took off a year and worked, my car is so old they don't make parts for it anymore. I squeaked through college and law school by the skin of my teeth whereas you took honors; Brie too. So you made a few bad decisions; it isn't the end of the world. I see a bitterness in you I never saw before. Please, Sela, don't let it eat at you. He isn't worth it. Start over and put the past behind you."

"Easy for you to say, but you're right, as usual. I really do wish you all the happiness in the world, Callie—I mean that. And I am so very proud of Brie, I could bust. I tell her that, too. She knows what I'm like. Real friends accept one another for what they are. The gowns *are* shitful though." She grinned wickedly. "Will you be coming back here after the wedding?"

"No. Most of my things were sent to Beaufort earlier in the week. Pearl's things are going there today. She'll pack the few remaining things tomorrow, and one of Wyn's employees will pick her up and drive her to the plantation. It's going to be hard for her to give this up. It's the only home she's ever known.

"Sela, look at the curtains," Callie went on sadly. "Pearl mended them so many times, the patches have patches. You can see the backing through the carpet. The floor is warped, and the windowsills are so rotten you can stick your fingers in the holes. The place is full of termites and powder-post beetles. It's not safe to walk on the second floor, and there are so many leaks in the pipes the walls are wet. The wiring is a fire hazard, and there's no insurance. Do you know how I got through my last year of law school? And you sit there and say you're jealous of me! Don't ever tell me that again," Callie said coolly.

"Wyn offered to pay for your schooling."

"The bottom line is I simply wasn't smart enough to hold a real job and study, too. I would never take financial help from Wyn. Never. When we move to Beaufort I am going to treat Pearl like a queen. I am going to wait on her hand and foot. I am going to bring her breakfast in bed. I am going to take her shopping and buy her fine dresses and good shoes. I am going to accompany her to church, and I am going to do the dishes while she watches me—and guess what? I'm even going to teach her how to drive, and I'll buy her a car when I start to earn money. I'm going to take real good care of her. What do you have to say to that, Sela?" Callie demanded, her face flushing a rosy pink.

"I think it's wonderful. She deserves the best, and I hope you follow through."

"Do you think I won't?" Callie screeched. "Do you think I just said all those things to hear myself talk? I meant every single word."

"Sometimes the best intentions go awry. What about Wyn? He's going to want to socialize. How are you going to do all those kind, wonderful things if you don't have the time?"

"I'll make the time. Pearl comes first. She does, Sela, don't look at me like that. Wyn understands. And if he switches up on me at some point, tough."

"Good for you, Callie," Sela said, hugging her friend fiercely.

"Ta da!" Brie sang from the bathroom doorway.

"My God, it's wearing a dress," Sela said in mock horror. "And its hair looks fashionable, and is that makeup I see on those freckled cheeks? Earrings, too. Lord have mercy!"

"You're an asshole, Sela. I told you that when you were six years old and I'm telling you it again now. My question is this: are you going to drive Pearl down here to see Bode? I can't exactly picture him pedaling that bike of his all the way to Beaufort. Did he ever get a car?"

"Yes, but he hardly ever drives it. He said he doesn't want to contribute to the pollution."

At that moment, Pearl appeared in the doorway, dressed in a colorful muumuu, her favorite daytime attire. A massive braid was wrapped around her head and fitted her like a crown. Once black, her hair was now streaked with gray to match her eyebrows. Her eyes were round, dark, and as shiny as new pennies. There was always a smile on her moon-shaped face, matching the one in her eyes. All she had to do was hold out her arms and all three young women would rush to her, grateful for the warmth and love she gave them. Her feet were big with calluses so thick and hard she wore them like a second skin. She hated shoes and only put them on when she went to church, which was seven days a week and twice on Sunday.

"Miz Callie, Mr. Wyn is on the phone," she said, dragging the curly wire from the kitchen into Callie's room.

Sela and Brie tactfully withdrew, Pearl's arms around their slim shoulders. "Melon and coffee?" she asked, placing pristine white linen napkins, expertly mended, in front of them. The china was from Wal-Mart as was the cutlery, the good stuff sold off years ago.

"Just coffee, Pearl," Sela said.

"Just coffee for me, too," Brie said.

"Lord have mercy. The two of you don't hardly make one

good substantial woman. Side by side you're still skinny.
Men like their ladies to have meat on their bones."

"I'm this skinny because a man made me so," Sela grumbled.

"I'm this skinny because I don't have time to eat. I'm out
chasing the bad guys all day long." Brie laughed nervously.

Pearl chuckled, a deep rumble starting in her massive belly
and working its way up to her robust chest. "Has Miz Callie
been filling your heads with all the fine things she's gonna be
doing for me? If she has, don't you go paying her no never
mind."

"She needs to do it for you, Pearl. Let her. Be gracious and
accepting. How's Bode's law practice? Do you think he'll ride
his bike to the wedding?"

"Well, his practice is fine . . . *was* fine. He makes money
and he gives me some, but I won't take it. Bode is a fine man.
He had some lady make me this dress I'm wearing. He knows
how I like pretty colors. But to be answering your question, I
don't know how he's getting to the wedding. Maybe he'll
take a taxi and maybe he'll walk and maybe he'll ride his
bike. As long as he gets there is all that's important."

"Hear, hear!" Brie said, holding her Wal-Mart mug high in
a toast. "To Bode Jessup, a fine man!"

"A mighty fine man," Pearl said. "There is none better
than my boy."

"Is he better than Wynfield Archer?" Brie asked slyly.

"Don't you be putting words in my mouth, young lady,"
Pearl said sternly.

"I think he's better," Brie said quietly.

"So do I," Sela said.

"I'll whop your behinds, the both of you, if you say that to
Miz Callie," Pearl warned.

"We'd never, ever . . ." they said in unison.

"Good."

"What time is the party?" Brie asked, holding her cup out for a refill. "I always really loved this kitchen. Still love it. I think part of it is because you're here, Pearl."

"That's a kind thing for you to be saying. I will miss it, too," she said, looking around the huge square room. "Course, I ain't seen Mr. Wyn's kitchen. It might be just as good as this one." Her bare foot scuffed at the old Charlestonian brick on the floor that she scrubbed with pumice stone three times a week. The cabinets and doors were old with iron hinges and so many coats of white paint they no longer closed properly. The walls were white, adorned by framed drawings that Pearl's "children" had made for her years and years ago. Bode's picture was of a sunrise and sunset, superimposed over a vast body of water that was as blue as a summer sky. Callie's picture showed a field of cotton with people picking the crop. The caption read: *white people picking cotton.* It had been drawn when she was five and still learning how to print and spell. Sela's picture was of two dogs as big as horses and labeled: *mother dog and baby dog.* Brie's picture was of Pearl with a chicken in her hand, a bandanna wrapped around her head. The crayoned words said: *my other mother.* Green plants and herbs hung from the rafters and dotted the windowsill. Pots of flowers, every color of the rainbow, in clay pots, lined the raised hearth of the fireplace. Curtains the color of freshly picked cranberries hung over the multipaned windows that held as many coats of white paint as the cupboards and matched the old Charlestonian brick to perfection. The butcher-block table was old, ancient really, and deeply scarred by the huge knives Pearl used to hack up chickens and vegetables. The chairs were just as old and scratched, the finish worn off long ago. Cranberry-colored cushions rested on the seats and the backs of the chairs, all sewn by Pearl. The rag-tied rugs by the sink and stove were made by Pearl from Bode and Callie's outgrown clothing. The appliances were old, the enamel chipped, black spots covered over with dabs of white paint that were now yellowish in color.

It was a kitchen of happiness and sorrow. Callie's father had died while sitting at the butcher-block table. Bode had kissed Callie on the cheek in the kitchen when she was ten years old. Sela's first skinned knee was treated in the kitchen, and Brie cried her eyes out there in Pearl's arms, the day of her mother's funeral. And it was in this same kitchen that Pearl had listened to secrets and then sworn on the Almighty never to reveal them.

"Did I ask what time the party was, or do I just think I did?" Brie asked.

"Two o'clock," Pearl said.

"The heat of the day." Sela sighed as she fanned herself with the napkin. "Let's go into town and see Bode," she said to Brie.

"Sounds good to me," Brie said, carrying her coffee mug to the sink. "Is there anything Sela or I can do, Pearl?"

"Git along with you. I have some packing to do for Miz Callie that will keep me busy. You be back here by one o'clock, you hear me now?"

"Yes, Pearl," Brie said, planting a wet kiss on her plump cheek. "I'm so glad to be home."

"I don't know what this world is coming to when a fine young Southern lady carries a gun in her purse," Pearl grumbled.

"I wear a holster, Pearl," Brie said solemnly.

"Are you funning with me, Miz Brie?"

"Nope, I saw it." Sela grinned. "It's a wicked piece of metal, I can tell you that."

"I never thought I'd live to see the day. I knew way back when you was running around here you were going to do something different. You didn't like doll babies and you were the one who always wanted to play cops and robbers," Pearl fretted as she filled the sink with hot sudsy water.

"Wasn't I always the cop?" Brie asked.

"And Bode was the bad guy." Sela laughed. "Callie was the damsel in distress, and I was the lady of the manor. God, that was so long ago . . ."

"Shoo, shoo," Pearl said, waving her soapy hands in the air.

"Your rented car or my rented car?" Sela inquired.

"Don' make me no never mind," Brie said, mimicking Pearl.

"Okay, mine," Sela decided. "God, this place is gorgeous. Do you remember the first time our mothers brought us out here and we rode down the road with all those angel oaks on each side, the Spanish moss dripping almost to the ground? I think my heart stopped beating for a few minutes. It's funny how we never saw how dilapidated the house was, or how things had gone to ruin, even back then. We were so happy, at least I was. I lived to come out here."

Sela turned on the ignition and drove the rental car down the rutted brick road that led to the main road. At the entrance to Parker Manor she stopped the car, perspiration beading on her forehead. She pointed a long, red-tipped finger at the ivy-covered brick pillars. Her voice was a hushed whisper when she said, "I used to dream about these pillars and the old oaks. In my dreams there was always a sign over the pillars that said *Sela lives here.* God, I wanted to belong here so bad I could taste it. Right now, this very minute, if someone said, 'This is all yours,' I'd get out a hammer, nails, and a scrub bucket and go to town on it. Is that crazy or what?"

"Nope," Brie mumbled. "I used to dream, too; but in my dreams I was always dressed up in my white dress and Mary Janes. I had a basket of flowers on my arm and . . . it was all so ethereal. God, I loved the flowers, the scent of the jasmine, the oleander, the camellias, the azaleas." Tears momentarily blurred her vision.

"Where was Callie in your dreams?" Sela asked carefully.

"With Bode," Brie said just as carefully. "Where was she in your dreams?"

"With Bode. Everything's wrong, Brie. Nothing feels right to me. How did we get on this subject anyway?"

"You mentioned your dream," Brie volunteered.

Sela shrugged. "Do you think we came out here because of this place and Callie and Bode—or was it because Pearl made us feel so loved? I love her. God, I really do," Sela said, her voice breaking. "She's getting old, Brie. What if she dies when Callie takes her to Beaufort? What if she misses Bode so much she dies of a broken heart?"

"I want you to shut up right now, Sela. I don't want to think about that. Bode won't let that happen." She turned then, to stare at the manor house where she'd spent so many wonderful days and hours.

Yesterday.

"I think," she said in a strangled voice, "we came here because of Callie, this place *and* Bode. But if you're asking me to single out one person, one thing, then I'd have to say it was Pearl. From the very first day, for me anyway, it was Pearl. She hugged me so tight that first time. She said I was as pretty as a moonbeam. At five I knew it was a lie, I called it a fib back then, and I loved her for that damn lie."

"She told me I was as pretty as the first star at night," Sela whimpered. "We were so homely and gawky, Brie."

"I know. Callie wasn't, though. She was the moonbeam and the star all rolled together. Do you remember, Sela, how

Pearl used to dude her up for her afternoon 'audience' with her mother, every afternoon at four o'clock?"

"I remember. Callie always said she knew someday her mother was going to hug her, but to my knowledge Mrs. Parker never did. Callie said she always gave her a wafer cookie, patted her on the head, and said, 'Now run along, dear, and be a good girl for Pearl. I have to take my medicine now.' She was a drunk. We didn't figure that out until we were fourteen or so."

"I want yesterday," Brie whispered.

"Me, too," Sela breathed in return. "I'd kill if there was a way to get it back. I mean that, Brie."

"We'll always be friends, won't we, Sela?"

"Always. Remember how we used to call ourselves the sisterless sisters?"

"We should make some kind of pact to get together every year or something like that," Brie said. "What we should do is pick a holiday and make certain we plan in advance. Let's talk to Callie and Bode about it."

"That means Wyn will be there," Sela said.

"Oh."

The matter was dropped and not brought up again.

"I love you, too, more than yesterday and twice as much as I'll love you tomorrow. Top that, Wyn Archer," Callie said, a smile of pure joy on her face. "I can't wait either. This time tomorrow I'll just be hours away from being Mrs. Wynfield Archer. I've never been happier. I'll see you this afternoon. Bye, darling."

Pearl's face was inscrutable as she dried the last of the dishes. Her back was to Callie, but she knew the minute Callie entered the kitchen. She didn't need to hear the click of the receiver in the cradle to know her darling child was with her.

"I swear, Pearl, I think Wyn is more jittery than I am. I

thought men were supposed to be calm and collected. Was my father like that when he and Mama got married? I was hoping it would cool off today. It's so sticky I'm going to need a second shower. It's going to be great, Pearl—Wyn has *central* air-conditioning. We'll never sweat again. Inside, at least."

"Ladies perspire, men sweat. Didn't you learn anything at all in those fancy schools?" Pearl groused.

"I certainly did. I learned that I sweated in the summer up North as much as I sweat down here. *Sweat,* Pearl. That's when you're dripping wet. Look at me. Even my hair is frizzing up. Where did Sela and Brie go?"

"To look around. I heard the car start up, so they must have decided to go for a spin somewhere."

Callie mopped at her face with a paper napkin Pearl handed her. "I thought you said no self-respecting Southern housekeeper used paper napkins."

"I did say that, and I still say that. I use them for spills and for young ladies to wipe the perspiration from their brows." Pearl turned to face Callie. "I've been thinking, Miz Callie. Why don't I stay here till you get back from your honeymoon? I'm not going to feel right moving into a new house without you there. I thought I'd ask Bode to come out here and stay with me, or I'd move in with him for a while."

"Pearl, I thought we had settled all this days ago. Are you having second thoughts?"

"You didn't answer my question, missy."

"Pearl, if you really want to stay here until I get back, it's okay with me. It's okay with me if you want to stay with Bode. I want whatever will make *you* happy. You miss Lazarus. You want to be close to him, to be able to visit his grave." She hoped for a smile, but Pearl's face remained inscrutable. "I guess that means you're going to stay."

"I thought you'd see it my way." Pearl smiled.

"You are coming to the party, aren't you? Bode said he was picking you up."

"A friend of Bode's is picking me up in his automobile. I'll be there. And speaking of the rascal, look who's pedaling up the driveway."

"Bode! Make us some breakfast, Pearl. Flapjacks and eggs for Bode. One scrambled egg for me. Hurry—if he sees you making it, he'll stay."

Callie was the same young girl she'd been earlier in her bedroom with Sela and Brie when she squealed Bode's name and threw herself in his arms. "It's about time! I thought . . . I'm glad you're here, Bode. Pearl is making us breakfast. Flapjacks and eggs." Yesterday was forgotten.

"I ate earlier, but thanks for the invitation." He smiled as he loped across the kitchen to hug Pearl. "How's it going, Mama Pearl?"

Callie's heart swelled. Her eyes misted over when she saw the look of happiness on Pearl's face. Was she doing the right thing by taking Pearl away from Bode? Pearl was the only mother Bode had ever known.

"Jest fine, Bode. I can't believe you're turning down one of my breakfasts." She squeezed Bode so hard Callie saw his eyes pop.

"I can't believe it either, but I . . . ." A look of desperation and something that looked like uncertainty crossed Bode's face.

This wasn't the Bode she knew, Callie thought. Bode was never at a loss for words, except for yesterday, in the car park. He would have been the world's best poker player because his face never gave away anything. That very look was an asset in the courtroom when he was summarizing his case in front of a jury. She felt a tiny curl of fear circle her stomach.

"You have to do *what?*" Callie drawled. "I'm upset with you, Bode. I've been home a month, and I've only talked to you once on the phone." Yesterday was better left alone. "I'm going to be working for you in two and a half weeks. Shouldn't we talk, go over things like where my desk is going to be, how much you're going to pay me? Something's wrong. I know you too well, Bode. When you don't want to deal with something you ignore it." *Like yesterday.*

Callie's heart started to ache when she stared into Bode's dark eyes. "Yesterday never happened, Bode," she whispered.

Bode grinned. "Never happened."

"Something's wrong, I can feel it. Spit it out, Bode." *Surely he wouldn't hold yesterday against her.*

"Well, it depends on one's interpretation of the word *wrong*. I had this offer. It's too good to pass up. I'm leaving in a little while. Some of my friends opened up a practice in New Mexico. It's a big, artsy-fartsy community and they offered me a full partnership and I don't have to put any money into the pot. I'm going to give it a try."

Callie backed up a step, her eyes going first to Bode and then to Pearl. Pearl looked like she was in shock, so that meant she hadn't known about Bode's decision. "When— aren't you even going to stay for the party, the wedding?" Damn, she sounded like she was begging. She could feel her eyes start to burn. How could he do this to her? "What about my job?"

"I can't, Callie. My plane leaves"—he looked down at his watch—"two hours from now, so I've got to get moving. A friend is waiting out by the main road to give me a ride to the airport. I'm sorry."

Anger, the likes of which she'd never known, rivered through Callie. "That sucks, Bode. You tell me all this today. I was . . . I thought we had a deal. I was going to work for you, we were going to be a team. Why didn't you just send me a certified letter? I might have been able to handle *that.* How dare you do this to me! How dare you! I wanted all my friends to be at my wedding. I wouldn't let *anything,* anything, Bode, stand in my way if it was your wedding. I can't believe you're doing this to me. I thought we were friends. Friends don't do things like this. I was wrong about you, Bode. Go on, go catch your plane," Callie sobbed as she ran from the room.

"You best be going, Bode. Miz Callie is never, ever going to understand what you jest did. Don't pay me no mind. Give me a big hug and let your feet take you out to the road." Tears glistened in the old woman's eyes as she held out her arms to the young man she thought of as her son. "I understand, Bode. I might be getting old, but I understand."

"I know you do, Mama Pearl. Give this to Callie before she leaves for the party. I want to go on record right now as saying this is a mistake." He handed Pearl the deed of trust Callie had asked him to draw up. "Tell Callie she owes me twenty-five bucks, and I'll send her my bill."

"I'll tell her, Bode."

"It's okay if I leave my bike in the barn, isn't it?"

"Course it's all right. You go on now; I'll take it out to the barn and put a tarp over it."

"That baby is going to be worth a fortune someday, Mama Pearl," Bode said with a catch in his voice. "I'll write. Not often, but I will write. I love you, Mama Pearl. Take care of her."

"I will, Bode. I love you so much," Pearl cried brokenly.

Tears rolled down Bode's cheeks. "All I am I owe to you, Mama Pearl. I couldn't have done it without your help. I just wish you'd let me do something for you. I'd work my ass off for you, you know that, don't you? I'd give you my last dime, the shirt off my back."

"My love isn't for sale, Bode Jessup. Now you git on out of here before I start to howl like a banshee."

She watched from the kitchen doorway as Bode walked out to the road. She saw him stop once and raise his eyes to the second floor. She knew he was remembering another time when he had stood there . . . waiting. Pearl drew in her breath, waiting to see if Callie would come running from the first-floor bedroom she now occupied. She wanted to scream to Bode, "You're looking at the wrong window!" but she bit down on her lip, tasting the salty tang of her own blood.

When Callie didn't emerge from her bedroom and when Bode was no longer in her sight, Pearl went outside and wheeled Bode's bike to the barn. The fine hairs on the back of her neck prickled. Callie was watching her, she was sure of it.

Inside the dark barn, Pearl's shoulders slumped as sobs ripped from her throat. "I should have told him." She dropped to her knees in prayer. "Lord, I'm just a poor, old, dumb woman with no brains. Keep my boy safe and make Miz Callie happy. If it's too much to ask, punish me some way. I'll pray harder, more, anything You want. I promise to wear shoes. You know how hard that is for me, but I'll do it if You keep my boy and girl safe. That's all I have to say, Lord. Oh, one last thing, don't let this here bicycle rust. I'd like it to be in good condition when Bode gits back. This is Pearl. You know I don't have no last name so I can't identify myself more. Just Pearl, from Parker Manor, Lord. Amen."

Callie watched Bode from behind the curtain in her room. Her hands were clenched into tight fists. "Look back, Bode, look back," she whispered. She wanted to shout his name, to tell him to wait, to say she wasn't angry; but she *was* angry. She wanted to run out to say good-bye, but her feet were rooted to the floor.

"You're never coming back, I know that, Bode Jessup. You

aren't my friend. You lied. You're turning your back on me when I need you the most. Friends share. I wanted you here so I could share my happiness, knowing someday you'd invite me to share yours. Damn you, Bode, I hate you. I'll hate you till the day I die. Go to New Mexico, see if I care. If you write, I'll send the letters back unopened. I hate you, Bode Jessup. I hateyouhateyouhateyou."

5

The overhead sign at the entrance to Archer Hall was worn and simple. The carving, done by some long-ago slave, had weathered with the years, blending perfectly with the long row of angel oaks that dripped Spanish moss, giving an eerie and yet beautiful impression to first-time visitors. The road was made of old Charlestonian paving that, over the years, had been restored, brick by brick. It ran in a straight line, as straight as the angel oaks that graced both sides of it. At the end stood Archer Hall, glorious in the summer sunlight. Its pristine whiteness, its massive white columns, made visitors gasp in delight, imagining all manner of antebellum soirées and carriage-driven guests arriving for festivities.

There were still soirées but the guests arrived in Lincoln Town Cars, Mercedes Benz automobiles, and Porsches. The food was the same, the recipes handed down over the years, and all of it simple and rich, with elegant desserts that were described as sinful to a lady's waistline.

Wynfield Archer reined in the gelding at the entrance to his home. Damn, he was running late, but this ride was important to him. Everything in life was important to Wyn. He never did anything he couldn't give one hundred percent of his attention to. He looked now at his riding partner, Kallum Trinity, who was also his business partner and best friend. "I'd die if I ever had to give this up," he said quietly.

"Then I suggest you curb your spending," Kal said just as soberly. "I told you months ago we have a serious cash-flow problem. Business is down twenty percent and you spent a fortune renovating the master suite in the house. Plus," Kallum said, holding up his hand to forestall what he thought Wyn was going to say next, "plus, I know weddings are important, but does this really have to be the wedding of the century? Jesus, Wyn, the last time I checked your bank balance, I— Fifty thousand dollars for a wedding is outrageous in my opinion."

"That's what I get for having a CPA and lawyer for a business partner. But, to answer your question about the wedding first, I want to give Callie the best, everything she never had, and I'm willing to go into hock, to bust my ass, to do whatever it takes to give her everything I can possibly give. That's how much I love her."

Kallum pushed the Braves baseball cap back on his head. "That doesn't sound right to me. It sounds like Callie wouldn't marry you unless you did all those things. Callie is a pretty simple person. I've never known her to ask for anything. If you want my honest opinion, I'd say all of this is a little overwhelming to her. I don't think she wanted it or expected it. You can be overwhelming, too, Wyn. You bulldoze ahead and don't think about the other person."

"Look, I'm never going to get married again. This is a once-in-a-lifetime thing for both of us. I want to do it. Money just isn't that important to me. I like things, I like giving. I like grandness. That doesn't mean I'm some kind of . . . of . . ."

"Jerk will do. While we're on the subject, don't you think

twenty-five thousand dollars is a lot to spend on a honey-moon?"

"Hell, yes, it's a lot. I'm the first to admit it, but again, I want to give Callie the best. I want us to have a memory we'll never forget."

"Why do I have the feeling Callie would have been happy going to Myrtle Beach or Hilton Head for a week? A trip to Hong Kong, followed by Bali, Singapore, and wherever else you're planning on going to . . . Listen, you never did tell me—did you consult with your wife-to-be, or did you just go ahead and make the plans?"

"I made the plans," Wyn muttered. "What's with this sudden inquisition, Kallum?"

"I don't care for the word *inquisition,* Wyn. I'm concerned. I think I have a right to be concerned. You need to develop more respect for money. I've said everything I have to say. When you get back, the purse strings are going to be tightened so hard you're going to gasp. Is it a deal?"

"Absolutely," Wyn said, stretching out his hand. "Listen, if I haven't told you lately, you are without a doubt the best friend a man could have. I hope we'll always be business partners and friends. Now, tell me, what's the latest business gossip?"

Kallum shrugged. "Everything pretty much slows down in August, as you know." He wasn't going to mention Bowdey Jessup's vacant office. He liked Bode, really liked him. What's more, he respected the guy.

Wyn took a deep breath. "Smell the gardenias, Kallum. They've bloomed three times this year. Callie's bridal bouquet is gardenias from Archer Hall."

"They make me sneeze," Kallum grumbled. "My eyes are already starting to itch. I'll see you at the party. Don't worry, I'll recognize you—you'll be the guy with the sappiest expression."

"Oh yeah?" Wyn drawled. "I saw a sappy look on your face when Callie told you you'd be Brie Canfield's partner. She's turned into quite a looker. She's . . ." Wyn's agile brain struggled for just the right word ". . . earthy. Don't try any tricks, either. She carries a gun and knows how to use it."

"I'll remember," Kallum said as he turned off to his own home two miles down the road from Archer Hall.

Wyn sighed as he slid from the horse and walked him the rest of the way to the stable. Normally he rubbed his horse down himself after a brisk ride, but today he handed him over to the groom, but not before he offered an apple to the gelding. He had just enough time to shower, shave, and drive to Summerville.

Wyn took time now the way he always did, to look over his house, trying to see it through Callie's eyes. He knew she'd want to redecorate, to get rid of some of the older furnishings, and it was all right with him. Whatever made Callie happy made him happy.

The windows were tall, with light streaming through the sparkling glass. Now, at this early hour, he could see how faded the brocades and damasks were. It had never bothered him before. Now, it did. The heavy, cumbersome sofas, the spindly, fragile chairs and thick, ugly tables . . . and all his innumerable ancestors, whose names he'd long ago forgotten if he'd ever known them at all, stared back at him from their tarnished silver frames.

The old photographs would be the first things to go. Callie would set up pictures of their wedding, framed candid shots of her and Sela and Brie. Not Bode. By God, not Bode. New beginnings should be new, not cluttered up with furniture and memories of the past. He could feel a knot form in his neck. Bowdey Jessup belonged in the past the way this old furniture did. He eyed the ancient Victrola and wished he could take the time now to carry it out to the barn. They'd get a CD system. He made a mental note to ask Kallum who he could get to wire the house.

The house itself was spotless, the heart-of-pine floors gleaming with hundreds of coats of wax. He cursed himself for not having asked Callie what kind of furniture she liked. God, what if she was into Danish modern or Chinese lacquer? Maybe he'd have to help her out, the way he'd helped select the dresses for the wedding party. He did love the purple wisteria that covered the grounds. Kallum had been nagging him for years now to cut it back, for it was choking off all the other plants, especially the priceless camellias. One of these days.

The staircase was made of ancient oak, polished to a high sheen, the steps covered with a thick carpet. He fondly remembered how he and Callie had slid down the banister, whooping and hollering like ten-year-olds. He'd caught her at the bottom, been delirious with laughter until she'd said how she and Bode used to slide down the banister at Parker Manor almost every day. She said Bode never caught her, though. His happiness had dimmed for a moment.

He hated Bode Jessup with a passion that was unequaled. These past years he'd tried to control his hatred for Callie's sake, but every time she brought up his name the fine hairs on the back of Wyn's neck stood on end. Of all the people in the low country, why did Bode Jessup have to be Callie's best friend? That, more than anything, was what bothered him. Kallum Trinity liked Bode. So did everyone in Summerville. Brie and Sela adored him. Callie said she loved him like a brother. No one to his knowledge had one bad word to say about Bode Jessup. Even Steven Bryers, who'd had his ass whipped by Bode, had only good things to say about Bode. Steven was a dentist now and boasted all over town that Bode had a perfect set of teeth and had never had a cavity.

Christ, according to Bryers he didn't even have plaque build-up! Pure and simply, he was jealous.

"Don't let Bode Jessup spoil your day, Wyn," he told himself as he mounted the stairs to the second floor. "You got the girl. Bode is out in the cold. Once Callie settles down and becomes a mother, Bode will just be a memory." He whistled as he shed his clothes, stomping his way through the meadow of carpeting to the huge modern bathroom he'd installed a year ago, complete with Jacuzzi and bidet. How Callie had giggled over *that*. He rather liked having his butt flushed with warm water.

He was happy about a lot of things, happy that he'd finally sold the family mansion in Charleston to a family with six children. He was tired of going back and forth at the change of the seasons, and with the monster air-conditioning unit he'd installed he was as happy as a pig in a mudslide. Thank God he hadn't lived back when the tradition of the low country demanded that one live in Charleston during the winter months and then summer in the piney forests. Something about a swamp fever. Not that he cared diddly-squat about fevers or anything else. This was his home, his niche, and he wasn't ever going to live anywhere else. His good fortunes were almost an embarrassment. Not that he cared about that either. All he really cared about was Callie and the wonderful life they were going to have. He would give her everything in his power. He would love her as no man ever loved a woman. Together they would have beautiful, wonderful children, two boys who looked like him and two girls who looked like Callie. They'd grow old together, their hair graying, rocking on the oak rockers on the verandah.

Wyn padded naked out to the cool bedroom, poured two ounces of bourbon into a glass, and took it neat. He sucked on his tongue from the bite and then started to whistle, a popular ditty that made him grin from ear to ear. Thirty minutes later he was dressed in a blue-and-white Brooks Brothers seersucker suit with a crisp white-linen shirt. He stood back to admire his reflection in the mirror. "You, Wynfield Archer, are as handsome as Callie is beautiful." He laughed uproariously, then sobered when he wondered what Bode would wear to the party and the wedding. Probably jeans, a white shirt, and those god-awful, black, ankle-high Keds sneakers he was born with.

"Go to hell, Bode Jessup," he muttered as he downed another ounce of Wild Turkey. He held the glass of powerful bourbon aloft. "To me. To Callie. To politics. To success!"

On the way to the garage he shook his head to clear it. Maybe he should have a cup of coffee. He had a buzz on, and all because of Bode Jessup. He *never* drank before four in the afternoon. Never. A quick glance at his watch told him he didn't have time for a cup of coffee. He'd just have to drive carefully and straddle the white line. He'd be fine as long as he was careful.

He was sweating when he backed the Cadillac out of the garage. He swore. He should have had the good sense to come out ten minutes earlier to turn on the air-conditioning. The bourbon he'd consumed on an empty stomach was making its presence known. He mopped at his brow with a square of linen that was so expertly stitched and laundered it looked like it came from one of the finest shops in Charleston. He swore again. Now he'd have to go back into the house for a fresh handkerchief.

Ten minutes later, Wyn eyed the Cadillac for a moment before he slid behind the wheel. He hated the car, which formerly he had loved. To him it was a badge, a symbol of his prosperity, but once Bode Jessup saw it and had made a derogatory comment in front of a group of businessmen.

They had snickered at Bode's bold tongue. Wyn remembered his words exactly, but refused to give Bode the satisfaction of trading the car in for a foreign model. "It looks like a pimp-mobile, Wyn. Did they give it to you, or did you actually pay money for it?" Thank God he'd had the wit to offer a comeback that made the men chuckle. For the life of him he couldn't remember what it was he'd said. One of these days he was going to remember. Maybe he'd share the experience with Callie, and then again maybe he wouldn't.

The tires squealed on the old brick as Wyn backed the big car around and headed for the road, his thoughts on Bode Jessup and how he was going to have to be polite to the bastard, even shake his hand. Well, hell, he could be magnanimous. After all, he'd gotten the girl. Your loss, Bode. Eat your heart out, you son of a bitch.

His anger was getting the best of him. He had to control it and ease up on the gas pedal. So what if he was a little late? The minister couldn't start the rehearsal without him, and Judge Summers couldn't start the party without the guests of honor. He watched as the needle dropped from seventy to sixty and then to fifty-five. He moved the lever for cruise control and fired up a cigarette.

Tomorrow was going to be the happiest day of his life. Today was running a very close second. The Reverend Neville said the wedding rehearsal would take twenty minutes; then it was on to the party. Judge Summers and his wife, Miss Nela, really knew how to throw a party, and the fact that the Judge himself was giving Callie away made it all the more prestigious. The local newspaper would cover the party, and print a glowing article on the soon-to-be Archers—an article Bode would read because it would be on the front page. Anything Judge Summers did made the front page, even if it was a fishing trip or acquiring a new camellia for his garden.

Aaah, life was wonderful.

* * *

Sela and Brie watched Callie pace the kitchen. She'd already walked around the butcher-block table nine times and was on her tenth trip when Sela barked, "Enough already, Callie. What's wrong?"

"Wrong? Nothing's wrong. Wyn is late. Pearl isn't ready. Pearl's *always* ready. I'm starting to sweat. My makeup is ruined. You two have been acting bitchy all day and—"

"And Bode's offices are empty," Brie said quietly.

Callie's head jerked upright. "He had no right to hurt Pearl like that. I hate him for doing this. In the whole of my life I never saw Pearl cry, but she cried today. She also told me she is going to stay here until I get back from my honeymoon. She wanted to stay because of Bode. I know it, and he knows it—and what did he do? He stood here, calm as can be, and said . . . and said I don't have a job and that he was leaving. How could he do that to Pearl? He even had the nerve to bring that damn bike of his and . . . and ask Pearl to store it in the barn! You should have seen her. She treated it like it was made of solid gold. I was watching her. Okay, I was . . . spying. I thought she was going to kiss the damn thing. He made her cry. I'll never forgive him for that," Callie spluttered.

"Looks like he made you cry, too," Brie said gently.

"Yes, he did. I would have cried if either one of you said you couldn't come to my wedding. I thought we were friends! I *wanted* him at my wedding. Would an extra two days have made all that much difference? He could have taken a flight out right after the wedding. Oh no, he slaps me in the face with this, and he made Pearl cry. Now she's going to be unhappy with the move and she'll start to blame me. I know in my heart she doesn't want to leave. You know how she goes to the cemetery to visit Lazarus's grave every Sunday. I told her I'd drive her back there, and she said no. If she stayed here, Bode would have taken her. Bode changed all that. I hate him, God, how I hate him for this! Why did he wait till today, the very last minute? It's unconscionable, that's what it is," Callie raged. She was on her thirteenth walk around the butcher-block table.

"Bode never does anything without a reason," Sela said. "God, it's like an oven in here. How do you stand it?"

"I stand it because I have to stand it. Where *is* Wyn? He's never late. I wonder if something has happened." She completed her fourteenth walk around the table, wringing her hands and muttering under her breath.

"You can just get the idea that something's happened to Wyn right out of your head. Nothing ever happens to the Wynfield Archers of this world. Society is programmed to believe the worst, did either one of you know that?" Brie spoke in a voice that was no different from the one she would have used to discuss Summerville's yearly rainfall.

Pearl took that particular moment to make her entrance into the kitchen. Wyn simultaneously tooted his horn as he swerved the big Cadillac to a halt alongside the steps to the back porch. The three young women gasped, their eyes agape at Pearl's splendor of attire.

"Pearl! How . . . beautiful you look," Callie said, rushing across the kitchen to throw her arms around her. She immediately backed away to stare in awe at Pearl's dress.

It wasn't just a dress, it was a creation. Loose and flowing, kaftan style, it was a patchwork rainbow of color. Some of the patches were square, some diamond-shaped, some circular . . . all vibrant colors of raw silk that came alive on Pearl's ample body.

"It's gorgeous," Sela said sincerely. "I want one."

"I think it's the most beautiful dress I've ever seen," Brie said. "It's so . . . so *commanding*. Wherever did you get it, Pearl? Don't tell me you made it."

"My boy gave it to me," Pearl said proudly. "He had it made special in Charleston. It's a one-of-a-kind. Hand-sewed. The stitches are finer than my own. I have another one, too. Bode said I needed two—one for today and one for tomorrow. Look, he even gave me a purse."

"Oh Pearl, it's so beautiful," Callie said, her eyes swimming in tears.

"My boy said I had to look good for the two most important days in my baby's life. I won't shame you, will I, Miz Callie?" she asked anxiously.

"You would never shame me, no matter what. If you want to go barefoot and wear your old green sack dress it's okay with me. Bode had no right to say that to you."

"Oh, shut up, Callie. You're just bent out of shape because Bode one-upped you," Sela grated.

"I want to take your picture, Pearl," Brie said, rummaging in her purse for her small camera that she was never without. "Maybe Wyn will take our picture with Pearl."

"That was a hateful thing to say," Callie snapped to Sela. She smiled wanly in Wyn's direction, offered her cheek for his light kiss. She frowned slightly when she smelled the alcohol on his breath.

"What's hateful, and I'll be delighted to take your picture," he said, and grinned from ear to ear. He held out his hand for Brie's camera.

"May I say you look lovely, Pearl," Wyn said gallantly as he motioned the girls to get closer to her. "Now, everyone say *cheese.*" The women obliged.

"Take four of them, Wyn," Brie requested. "I want us each to have one. I'm going to frame mine and put it on my desk. Maybe I'll get it enlarged and have one of those calendars made up. Would you like one, Pearl?"

"Yes, I would," Pearl said.

"Get me one, too," Callie said.

"And me," chimed in Sela, fingering the material in Pearl's dress. "I bet this cost Bode a fortune. Show me the other one, Pearl."

"I'd like to see it, too," Brie said, her eyes going from Wyn's questioning gaze to Callie. She sensed something wrong as she followed Sela and Pearl into her spartan room. Since she was the last in line, she overheard Wyn's hushed words. "You didn't tell me Pearl was coming. How's it going to look, Callie? She's so big, there's not enough room in the car. If you'd told me you were inviting the servants, I'd have brought along mine, too. What were you thinking of, darling?"

"Pearl's not a servant, at least to me she's not. She's like a mother, and she's my best friend. Brie and I can sit in the front seat since we're the smallest. Sela and Pearl can sit in the back. It's not a problem, Wyn, unless you make it one." How tight and angry Callie's voice sounded.

"It's just a wedding rehearsal, darling. And the party the Judge is giving is just a little gathering. Is this one of those female things I'm not supposed to understand?" Brie heard Wyn ask lightly.

"It's important to me, Wyn," Callie hissed. "If my parents were alive, they'd be at the rehearsal *and* the party. Pearl is my only family, so I want her there. Don't spoil this for me, please."

"Not in a million years. I'm sorry, darling. Of course there's room for Pearl."

Pearl's hands trembled when she opened the shiny white box Bode had brought her earlier in the week. She'd heard every word. Her fingers worked at the thin tissue paper, worked loose the huge crimson seal that was the seamstress's trademark. Tears burned her eyes when she withdrew the dress she was to wear to the wedding. She barely heard Sela and Brie's ooohs and aaahs as they fingered the costly material and marveled over the tiny stitches.

"French seams. Who is this lady and how did Bode ever find her?" Sela asked.

Her voice husky with unshed tears, Pearl said, "She only sews for special people. I think she's a client of Bode's."

The most intuitive of the three women, Brie said, "Listen, I have an idea. What do you say we let Callie and Wyn go along by themselves and us three go together. We can jabber to our hearts' content and then Pearl, you can give us the *real* lowdown on Bode."

"Good idea," Sela agreed when she felt Brie's kick to her ankle.

"Is that okay with you, Pearl?"

"Oh yes, Miz Brie," Pearl said gratefully, her eyes still wet.

"Then I'll tell Callie." She kicked Sela again as she called out to Callie and Wyn.

"But . . . there's plenty of room. Wyn's car is air-conditioned," Callie objected when she heard their plan.

"So are the rental cars. They come that way from the factory," Brie said tightly. "Sela wants to change her dress. We'll be there in plenty of time. Go ahead, you two."

"But . . ."

"Darling, it's the wise decision. Brie's right. Come along."

A devil perched itself on Brie's shoulder. She didn't mean to say it, she didn't want to think about saying it, but the words tumbled out of her mouth before she could order her tongue to remain silent. "Yes, darling, run along before I put a ring on the *other* side of your nose." She gasped then, and fled into Pearl's room, slamming the door behind her.

Pearl and Sela stared at Brie's blazing cheeks. "What did you do?" Sela demanded. Brie told her.

"My God!"

"Shame on you, Miz Brie. I taught you better than that," Pearl said, wringing her hands.

"You know what? I don't care. I don't like him, and I'm

tired of pretending I do. He damn well does have a ring through Callie's nose and how she can't see it is beyond me."

"Now if I'd done what you just did, neither one of you would be speaking to me," Sela said. "Callie loves him, and it's none of our business. Wyn does love her. All you have to do is look at him to see how much. In the end that's all that matters. Isn't that right, Pearl?" she asked anxiously.

"When two people love each other, that is all that matters and you, Miz Brie, need soap in your mouth. Shame on you," Pearl said, with a catch in her voice.

"Go ahead, pick on me. I just said what both of you have been dying to say all day. Furthermore, if I knew where to get hold of Bode right now, this damn minute, I'd stick my face in his and give him what for. Where is he, Pearl?" she asked viciously.

"He said he was going to the airport."

"Well, let's just see if Bode turned into a liar or not," Brie said, stomping her way out to the kitchen, where she dialed Information and asked for the number of the airport. She repeated the number, broke the connection, and dialed, her eyes on Pearl's. "This is Detective Brie Canfield from the San Diego Police. My badge number is . . ." Sela gasped, and Pearl reached for the back of the kitchen chair for support. "I need some information, and I need it *now*." Five minutes later she gave a thumbs-up sign and grinned. "You take Pearl to the church, Sela. I'm going to the airport."

"Miz Brie, you can't do that!"

"Why not? Bode didn't tell us good-bye. He owes us that. He's ruining Callie's wedding day. I can't let him do that. I *won't* let him do that. You're good at telling lies, Sela. Say I twisted my ankle or something. I'll get there when I get there."

"Is this how you do things? You just bulldoze ahead and take matters into your own hands?"

"Not usually. I have backup most of the time. I hardly think Bode Jessup is going to attack me, but if he does I'm ready," she said, brandishing the gun from her purse.

"Oh my God!"

"Lord have mercy," Pearl whispered.

A moment later she was gone, the rental car spewing up gravel and clumps of overgrown grass in its wake.

"I guess we better get going. I need a drink, Pearl. Is there anything stronger than ice tea here?"

Flustered and out of control for the first time in her life, Pearl pointed to the kitchen cabinet.

"What is this?"

"The last of the elderberry wine Lazarus gave me."

"Really, Pearl."

"You be careful, Miz Sela, that wine has the kick of a mule."

"That's about what I need, Pearl. You too." She poured generously into two water glasses. "What should we drink to, Pearl? I know," Sela said happily. "First let's drink to Brie shooting Bode's balls off. Then let's drink to that dickweed Wynfield Archer. Then we can drink to Callie coming to her senses, and if there's any wine left we'll drink to the fine, up-standing man who made this wonderful wine, Lazarus him-self. Drink up, Pearl," she said, clanking her glass against the old woman's.

Pearl sipped. Sela gulped and upended her glass.

Sela poured, again and again. When the jug had less than two inches of dark wine remaining, Pearl fumbled with the cork before she took the bottle from Sela and stuck it back in the cupboard.

"Why'd you do that?"

"Because I need something to remember Lazarus by."

"You should have married him, Pearl. Callie said he loved you. Did you love him?"

"Don't make no never mind now. He's gone. I prayed over his grave and sang a hymn in church for him. A woman can't marry a man who don't have no name. A man can't marry a woman who don't have no name. Their children will come into the world and not have a name. God didn't see fit to give Lazarus and me names. The manor house name ain't the same as being born with a name. If you don't have a name, you can't get social security. Lazarus didn't have any. He died a poor man with no name and no social security and no one to grieve but me."

Sela's head bobbed up and down. "I see what you mean. Does Bode feel the same way?" She tried to look at the hands on her watch, but she couldn't make out the small numbers.

"Bode give himself his name. He has two names, the one he was born with, but he don't know that name, and the one he give himself."

"We have to call a taxi," Sela said, getting up from the chair. "Are we late, Pearl?"

"Yes'm, real late."

"Maybe we shouldn't go," Sela said, sitting back down. "I wonder if Brie shot Bode. Turn the radio on, Pearl. I bet she handcuffs him and drags him back for the wedding."

Pearl said, "My head feels like a bowl of Jell-O without the bananas."

"Wait till your stomach starts going one way, the Jell-O the other way," Sela singsonged. "Lordee, lordee, lordee." She started to giggle.

Pearl, her eyes crossed from the amount of wine she'd consumed, shook her dress down over her ample bosom and announced, "I hear a car coming."

"It must be the taxi," Sela said, struggling to get up.

"You didn't call no taxi, Miz Sela."

"What time is it?" Sela squinted at the kitchen clock.

"We missed . . . I hear voices."

"That's because people are talking," Sela said smartly. "Oh look, it's Brie and Bode. They came to fetch us."

Pearl sat down and started to cry. Sela joined her, both of them sobbing into their sleeves.

"Jesus Christ!" Bode spluttered.

"I'll whip you, Bode Jessup, for taking the Lord's name in vain," Pearl blubbered.

"Do you know what time it is?" Brie yelled, trying to drag Sela off the chair. "Go in the bathroom now and throw up. Get it over with," she ordered her.

"Mama Pearl, what happened?" Bode said, dropping to his knees.

"I got to feeling sad and Miz Sela said we should have a drink of Lazarus's wine, so I said it sounded like a fine idea. That's why Lazarus give me the wine. To drink when things were going poorly, he said. Why'd you come back, Bode?"

"Because this . . . this *cop* said she'd blow my lower extremities off if I didn't. I came back because I didn't want her to do something she'd regret later in life. Besides, she has no jurisdiction in South Carolina. And she said you needed me. Do you need me, Mama Pearl?" There was such anguish and hope mixed in Bode's voice that Pearl could only say yes.

"The phone's ringing," Bode shouted in the general direction of the bathroom.

"Do what I do, you asshole, and answer it," Brie shot back, her voice full of rage.

"I'm not answering it," Bode said.

"Pick up the receiver and hand it to Pearl. You're a devil come to life, Bode Jessup," Brie shouted.

Bode picked up the receiver and held it to Pearl's ear. He could hear Callie's angry voice on the line.

Pearl started to cry the moment she heard Callie's voice.

Disgust written all over his face, Bode took the phone and put it to his ear. "Callie, it's Bode. What can I do for you?"

"Why is Pearl crying? Where are Sela and Brie? No one showed up for the rehearsal, and we're late for the party. What is going on, Bode? What are you doing in my house? I want you out of there right now. You're not my friend. You aren't the person I gave you credit for being all these years. Put Pearl on the phone. I hate you, Bode Jessup."

"Pearl is drunk," Bode said coolly. "Sela is puking in the bathroom. Brie is trying to . . . I don't know what she's doing. She came to the airport and threatened me. That's what I'm doing here. Now, if you can just come home and get your family and friends straightened out, I'll be on my way. Well, what do you have to say for yourself?"

"Wyn said you'd screw things up, and he was right," Callie said bitterly. "I can't come all the way back there now. The minister is—well, he had an unholy fit. The Judge and his wife spent a lot of time and effort on this party, and I can't just walk away. How drunk are they?"

"I don't know too much about drunks," Bode drawled, "but I'd say they're pretty far gone. Wyn would know more about that sort of thing."

"You are so hateful, Bode Jessup. I'm never going to forgive you for this. Never."

"Is that your last word, Mrs. Soon-To-Be-Archer? If so, I'm outta here. I wish you the best, Callie. Have a good life."

Brie was back in the kitchen, her hair in straggly strings around her face, her makeup streaked. Huge patches of perspiration bracketed the underarms of her linen dress. Her eyes spewed anger. "You're really leaving?"

"I have to leave, Brie," Bode said quietly.

"You're breaking Pearl's heart. Can't you see what you're doing to her? What's gotten into you, Bode Jessup?"

"He's a man. All men stink. None of them are any good," Sela said hoarsely. She looked ghastly.

Pearl continued to whimper at the table. "Go, Bode, just

go. Don't you pay them no never mind. My heart's been broke and mended so many times it's tough as the leather on these here shoes. You do what you have to do."

Tears sparkled in Bode's eyes as he stared first at the girls and then at Pearl. His eyes pleaded for understanding.

"You love Callie. That's what this is all about, isn't it?" Sela whispered. Her face was full of awe. "Well, I certainly understand a thing or two about unrequited love. You shouldn't have forced him to come back," she said to Brie.

Bode stared hard at Sela and Brie. He purposefully avoided Pearl's tearful gaze. In one fluid motion he grasped one of the sturdy kitchen chairs and spun it around before straddling it. He was angrier than either girl had ever seen him. "Over the years, Sela, you have said some stupid things, but this is the worst to come out of your mouth. Never say anything you can't back up one hundred percent. As an attorney, that's probably the best advice I can give.

"Listen to me very carefully. I came back here because Brie charged into the airport, her hand *inside* her purse. She was wild. Dealing with high-strung females who tote guns is not my idea of a proper farewell. Now I could have taken you with one hand behind my back, Brie, but I didn't want to cause a fuss. I also didn't want to humiliate you. A gentleman never embarrasses a lady in public. I have too much respect for you, Brie.

"None of this is my doing. We all care for Callie, and because she's such a good friend, I didn't want to be a party to ruining her wedding. It's no secret that Wyn Archer hates my guts. I don't much care for him either, but that's beside the point. I would never do anything to spoil Callie's wedding. When the offer came to move to New Mexico, I jumped at it. Sometimes it's just time to move on, and this is that time. My friends sent me the airline ticket. I suppose I could have changed it at a hefty fee, but I didn't. You're all making too much of this, blowing it way out of proportion.

"You're both right about one thing, though—I should have stayed long enough to see Mama Pearl in her new dress. Being a man, I'm stupid, I guess. I thought giving it was enough—it wasn't. Seth Williams was to pick up Mama Pearl. I made the arrangements. He's going to look out for her until Callie and Wyn get back from their honeymoon. I thought this through. For God's sake, I even sent a wedding present to Beaufort! I cannot believe that you two, who I considered to be my best friends, would think so ill of me.

"And you, Sela, how could you have gotten Mama Pearl liquored up like that? I know you're no stranger to the sauce, but you had no right to do that to her. In closing," Bode said in his best courtroom voice, "if anyone here is ruining Callie's wedding, it's you two. I know you probably meant well, but that just goes to show your immaturity. Grow up. Now if you'll excuse me . . .

"Drink lots of black coffee, Mama Pearl. You sashay into that party like the queen you are. I love you so much. Whatever I am, I am because of you—and don't you ever forget it because I sure won't. You look more beautiful than the first star at night. When I think about you, which I will do every single day, I'll think of you in this dress." He kissed her, hugged her, then held out his arms to Sela and Brie, who were both sniveling.

"It's okay," he whispered. "You meant well, but you have to learn to mind your own business. I could have taken you, Brie." He chuckled.

"Not on your best day, Bode." She hiccupped. "I'll drive you back to the airport."

"No, you won't. I'll call a cab or hitchhike. I can't handle your kind of help, well-meaning or not."

"Some small part of you has to be glad I did, though. If I hadn't gone after you, we'd all be thinking you're a first-class son of a bitch, and you aren't that at all. I'm sorry, Bode. I really am. If it's any consolation to you, I would have shot you in the foot, not where I said. I would have lied and made up some story."

"I know. Friends, okay?"

"Yeah," both girls said in unison. "Write, Bode."

"You bet."

"Liar," they both said.

Bode grinned.

All three women watched him walk out to the main road. Pearl sobbed, the girls' arms around her broad shoulders.

"He'll never come back. I know it in my heart," she wept.

Sela and Brie looked at one another. "Time takes care of everything, Pearl," Brie said gently. "Eventually he'll come back. We still come back from time to time. Bode will, too; but not for a while. Everyone wants that one place called home to be able to return to. Don't lose faith, Pearl. Bode won't let you down."

"And on that note I think we need to clean up again and sashay our way to the Judge's house and partake of that scrumptious spread his wife will have surely put out. It's probably all picked over, but we have to show our faces. Brie can drive since she's sober," Sela said.

"Miz Callie is never going to forgive me," Pearl cried.

"She's already forgiven you. She loves you, Pearl, more than life itself. I say we get up and head out for the party. That dress is too gorgeous, Pearl, not to be seen. Here, let me wipe your eyes." Sela softly dabbed at Pearl's eyes with one of the linen napkins from the kitchen drawer.

"Brie and I love you just as much as Bode and Callie love you. You need to believe that, Pearl."

"I do, Miz Sela. I love all my children. Let us get fixed up so we can walk in with our heads held high. I don't want anyone saying we look like low country trash."

"I'll shoot them if they even look like they're thinking such a thing." Brie giggled.

"There you go," Sela said.

Pearl smiled benignly—and that's what it was all about: Pearl's happiness, now, at this point in time.

6

The radio had been playing softly for the past ten minutes. Neither Wyn nor Callie had spoken a word to one another in that time. Callie sat close to the door, her back stiff, her eyes straight ahead. Everything was wrong; nothing was working out right. She was supposed to be happy. Instead she was more miserable than she'd ever been in her life. Right now she felt like calling the wedding off. All she wanted to do was run to Pearl and have her make the hurt go away. What kind of friends did she have anyway? The kind that couldn't be bothered to show up at the wedding rehearsal when they were in the wedding party. It was those stupid dresses, she was sure of it. She should have said something to Wyn earlier, but it was too late now. She felt so alone, like she had when she was a child and Pearl dressed her up for her afternoon audience with her mother. She always wanted to cry when she stood outside the door, all alone, dreading walking into the dim bedroom. When she'd shared her feelings with Bode he'd told her to imagine something pleasant and hold on to the thought. She'd tried it and sometimes it worked. Sometimes it didn't.

What she'd done was sort of skip into the room, wave her

arms about, and transfer her thoughts to the pond where Bode had his jumpers: four frogs named Alexander, for Alexander the Great, Abraham, for Abraham Lincoln, Star, for the first star at night, and Rogerina, because Bode liked the way the name sounded.

Think of something pleasant. Think about being married to Wyn. Think about how wonderful it's going to be.

He was angry and upset, not for himself, but for her. He wanted everything to be perfect, and her friends had spoiled it. She needed to say something, anything, to break the miserable silence between them.

"Wyn, I feel like I should apologize to you, but part of me doesn't want to. I didn't do anything wrong. I don't want us to be this way. We haven't spoken since we left the church. Please, say something."

"I thought you were angry with me," Wyn said, the words exploding from his mouth like bullets.

"How could you think such a thing? You didn't do anything. I was upset with Sela and Brie and yes, with Bode, too. It's over, let's put it behind us. They'll be at the party, and things will be fine."

"Does that mean you're feeling better about it all? Look, I don't mind going back to the church for the rehearsal after the party. Things always go wrong at the last minute. Reverend Neville said he didn't mind so why should we mind? I'm just glad you're talking to me. I was beginning to think we were going to walk down the aisle not speaking to one another." His tone was light, but there was no smile on his face that Callie could see. She did her best to match his tone when she replied.

"And then leaving for our honeymoon still not talking to one another." She giggled, in spite of herself, and Wyn allowed himself a small smile. "A few days from now we'll laugh about all of this. It's a memory, Wyn. We have to store it away."

"You're absolutely right, darling."

The Cadillac slid over the bumpy road with hardly a jar, continuing down the road, past the azalea gardens and then turned right on Fifth Street.

Judge Avery Summers and his wife, Nela, lived on Sumter Avenue. Like Wyn, he'd long ago sold his big house in Charleston and moved permanently to Summerville. He liked living in the Historical District. He'd restored the house to its original splendor and could be seen after hours working in his gardens or dabbing paint anywhere it was needed. The house gleamed now, its pristine whiteness shining in the late-afternoon light, like a beacon to welcome guests.

Avery Summers was to give her away. It was his duty, he said, because he'd been Callie's father's closest friend and her guardian. It was his duty also to host the party since he and Nela were standing in for Callie's parents. After all, the young woman was going to work for him—a job Bode Jessup had insisted he create. It had taken Bode all of seven and a half minutes to explain the situation and to beg the Judge to hire Callie. He'd even promised to send half of whatever the Judge felt she deserved by way of salary, the details to be ironed out through the mail or via fax.

He'd given Bode a stern lecture, and then Bode had given him a stern lecture in return. In the end they'd shaken hands, puffed on expensive cigars, sipped some excellent brandy, and finally said good-bye. Neither had spoken about what was to happen a year from now when the Judge retired.

"We're here," Wyn said. "The Judge is doing it up regally. Valet parking. He does love to put on a show. Bet the food is something else. Nela loves a good party."

"I feel guilty letting them do all this. I wanted a little dinner in Charleston, just the wedding party, but the Judge insisted. I couldn't say no."

"It makes him happy, Callie. After all, he is your guardian."

"I know, and I really am grateful, but now I'm going to feel obligated. I hate feeling obligated. I don't see Sela's or Brie's car. I'm going to call as soon as I get inside."

"I can go get them if you want. It's your decision, Callie."

"Let me see how things are going before you do that."

At first glance, and after the welcoming embraces by the Judge and Nela, Callie thought the entire town had turned out for what Judge Summers said was just a small get-together. With Wyn at her side, she smiled and spoke with people she'd known all her life.

The Judge, a portly man with snow-white hair, a handlebar mustache, and a booming voice, hugged her to his ample chest. With his arm still around her, he allowed his wife, Miss Nela, a tiny woman, no bigger than a mouse, Avery constantly teased, to peck Callie on the cheek.

"The child needs to circulate, Avery, so I'd be obliged if you'd let her go before you snap her ribs in two." Nela shook her head, her pageboy bob swinging as she tugged at Callie's arm.

The rooms passed in a blur as Nela escorted Callie through the guests toward the sunroom, where a magnificent spread of food was being laid out. She barely had time to notice the hodgepodge of three-hundred-year-old antiques vying with Wal-Mart knickknacks. She knew some of the carpets were priceless Persians while others bore the Pier 1 Imports label. Pots, jugs, vases, as well as old milk cans held green plants mixed with silk branches, also from Pier 1, along with eucalyptus branches sticking out of the arrangements at crazy angles. The smell was overpowering.

"Foods's food," Miss Nela said happily. "I just brought you out here to see if you're really all right. Avery said you are, but I wanted to see for myself that Bowdey hasn't spoiled the day for you. I do like Bowdey, I can't get around that. Avery gave that boy a send-off luncheon a few days ago, and the whole town turned out. It was a good thing he took over Shoney's; otherwise, people would have been turned away. Everyone came, 'cepting you and Wynfield and your friends. Why was that, Callie?"

"I didn't know about it. Pearl didn't know either. She would have told me," Callie said, her voice stunned.

"I heard Avery calling Wynfield myself, Callie. Of course he didn't have to go, I didn't expect him to, but I surely thought you would have been there." The pageboy bob was moving again, swishing against Nela's high-necked lace collar. Her round, wire-rim glasses jiggled on her nose.

Callie eyed the array of food on the table, felt the whirring of the paddle fan overhead tease at her hair. "Avery was a tad upset that you weren't there. Just a tad," Nela said, her round rosebud mouth pursed in disbelief at what she considered to be Callie's disrespect for an old friend.

"I didn't know," Callie said again, her eyes miserable.

"All the lawyers in town, Avery included, chipped in and bought Bode one of those fancy mountain bikes. I heard early this morning from Ester down at the courthouse that Bode pedaled that bicycle down to the police station and turned it over to the PBA to be raffled off for some youngster. Now, isn't that just like Bode?"

"Yes, that's just like Bode," Callie said quietly. "There's so much food here, Miss Nela."

"I know. Men do love to eat, don't they? We're all going to miss Bode. Are you going to miss him, Callie?"

"Very much, but not as much as Pearl. I don't understand any of it. He never even . . . oh, it's not important."

"We should be returning to our guests. The food does look pretty, doesn't it?"

"It's very nice. I can feel the pounds going on just looking at it."

"I understand y'all have to go back to the church again because of some mix-up. Avery is going to fret over that. He likes to plant himself in that recliner I got him at Wal-Mart after supper and not move till it's time to go to bed."

"I'm sorry about that, too, Miss Nela. You know what they say."

"No, what?" Nela said curiously.

"That nothing ever works out right until the actual moment. Rehearsals and things like that always go awry. I think there's some kind of old saying about show business—you know, if the rehearsal is a disaster, the opening night will go well." Callie's words trailed off lamely as Nela stared at her.

"I'm not sure I ever heard that, but if you say so, I'll take your word for it. What will you do when Avery retires?"

"Why . . . I suppose I'll get a job someplace else or maybe I'll open my own office. I don't intend to let my education go to waste."

"What if you have babies?"

"I'll get a nanny for them. Women don't stay home anymore."

Nela clucked her tongue. "I imagine Wynfield will have something to say about that."

Callie drew in her breath. "Yes, Miss Nela, I imagine he will. We'll work it out. Wyn is very open-minded."

"I'm real glad to hear that, Callie."

"I need to speak with the Judge, Miss Nela. Is there someplace we could speak in private?"

"Avery's study. You know where it is. You go along, and I'll send Avery in."

"Wyn, too, please, Miss Nela."

Callie threaded her way to the rear of the house, to the

Judge's domain, where no one, not even Miss Nela, entered unless invited. He smoked his cigars there, ate his chocolate kisses, and drank his bourbon in peace and quiet, often in his bare feet, with his shirtsleeves rolled up.

The Judge's study was a nice room, a man's room, a Judge's room. The furniture was mahogany as were the bookshelves loaded with leather-bound books and stacks of periodicals heaped every which way. The plants were dusty, the ashtrays full. Dustballs were all over the floor. Once the Judge had said, rather proudly, that he cleaned his office every Saturday morning. If he felt like it. If he didn't, he said, he waited until the following week.

Callie gave the green recliner a hard thump. Dust spiraled upward. No wonder the Judge was always wheezing. Her index finger traced a line in the thick dust down the center of the television screen. She shrugged. Pearl would have this room spick-and-span in an hour's time.

The door opened. Callie almost jumped out of her skin when Wyn said, "I sense a secret of some sort. I've been looking for you. Miss Nela said my presence was required *immediately.*"

Callie's eyes burned. This was supposed to be such a special moment, and now it felt flat. She wanted to run away, as far and as fast as her feet would take her. Instead she smiled and allowed the Judge to embrace her.

Judge Avery Summers was a one-size-fits-all shape. He favored white suits even in the winter, and wore them well. He was a good man, a fair man. She'd only heard him raise his voice once in all the years that she'd known him. It happened when Bode brought in the deed of trust for him to look over. As Bode said later, the Judge went ballistic for all of ten minutes. In the end, with Bode's logic and her persistence, the Judge had calmed, but it was obvious he didn't approve of her deeding the manor house and property to Wyn. "The bottom line, Judge, is Callie wants this. As far as I'm concerned, it's a done deed," Bode said. Bode hadn't approved either. Pearl had just pursed her lips and refused to comment.

Tears burned Callie's eyes. Was she making a mistake? No. Not at all. It was to be a surprise. She had to give something in return for the good life Wyn was going to be giving her. It was all she had. It was also fitting that she give it to Wyn. It would still be hers. At least, half of it would be hers. Marital property.

The envelope was in the Judge's hand. He opened the clasp and withdrew a sheaf of papers. He handed them to Callie who passed them to Wyn.

"It's a poem, right?" Wyn grinned, reaching for the papers with one hand as he set down his drink with the other. She heard his gasp, saw his eyes moisten. "Callie, I . . . this is yours. It's a wonderful thing you're doing, but I . . . oh, my darling."

"It's not worth much, Wyn, but it's all I have to give," she said, her voice choking up. "I want you to have it."

"Callie, I don't know what to say. No one has ever given me anything like this. However, I don't intend to let you outdo me. Wait here, I saw Kallum arrive, just as the Judge and I started back here. He has a few things, too. I'll be right back."

"I think your plants need to be watered, Judge," Callie said for something to say.

"I'll do it tomorrow morning. Did you happen to see Dora Witfield? If that fool wife of mine has allowed her to have two rum punches she's going to be taking off her shoes and Lord knows what else," the Judge said, his eyes everywhere but on Callie.

"As long as she doesn't get to her sweater it will be all

right," Callie said. "I'm doing the right thing, Judge. Please don't be upset."

"I'm not upset, although it's time enough, in my opinion, to be doing things like this after you give birth to a child. That's all I'm going to say on the matter. Missed you at the luncheon."

"I didn't know about it, or I would have contributed to the gift. Why didn't you tell me?"

"Told Wynfield. I asked him to tell you. I guess he forgot in the rush of things."

"I guess so," Callie said quietly. That alone, she thought, might be reason enough to explain Bode's attitude. "When I get back I'll drop Bode a note and explain. You have his address, don't you?"

"As a matter of fact, I don't. Bode said he'd write after he got settled. I don't believe for one minute that he'll write or come back here. He's rid himself of us. He's going to be missed. Bode is a fine attorney. A fair man, a just man. He's got more compassion in his little finger than half the people in that room out there."

"It's funny you should say that, Judge. Bode said the same thing about you."

"He did, did he?" The Judge preened himself.

"More than once."

"Good man, none finer." The Judge continued to look pleased.

"Judge," Wyn said, closing the door behind Kallum, "Dora just took off her sweater."

"Lord!" he exploded. "What's my wife doing?"

"Holding it for her." Kallum chuckled.

"Y'all don't need me anymore, do you?"

"No. We've got it covered, Judge," Kallum said.

"What do you have covered?" Callie inquired.

"This," Wyn said, holding out a beige folder with a tab on the end that said CALLIE in capital letters. "It's half of everything I own. There's a copy of my will, my insurance policies. As of tomorrow, Calliope Archer will be my legal heir. Kallum will put your name back on your deed tomorrow. I wanted it all signed today, but Kallum said it has to be done when you're Mrs. Archer. I did my best to finish it off today, but two of the deeds didn't arrive. They're being messengered to the house in Beaufort. I'll look them over this evening and Kallum will bring them by tomorrow so you can sign them as soon as the wedding is over, and before we go off on our honeymoon. We'll go into the vestibule before we have the pictures taken. Is that okay with you, darling?"

"Yes, Wyn, but we can always do it after we get back from our honeymoon."

"That's what I told him, but he wouldn't listen. Did you ever in your life see a man so eager to share his holdings? I say we make a toast to yours and Wyn's long and happy lives," Kallum said.

"Hear! Hear!" Wyn cried, holding out his glass. Kallum poured lightly until Wyn said, "Tilt the bottle, Kal. If I'm going to drink to a long and happy life I want to taste it, not smell it."

Kallum frowned, but did as instructed. Wyn took his seat. Callie sipped. Kallum just held his glass to his lips, Callie noticed.

"Guess I'll be driving to the church," Callie said.

"Looks that way." Wyn grinned. "Now, let's go and enjoy our party. Miss Nela said she personally made a pot of crab stew just for me, with thirteen ounces of bourbon. She soaked the crackers in another four ounces for two whole days and then let them dry in the sun."

"Forget driving. You'll be asleep in Miss Nela's spare room

for two days if you eat that mess," Kallum grumbled. "You are the only person besides Miss Nela who can abide that stuff."

"It grows hair on your chest." Wyn laughed. "Come along, darling, we need to circulate, and then we'll eat."

Outside the Judge's office, the house was full of life. Music was being played, but the babble of voices was drowning out the lyrics of Waylon Jennings, the only artist the Judge listened to; Miss Nela, too, although she professed to like Willie Nelson and had a secret stash of his recordings in her sewing room.

"You head toward the sunroom, Wyn, and I'll take the front. I'll meet you in the dining room in let's say, forty minutes," Callie said.

"I haven't seen Brie or Sela," Kallum remarked, following Callie to the huge living room.

"They'll be here. They promised," Callie said tightly.

"Is everything all right, Callie?"

Where are my friends? "Why do you ask?" she said, staring straight ahead.

"You seem on edge. There's no laughter in your eyes. Oh, you smile, but that smile doesn't reach your eyes. Wyn seems off-track, too. Is this what weddings do to people? If so, I'm going to remain a bachelor. By the way, how is it you were a no-show at Bode's luncheon?"

"Damn it, Kallum, I wasn't invited. Miss Nela said the Judge invited Wyn, and he was to tell me. Well, he didn't. And I don't want to talk about it, if that's all right with you."

Kallum shrugged. "Look, there's Brie and Sela now. Oh my, is that Pearl?"

"Yes, that's Pearl, and Kallum, I'd appreciate it if you wouldn't be such a damn snob. You remind me of Wyn sometimes. Another thing: Brie feels the same way I do about Pearl, so unless your attitude changes within minutes, I'm going to whisper in her ear."

"Jesus, Callie, I didn't mean anything. I don't feel any particular way."

"Don't you ever talk about Pearl, not ever again. To me, Pearl is . . . I'd take her over every single person in this room. Do you hear me?" Her voice stopped just short of being shrill.

"Even Wyn?"

"Yes, even Wyn," Callie said, stalking her way to the center of the room, where Sela, Brie, and Pearl were being welcomed by Miss Nela. She was in time to hear her hostess say, "We can get on with the party now, but you've missed all the action. Dora took off her shoes, her sweater, and her wig, and is now sleeping on the back porch."

"Why don't we *all* go outside and have a cigarette?" Callie suggested through clenched teeth.

"Good idea," Brie said,

"The best," Sela echoed.

"I told you girls to stop smoking. You promised," Pearl said.

"It's my New Year's resolution," Brie said.

"I can't quit, it's my security blanket," Sela said, groaning.

"I don't want to quit," Callie said defiantly.

Outside in the garden, smoking cigarettes none of them wanted, Callie said, "Somebody tell me what's going on. Now!"

They told her. All of them had the grace to look ashamed.

"I don't believe this. How could you do this to me? Today of all days."

"Believe it or not, we thought we were helping. At least, I did. Bode made me so damn mad. He gives Pearl this absolutely gorgeous dress and then takes off and doesn't wait to see her in it. It wasn't right. I didn't like him walking out on you like that either. So, I presumed on our friendship and took matters into my own hands," Brie explained. "At least he got to see Pearl. Then he hitchhiked back to the airport."

"I tried to trick him into saying he loved you, but he cut me down to size, and I deserved it," Sela said. "You can rest easy; he doesn't love you."

"I could have told you that," Callie snorted. "There's only room for two things to love in Bode's life—Mama Pearl and the law."

"He made that clear," Brie said. "Guess Wyn is upset that the rehearsal had to be rescheduled."

"He took it well," Callie said quietly. "Let's get to the drinking bit."

"My fault. I asked Pearl for some of Lazarus's wine and before we knew it we were snookered. It's all my fault," Sela said.

"Are you all right, Pearl?" Callie asked.

"I'm jest fine, Miz Callie. I think it's best if we forget what happened and don't speak about it again. It pains me to see you unhappy. These people made this fine party, and we spoiled it for you. I'm real sorry."

"Yeah, me too," Sela mumbled.

"Me too," Brie said.

"Then do you think we can all go inside and smile and pretend we're having a good time?" Callie said tartly.

"I'm real good at that," Sela offered.

"I hate a phony," Brie said, stomping ahead of the others.

"I hate everything and everyone," Callie muttered under her breath.

"Amen," Pearl groaned, her black laced shoes rubbing against her heels and toes. "Amen."

Callie waved her friends ahead. She drew back, her hand

on Pearl's arm. She guided her deeper into the garden, where the scent of the flowers and the lush pines calmed her jangling nerves.

"Pearl, I need to ask you something. I don't want to ask, but I have to, for my own peace of mind. Today . . . well, today is almost over and tomorrow will be here before I know it. I wanted to talk to you, to ask you so many things, but you know that look you give me from time to time when I step over into what you call your personal business. Pearl, I need to step over that line right now."

"Curiosity always kills the cat—you know that, Miz Callie." Pearl turned away to pluck at a blossom on the crepe myrtle tree. If she'd looked at that moment she would have seen the quiet desperation in Callie's eyes. When she did turn, she held out the bloom and smiled. "I always said you were prettier than these blossoms, Miz Callie."

"Yes, Pearl, you always said that. I can't let you put me off anymore. Do you like Wyn? I want an answer, Pearl, and I also want to know why you let Sela and Brie talk you into opening that wine Lazarus gave you."

"None of this is important, Miz Callie. You don't need to be talking and thinking about such things today. Or tomorrow or the day after tomorrow. Unless you have a mind to call off your wedding."

"There you go again. I'm not leaving this garden until you give me straight-out answers. I mean it, Pearl." The blossom in her hands was a mangled mess. She dropped it to the ground and picked another.

Pearl slapped it out of her hand. "Mr. Wyn is a fine man. Everyone says so. *You* say so. You must believe it or you wouldn't be marrying him. It don't make no never mind what I think of Mr. Wyn."

"Damn you, Pearl, that's not what I asked you. *Do you like him?*" She snapped off a whole branch from the crepe myrtle and waved it crazily in every direction. The desperation was still in her eyes. Pearl saw it this time. Her shoulders slumped.

"No. No, I don't," Pearl murmured.

"Now what was so hard about that?" Callie said. "Am I breaking your heart, Pearl?"

"I should be fanning your bottom for making me puddle up like this," Pearl said, wiping at her eyes with the back of her hand.

"You have secrets, Pearl, I know you do. I always shared mine with you, but you never shared yours with me. Why? I'm stepping over your line—and you know what, Pearl? I don't care. I'm all grown-up now." She wiped at her own eyes with a tissue from her pocket, then handed it to Pearl. Her foot inched out, gouging a deep line separating her from Pearl. "You see this line? Well, this is what I think of it." The white-linen shoe dug deeper and then scuffed at the line. Then she dropped to her knees and dug at the line.

Pearl raised her eyes, and said, "Lord, this chile be crazy. She don't know what she's doing. Be kind to her." She reached down to grasp Callie under the arms and pulled her behind the crepe myrtle that was hundreds of years old.

"Look at you! You're a fine mess. You're shaming me, Miz Callie. I spent hours ironing that linen dress. Now you have grass stains all over it, and them shoes is ruined. All them fancy people in there are going to say I don't take care of you right."

"I don't give a flying fuck what those people in there think. I care what *you* think! Are you going to slap me now for saying dirty words?" Callie mumbled, burrowing against Pearl's chest.

"I should. Maybe later I will. Or maybe I'll just pretend you didn't say what you said. That Miz Sela shouldn't be teaching you such things."

"Pearl, don't blame Sela. Bode says it all the time. Well, he says it sometimes. Under his breath, not out loud," she said when she saw the outrage in Pearl's face. "I'm lying; Bode never says it. Not ever. Wyn says it. So does Kallum. I'm sorry," Callie wailed. "Don't be ashamed of me, Pearl. Please."

Pearl led Callie deeper into the garden. "I think it's time for you to tell me what's wrong, Miz Callie."

"I want to kill Bode. I want to scratch his eyes out. I want to curse at him, kick him in the groin. I want to pound him until he squeals for mercy. I don't want to get married. I love Wyn, but I don't . . . I'm not ready . . . I can't back out, Pearl, I gave him our house! I guess the Judge could get it back for me. I do sort of love him. He's dear. He promised me every-thing under the sun. He'll do anything for me, but he won't accept Bode as my friend, and he won't give up racing those dogs. If he really loved me, he'd do that. He would, wouldn't he, Pearl?"

"I can't be answering something so important, Miz Callie."

"Tell me, Pearl. I want to hear you say it out loud."

"Don't you be putting words in my mouth, young lady. And I'm not funnin' with you either. I want to go home."

"Well, I can top that. I want to go home, too."

"Which home?" Pearl said.

"*Our* home."

The two women stared deeply into each other's eyes. Love and devotion was mirrored there for them both to see. Callie smiled happily. Pearl grinned from ear to ear.

"I guess we can scrape together enough money to pay Wyn rent until the Judge rescinds the deed of trust. Wyn won't make things difficult. What *is* going to be difficult is telling him the wedding is off. God, Pearl, I feel like the weight of the entire universe has been lifted from my shoulders. I feel like dancing a jig. Let's dance, Pearl," Callie said, pulling at her dress. She yanked at her panty hose and had them off in the time it took Pearl to blink. Pearl hooked her fingers in her knee-highs as the ugly black shoes flew in separate directions. Holding hands, the two women laughed as they danced deeper and deeper into the garden.

"I wish Lazarus could see us," Callie chortled. "If Bode was here, you know what he'd say, Pearl?"

"No, what would my boy say?"

"He'd say it's about time I got my shit in one sock. That's not really a bad thing to say, Pearl. It's just a saying. Everyone says it. Okay, it's not nice. I lied again: Bode wouldn't say that at all. What he'd say is, it's about time I came to my senses. Yes, that's what he'd say!"

"No, Miz Callie, Bode would say just what you said. Don't you go trying to make my boy look better than he is. Lord, forgive me for saying such things."

Callie hooted with breathless laughter as she dropped to the ground, Pearl next to her.

"It's just you and me, Pearl. I'll get an extra job. Maybe we can do bits and pieces on the old house. I have my whole life to redo it. I'm a good lawyer, Pearl. I can earn us a living, I know I can. We'll make a budget and really stick to it. If the house falls down around us, we'll move into an apartment in town. I'll make it work, Pearl, I really will. Listen, when we write to Bode, I'll tell him he has to share in the expenses. It's his home, too. He'll do it. He will, won't he, Pearl?"

"Yes, my boy will do it. Bode's a good soul."

"I feel wonderful, Pearl. How about you?" Pearl nodded. "Okay, here's the deal. You know, everything happens for a reason. Y'all being late, canceling the rehearsal—it was meant to be. I'm going to have Sela and Brie drive you home. Not a word to them. I'll tell them myself when I get there. Stall them as long as you can. Don't let them leave for the church. I'm going to tell Wyn when we leave here. He . . . he said he has to deliver some keys to a family in Walterboro.

We were going to do that before we headed for church. I'll tell him on the way and he can drop me off at home. I can do it, Pearl. Why did you open Lazarus's wine? Is there any left?"

"It seemed like I was supposed to do it. Miz Sela said to open it. I can't deny you girls anything you ask of me. The wine isn't important."

"It is so. Sela knew that, so did Brie. Lazarus gave you that wine so . . . you know."

"Well, I ain't about to die, so don't you be worrying about drinking at my funeral. The old fool give me wine I wasn't supposed to drink. What kind of gift is that? Wine goes sour like vinegar if you keep it too long. There's enough left for you to drink when I go to my Maker."

"But it's been opened. It will go bad. It doesn't matter— I'll drink it anyway. Is there enough for Bode, too?"

"There's enough, and I'm tired of talking about dying."

"Pearl, in the morning we are going to call Bode. Do you think he'll say I'm doing the right thing?" Callie sounded anxious.

"Chile, Bode will tell you what he thinks. Bode has never told a lie. Leastways, I don't think he has. You need to stop stretching the truth or the Lord will fork your tongue and stick it between those pretty teeth of yours. You mind me, Miz Callie?"

"Yes, ma'am," Callie said, her eyes sparkling for the first time in many months.

"You go along now and fetch Miz Sela and Miz Brie. I need to put on my shoes."

"I'll help you. Lord, Pearl, look at those blisters. You can't put those shoes back on."

"Can and will. I won't be shaming you, Miz Callie."

"Damn it, Pearl, you could never, ever shame me. Hell, I'll walk barefoot right alongside of you. You are *not* wearing those shoes. Your blisters have blisters. Why didn't you say something?"

"I'm saying it now. I'm putting on these shoes and I'm walking out to Miz Sela's car and when I'm inside I'll take them off. You need to be thinkin' about those grass stains and your own shoes," Pearl snapped.

And that was the end of that.

"Jesus," Sela said on seeing Callie. "What happened to you?"

"Wyn was looking for you," Brie said. "He said you guys are leaving early—something about dropping off some keys before the rehearsal. You are kind of messy, Callie."

"I slipped on the grass. Pearl and I were out behind the crepe myrtles. I went down, but I kind of skidded. Listen, will you drive Pearl home? And stay there, okay?"

"Stay there as in stay there and don't go to the rehearsal?" Sela asked, and Callie nodded.

"Is Pearl all right?" Brie was worried.

"No, she's not all right. You should see her feet—she has blisters all over them. At the house she has some kind of concoction she plasters over everything. Do it for her before her feet get infected, will you? Wait on her, and I swear to God I'll kill the both of you if you drink any more of Lazarus's wine. You knew that bottle was for after . . . after Pearl's funeral. How *could* you?"

"God, Brie, I forgot about that," Sela said, guilt-stricken. "She said it was okay. It's my fault, I take the blame. Poor Pearl. I'll try and make it right, I swear I will."

"It's not Sela's fault," Brie interrupted. "It's mine. I'm a crazy person these days. I really did forget about the funeral part. Because I can't imagine . . . can't bear the thought that Pearl might someday . . ." Her voice trailed off.

"Don't say it," Callie said through clenched teeth. "Pearl is not going to die for a very long time. Do you hear me? Not for a *very* long time."

"We'll take care of her, Callie. You go ahead and do whatever you have to do." Brie hugged her friend and whispered in her ear, "If you're about to do what I think, you have my blessing. Do it. Life is just too damn short to make mistakes early on. We'll see you at the house."

"Are you two whispering about me?" Sela asked suspiciously.

"Come off it, Sela, you aren't worth whispering about. Move that skinny ass of yours or I'll shoot your foot off. Here comes Pearl. Everyone smile. You know how she is about us wearing what she calls our happy faces." Brie looked at them. "Ready, Pearl?"

"Yes'm, I truly am ready to go home."

"Well, guess what, so are we," Brie chortled as she led Pearl down the garden path and out to the garage area where Sela had parked the car. She waved offhandedly to Callie, who waved back.

"Kallum, will you do me a favor?" Callie called to Wyn's friend, who was smoking a cigar by the back porch.

"Of course. What happened?" he asked, eyeing her grass-stained dress.

"I slipped and fell. I can't go back inside looking like this. Can you fetch Wyn and explain? We still have to drop off his client's keys and then I can . . . We still have time," she said, looking at her watch.

"Callie, are you okay? Your face is flushed."

"I'd appreciate it if you'd hurry, Kallum," Callie said brightly.

"Fine. Here, hold my cigar until I get back."

"These things are so putrid-smelling," Callie said, holding the cigar out in front of her like it was a snake.

"Your soon-to-be husband gave it to me. He's been passing them out for the past hour or so. The house reeks. That's why I came out here to smoke mine."

"Miss Nela is allowing cigars to be smoked in the house? Good Lord!"

"Miss Nela is snookered, Callie."

"No!"

"So is your intended."

"Don't tell me that," Callie snapped.

"Fine—pretend I didn't say it. Do you still want me to fetch him for you?"

"Yes. I knew I was going to have to drive. Why did he do that?"

"Because he's happy in love and he's celebrating. You don't look to me like you're happy in love, Callie."

"Are you some kind of expert, Kallum?"

"In a manner of speaking. I've been around the block."

"You don't like me, do you, Kallum?"

"That's a terrible thing to say, Callie. Of course I like you. It's very easy to like you. Wyn loves you very much. I can't help but wonder if you love him as much as he loves you."

Callie threw his words back at him. "That's a terrible thing to say. However, I respect your forthrightness. Fetch Wyn, please."

He doesn't look drunk, Callie thought as Wyn approached her in the back driveway. He was smoking a cigar and looked like he could have posed for an ad in *Country Gentleman.* When she said so, Wyn laughed in delight.

"Give me the keys, Wyn, I'll drive," she said quietly.

"We're not married yet, darling. Until you say 'I do,' you can't give me orders."

"I didn't mean it to sound as though I was giving you an order. You know how I feel about drinking and driving. Kallum said you were snookered. I really don't mind driving."

"I'm a better driver," Wyn boasted.

"I can manage. Please, Wyn, don't make a scene."

"I have no intention of making a scene. I'm driving. I'm

not drunk, Callie. I won't be a hazard on the road. I'm surprised you have so little faith in me, and Kallum had no damn business telling you I was snookered. Jesus, he's my best friend, my business partner. I'm fit to drive, honey."

"Kallum doesn't like me. Why didn't you ever tell me that, Wyn?"

"You know I don't care what people think. Did he tell you he doesn't like you?"

"Of course not, but I'm not stupid. He thinks I'm not good enough for you."

"Darling, you are the best thing that has ever happened to me. I love you more than life. There's nothing I wouldn't do for you. I want us to have the perfect life. I'll work day and night to make you happy. I mean that, Callie."

"Then let me drive."

"Anything but that. You're questioning my ability. I know I'm capable of driving. Get in the car, Callie, or we really will be late. Make sure you fasten your seat belt."

She didn't want to get in the car, knew she shouldn't get in and buckle up. He was drunk. If he was sober, he would have noticed her stained dress and shoes.

"The seat belt isn't working again," Callie said.

"It worked on the way here. You're probably not doing it right. Try it again."

"The catch isn't catching. And for your information, Wyn, it wasn't working on the way here. I told you about it then."

Wyn frowned. "That's right, you did. Here, let me try it."

Callie leaned back against the plush velour of the seats, hating the scent of Wyn's breath as he struggled with the seat belt.

"Try it now," he suggested.

"Well, it's in the buckle, but I don't know if it will hold."

"You sound like you're anticipating an accident," Wyn grumbled.

"I'm doing no such thing. I'll keep my hand on it. You have to remember to get it fixed."

"First thing I'm going to do when we get back from our honeymoon."

"Wyn, after you drop off the keys can we stop somewhere, or will you drive me home so I can change my dress?"

"Absolutely," Wyn said, puffing on the cigar. Callie rolled down the window. "But if we go all the way back there, we'll be late for the rehearsal again. We're probably going to be the only couple ever to get married without a rehearsal. As far as I know, we are the only couple who had a party *before* the rehearsal. It must be like show business . . . everything ass-backwards and it works out fine in the end."

"Wyn, you're tailgating, and the light is starting to change. Slow down."

"Whatever you say, darling," Wyn said, cruising through the amber light on Carolina Avenue.

"That wasn't funny, Wyn."

"It wasn't supposed to be funny. That's the longest light in town, and I damn well hate sitting there while everyone makes up their mind which way they want to go. I didn't do anything dangerous."

"Slow down, Wyn, I said slow down! If you don't slow down, I'm going to open this door and jump out and take my chances. I mean it, Wyn. *Slow down!*"

The panic in Callie's voice made Wyn ease up on the gas pedal, but it was too late. A bright blue Bronco was halfway into the curve as the Cadillac misjudged the depth of the crescent. The impact was sudden, spinning the Cadillac completely around until it was facing the Carroll Court gravel road. Just as her seat belt snapped open, Callie saw the Bronco roll over, glimpsed the face of a baby in the infant seat and the monster live oak tree directly in front of the Cadillac.

And then there was nothing but total blackness.

Wyn saw the same things Callie did and then he saw Callie sucked through the opened door. She was a rag doll, her arms and legs flapping every which way before she hit the ground to the left of the huge oak. He scrambled from the car, felt blood dripping into his eyes from the gash on his forehead. The cigar was caught between his shirt and tie, scorching his flesh. Wyn tossed it away; he saw that his hand was bleeding, too.

"Callie! Callie," he shouted over and over as he crawled toward her. He wanted to pick her up, wanted to hold her to him, but he was afraid to touch her. He struggled to find a pulse, but his hand was shaking too badly. People were coming out of their houses, their voices shrill with panic. Above the babble of voices, he heard himself shout to anyone who was listening to call an ambulance.

Again and again he called Callie's name, begging her to open her eyes. "Please, Callie, open your eyes. I won't let you die. Goddamn it, I won't let you die. I'm here, I'll make sure everything is done. I'm sorry. Please, Callie. Please God, I'll stop racing the dogs if You let her live. I'll kiss Bode Jessup's feet, I'll do anything, just don't let her die." He wanted to shake the lifeless form on the ground, wanted to yank at Callie's hair to make her move. "Where's the fucking ambulance?" he shouted hoarsely, tears streaming down his cheeks.

"They're on their way," a woman told him. A big burly man was squirting foam over the back end of the car.

"They're dead. My God, they're dead!" another woman's voice cried.

Callie couldn't be dead, but he knew she was.

"The woman and the baby in the Bronco. They're dead," the same voice said. Wyn thought she sounded like she was in shock.

"Oh my God," he sobbed. He covered his face with his hands. How had this happened? The woman with the baby must have run the stop sign.

"Here come the police," the man with the foam said. "The ambulance is behind them."

Wyn felt himself being lifted away from Callie's body. He tried to struggle, but gave up and let himself be propped up against a chain-link fence. He did his best to focus on the men working over Callie. He watched as she was lifted onto a stretcher. He knew she was dead. She was too still, too ashen to be alive. He had to think. Someone was talking to him. Maybe they were going to tell him Callie was dead. He didn't want to hear the words, didn't want to stare into the person's face while he was telling him his reason for living was gone. Like ashes in the wind. This couldn't be happening. He was asleep and was going to wake up any minute. He pinched his arm, saw the blood on his hand, and knew he wasn't sleeping.

Wyn tried to move away from the chain-link fence when he heard voices. A man and a woman were talking, the woman's voice hateful-sounding. "He's drunk, I can smell him from here. A woman and her baby are dead. I told you, Elton, never to drink and drive. This is right in our front yard. Now, will you listen to me? Just think about that lovely young lady lying in our front yard. She's dead, too, Elton. If you ever take another drink when you're driving I will kill you myself. That man is a murderer. Look at that fancy big car, look at the clothes he's wearing. Elton. I don't want to live here anymore. Every time I come outside I'm going to see these dead bodies. If that man hadn't hit the oak, we'd be dead, too. That car would have crashed right into our living room where we were sitting. Listen to me, Elton!"

"Sir, sir, would you mind stepping over here," a young police officer said, notebook in hand.

Wyn placed one foot in front of the other. He thought he was moving. He was away from the chain-link fence and the hateful voices. *Murderer. Three times over.* Callie was dead. The woman said so. He hadn't been able to find a pulse. All because of him. *Murderer.* Callie was dead. He would have to tell Pearl. God didn't want him to kiss Bode Jessup's feet, he thought crazily.

Wyn was aware suddenly that it was dark. Lightning bugs were moving in front of him. Voices were coming from every direction. Lights flashed all around him. Then he saw the damage the Cadillac had done to the historic oak tree that he knew had to be at least three hundred years old. He'd ruined everything—lives, the tree, the faceless existences behind the chain-link fence. Elton would probably never take another drink.

"Sir?"

"Yes, officer?"

"The paramedics want to look at you."

"I'm okay; I can walk. Nothing hurts except my heart. They need to take care of the others. I can get checked over later." It wasn't his voice speaking. It was the voice of a murderer. A *drunken* murderer. "She can't be dead, we were supposed to get married tomorrow," he rambled on. "We were on our way to the wedding rehearsal. It was meant to be earlier in the day, but there was some kind of mix-up so we changed it to this evening. I had this stop I had to make in Walterboro . . . and . . ."

The shrill sound of the ambulance siren roared through the quiet evening air. Wyn shuddered. "I guess I need a ride to the hospital. How can I get there, officer?"

"I'll drive you, but first I have to fill out a report. I need to know what happened."

What happened? Elton's wife had spelled it out earlier.

DWI: driving while intoxicated. She said he was a murderer, three times over. He felt light-headed. What happened? DWI. His life was over.

"Sir? Who was driving this vehicle?"

He didn't stop to think, didn't stop to weigh the consequences. Callie was dead. He was alive. Life would go on, no matter what he did or said. "Callie. She was driving because I had had too much to drink at the Judge's party. She insisted. Callie wasn't wearing her seat belt. I don't know how it happened—I was dozing. I heard her scream and . . . and that's all I know."

His eyes followed those of the young officer when Elton said to his wife, "Jesus, look at that infant car seat. It looks like an accordion." Wyn turned, staggered over to the fence and threw up. *And all you can do is throw up a lie.*

"I want to go to the . . . wherever they took Callie. I want to go now."

"In a minute, Mr. Archer. I know this is difficult, but it has to be done. Is there anyone you want me to call?"

Hell, yes there is. Everyone in the goddamn world. Pearl, Sela, Brie, Kallum, the Judge. Even Bode.

Wyn's stomach lurched again. Bode would kill him with his bare hands, if Pearl didn't beat him to it. Bode would stalk him like a wild animal and then . . . and then he'd close in and torture him until he died. *Fuck you, Bode Jessup. I was going to kiss your feet.* As for Pearl . . . God, what would she do? Put a hex on him, a curse, or else she'd choke the life out of him with those big black hands of hers. Either that or she'd stomp him to death with her big callused feet.

What the hell did it matter? Callie was gone. Wyn's shoulders slumped. Tears rolled down his cheeks.

"Sir, is there anyone you want us to call?" the officer repeated patiently.

"No. I have to do it. What about the . . ." He pointed to the blue Bronco.

"Mr. Seagreave has been notified. He's on his way with one of our officers. I expect he's in shock like you are. I need to know your insurance company so we can call them. Your car is totaled. Not that that's important right now."

Insurance company. Drunk driving. Death. Three deaths. They'd take away his insurance, his license. He couldn't exist without a driver's license. Callie's insurance, then his would kick in. Maybe. It was his car—or was it? He'd told Kallum to put the luxury auto in Callie's name over a month ago. The Cadillac was registered in Callie Parker's name. Callie had refused to drive it, though. She said she'd be jinxed if she drove it before she was Mrs. Archer. He'd humored her and put it in her name anyway. He'd paid the premium in her name, too. She'd only driven the car once, said she couldn't get the hang of such a big vehicle. Her car, her insurance. "The papers are in the glove compartment." It made sense. Callie's car. She was driving. *You son of a bitch.* They'd cancel her policy within thirty days. What the hell did that matter? You couldn't drive if you were dead. He hadn't taken out the max on insurance because he'd known in his gut Callie wouldn't drive the Caddy. She wanted a Honda to, as she put it, scoot around in—or had she said something else? It didn't matter.

Wyn watched the activity around him. He reached out for one of the lightning bugs and when it settled on his index finger he felt like he imagined the first moonwalker felt. A dog barked from down the road and then another and still another. A chorus of sounds split the air. He felt dizzy, lightheaded.

"I need a lawyer," he murmured. Who? The Judge? Kallum? No one would mess with the Judge. Kallum was good, but not as good as the Judge. Maybe he didn't need a good lawyer at all. Maybe he didn't need any kind of lawyer. Insurance companies handled everything. Callie's insurance company. *You son of a bitch.* Callie's dead, and all you're worried about is your own skin. Where's your remorse, your grief? Dead with Callie. Life has to go on. *I'm so sorry, Callie.*

The cacophony of sound rushed into his ears again. All the neighbors were out now, huddled together, their children and pets racing up and down the dirt road. He didn't think he'd ever heard so much noise at one time in his life. The fireflies were swarming about him. He wanted to catch them all and didn't know why. Was the oak going to die? Suddenly it was important for him to know if the ancient oak would survive the accident. He wanted to ask someone, but he didn't.

Wyn felt himself being led away, helped into the police cruiser. He was told to buckle up. He did. He stared straight ahead as the officer turned the car around and headed down Route 17. They were probably going to ask him to identify Callie's body. Procedure. Everything was going to be procedure now.

His mouth was dry. Too dry. Could he identify Callie? He'd told them who she was. Maybe this was a formality of some kind. Mr. Seagreave might want to punch out his lights. He had it coming. He could live with a broken nose and a few cracked ribs. Mr. Seagreave was entitled to do whatever he had to do.

"All I want to do is die." He didn't realize he had said the words aloud until the officer reached over to pat his arm in sympathy.

Hours went by, and Wyn had no idea what he did during that time, other than to sit on a hard wooden bench and drink coffee that came back up as soon as it went down. He didn't ask questions. He didn't volunteer any additional information, for the simple reason that no one came near him.

It was twenty minutes past midnight on his wedding day, when he felt a tap on his shoulder. He raised bloodshot eyes to stare into the kindly face of a resident doctor.

"I'm sorry, I don't have good news. She's barely alive and in a deep coma. We've done all we can for now. Go home, Mr. Archer."

Wyn's head snapped backward. "Callie's alive!"

7

Bode parked his brand-new, leased BMW in a parking space that said in bold, black letters BOWDEY JESSUP. Hatch was going formal on him. He knew he was conforming, for the first time in his life. He wasn't sure if he liked the feeling or not. Bicycles, scooters, and Harleys were unacceptable, Hatch had said firmly. Suits were required for court. A dress jacket and jeans were frowned on, which meant they, too, were unacceptable. The string ties could stay. So, here he was in a suit and a button-down shirt complete with pointed collar.

His office was state of the art, complete with wide-screen television, VCR, and a CD system. A bar was snuggled underneath the breakfront that housed the sound system, and it was stocked with every drink imaginable. For clients. Grape soda for him. Snacks were in a separate cabinet—potato chips, something called squiggies, pretzels, and an assortment of chocolates and gumdrops, all his favorites. He certainly wasn't going to starve.

A huge, round table held the latest law periodicals and a monstrous bowl of fruit. He grinned when he saw a copy of *People* magazine. Hatch did love Hollywood gossip. A sofa and two deep, comfortable chairs flanked the round table. Bode tried them out, bouncing on each of them. Comfortable, but not so comfortable clients would want to stay beyond a reasonable length of time. At three hundred bucks an hour, why would they even want to sit down? He laughed.

Bode was still smiling when he walked the length and breadth of the new office that had his name on the door. It was, according to the walk off, thirty feet by twenty-five. A monster room. He could probably raise a family here if he wanted to. He laughed again.

He loved the rich paneling, the perfectly hung drapes, the matching fabric on the furniture that complemented the deep, chocolate carpet. The green plants added a human touch, as did the ornate and colorful fish tank in the corner. Hatch had deliberately put five fish in the tank. A tiny plaque glued to the side said: *Mama Pearl, Callie, Brie, Sela, Bode.* He stared at the fish swimming so gracefully in their tank. A reminder of his family, a reminder that they would move on with their life even though he wasn't there to supervise it. At least, he told himself, that's what he was getting out of the tank. He studied the fish for a full ten minutes before he was comfortable with the names of each one. Now, he could sit back in his brand-new swivel chair and talk to his new family. And the plants.

The bookshelves were elegant and matched the burnished paneling. It all smelled so new. So unused. Well, he could create a mess with the best. By the end of the day he knew the office would look used and lived in. He leaned back in his brand-new chair, swiveled around, and yelled, "Yippeeeee!" He eyed the computer with hatred. The printer and optical scanner were right next to his desk. He viewed those with *deep* hatred. The telephone system looked to him like he might need an aerospace degree to master it. He punched buttons, listened to the beeps and whistles, and said, "Shit!" He said his favorite word again when he peered down at his desk. A calculator as big as a legal pad was under glass. He touched numbers and watched it light up. "Whoa," was all he could think of to say. Great for billable hours, but Hatch said he didn't have to worry about billable hours. "Hot damn."

The door carved into the paneling across the room beckoned him. He was like a kid when he stood before it, his hand on the brass knob. Inside was a bathroom so elegantly appointed he found himself sucking in his breath. A glass-enclosed shower, thick, thirsty-looking towels, a toilet raised off the floor. He bent over to peer under it. He sat down gingerly. Mama Pearl should see this. The vanity basin with its walled mirror would be the envy of any woman. He preened in front of it, running his fingers through his dark curls. He looked down then and saw the yellow wall-to-wall carpeting. Hatch did love yellow. Something about corn and Reservations.

A second door in the bathroom led to a closet that was bigger than his whole apartment back in South Carolina. Everything was built in—shoe racks, drawers for everything imaginable, and it would have to be imaginable because he didn't have much. A chair, table, and lamp and a small kitchen that was so perfectly camouflaged he did a double take. A hideout, for when he didn't want to sit in his office or maybe wished to hide from Hatch. The guy had a wacky sense of humor. The same intricate phone system was on a long table with stacks and stacks of legal pads. Cups of pencils, pens, trays of paper clips and rubber bands were neatly lined up. But it was the picture on the wall, blown up to ten times its original size, that made him double over and roll all the way across the room. Laughing and gasping for breath he finally managed to get up and salute the picture in the elegant gold frame. "Here's to you, Miss Priceless."

"So, you found it. Every office has one. I got them for nothing. So, did I do good or what?" Hatch rumbled with laughter.

"How the hell do you explain this?" Bode demanded.

"I don't. These pictures are for partners only. Guess what, they didn't even ask. None of them has one ounce of art sense. This is art, Bode, make no mistake."

"Jesus," was all he could think of to say.

"Is it okay, Bode, do you like it?"

"God, Hatch, what's not to like? Does this firm really take in that much money? Who the hell *are* your clients?"

"I told you, most of them are high rollers from Nevada. They pay. They also give out bonuses. Don't for one minute think this firm does anything illegal. I've got the best of the best and those guys pay for it. I love showy stuff. I told you I worship money. This building was in *Architectural Digest*. The architect is a client. Megaretainer. All retainers are of the megatype. We do *pro bono* work, too. You do that between seven and nine in the morning and from six to seven at night. Weekends are yours if you want to do more. I try to encourage the partners to do as much as they can. I have fifty cases right now of my own. When I can't win them, I just give them the money and do a little razzle-dazzle with legal terms and they go away happy. You can do the same thing. We have a fund for . . . you know."

"Giveaways. I'm proud of you, Hatch."

"Yeah, sure. You did the same thing. And you were stupid enough to tell me. Where do you think I got the idea?"

"Not from me. I got it from you way back when. You said you were going to do it someday if you were ever in a position to help the needy. What I did was hardly a spit in a bucket."

"It doesn't matter, you did it. I'm doing it. Now, *we're* doing it. All the promises we made to each other back in school are coming true now. Jesus, I'm glad you're here."

"I don't think you've forgotten anything except maybe a caseload. When am I going to see my first client?"

"Ten o'clock. Your secretary will fill you in when she gets here. Her name's Medusa—I swear to God. She makes the best coffee and she bakes ladyfingers for me. You're gonna love her. Wanna go out to lunch?"

"Well, sure."

"Great," Hatch said, clapping his big hands together. "Do you need anything? Would you rather wait and start tomorrow and maybe do some shopping? We have some really great stores. I can have someone come to the office. Whatever you want, Bode."

"You know what I really want?"

"Tell me and it's yours," the big man said happily.

"I want a cup of coffee and I want to practice law. Get the hell out of my office so I can count my paper clips."

"You got it. Lunch is twelve-thirty. I insist everyone go out to lunch. We actually close the office from twelve-thirty till two. It's a perk."

"GO!"

Bode made his way to the chair behind the massive mahogany desk. He leaned back, his eyes on the phone. Maybe he should call Mama Pearl and tell her all about his new offices and ask her how the wedding went. He should do that. It was the decent thing to do, and Mama Pearl would want to know he had arrived safely. He leaned over to study all the buttons on the phone. Maybe he could figure it out by four o'clock, if he was lucky. In the meantime he'd have to wait for someone to call him. Tomorrow was another day. He'd call tomorrow, he promised himself.

She was beside his desk and he hadn't seen her come in. She was as soundless as Hatch even when the big man was on a rampage. She wasn't tiny, she was a miniature—of what, he didn't know. Seventy-nine pounds tops. A tiny little lady with a smile as big as the world. Soft, brown eyes with gold flecks in them that matched the long, thick braid that hung down to her waist. A cluster of tiny little bells hung from her ears. They hung around her neck and wrist, too. So, if they tinkled, how come he hadn't heard her come in? He was about to look down to see if she had them on her ankles when she said, "No, I don't wear ankle bracelets."

Flustered, Bode said, "I didn't hear you come in."

"You didn't hear me come in because I didn't make any noise. I'm Medusa, Mr. Jessup. Should I call you Mr. Jessup or would you prefer me to call you sir?"

"How about Bode? It's my name."

"I know all about you, Bode. Hatch, as you call him, filled me in. His mother and I were friends. It's a pleasure to finally meet you. He used to talk about you all the time; he still does. I'm very proud of him."

This lady was Hatch's Pearl, he was sure of it. Maybe not from his early years, but certainly later, after his parents' death.

"These," Medusa said, placing a stack of folders on his desk, "are your *pro bono* cases. I believe there are twenty-three. Some of them are very interesting. Your first client is due in ten minutes, and your coffee is now ready. Is there anything else I can do for you, Bode?"

"Explain to me how this . . . this phone works."

"You do this, this and this . . . then you press nine. Nine is an outside line. You're number four. That means when four lights up you press it, but first you have to press zero. I'll type up a little sheet and tape it to the desk for easy reference."

"What if I just want you?"

"Shout"—the little woman smiled—"or press zero and one."

"What, no smoke signals?"

"We do that at high noon, just look out the window," Medusa said. "You have a luncheon engagement with Hatch. I'll remind you fifteen minutes ahead of time so you can wash your hands."

"You sound like Mama Pearl," Bode grumbled.

"I'm flattered," Medusa said, closing the door behind her. Bode opened his battered briefcase, his first present from Brie. His first real present. Although she'd given him a traveling case when he left for college. He still had that, too. A smile played around the corners of his mouth as he watched Medusa set a steamy cup of coffee next to him. "You have five minutes to drink that coffee. Your first client is waiting in the outer office. Five minutes."

"Fine, send him in and bring him some coffee." Medusa frowned but nodded, the tiny bells silent.

"Mr. Jessup, this is Maxwell Thornton," Medusa said, ushering in a tall, distinguished-looking man in his sixties. She quietly withdrew, the door closing softly behind her.

Bode walked around the side of the desk, his hand extended. Thornton's handshake was firm and hard. "Please sit down. Coffee?"

"I've had my caffeine fix for the day. Go ahead and drink yours."

"It will wait. What can I do for you, Mr. Thornton?" He leaned back in his chair, his fingers making a steeple as he prepared to listen.

Thornton cleared his throat. "No matter how I say this, it's going to come out sounding . . . terrible. I guess I should just go ahead and try for some kind of chronological order."

Bode nodded. "Take your time," he said quietly.

"Twenty-five years ago, my wife and I adopted a child. It wasn't done through an agency; it was private. Then, two years later we adopted another child the same way. Connor is thirty now and Madeline twenty-eight. A week after we brought Madeline home, my wife, Caroline, found out she was pregnant. She gave birth to twin girls seven months later, Amy and Andy."

"It sounds like you have a wonderful family, Mr. Thornton."

"It is. We've always done everything together. The children work in my business. Connor pretty much runs the company. He has a good head for business. Madeline is the comptroller. Amy and Andy run the offices. My firm manufactures cardboard cartons. It's very profitable. I'm the second largest firm in the country. Containers are . . . profitable."

Bode leaned forward. He knew what was coming next. His guts started to churn as he waited, feeling Thornton's embarrassment.

"I'm seventy-two years old. Caroline is seventy. My heart isn't what it should be. My wife isn't well either. I set up trusts years ago, bought tons of life insurance. Everything is taken care of, except that now, my wife has decided she wants our estate to be left to our natural children, with bequests to the adopted children. Sizable bequests," he added swiftly, shifting position in the chair, his eyes everywhere but on the attorney facing him.

"And your feeling is . . . ?"

"I don't think it's right, but my wife . . . it's very important to her that we do this. She's already spoken to Andy and Amy, and as much as I hate to say this, I think they're encouraging her to put pressure on me."

"Once adopted, children of that adoption have as many legal rights as biological children. You're right, Mr. Thornton, what your wife is proposing isn't right, morally or ethically—in my eyes and yours, too, it would appear. What exactly is it you *think* you want me to do?"

"To tell me it can't be done, I guess. Everything in life can be undone if you have the time, the patience, and the stamina. Isn't that right, Mr. Jessup?" Bode noticed beads of perspiration dotting the man's brow.

"That's often the case, but I need to know why. The courts are going to want to know why, too. I would suspect that Connor and Madeline will want to know why, also."

"I love them both like they're my own."

"They are, Mr. Thornton. It doesn't sound fair to me. Why don't you think it through some more and come back when you've finally decided. I have the feeling you want me to make your decision, and I cannot and will not do that. If you feel that way, how does your wife feel?"

"Once our own children were born she changed. She said I couldn't possibly understand since I wasn't a mother. As I said, the bequests are sizable. They were my wife's idea."

"What do you consider sizable, Mr. Thornton?" Bode asked with an edge to his voice.

"My wife feels half a million each is more than enough. Andy and Amy say that's too much. I myself don't feel it's enough, and I really don't want to do this. I came here hoping you'd talk me out of it or tell me I can't do it."

"You can do anything you want, Mr. Thornton. It's your money. Would Connor and Madeline contest the will?"

"No, they aren't like that."

"They sound like fine children, people to be proud of. What do they call you?"

"Call me?"

"Yes. How do they address you?" The edge was still in Bode's voice, his eyes narrowed as he stared at his first client across the desk.

"Connor calls me Dad, and so does Madeline. Amy and Andy do, too. Why?"

"*Are* you Dad? Do you deserve to be called Dad? How did you feel the first time they called you that? I'm asking you for personal reasons so don't feel you have to answer me. You see, I never had a father. A very kind, generous man took me into his home, but while he provided for me, we never really had any personal interaction. In my secret thoughts I called him Dad, thought of him as Dad, but the word Dad never, ever passed my lips. I wish it had. You have no idea how much I wish that. I don't think I'm the person to help you, Mr. Thornton. My own background is too cloudy for me to deal with you on a legal level. I can arrange for you to work with one of the other attorneys. Are you agreeable to that?"

"Hell, no, I'm not. Mr. Littletree said you were the best. I need the best. It sounds to me like you're just the man to help me if you can relate to what I'm telling you. I don't want another attorney," Thornton said adamantly. "Just tell me how I can divide my estate equally. To answer your question earlier, it felt great, wonderful actually, when the kids called me Dad. Jesus, I went out and bought footballs, baseballs, bats. I had a basketball hoop put up in the driveway. I went the whole nine yards. I was Connor's dad from day one."

"Then act like it," Bode snapped. *I didn't say that, somebody else said that.* "Maybe you need to give some thought to sizable bequests to your wife and natural children. It would certainly give them something to think about." *Jesus, this guy is going to take me before the bar and have my license.*

"My wife, their mother . . ." A second later he was up off the chair, wringing his hands and pacing the large office, his eyes full of misery.

"Let me tell you what a mother is. Sit down." It was a

command full of iron and steel. The older man blinked, but did as he was told. Bode's voice rang with love and emotion when he spoke of Pearl and the girls. When he finally wound down he felt like smoke was coming out of his ears. He stood up, the palms of his hands braced on his desk. He leaned over, his eyes shooting sparks. He spoke slowly, enunciating each word carefully and slowly. "Don't think, even for a minute, that Connor and Madeline don't know what's going on. Do not allow yourself that luxury. In their eyes it must be unconscionable; my eyes, too. When you commit, you commit one hundred percent where children are concerned. Anything less is totally unacceptable. Now, please leave my office and when you're ready, if you're ever ready, to act like a man, a father, you can come back." *And there goes my law career. Sorry, Hatch.* He started to pack up his briefcase. "You can leave now, Mr. Thornton." He was angrier than he'd ever been before. So angry he wanted to smash something, to use his fists, something he'd never done in the whole of his adult life.

Outside, Hatch Littletree had his ear pressed to the door, his face full of glee.

"The spirits of our ancestors will send you up in smoke. Momentarily, Shunpus," Medusa hissed.

"If you'd listened like I told you, I wouldn't have to disturb my ancestors." He moved away from the door though. "What did you hear, Medusa? I know you have the ears of a deer."

"Your friend is upset. He's packing up his briefcase because he thinks he's done something wrong, that he acted in an unprofessional manner—something you do every day, Shunpus. You need to put him out of his misery."

"You heard all that, sitting way over here at your desk?" Hatch said in awe.

"When one is silent, one can hear everything. You are a disgrace. You make more noise than a herd of wild buffalo."

"Ah, Mr. Thornton, did things go well?" Hatch asked politely.

"You said he was the best. I believed you."

"And?"

Thornton slapped down a check on Medusa's desk. "I'll reschedule an appointment."

"Anytime, Mr. Thornton." He watched the man leave. "And where the hell do you think you're going, Bode? It isn't lunchtime yet."

"I blew it, Hatch. My first client and I lost him. I let my personal feelings get in the way of my professional duties. The guy is probably calling the ABA as we speak. I'm sorry, Hatch. Hell no, I'm not sorry. I'd damn well do it again. What the hell are you smiling at?"

"You. I love you, Bode Jessup. You practice law like I do. Take a look at this," Hatch said, holding up Thornton's check. "Twenty-five big ones."

"For what?"

"For what, he asks," Hatch cackled. "That's what we charge for a retainer. We use it up in a heartbeat, and then we get another one. That's how we do business. I knew you two would get along as soon as I heard what his problem was. *Now* we can go to lunch." His big hand was about to clap Bode on the back, but he thought better of it and reached down to take his friend's hand. "Let me show you the way, O Great Father," Hatch intoned, roaring with laughter. "Don't sweat it, he's going to reschedule. She's doing a victory dance in there, you know."

"How do you know that?" Bode demanded. He shook his hand free of Hatch's.

"I know that because I have the eyes of an eagle and the ears of a deer. It's my heritage. I know everything."

"Bullshit. You were listening at the door."

"That too." Hatch's laughter boomed through the offices. In spite of himself, Bode joined in.

The first thing he was going to do when he got back from lunch was to call Mama Pearl.

8

It was four days before Bode had a chance to draw a deep breath and do anything but work. Mama Pearl was on his mind as well as Brie and Sela. There was no point in thinking about Callie, the wedding, or her honeymoon. That all belonged in the past now.

Bode stuck his pencil behind his ear, fired up one of his rare cigarettes, and placed it in the ashtray before he took a long pull from a frosty bottle of grape soda. Medusa learned quickly to anticipate his need for the soda and would put the bottle, the cap slightly open, in the freezer so it got thick and slushy. He did love grape soda. Orange, too, and sometimes lemon and lime. He was drinking seven bottles a day according to Medusa. Hatch was having it delivered by the case these days. These days. Four days and already the big guy knew his MO.

He dialed the number at Parker Manor and waited for Pearl's voice. When he didn't hear it after the fifteenth ring he frowned. Where was she—in Beaufort? Did she go to the market or church? He looked at his watch; it was two hours later in South Carolina which meant it was four o'clock. Pearl always started to fix dinner at four o'clock. Unless Brie and Sela had left and there wasn't anyone to fix dinner for. No, she must be in Beaufort at Wyn Archer's. After the eighteenth ring he hung up and dialed information for the Archer number. He made the call person-to-person. He frowned again when he heard a voice so like Pearl's say, "Pearl doesn't live here."

Brie would know, so would Sela. He dialed Brie's number in San Diego, listened to her message, then hung up without leaving one of his own. He tried Sela, got her answering machine. He hung up again without leaving a message. He tried the number at Parker Manor a second time and let the phone ring twenty-five times before he hung up. Once he'd suggested an answering machine and Pearl had just looked at him like he'd sprouted a second head. She'd said, "Now why would I be needing a piece of machinery like that? All they do is confuse a person with all them bells and screeches. If anyone calls me and there's no answer, that means I'm not home and they can call back. I don't have any important business." And that had been the end of that. The phone had rung, which meant it was still connected. Pearl must just be out visiting. She did like to do that when she had the time. Or, she might have gone to the cemetery to put flowers on Lazarus's grave.

"Your two-thirty client is here, Mr. Jessup," Medusa said from the doorway. He nodded as he dropped his soda bottle under the desk and slid the ashtray into his top desk drawer. He blew at some stray ash before he got up from his desk to greet his new client.

The afternoon passed with barely a moment between clients, and it was six-thirty before he knew it.

Bode leaned back in his chair, a wave of tiredness swimming over him. Something was happening to him. He'd just sent a client on his way because he wanted to initiate a suit based on principle. He'd always acted and fought for principle. "Ten thousand," he'd told the client, "right up front and there's a ninety-five percent chance we'll lose. If you have nothing else going on in your life, if you have money to burn, if this case eats and burns at your soul, then we'll start the suit. By the time it gets to court, in say, three years, the chances are you won't remember half of what it's all about. From start to finish your legal fees and court costs will be about fifty thousand dollars." The man had stood, looked at him, and with absolutely no emotion showing on his face had stated: "I always said you lawyers were slimeballs swimming around in a sea of pus. I heard that on some television show. I got up and cheered." He'd gone on to call him a maggot and a few other names Bode would rather not remember. Then he did show some emotion. He kicked the chair and sent a luscious green fern sailing across the room before he stalked out. Bode had watched the dirt spiral upward, seen the graceful fronds of fern break in midair and float downward. There were little pills of some kind of white stuff mixed with the soil that peppered his desk.

Everyone is entitled to his day in court, Bode Jessup, and that includes Hiram Overglace. Yeah, yeah, I know that, but the courts are backed up enough without frivolous suits like this. It's my job to point out to a client . . . certain things. Like spending fifty grand for pure bullshit. Fifty grand is enough to give some kid a solid education, enough to buy a small house somewhere. If he wants to piss his money away on nonsense, let him get some other lawyer who doesn't give a shit about the courts, or his bank account, and is interested only in billable hours. It's not my bag. I'm going to live with it, and Overglace is going to live with it, too.

"Yo, Bode, how'd your day go?" Hatch said, poking his head in the doorway. He looked around at the dirt and the little white things all over the furniture. "Like that, huh? Five bucks says it was a guy named Overglace. He comes in at least once a month for something or other. The results are usually the same."

"How come you sicced him on me?" Bode complained.

"Because he's already been through every guy in the firm. You were the last. I think it's that free consultation we offer. You working late?"

"Yeah, and I want to call Mama Pearl. I've been trying for days, but there's been no answer. See you tomorrow."

"I love it when the partners work late," Hatch said gleefully. "By the way, that white stuff is called vermiculite and you get to clean it up. Trust me when I tell you it's an experience. The stuff is like fairy dust, you can't catch it. Say hello to Mama Pearl."

Bode nodded as he tried to pick up one of the little white circles on his desk. It was elusive. He spit on the end of his finger and tried again. He felt pleased with himself when he held his hand over the wastebasket. He watched in dismay as the little white ball fell off his finger and settled on the floor. "Ah, shit!"

He placed his call to Parker Manor and let the phone ring twenty times, his fingers drumming on the desk. Where was Mama Pearl? It was too early for church. Maybe she'd gone visiting to see Lazarus's family or maybe she went to see Arquette, her best friend. Maybe she'd taken a vacation. That was just too silly for words, about as silly as her going on Callie's honeymoon. He tried Brie's number and then Sela's. Both times he got the answering machines. He didn't leave a message.

He was on his feet, pacing, his face puckered in worry. Maybe he should call the Judge. Then again, maybe he shouldn't call the Judge.

Bode stared at the phone a moment longer before he punched out Brie's number in California. He waited for the brief message, the beep. He wanted to say, "Brie, it's Bode. I called twice earlier so those hang-ups are mine. I hate these damn things, talking into them, I mean. Listen to me, Brie. I don't love Callie Parker. I might have had a crush on her when we were kids growing up. That's a lot different than being in love with someone. A strange thing happened to me before I left, that Friday. I was leaving the office. I hate saying stuff like this over the phone, but I really do need to talk to you. Callie showed up in the parking lot and . . . listen, I can't talk about this on the phone, I'll keep trying you till I get you." Once again he didn't leave a message and didn't know why. He dialed Sela's number again and then Parker Manor. There was still no answer at either number.

He rummaged for a cigarette. He felt wired, antsy, out of control for some reason. He wished Brie had been home. His heart skipped a beat just the way it had done the day she showed up at the airport madder than hell and packing a gun. Jesus, if he lived to be a hundred, he'd never forget it. For one brief second his heart had leaped in his chest at the sight of her, until he saw the expression on her face. Then his heart had thudded.

He should have stayed for the wedding, it was the decent thing to do. Well, he was damn tired of doing the decent thing for other people. It was time to do what Bode wanted.

Hatch was back, his eyes troubled. "Want to talk?"

"Yeah, yeah, I do. I need to know why I feel so guilty. It was a pretty cowardly thing for me to do, cutting out like that. A few more days wouldn't have made that much difference. Do you think, Hatch, that if I had stayed I would have . . . done something?"

"Like what?"

"Like I don't know, that's what. Wyn Archer is a decent

kind of guy, and he loves Callie. He's what he is. If looking down his nose at me makes him happy, that's okay, too. Inside, he's decent. He's jealous of me, at least that's what Callie said. Of our friendship."

"Or what he perceived to be more than a friendship? I don't like to cast aspersions on your old friend, but did it ever occur to you that maybe Callie told him things that were not quite true? Ah, I see by the look on your face that either it did occur to you or you know it for a fact. What *is* our problem here, Bode? Don't tell me it's still that trash business, the lack of knowing your real roots and being an orphan. I thought we put that behind us after we talked it to death."

"It will always be there, Hatch. It's not going to go away. Ever."

"That's a long time," the big man said quietly. "What say we finally do something about it? Let's start a search. We have six private dicks on our payroll. Good guys, they never come back empty-handed. Do you want to talk about it or do you want to do something about it?"

Bode's face drained. Did he? "What if—"

"That's the chance you take, Bode. You haven't asked for my opinion, but fearless man that I am, I'm going to offer it anyway. It won't change you. You are who and what you are. That's a piece of your personal puzzle, the one God created. We all want all the pieces, but sometimes those pieces aren't . . . What I'm trying to say is, they don't fit the whole of the puzzle anymore. Maybe once, in the beginning. Things expand and grow. Your call, Bode."

"I have to tell Mama Pearl. The only problem is, I can't get hold of her or Brie or Sela."

"Write her a letter and keep on trying to call her. She'll want whatever makes you happy."

"Let me think about it."

9

The sterile surroundings, the deep quiet, and the weary man in front of him forced Wyn backward so that his knees hit the dull, gray chair behind him. He toppled backward, his face full of shock, his eyes glazed. "I want to see her," he managed to croak.

"I know you do, but it will serve no purpose now. It's too soon to say anything other than Miss Parker is in critical condition. You've been through a terrible ordeal. Go home, rest, get something to eat and come back around noon. We'll talk then. I've been working round the clock for the past three days and I need some rest myself. Noon, Mr. Archer," the doctor said wearily, and walked away.

Wyn stared after the man, his face full of stunned surprise. Go home. Eat. "In your dreams, Doc," he muttered. He wasn't going anywhere. He was going to stay right there. For the rest of his life if he had to.

It was his fault Callie was lying in a coma. He racked his brain to remember what he had read about comas. Deep sleep. Barely alive . . . *Barely alive* meant she wasn't dead! If you weren't dead there was hope. The rush he felt left him weak. He'd told so many lies. He had to make it right.

Pearl.

He bolted then, his leather-soled shoes slapping the tiled floor as he ran to the front desk. "I need a cab. Now. Right away."

"One just pulled up, sir," the receptionist said, pointing to the white cab nestled next to the curb under the overhang.

Wyn sprinted through the opened doors. "I need to get somewhere quick, but don't break any speed laws. Please, hurry."

He'd tell Pearl, hold out hope—Callie was alive. Pearl was going to fall apart, for Callie was her life. She would blame him. Not with words, but with her eyes. He wouldn't be able to meet those dark eyes, not now, not ever. Pearl would take one look at him and know he was responsible for the accident. Callie said Pearl could see into a person's soul. Pearl and her goddamn superstitions. She'd filled Callie's head with the old sayings, muttering and mumbling about curses and hexes. The only thing worse than Pearl and her crazy beliefs was Callie's believing in them, too.

He recalled the day Callie had stopped him from planting a cedar tree. He would die when the tree was large enough to shade a grave, she'd warned him—in about six years' time. He hadn't planted the tree because his darling's eyes had pleaded with him not to. He felt silly as hell, but whatever made Callie happy, he did. For instance, she would never use the same towel as he, even at the beach. Their friendship would be broken forever, she said solemnly. He always made sure they had extra towels, and he also made damn sure he never touched hers. Pearl had a ditty for everything.

The day he'd placed his hands on the back of a rocking chair on the Parker verandah, and given it a hard rock, Callie had almost jumped down his throat. Now, she'd whispered in terror, someone was going to die. If it was possible for

Pearl's black face to turn white it would have. Lazarus died two days later.

And that's why Pearl of Parker Manor hated him. He'd wanted to pension her off, but Callie wouldn't hear of it. She'd as much as said: "Pearl comes with me, or I don't marry you." He'd agreed. He would have agreed to anything, as long as Callie smiled and said she loved him. Marrying her was the best thing that could ever happen to him. Now, he'd screwed that all up, and Pearl was going to know. He would goddamn well beat her to the punch. First thing in the morning he was going to call the police and admit to everything. He'd say he hadn't been thinking clearly, that his brain had been fogged up by alcohol. The truth was always the best defense. If Callie didn't make it, it wasn't going to matter what happened to him.

Bode.

"Jesus *fucking* Christ!" he muttered under his breath. He had to call Kallum. Kallum was a lawyer; he'd know what to do. Wyn would call him from Callie's house and arrange to meet him back at the hospital.

Callie's house—*his* house. Callie had given him the rundown, decayed plantation. Wyn groaned when he thought about the insurance premiums. Better to get a wrecking ball and start over, but that would devastate Callie. No matter what, she'd never take Pearl's home away from her. Even if it meant the woman only visited on weekends.

Wyn rolled down the window and the humidity of the night slapped him in the face. He blinked, tried to get his bearings. "Can't you go any faster?"

"You told me not to break any speed laws, sir."

"That's right, I did say that. If you see a phone booth along the road, stop. I need to make a call."

"One's coming up on the right there by that gas station."

"Stop. Listen, driver, do you have any change?"

"Plenty," the driver said, counting out three dollars' worth of quarters. Wyn handed him a five-dollar bill from a gold money clip.

Wyn was all thumbs as he tried to drop the money into the phone slot. He listened to the ringing on the other end. "Pick up the damn phone, Kallum," he snarled. The minute he heard the attorney's voice his shoulders sagged in relief. He babbled, knowing he was incoherent. "Just meet me at the hospital, Kallum. I'm on my way to pick up Pearl and the girls. I'll drive back with them. By God you better be there when I get back. I need you. I'm not going up against Pearl on my own. That woman scares the shit out of me."

A moment later he was back in the cab. "I'd like some air-conditioning, if you don't mind."

"Ah don't mind at all, but ah don't have any," the driver said.

"Don't your passengers complain?" Wyn said, just to have something to say.

"All the time, but they're so happy to git where they're going they forgit about it."

Fifteen minutes later, the driver slowed at the massive stone pillars that marked the entrance to the Parker place.

Wyn pulled off two twenty-dollar bills and handed them to the driver. "I need the exercise. You can turn around here and head back."

The moment the car's taillights were tiny dots in the dark night, Wyn ran, his legs pumping furiously, down the rough brick road. Yellow light beckoned him from the back of the house. He was breathless when he climbed the porch steps. Pearl, Sela, and Brie were seated at the kitchen table, coffee cups in front of them. The screen door creaked, the loudest sound he'd ever heard. Three pairs of eyes searched his face.

As one they said, "What happened?"

"There was an accident. Callie's in the hospital. This was . . . I couldn't leave until I knew . . . I took a cab." He carefully avoided looking at Pearl and directed his voice at Sela and Brie. "We need to go back. My car was totaled. I think one of you should drive."

"I'll drive," Brie said quietly.

"Get a clean hanky, Pearl." Sela raised defiant eyes to Wyn. "Pearl never goes anywhere without a clean hanky."

"Yes—and wear your slippers, Pearl. No one is going to look at your feet. You wait here, I'll get them for you. Tell me where the hankies are, and I'll fetch one for you as well." Brie was shocked, but efficient.

"Is my baby all right, Mr. Wyn? How bad was the accident?"

"Callie's alive. The accident was real bad. Callie . . . Callie's in a coma." Once again he avoided Pearl's eyes. He watched as Brie carefully fitted the soft felt slippers over Pearl's large feet. How tender she was. She offered the hanky to the old nanny with the same tenderness. How loved this old woman was. Why didn't he love her the way they did? Callie said it was because he was jealous of Pearl. Maybe he was.

"What's a coma, Mr. Wyn?" Pearl asked, but she didn't wait for an answer. Her eyes rolled back in her head and Wyn had to strain to hear the words she muttered. "I never should have transplanted the parsley. I did it outside, back by the stable. I only did it in little pots because Miss Harriet down at the library wanted some fresh parsley. Now my chile is going to die because I transplanted it. It's my fault." To Brie she said urgently, "Find the mustard seed so I can sprinkle it around my baby's bed."

"The hospital bed?" Wyn said stupidly. "They won't let

you do that. Hospitals are sterile. It was a car accident and I— Planting those damn herbs didn't have—Oh, forget it," he said when he saw the angry looks on Sela and Brie's faces.

"I have it, Pearl," Brie said as she poured mustard seed from a small shaker bottle.

"I didn't hear no hoot owl last night, did you?" the old woman asked fretfully.

Brie's eyes met Sela's over the back of the chair. The owls had screeched all night long, but Pearl's hearing wasn't what it had been, and she played gospel music until she fell asleep. Not for the world would either girl admit to hearing the owls, for to do so meant Callie would die. Someone always died when an owl hooted. It was just an old superstition, Brie told herself, but her eyes locked on the little bag of mustard seed clutched in Sela's hand. "Don't lose that," she said quietly.

"Don't you worry," Sela murmured.

Wyn snorted in disgust. "Callie is unconscious, in a coma," he said harshly. He had to stop this ridiculous nonsense.

"A coma is a very deep sleep," Sela said. "You should have called, Wyn. We've been sitting here for hours. I think we all knew something terrible happened. You should have called, or at the very least had someone else call."

"Easy for you to say. You weren't there. I didn't think about anything but Callie. If you're ready we should be leaving."

"When will my baby wake up?" Pearl asked, her eyes full of fear.

"I don't know," Wyn admitted.

"Sometimes it takes a while," Sela said.

"Weeks," Brie commented grimly as she searched for her keys.

They were still in their party clothes, Wyn noticed, and he

wondered why they hadn't changed. He gave voice to his thought.

"Because we were too damn worried to think about our clothes. I can't believe you'd say something so crass," Sela snarled.

Sela helped Pearl into the backseat of the rental car before climbing into the front seat next to Brie. "The keys to Callie's Beetle are in the car," she told Wyn. "I'm sure you can manage. Obviously you are going to need some wheels. It's over there, under the oak."

It wasn't until he was out on the main road that it occurred to Wyn that he could have had Kallum drive him back to Beaufort. Now he was stuck with this rusty bucket of bolts. He cringed each time he shifted the gears. And yet Callie preferred this ancient vehicle over his Cadillac. Bode's influence? he wondered. The guy rarely drove a car, preferring to pedal a bicycle. *Shit, why am I thinking about Bode Jessup now? Because,* he answered himself, *every time I think of Callie I think of Bode Jessup.* How long would it take before Bode appeared on the scene? Hours? Days?

Ahead of him, through the windshield, Wyn could see Pearl's head with its coronet of braids. Either Brie was driving slow or else this Beetle had more power in it than he'd thought. Why Callie would prefer it over the Caddie was still a mystery to him. He'd told Kallum to make sure a bright red Honda was sitting in front of the house when they returned from their honeymoon. With a huge silver ribbon on top. Callie would have smiled and hugged him. It was supposed to have been wonderful, and now he'd ruined everything.

Bode.

When Bode found out—and he would find out—that Wyn had lied to the police, lied about Callie, the woman he was going to marry, Bode would beat him within an inch of his life. Everyone in the whole damn world knew Bode Jessup loved Callie Parker, except Callie and Bode. Bode would never admit to anything.

Wyn wished for sound then, anything to drive the thoughts from his head. He switched on the tinny-sounding radio and waited for some late-night DJ to play a song he could relate to, but all he heard was static. Callie said she sang to herself while she drove—now he knew why. He wished time would go faster. Wished Brie would drive faster so he could get to the hospital quicker. Kallum always said if you had one foot in today and one foot in tomorrow, then you pissed on today. Jesus, where did that thought come from? Never wish your life away.

A sob caught in his throat. His eyes filled up and overflowed, and his shoulders started to shake just as Brie swerved onto the road that led to the hospital parking lot.

The parking lot was almost empty, for it was after one-thirty in the morning. Most of the cars probably belonged to patients who were at the hospital on an emergency basis, Wyn decided.

When he climbed from the car, in an instant he correctly interpreted the situation. It was them against him. He felt like crying again, but squared his shoulders and motioned the women to follow him. No one said a word as they trekked through the humid night air to the entrance of the hospital.

Inside, it was a different story. Brie took charge, marching over to the receptionist and offering her badge for inspection. Wyn could hear her speaking in low tones, heard her ask for the police officer's name. He saw her write it down in a tattered little notebook. His stomach rumbled. He felt his throat constrict, felt the overpowering urge to run. Fast. He had the crazy notion Brie would shoot him dead on the spot the moment she found out he'd lied about the accident. Well, let her. He damn well deserved to die for what he'd done.

Never mind waiting until it got light. He'd check on Callie, then drive down to the police station and confess. It was after the fact now, he knew, since Brie would ask to see the original police report. She'd read the amended one, too. She'd call him a lying sack of shit, and he'd deserve it. But what was worse, she'd tell Bode Jessup.

Brie walked over to where he was standing, slightly apart from Pearl and Sela. Brie's dress swished angrily against her knees. She had nice legs, he noticed. Her face was unreadable. She had no jurisdiction in Summerville, he needed to remember that.

"All we can do is speak with the night nurse in the intensive care unit. Callie is listed as critical." This last was said as she put her arm around Pearl. Instinctively, Wyn reached out when he saw Pearl's eyes go from dark to white. He caught her, and helped her to one of the leather benches against the wall.

A moment later, Sela was holding out a small paper cup with water. Her hand was trembling so badly she dribbled the water down the front of Pearl's dress. "Oh shit, I can't do anything right. I never could. I feel so helpless. This is like when my husband told me he was leaving. I couldn't do anything then either to make it right."

"The Lord will make it right," Pearl whispered.

"Yeah, sure," Wyn muttered. Praying wasn't something he did on a regular basis. He didn't do it on an irregular basis either. Kallum said he was an atheist even though he went to church. But he only went to church so he could say he went. He never prayed, never bowed his head, never sang the hymns. He did shake the minister's hand on the way out of church though.

"Maybe they'll let us look at Callie through the ICU window. In California they let you do that. I've done it lots of times when a suspect or a victim was in ICU," Brie said.

"I'm not sure I want to." Sela fretted.

"Pearl?"

"I'm not leaving here till I see my baby. They can't make me leave, can they, Miz Brie? I forgot my string bag."

Brie swayed dizzily. Pearl never went anywhere without her oversize string bag—what Callie called her bag of miracles. She'd remembered the hanky though. Damn. The string bag was Pearl's storehouse for all her charms. Once, when they were little, Pearl had let them look into the depths of her most secret possession. She glanced at Sela now and knew her friend was remembering the same things.

Brie fondly recalled Pearl chewing, ever so vigorously, John-the-conqueror root. Lazarus's sister had sent it from Natchez years and years ago, and it was replenished on a yearly basis. Pearl chewed it to bring her good luck.

Also in the string bag was a buckeye, polished and shiny. Sometimes Pearl wore it around her neck, but only on special occasions. A penny with a hole in it, threaded with red ribbon and worn around the ankle to ward off stepping in devil's dust, was worn on the way to church. A small sack of saltpeter and bluestone rested in the zippered compartment of a large purse. To bring health and happiness, Pearl said.

It was the left hindfoot of a rabbit that Pearl wanted now, Brie knew. She'd put it around Callie's neck—providing some nurse kindly allowed it. Or maybe it was the chunk of sandalwood she was after. She'd cut off a sliver with the rusty knife in the bag and slip it between Callie's lips. If she died, Callie would go to heaven. "Oh God," she whimpered.

"Miz Brie, they can't make me leave, can they?" Pearl pleaded.

"I don't think so. If you're feeling better, we can take the elevator up now. The receptionist said there's a small waiting area with some comfortable chairs and a television. I'm going to see Callie and then go to the police station. I'll bring your bag to you."

"Are you going to stir up trouble?" demanded Sela when they arrived in ICU. "That's just like you, Brie—stir up a mess and then walk away. It's Wyn's place to go to the police. Or Pearl's place. Why can't it wait till morning? We should all be here. I read somewhere that for twelve hours after a trauma of any kind, time is crucial. So go fetch Pearl's string bag, but forget the police."

"I never read that," Brie said calmly, "and I'm going to the police."

"That's because the only thing you read are police manuals. When was the last time you read *Cosmo?*"

"I never read *Cosmo.*"

"I rest my case. You can learn a lot from *Prevention* magazine. I read it when I'm standing in line at the checkout counter in the grocery store." Sela was talking nonsense in her distress. "I think you should stay here with us. Wyn can tell you everything that happened. He was there, for God's sake!" she snapped.

"Shhh," the nurse behind the desk said reprovingly. "It's very late. Please don't make noise."

"Can we see Callie Parker? Through the window?" Sela asked. The nurse shook her head.

"Please," Pearl begged, her eyes filled with tears.

"It can't hurt anything," Brie said, flashing her badge at the woman. "Miss Pearl has raised Callie since she was a baby. She's like her mother. Surely you can't deny her this." The nurse relented, and they followed her in single file to stand before the window.

"One minute only," the nurse warned, backing up a step.

Four pairs of hands went up against the window as though touching the glass would somehow make Callie open her eyes, let her know they were there.

"Oh God," Sela breathed.

"My baby looks like she's *daid*," Pearl whimpered, reverting to the comfortable Southern patois of her childhood.

"She's not dead, Pearl. She's just in a very deep sleep," Brie whispered.

Wyn struggled for words, but his tongue seemed to be three times its normal size, and the words wouldn't come. He was the first to turn away. He wanted to run into the room, to shout he was sorry, to breathe his own life into her body. He wanted to scream at her to wake up. Instead, he walked away. He was standing by the elevator when the women joined him. Maybe he could hitch a ride with Brie instead of driving the Beetle, if she was going to the police station. He'd tell her the truth on the way. Maybe she would understand.

The elevator swished open, and Kallum stepped into the hall. Wyn drew him aside. "Let's go downstairs, I need to talk with you." He heard Brie tell the others she would be back in an hour or so. It didn't matter—Kallum could drive him to the police station or he could drive himself. Wyn could feel the old woman's eyes on his back: his skin prickled. He moved quickly to the second elevator and pressed the down button.

"You look like you've been to hell and back," Kallum said.

"And you look your usual natty, debonair self," Wyn snarled. "How the hell do you manage to look like a magazine ad at two in the morning?"

"I work at it," Kallum said curtly. "I don't like talking in public places even at this hour. Let's go out to my car and talk."

Both men watched as Brie's rental car came to life. Neither said a word until they could no longer see the red glow of the taillights.

"How is Callie?"

Wyn shook his head.

Kallum held the car door open. "Talk to me, Wyn, and don't leave anything out. Take it from the time you walked out of the Judge's back door. By the way, where's Brie going?"

"To the police station. She's a cop, remember?"

"For what purpose? Wouldn't morning be soon enough? Maybe it's instinctive. You know, her cop nose at work, or whatever . . . Don't leave anything out, Wyn."

Kallum was cross. From long years of friendship, Wyn knew Kal didn't like to intrude into his private life, hear about Wyn's personal problems. His own tidy life was such that it made Wyn cringe, and on more than one occasion he'd said, in all seriousness, "Don't you *ever* do anything that isn't choreographed down to the last detail?" And Kallum's reply was always the same. "If you don't take the time to think things through, you make mistakes and run into trouble. If you do take that time, then you make a plan and stick to it, you have a handle on things. It's when you go off at half-cock that problems occur."

"I wish you wouldn't smoke in the car, Wyn," was all he said now. "If you really need to smoke, let's stand outside."

"You're a pain in the ass, Kallum," Wyn mumbled as he dutifully climbed from the Jaguar. He held out his lighter when Kallum withdrew a filter-tipped cigarette from his jacket pocket. Both men inhaled and blew clouds of smoke in each other's faces.

"Callie's in a coma," Wyn began. "It doesn't look good. She's alive though. I thought she was dead. I honest to God thought she was dead. I couldn't find a pulse. Jesus, I wanted to die right there with her. A mother and baby were killed. Outright. I was driving, Kal. I should have listened to Callie. She said I had had too much to drink, and she was right. I thought . . . I didn't *feel* drunk. When the police talked to me

I . . . what I said was . . . Jesus, I still can't believe it! I said Callie was driving because I had a snootful. The cop seemed to believe me. I thought Callie was dead, Kal. I couldn't find her pulse. I . . . all I could think about was the mother, the baby, and Callie and me driving drunk. I know it wasn't right, me saying she was driving, but I thought she was dead. If she was dead, it didn't make a difference. If I'd told the truth, my life . . . My mind was going a hundred miles an hour. You registered the Caddie in Callie's name. The insurance was in her name. It seemed . . . it seemed like the thing to do at the time. Now that I've had time to think about this I know how wrong it was. Hell, I knew it was wrong at the time too, but . . . I'm going to the police, Kal. I shall tell them the truth. At first I was going to go with Brie, but then decided to wait for you. I don't want to live with this hanging over my head. I can't let everyone think Callie was responsible for the Seagreaves' death. My God, Kal, I killed a woman and a baby! Callie might die, too. I can't live with that on my conscience."

"Callie told me she was going to drive," Kallum said thoughtfully. "If I'm not mistaken, Mona and Jed were sitting on the back steps. I imagine they heard us. Did the boy parking the cars see you drive away?"

"No, he had gone to fetch someone else's car. I had parked in the Judge's driveway, so I didn't have to do any maneuvering to get out. Besides, the hedges cut off the view from the driveway. We walked through the open garage. What are you trying to say, Kal?"

"Maybe you shouldn't be so hasty. This is going to sound cruel, Wyn, and I don't mean it that way, but if Callie doesn't make it, no one needs to know. You can make amends in other ways. This way, your life won't be ruined. You won't be in the courts for years."

Wyn stepped on his cigarette. "I can't believe you're saying this. What if someone else finds out? If I confess now as opposed to later, it might not go so hard on me. Jesus, don't forget eagle-eye Brie. She's going to be like a bloodhound. If she even *thinks* something isn't right, she'll go the whole nine yards."

"There's nothing for her to find out. She's going to read the police report, and she'll make some noise; then she's going to get on a plane and go back to her life in San Diego. I'm not saying she won't think about this a lot, but she does have a life and a job she obviously loves. Stop using the word *confess*. It makes me nervous."

Wyn fished for a second cigarette. "You might be right about Brie, but what about Bode? They'll be on the horn with him soon. He's going to come charging back here. Hell, you know Bode. The police are his friends. Everyone in town is Bode's friend."

"He's not God, Wyn. He's a damn fine attorney, but that's as far as it goes. It's my job to look ahead to any problems that might crop up."

"Are you telling me you're prepared to deal with Bode Jessup, one-on-one, if he comes back here? Attorney to attorney is what I mean. For Christ's sake, Kal, he can run rings around you—you said so yourself! The Judge loves him. You better think about that. Look, I see this blowing up in my face somewhere along the way. I screwed up. I want to make it right. The worst thing Bode can do to me is beat me senseless—and Kal, I deserve it."

"It all comes down to money, Wyn. The insurance will pay off for the mother and child. They'll pay off for the Caddie. They'll pay the hospital bills for Callie for a very long time. They'll give you and Seagreave loaner cars until you get new ones. They even pay for funerals. Your legal fees will be honored. It's all about money, Wyn."

"The hell it is. It's about honor—mine. I killed those people, not Callie, and now she might die because I was like every other drunk who thinks he's in control. If you're not going to drive me, I'll walk."

"What if Callie dies, Wyn? You said that was a possibility."

"I'll deal with it."

"How will you deal with Bode if Callie dies? He'll be your worst nightmare come to life. Bode will accept things as they are, but not if you change your story and Callie dies. Decide now, Wyn."

"There's Pearl to consider, too."

"What about Pearl? What can she do? She's an ignorant black woman who can barely read and write. Think about this, Wyn. You can call in every specialist in the world. You can make things easier for Pearl. You can give Callie the finest care there is."

"It won't change what I did, who I am," Wyn said, his shoulders shaking with torment.

"That's true, but you can go on to make a better life for yourself. You can educate others about drinking. You're real good about crusades. Make this your personal crusade and you'll be South Carolina's next governor. Instead of ruining four lives, you'll have saved one. Yourself. If Callie recovers, it will be because of all you've done. Bode can't find fault with that."

"Governor?" Wyn said weakly.

"Down the road. I see the U.S. Senate first. We talked about this before, Wyn."

Wyn's shoulders straightened imperceptibly. "And you'll be my lieutenant governor?"

"That was our plan."

"And if I go to the Senate?" He was dreaming. He wasn't having this conversation.

"Your most trusted aide. I'll be working behind the scenes to pave the way for the time you agree to run this state. Don't go weak on me now."

"Then you'll have a hold over me for the rest of my life."

"That's stupid talk, Wyn. We've been friends since we were six years old. If that's how you think of me, I'll drive away from here right now. Look at me," Kallum said, as he placed both hands on Wyn's shoulders, "and listen to me carefully. It is not in your own best interests to change your story at this point in time. From now on, refer all inquiries to me. That goes for the police, the insurance company, the Judge, Bode—anyone who even mentions this accident. Now, do we have a deal?"

Kallum wasn't his friend. Jesus, how could he have been so damn blind? He wished he was man enough to stand up to him, to follow through with his decision to go to the police. He would do exactly what Kallum said because he didn't have any guts. He wished he could die, right then, that very second.

"All right," Wyn said wearily.

"I thought you'd see it my way," Kallum said coolly. "I think you should go back inside and comfort the ladies. I'll wait out here for Brie to come back."

It was an order, Wyn thought in stunned surprise. It used to be the other way around. Actually, he never gave Kallum orders; he simply suggested certain things. He stared at the man he'd called friend for so many years.

Kallum was tall, lean, and fit. He had pale blue eyes enhanced by contact lenses. Callie called them summer blue eyes. His short, wheat-colored hair was just long enough to be brushed back carelessly. However, Wyn knew he blow-dried it daily and then spritzed it with something called Freeze & Shine. When the goop dried he ran his fingers through it and *voila`!*—the ultimate in casualness. He'd never seen him in anything but white shirts, open at the neck or buttoned with a tie. His clothes came from Armani, Ralph Lauren, or Brooks Brothers. He boasted of owning nine pairs of Brooks Brothers shoes. Once, Callie had naughtily suggested they should break into Kallum's town house and steal all the tassels. Callie had said a lot of things about Kallum. Now he was going to have to try and remember them. Suddenly, Wyn didn't like Kallum.

His life was changing in front of his eyes, and he didn't have the guts to stand up for himself.

He wasn't fit to kiss Bode Jessup's feet.

An hour later Wyn knew he was in the way. Neither Pearl nor Sela wanted him in the small waiting room. Well, he wasn't going to leave. He had as much right to be here as both of them. More, since today was to have been his wedding day.

"How long are you planning on staying here?" Wyn asked.

"Until my baby wakes up," Pearl said.

"Until they boot me out," Sela said. "You better give some thought to notifying the guests that the wedding is off. How long are *you* going to stay?"

"As long as I have to. I'll call the Judge at six o'clock. Miss Nela can phone round all the guests and tell them. It will give her something to do. What does Brie hope to . . . to learn at the police station?"

Sela shrugged. "You know what a methodical mind she has. I guess she wants a copy of the report so when we call Bode and he starts asking questions, we have the answers."

"Do you think he'll come back?"

Sela smiled disdainfully at Wyn. "If you were Bode, would you come back? Ah, I see by the look on your face you would. Then I guess you have your answer."

"The doctor told me he'll talk to me at noon today. When the shift changes I'm going to speak with the charge nurse and then I'm going home to change." He addressed his next comment to Pearl. "Do you mind if I bring some clothes to the manor house and leave them there? That way I won't have to go all the way to Beaufort to shower and change."

Pearl looked at him for a long time before she answered. "The house belongs to you, Mr. Wyn. I'm the one who needs to ask you if you mind if I go back and forth to change."

"Oh no, that's— Well, maybe it is, but it doesn't mean anything. I'll have Kallum deed it back today. Tomorrow, today is Sunday. It's your home, Pearl. Then it's all right with you if I shower and change? I can use Callie's room."

"It's your house, Mr. Wyn. You can't be giving it back. Miz Callie wanted you to have it. It's not right to give it back. Miz Callie don't know what's going on," Pearl said flatly.

"Guess you have your answer, Wyn," Sela said, staring ahead of her. "Brie and I will be availing ourselves of your hospitality until it's time for us to leave."

The hours dragged by.

Brie returned at four-thirty in the morning to plop down next to Pearl. She handed over the string bag.

Wyn stirred himself long enough to ask, "What did you find out?"

Brie snorted. "You were there. What do you think I learned?"

"I don't know, that's why I asked."

"I learned that Mrs. Seagreave was seven months pregnant. The baby died. Mr. Seagreave asked the investigating officer for Bode Jessup's address. Guess he wanted to engage him. He started to suffer chest pains and had to be admitted to this very hospital. Mrs. Seagreave's parents live in Lancaster, Pennsylvania, and are on their way. It's a tragic, nasty business. I have the insurance agent's name and phone number. I'm going to call him first thing in the morning. The investigating officer had the feeling the agent thought there was something odd about the accident. Do you know what that might be?"

Wyn felt light-headed. He was reliving the accident, second by second. He shook his head. He didn't trust himself to speak.

"Do you mean some kind of funny business?" Sela said harshly. Pearl's head jerked upright, her licorice eyes full of silent accusation.

Wyn wanted to confess to all wrongdoing right then and there. He wanted to drop to his knees and tell these three cold-eyed women how sorry he was. His eyes started to fill. He wiped at them angrily and did his best to stare them down. In the end all he could do was jam his hands in his pockets, and pace about the room.

"I'm going to see if I can find out anything about Mr. Seagreave," Brie said.

"Why? What's wrong with you, Brie? Why do you have to keep doing things like this? I, for one, would rather not have known, right now, about Mrs. Seagreave's pregnancy. Don't we have enough to deal with as it is? When the sun is out, things aren't . . . they don't seem so terrible. What I mean is, I'm not trying to make light of this. It's just that . . . Oh, go on. Do what you have to do," Sela said wearily.

"I intend to," Brie said, walking away.

Wyn watched her go. *And the body count can go to four if Mr. Seagreave dies. Kallum, you son of a bitch! I should have gone to the police.*

"What does that mean, Miz Sela?" Pearl asked anxiously.

"What that means," Sela said gently, "is, if Mr. Seagreave dies from his heart attack, Callie is responsible for four deaths."

Pearl lumbered to her feet. She hobbled over to where Wyn was staring out at the dark night. "You need to be telling Pearl how this happened that my chile is responsible for all these deaths. Miz Callie is a good driver. She's careful and she don't drive fast. Bode said she was good, so you need to tell me all about how this happened." Her hands on the string bag quivered.

"She misjudged the depth of the curve. Mrs. Seagreave ran a stop sign—at least I think she did. Callie didn't like driving the Cadillac. It was too big a car for her to handle. That's all I know." *You lying sack of shit. Pearl's God is going to fry your ass in hell. Get it together, Archer, Pearl's just an old woman who sees problems where there are none.*

"My chile didn't do that—what you just said. Miz Brie don't believe it neither."

"Do you think I'm lying, Pearl?" Thank God his voice sounded properly outraged. She had her panties in a wad because the manor house was turned over to him. That's what this was all about. Jesus, he'd just offered to deed it back. Did she want his blood? He had to look her in the eye now because she was going to say something to him. For one brief second he thought he was going to drown in the dark licorice pools.

Wyn backed up a step when, without taking her eyes off him, Pearl waved her arms up and down, ever so gracefully, up and down the length of him. Jesus Christ, she was probably putting an impotency curse on him. She stared at him a few seconds more before she returned to the leather bench. '

'What did you do?" Sela hissed to Pearl. "Besides scare the hell out of him?"

"I gave him pain and sorrow."

"You didn't!"

"Yes'm, I purely did. The same pain and sorrow my baby is feeling."

"He doesn't look like he's in pain. I'll give you the sorrow part, but personally, I'd like to see him double over or something similar," Sela whispered. "I think Callie told him the wedding was off, and they were arguing and she . . . lost control or something like that. Of course he isn't going to admit to that."

"That's not what happened," Pearl said quietly.

"Do you *know* what happened?"

"Not yet. I'll have to wait for Lazarus to tell me."

"Pearl, don't start that spirit thing again."

"If you don't want to hear, then why do you ask me?"

"Pearl, it was an accident. I know how much you love Callie, and it's hard for you to accept what happened. None of us are perfect. Things happen. Accidents . . ." Her voice trailed off lamely.

Pearl folded her hands and closed her eyes.

Brie stood in the open doorway. *We're like a family,* she thought, *waiting to hear about a beloved family member.* She wanted to cry. But cops didn't cry, at least in public. She wished Bode was here. Bode would . . . what would Bode do? He'd be sitting here just the way Pearl and Sela were sitting. Maybe he'd be standing at the window staring out at the night like Wyn was doing. Or, maybe he'd be standing here in the doorway dreading telling them what she was about to confide.

"Steven Seagreave is down as DOA; that means dead on arrival. It was a coronary. He was only thirty-seven years old. It doesn't seem right to die so young. But his family is gone. Maybe God wanted him to die. There's a reason for everything. You always say that, Pearl."

Pearl's eyes remained closed. Sela picked at the bloodred

polish on her nails. Wyn's back stiffened, but he didn't turn from the window. Brie sat down. Tears dripped down her cheeks.

"What are we going to do?" Sela asked.

"I don't know. Call Bode when we go back to the house?"

"I've been thinking about that, Brie. Maybe we shouldn't call him—I mean, not yet. I truly do not think Bode could handle this. The wedding proved too much for him. Maybe we should wait, keep Pearl company."

"God, I'm tired. I think you're right. We can decide later on if it looks like Pearl . . . we'll talk to her. It has to be her decision. You know how she feels about people trampling over what she calls her private business. I'll tell you one thing, though. I want to be here when Wyn talks to the doctor. He said noon. Let's go home and shower and have some coffee."

Pearl refused to go with them.

Wyn nodded curtly when Brie told him they were leaving. "I'll be going shortly myself. Is it okay to leave Pearl alone?"

"I think she wants to be alone right now. We won't be long."

"Take as long as you need. I'm going to stop by the Judge's house. I should be back here myself by ten."

They didn't say good-bye.

Pearl's worn, callused hands plucked at the threadbare string bag in her lap. It was an old bag, belonging first to her great-grandmother, then her grandmother and then her mother. It was the only thing her mother had to hand down to Pearl, and she treasured it as much as she treasured her love for Bode and Callie and the girls. The bag had been mended by her ancestors, oftentimes with strands of vines that grew in the live oaks; bits of hemp and string, all with minuscule knots holding the contents secure.

Pearl looked around the quiet waiting room as her fingers sought those tiny knots. She counted quietly, seeming to gather a measure of comfort from the little lumps. The string bag was lined with a square of flowered material from a flour sack, its pattern faded and worn. Each generation sewed a new lining. She'd meant to replace the lining, even had the square of material from one of Callie's old dresses, but she'd never done it.

Pearl turned now, her huge body shielding the bag and its contents from the two people sitting in the far corner of the waiting room. Her eyes were closed, her fingers busy now with the two small leather pencil cases that had once belonged to Bode and Callie. Who would she leave this string bag to when she passed on? She had no blood children. To leave it to Bode would cause Callie to cry. To leave it to Callie would bring sadness to Bode's eyes. She wanted to cry, needed to cry, but she couldn't do it here in this quiet room with the shiny floors that smelled like a medicine bottle.

She didn't like this place. Lazarus hadn't liked it either. He'd made her promise not to bring him here if he got sick. She should have let Lazarus give her a baby. *Don't think about Lazarus and death,* she told herself. *Think about Miz Callie lying so still upstairs in that terrible room with all the machines.*

The snap on one of the leather cases opened without a sound. It was softer than butter, almost twenty years old. Callie didn't even know she'd saved it. Bode didn't know she had his either. Bode's case was the one with the secret papers. Callie's father had given them to her on a bright sunny day, long before he died. He'd said, "You keep these, Pearl, until I ask for them." It was understood that it was not to be spoken about, and she'd honored that promise. Whoever it was that would get her string bag would also get the papers. They would read them, but she'd never know what they said because she'd be dead.

The papers weren't important now. It was the buttons, all forty of them, all but one with four holes, that were going to make her baby sit up and smile.

It had taken her years to save up forty buttons. Some were from Bode's shirts, some from Callie's dresses, two from Lazarus's shirts that she washed once a week. There was one from Callie's mama's prettiest dress and one from her father's dress jacket. She'd snipped it off his dead body before they closed the coffin for the last time. It was probably, she thought, the most powerful button in the pencil case because it only had three holes in it. A three-holed button was magic in itself. Her fingers played with the buttons until she located the black one with three holes. She'd never used it before, never used any of the buttons because there was no need. With Lazarus, there had been no time. One minute her man was talking to her and the next minute he was lying on the ground, dead as the last leaf in winter.

The buttons were in her hand, light as a feather. She squeezed her eyes shut as she muttered and murmured under her breath. When she opened her eyes she dropped the buttons into her lap, her eyes going to the three-holed button and where it rested next to the others. Again and again she dropped the buttons in her lap, the three-holed button staring up at her like a monster eye. Tears rolled down her cheeks. Her baby wasn't going to sit up and smile at her. Not now, not ever.

Pearl drifted off into a silent orgy of disbelief. Her foot tapped slowly on the shiny tile floor. It was her way of calling on the good spirits to come to her aid.

It occurred to Pearl as she entered into a half sleep, half trance, that there were no buttons that belonged to her in the pencil case. The reason being, she had never owned anything with buttons, with the exception of this new dress Bode gave her. It was an omen, she was sure of it.

The tears rolled on down her weathered cheeks.

Pearl grieved. It was the only thing left for her to do.

10

All three doctors look alike, Wyn thought. *How is that possible? Doctors, like other people, should be individuals.* Maybe it was the long white coats, the stethoscopes. Maybe it was the prematurely gray hair, or maybe their tired eyes that saw so much death. *Triplets,* he thought crazily. He tried to pick out the doctor he'd spoken to last night. His face had been a blur then; it was still a blur. All he could remember was the man's weary eyes and exhausted voice. He waited now, behind Sela, Brie, and Pearl, for one of the doctors to speak.

The orthopedic surgeon and the trauma specialist took a step backward. The neurosurgeon took a step forward and addressed himself to Wyn.

They all listened to the discouraging words. Callie wasn't going to get better; she was in a deep coma. They would, of course, do what they could to make her comfortable. In unison the triplets said, "I'm so very sorry."

"*Bullshit!*" Wyn raged. "I want every specialist, the best the world has to offer. I don't care what it costs. Get them, and if you can't get them for me, I'll do it myself. Now! I want the calls to go out *now!* I want physical therapy around

the clock. I want everything. Do you hear me? I want everything that can be done to be done, and I want it done starting
now." He deflated with his words and sat down.

Brie walked over to the small group of men and identified
herself. "Mr. Archer is right. We'd like a second and a third
opinion, as many opinions as we can get. It's not that we're
questioning your abilities. We want a consensus of opinion.
Callie is so young—too young, to have her life snatched like
this. We need to know that everything that can possibly be
done *is* being done. We need . . . a miracle," she said.

"We can only do our best," the trauma specialist said
softly.

"We've already called in the best in their field," the neurosurgeon explained, "on the off chance we may have missed
something. The team will arrive tomorrow. It is our considered opinion," he added as he agitatedly finger-combed his
hair, "that a miracle is almost certainly ruled out. We can't
offer you hope where there is none. That wouldn't be fair to
you or the patient. If you follow me, you can see Miss Parker,
one at a time, for five minutes each. Then I want you all to go
home and come back during visiting hours."

At the nurse's station outside the ICU ward, Wyn charged
ahead, but Brie's arm snaked out and jerked him backward.
"Ladies first, Wyn. Pearl goes in before us."

"Yes, yes, you're right. I'm sorry, I wasn't thinking. I'm
sorry, Pearl. God, what does she carry in that bag?"

"The mysteries of the universe," Sela said tiredly.

"I had the chance to look, but I didn't," Brie said. "If I had,
I wouldn't have been able to look Pearl in the eye. Is it important for you to know, Wyn?"

"I don't want her plastering Callie with any of that stuff.
Callie told me about her spells and all that other bullshit she
uses. It's goddamn voodoo if you want my opinion. She bet-

ter not be putting any of those dirty old charms around Callie's neck."

"And if she does, Wyn, what harm is there in it? The doctors aren't offering any kind of hope, and if it makes Pearl feel better to do whatever she feels she has to do, what right have any of us to tell her she can't? She's going through a terrible time just the way you are. Let it be, Wyn," Brie said tightly.

"I can't believe you go along with that nonsense. I know you girls were brought up on that foolishness, but it's hocus-pocus, pure and simple."

Two minutes later, Pearl came out of the room with tears drizzling down her cheeks. Both Sela and Brie rushed to put their arms around her. She sobbed then, the sounds ripping at both women's hearts.

"You can take my turn as well, Pearl," Brie offered.

"Mine too. You can have another ten whole minutes, Pearl," Sela said as she dabbed at Pearl's cheeks with a tissue.

"I can't be doing that," Pearl said, sobbing.

"We want you to. Tell Callie we're out here. We'll say a prayer for her. Tell her that, too," Brie said.

"If you're sure . . ."

"We're sure," Sela said. "When you come out, we're taking you home. We'll come back later. Is it a deal?" Pearl's head bobbed up and down.

His eyes misty with tears, Wyn shuffled from the intensive care unit out to the nurses' station, where he stared at Brie and Sela with blinded vision. He sensed Pearl move past him and knew she was taking Brie and Sela's turn. "That was nice of you, but it has to be torture for her. I'm not sure you did her a favor by giving up your turn."

"Pearl's a strong woman," Sela said.

"Did you call Bode?"

"We're going to wait for the second and third opinions," Brie said.

"I think that's a good idea. When you pay for the best you get the best. I'm not saying these fellows down here aren't good, but sometimes . . . most times there is someone better. You just have to find that particular someone. I'm really counting on a miracle."

He looks so damn vulnerable, Brie thought.

"And if these new doctors, these best of the best, if they can't give us the miracle, then what?"

"I can't allow myself to think along those lines. I need to believe something can be done. If I don't believe that, then I'm lost. I've read about people being in comas for months, sometimes years, and then they come out of them. Callie could be one of those people. She could wake up tomorrow. Those doctors we spoke with, they aren't God. They aren't even good stand-ins. Until someone positively tells me there is no hope at all, I will believe something can be done. I'll hunt this earth over, a dozen times, until I find someone to help her. This was supposed to be my wedding day."

Sela nudged Brie, ever so gently. She bit down on her tongue so she wouldn't blurt out the decision Callie had made and shared with Pearl in the Judge's garden. She felt Brie's breath explode in a loud sigh next to her. Obviously, Brie was expecting her to do just that.

"Please, you have to leave now," an orderly said as he inched a gurney around the threesome. The door to ICU was suddenly opened. The gurney swept through and minutes later was wheeled past them, the still form covered from head to toe. A cleric walked through the door, smiled tiredly at them before he headed for the elevator.

They bolted.

Brie and Sela turned away from the double doors to stare at the flowers sitting on the shelf above the nurses' station.

They looked badly in need of water, their petals dropping, the greenery brown at the edges. "I think," Brie whispered, "everything on this floor dies."

"Everything . . . and everybody, but not Callie," Sela said. "We should be doing something. Praying . . . crying. Talking about our memories. Standing around like this seems so wasteful, so useless."

"Do you think she's going to come out of it?" Brie whispered.

"No. Do you?"

"The doctors . . . miracles do happen."

"When was the last time you heard about a miracle?" Sela said, blowing her nose vigorously. "I just keep thinking about how nasty I was. I didn't have one kind word to say to her. I kept baiting her and . . . Oh, shit. I want to take it all back."

Brie patted her friend's shoulder. "Callie understood that you were only reacting to your own problems. Callie was— is—always good about understanding. She was so troubled about that business with Bode. I wish I knew what she was thinking and feeling before the accident."

"How long are you staying?" Sela asked.

"I was supposed to leave tonight, but I'm going to call and ask for a few more days. I can take time if I want to. The thing is, will I be a help or a hindrance? We need to get Pearl settled. What about you?"

"I was going to leave in the morning. I, too, can stay a few extra days. My real-estate class starts on Thursday. Maybe I can come here on weekends. I can make the drive in thirteen hours. I'm willing to do it if you think it's a good idea. Maybe when I finish the course I can relocate here. One place is as good as another for me at this point in time. Do you have any suggestions?"

"The airfare is outrageous from California to here. I can't come back and forth too much. Maybe once every six weeks or so. If I knew there was something I could do, something that would make things better for Callie, I'd do it."

"I'm not doing it just for Callie. If I come back here, it will be to help Pearl. I don't mean that the way it sounds. She doesn't look well to me, Brie. I've seen her clutch at her chest, and she gets breathless from time to time. Has she, to your knowledge, ever been to a real doctor?"

"I don't know. Callie never mentioned anything in her letters. We'll talk to her. If she isn't well, then I won't think twice about moving back here. We'll have to be devious though. Pearl will try and fool us. Shhh, here she comes."

"My baby is too still. I picked up her hand and squeezed it. I wanted her to feel me next to her bed. My sweet baby love didn't know I was there. She looks *daid*."

"She's not dead, Pearl, she's in a deep sleep and she can—she *will*—wake up when it's time. We're taking you home now. You need to eat something, and you definitely need sleep. We're both going to stay on at Parker Manor a while longer to help out."

"Bless your hearts for doing this for old Pearl. I do need you. Where will Mr. Wyn be staying?" she asked tremulously.

"Not with us, that's for sure," Brie snapped. "You two go out to the car, and I'll tell Wyn we're leaving."

"It's okay, Brie," Wyn said when she told him their plans. "I dropped a bag off at the Holiday Inn. I'll shower there. I plan on staying in Summerville. The Judge told me to stop by the house for meals. Don't worry about me bothering Pearl, or you and Sela. Somewhere, somehow, we all got off on the wrong foot, and it's probably all my fault. If you don't believe anything else, Brie, believe I love Callie with all my heart. There wasn't anything I wouldn't have done for her. If I don't make a lot of sense now and if I seem to do things that you find contrary, chalk it up to this utter hopelessness I feel."

Brie nodded. She believed everything he said. She acknowledged the misery and hopelessness she saw in his eyes. But there was something missing, and she didn't know what it was. As Pearl said, everything in its own good time. Sooner or later she'd figure it out.

The midafternoon sun was gone when the three women exited the hospital, the blanket-wet humidity like a shroud. Sela raised her eyes. "Drive like hell, Brie, or we're going to get caught in some heavy rain. You remember what the August rains are like—you can't see your hand in front of your face." She settled Pearl in the backseat. When she had made herself comfortable in the front seat of the car with a cigarette between her lips, she said, "It feels ominous, doesn't it?"

Brie craned her neck to see the dark gray clouds scudding overhead. It was going to rain. She wished for sun and dry air. *San Diego,* she thought, *has perfect weather.* "I think we might make it. If not, don't worry. I've taken defensive driving."

"It's not you I'm worried about, it's the other nutcases on the road," Sela groused. "I hate rainstorms. Once when I was first married . . . Oh never mind. That's a whole other story."

"Great. I'm not in the mood for stories. It helps if things are quiet."

Forty minutes later, Brie pulled the rental car alongside the steps on the back porch. Fat raindrops splattered on the windshield as Pearl lumbered up the steps. Sela ran on ahead, her shoulder purse flopping against her leg, while Brie stayed behind to roll up all the windows. She didn't care about the warm rain, didn't mind getting wet. She sat down on the top step, her legs stretched out in front of her. The rain, at first, was like a gentle waterfall, covering her completely, cleansing her. "Please, God, make this all come out right for Pearl," she prayed, "and for all of us."

The screen door opened. "I always said you were nuts. Anyone who sits in the rain and ruins her dress must be crazy. Brie, what the hell are you doing?" It was Sela.

"Actually, I was praying before you interrupted me. You sound like one of those screech owls. The rain feels soothing, sort of like a balm if you know what I mean. Why don't you join me? We need to talk, Sela. Where's Pearl?"

"Taking off her dress. I told her to have a nap, but I don't know if she will." She sat down next to Brie, and extended her legs like Brie's. "This dress cost four hundred dollars, the shoes two hundred and fifty."

"Bet you wish you had that money in your hand, huh?"

"Damn right. I always loved this place. If I was as rich as sin and I owned it, I'd turn it into a showplace."

"For who to see?"

"Me. Just little me . . . Oh, Brie—the only person who ever really loved me was Pearl. That's a hell of a thing to admit, isn't it?"

"Yeah, but I'm in the same situation. I know where you're coming from. What are we going to do about Bode?"

"You girls are plumb out of your minds," Pearl said, settling herself on a wicker chair behind them. "I hear you mention my boy's name."

"We were wondering if we should try and get in touch with him. What do you think, Pearl? It has to be your decision."

For the first time ever, the girls saw Pearl flustered. "I jest don't know, Miz Brie. Parts of me want him to know and parts of me don't want him to know. His heart's been broke so many times already. He *cain't* do nothing for Miz Callie but sit by her bed. I can do that for both of us. If we disturb his life, he's going to be that far behind when it's time for him to become a judge."

"Bode's going to be a judge! How do you know that,

Pearl?" Brie said as she wiped at the rain pelting her in the face.

"I seen it in the . . . I jest seen it," Pearl said, her voice stubborn-sounding. Brie and Sela looked at one another.

"Okay. That means we don't call him, right?" Sela said.

"I don't have a telephone number," Pearl said. "If he wanted me to have his telephone number, he'd have given it to me. That means he don't want no calls."

"This is different, Pearl," Brie said gently. "Will he forgive us when he finds out? He might see or meet someone from here, someone who still has ties. It will be a hard thing to forgive, Pearl."

"I know that," Pearl said. "It's not the time to be calling my boy. Give me your word."

They gave it in unison.

"We need to make arrangements for you, Pearl. You're going to want to spend as much time at the hospital as you can. This is what I propose. If you go along with it, we'll take care of it first thing tomorrow. We'll get you an apartment close to the hospital. This way you can walk instead of taking a cab or depending on someone to drive you."

"Miz Brie, I don't have money for that. My people will see that I git there. Don't be fretting now."

"I'm not fretting, Pearl. This is best. I'll stop and see the Judge; he'll take care of things. Callie had a small bank account. He can speak to the bank and get their permission to use it. I have some money I can add to the account and when Sela becomes solvent she'll contribute. This . . . it could be a very long time, Pearl. This will make it easier. We can't do anything for Callie right now so we have to do what we can for you. I'm going to call later and ask for an extra week. Sela can stay till Wednesday night. We agreed to come back and forth to do whatever we can. Now, is this okay with you?"

"I *cain't* be spending my baby's money on myself. It ain't right, Miz Brie," Pearl sniffed.

"You aren't doing it—*we* are. Callie would want it this way."

"Will Mr. Wyn let me stay at the hospital to take care of my baby?" Pearl asked, her voice shaky.

"Wyn wasn't married to Callie—*you* are her next of kin. The Judge can make that legal. Wyn isn't her guardian. You come first, Pearl. We all know Callie was going to cancel the wedding. We'll tell that to the Judge, and he'll do what's best for both you and Callie. He's a fair, honest man. You have to trust him, Pearl."

"What about this house, the property?" Sela said.

"Belongs to Mr. Wyn now," Pearl said.

"We'll see about that," Brie said. "When Callie deeded it to him, she believed in her heart she was going to marry Wyn. I'm sure she would have asked for it back. Heck, she probably wouldn't have had to ask! Wyn is an honorable man, he'd have given it back. He already offered. The Judge will take care of it. I think that's the least of our worries. Are you okay with all this, Pearl?"

Pearl nodded. "My people from church will look after the grounds and the good rooms in the house. Will it be all right if I come back here once in a while?"

"Of course. You're in charge, Pearl. Sela and I are both going to give you our telephone numbers and you call us collect anytime you want. Sela said she might move back here after she completes her real-estate course. What I'm trying to say, Pearl, is that you can count on us."

"The Lord will bless you both," Pearl cried. "You look like drowned cats, each one of you." She wiped her eyes on the sleeve of her cotton dress.

"In that case"—Sela grinned as she ripped off her shoes and panty hose—"I see a delicious puddle that's just crying out for our feet to stomp in it."

"Is it a *mud* puddle?" Brie squealed. She had her shoes off and was down the steps in the time it took Pearl to heave herself up and out of the rocker.

They were lunatics, stomping and splashing and throwing mud in every direction.

"You girls stop that now, you hear me?" Pearl shouted.

"We hear you, Pearl," Sela panted as she pushed Brie hard so she landed in the mud, facedown.

"My oh my, those fine dresses is going to be nothing but rags. Pearl is going to take a switch to your bottoms if you don't come up on this porch right now."

"Do you think she means it?" Sela hissed.

"Hey, we're all grown-up now. Yeah, she means it." Brie giggled.

"I wish Bode and Callie were here. Bode made the best mud pies; his always stuck together. Callie always decorated hers. Mine never had any substance—kind of like my life," Sela said as she sprawled in the mud. "Yours were always thick and hard like a rock. I think that means something."

"This isn't about mud pies, is it?" Brie asked, shaping a mass of mud into a round circle.

"No. If we were men, they'd probably say this is where you separate the men from the boys or something like that, but since we're women, I have no idea what this all means. Maybe that we're finally coming of age?"

"I think the word is mature. Tragedy does that to people. Did you say my pies were always rock-hard?" Sela nodded. "Then how do you account for this?" Brie said, slapping Sela in the face with the messy mud pie.

"You girls best be gitting your fannies up on this porch right now or I'm coming to git you," Pearl bawled.

"In a minute, Pearl," Sela gasped, as she pushed Brie backward again and then sat on her chest, her victim's arms flailing in every direction. "Some cop. You didn't even see it coming."

"Up yours, Sela. I let you take me because I slammed that pie in your face. We're even now. What do you think she'll do to us?"

"She still keeps that willow switch by the back door. God, did that sting! I want to be a kid again. We were, for just a little while."

"I want yesterday," Brie said as she struggled to get to her feet.

"Me too, but it's gone. Maybe tomorrow will be better than yesterday and today. Uh-oh—here she comes and she has that damn switch!" Sela shivered.

"Git in that bathroom, the both of you. It's going to take me hours, pure hours, to scrub you clean. You hear me, git along!" Pearl said as she whacked the switch first on Sela's behind and then on Brie's mud-soaked rear.

"Yes, ma'am," both women said happily as they raced for the bathroom.

Pearl was as good as her word. She showered them off, lathered them up, one by one, rinsed, scrubbed, rinsed again and again until their skin was red and puckered. "Now, you git yourselves dressed while I make us some supper."

"Yes, ma'am," they both chorused again.

"She had a good time," Sela said when Pearl had bustled off. "For a few minutes she forgot about—"

"Yeah, but my skin is never going to be the same," Brie grumbled. "Couldn't you have thought of something a little less painful?"

"I was never the brains of this outfit, and anyway, I didn't have a whole lot of time to come up with something."

Brie laughed as she pulled a thin cotton nightshirt over her head. "The last time I was this clean was when we did exactly the same thing and we were nine years old. We got two lickings that day, one for playing in the mud and the other when we tried to peek in the bathroom while she was cleaning up Bode. Oh, how I wish Callie and Bode were here," Brie wailed.

"The tough California cop has real feelings," Sela teased gently, putting her arms around her friend. "Go ahead and cry."

"I can't; that's the problem."

"When it's time for you to cry, you will. Now, put something on your feet, or Pearl will take a fit."

Brie pulled on a pair of Callie's old socks. Sela did the same.

Scrubbed and shiny as new pennies, they looked at one another, then burst into hysterical laughter.

"I have an idea. After dinner let's play secrets. A real, sharing, three-way secret. Pearl likes to play secrets."

"Jeez, we haven't played that since a long, long time ago. Bode always had the best secrets. Sometimes I think he made them up just to get over on us. Callie's were pretty good, too. Ours were boring." Brie giggled.

"Do you miss your parents, Brie?"

"In a manner of speaking. My father is working for some oil company in Saudi Arabia. He never calls or writes, even at Christmas. What kind of father is that? It was hard when Mama died. How about you?"

"As you know, my mother drank herself to death. When she died, all I felt was this overwhelming relief. I know that sounds terrible. She wanted to belong, to be somebody. Well, she was, she was a drunk. I have no idea where my father is. I suppose one of these days he'll show up. But, to answer your question, no, I do not miss them. I always thought of this as home—my *real* home. That nasty little apartment we lived in was someplace to stay until I could come here. I wasn't loved or wanted. You weren't either. And you know what?

Nobody loved Callie and Bode either. Just Pearl. She loved us all. It's amazing how much love she had to give four kids."

"Supper's ready," Pearl called from the kitchen.

The meal was plain and substantial: fried pink ham, grits with pools of melted butter, fresh peas, and sliced tomatoes, along with warmed-over biscuits. For dessert there was peach pie, followed by sweet black coffee.

"This is delicious." Brie sighed, stuffing her mouth.

"I haven't eaten this well since I was here the last time," Sela said, buttering her third roll. "And, to show my appreciation, I'm doing the dishes."

"Hear, hear," Brie said, reaching across the table for a fourth slice of ham. She waved her fork in the air as she tried to make a point. "You need to eat, too, Pearl. You're going to need all the energy you can conjure up in order for you to trek back and forth the way I know you are. You have to eat, three times a day. Promise us."

"Yes'm," Pearl said solemnly. They all knew she wouldn't keep her promise.

"If I was wearing a belt, I'd have to loosen it," Sela said.

"Me too," Brie said, fingering the cotton nightshirt.

"Don't make me no never mind," Pearl said. "I don't own a belt. They squeeze the life out of a body. You best be starting on the dishes, Miz Sela, 'cause I know you girls want to play that silly game you're so fond of, and we *cain't* play until the dishes are done. While you're doing that I'll be resting my eyes and thinking about which one of my secrets I'll be telling."

"I hope it's a good one," Brie said, pushing back her chair.

The moment Brie hung up the dish towel and Sela rinsed the sink, Pearl said, "It's stopped raining. That's a good sign for telling secrets. We *cain't* be sweeping the floor now, it's after sundown. We don't want to look for bad luck."

"Of course not," Brie said, putting the broom back in the closet.

The girls settled themselves at the table while Pearl rummaged in the pantry for a fat pink candle that she placed in the center of the table.

"Who goes first?" Brie asked.

"Me, since it was my idea. Let's make sure we have the rules down pat here. I have to guess your secret or the category it belongs to, right?" Brie nodded. "Then you guess Pearl's, and she guesses mine. If we don't get it on the first round we each have to give out a second clue. If no one guesses on three, then we have to tell the secret."

"Why don't we just tell the damn secret and be done with it, instead of dragging it out? Pearl looks tired, and I know I am. We also have to call the hospital to check on Callie. We could even go back later."

"Okay," Sela said agreeably. Brie looked at her suspiciously. So did Pearl. Sela shrugged. "My secret is, I won three thousand dollars on a horse bet."

"No kidding! What are you going to do with it?" Brie demanded.

"Give half to Pearl. Pretend I don't have the other half; maybe I'll put it in an IRA. Your turn. Tell us already," Sela demanded.

"I got a special commendation for . . . you know."

"Brie, that's wonderful," Sela said sincerely. "And now the FBI! That's the big time. I'm proud of you, Brie."

"Chile, are you sure you want to be doing that? I see what those agents do on the television. You could get yourself killed. Guns that go bang, bang with no stopping. They look like they're too heavy to hold."

"I think I can handle it, Pearl." Brie grinned. "My biggest worry is, will the men accept me?"

"And why not? You are one smart girl, Brie. Will you get

to wear one of those black jackets with the big initials on the back?"

"I guess so. Thanks, Sela, for what you just said." Brie looked stunned by her friend's compliment.

"That was a good secret, better than mine. Pearl, it's your turn." Sela smiled.

Both girls cupped their hands under their chins waiting for Pearl's secret, their eyes wide with anticipation.

Pearl rolled her eyes from side to side before one big hand reached up to pat the coronet of braids on top of her head. "I," she said, "have a three-hole button. A black one."

"You're funning with us," Brie and Sela said in unison, using one of Pearl's favorite expressions.

"I'm truly not." She folded her hands in front of her as if to say, "Top this!"

"Can we see it?" Brie asked, excitement ringing in her voice.

"Is it flat or does it have a ridge?" Sela inquired breathlessly.

When they were children, Pearl had regaled them with her old beliefs, and the three-holed black button was the one that generated the most interest. The "three-holer," as Bode called it, was a cure for just about everything in the world. It could cure snakebite, bring happiness, bring love, cause death, make the birds fly—anything a person wanted. Provided, when tossed with thirty-nine other buttons, it fell between four white ones. Out of Pearl's hearing, Bode said you had to keep throwing the buttons until you got them to come out the way you wanted them. Once, he said, Pearl tossed the buttons for two whole days before they came out the way she wanted them to, but the truth was, according to Bode, you had to cheat to get the three-holer next to four white buttons. It didn't work if the white buttons only had two holes.

"Ridge on one side, flat on other." Pearl beamed.

"Does anyone but us know?"

"Bode and Callie knows I gave my mama's button to Hester over at the church when I came on my own. My mama's button wouldn't work for anyone but her. *Onliest* person my button works for is me and Miz Callie 'cause I snipped the button from her papa's suit when he laid *daid* in his box."

Neither girl truly believed in Pearl's rituals, but humored her because it meant so much to her. Now, in spite of herself, Brie asked, "Did you . . . you know, toss the buttons at the hospital? Will Callie be okay?"

"I sprinkled them in my lap four times. They didn't come out right. It's a worry on my shoulder," Pearl confessed.

"But you said it had to be done at noon when the Angelus rang," Sela remembered. "You said it had to be done three times and the Angelus had to be ringing."

"Bless you chile, I *did* say that! Now how could old Pearl be forgetting something so important? I *cain't* say it don't make no never mind 'cause it does. Tomorrow I'll do it again."

"You win, Pearl. Yours is the best secret."

"I know," Pearl said smugly. "Ain't nobody at the church knows 'cepting Hester, who has a three-holed button and I give it to her, so her good luck will come my way, too."

Brie nodded sagely. "I'm going to call the hospital and see how Callie is doing."

Moments later, Brie said, "She's the same. Wyn is still there, and he goes to see her on the hour for five minutes."

Pearl's eyes puddled up. "I should be there with my baby. No one is sitting by her, no one is holding her hand. It isn't right."

"Tomorrow is another day, Pearl," Sela said gently. "Other specialists are coming; everything is being done. Wyn is seeing to that, thank God."

"Would he be doing all this if he knew my baby wasn't going to marry him?"

Sela shrugged.

"We don't know the answer to that, Pearl," Brie said.

"I don't claim to know about money and fy-nances. What's going to happen to my chile when the in-surance won't pay any more? What will the hospital do?"

"Well, Pearl, I don't think we should worry about that for now. Let's hope and pray Callie comes out of her coma before that happens. There are programs that help people. Funds . . ." Sela's voice trailed off lamely. "Medicaid."

"We'll help all we can," Brie said. "Don't worry about that, Pearl, it's a long way off. In the meantime we can check everything out before we leave."

"Bless you girls. What would I be doing without you?" Pearl cried.

As one they smothered her with kisses and hugs and dried her watery eyes with the hems of their nightshirts.

Pearl allowed herself to be led to her room, permitted herself to be tucked in, smiled when she was kissed and told to dream sweet dreams.

"Don't you dare get out of this bed until I ring the breakfast bell," Brie said sternly.

"Yes'm," Pearl said, her eyes closing wearily.

"Let's go out by the barn and have a cigarette," Sela said quietly. "We really need to talk."

The night was like warm, soft velvet, with only a crescent moon to light the way. Everything was clean-smelling after the heavy rain. The tall pines gave off a pungent scent that was both heady and tranquil. The monster oaks, the branches heavy and wet from the rain, bowed with the weight of the Spanish moss hanging like huge silvery garlands in the ebony night.

"This is one of the things I miss most about living up

North. I love these old trees and the Spanish moss, don't you?" Sela said as she tweaked her fingers at a clump that was trailing almost to the ground.

"You've been away too long, Sela," Brie said, pulling her back from the moss. "Pearl said that stuff is full of birdlice."

"Yuck," Sela sputtered as she scampered away from the tree.

"What is it you want to talk about?" Brie asked, sitting down on an upended milk box.

"Stuff. Things. I want to know what you think about the accident and why you felt you had to go to the police station."

"It's the cop in me. You never turn it off. Callie's driven that road thousands of times. When you live someplace and there are danger spots, you learn to live with them and respect them. Callie knew all about that curve: we used to creep around it. It's like the people who live on Carroll Court—they know they have to cross it, dead center. They respect it. Nor is the curve all that far from the Judge's house. I just don't see Callie laying it all on Wyn the moment she got in the car. In my mind that rules out them arguing. Wyn said, according to the police report, that he was dozing because he'd had too much to drink. That means Callie was paying attention. Even if her mind wandered, say to Bode and how he'd split, she'd still be paying attention to the road. Mrs. Seagreave, according to Wyn, ran the stop sign. How did he know that if he was dozing? Does a woman who has lived in the same area since she was born run a stop sign with a baby in the front seat? There's no one to speak up for Mrs. Seagreave. Callie can't tell us what happened. So, all we have is Wyn's version, and I'm not saying it didn't happen the way he said it did. I'm saying, to me, it doesn't compute."

"Are you going to kick up a fuss?" Sela asked.

"Guess not."

"But you aren't going to leave it alone either, are you?"

"Nope. Callie was . . . is . . . so conscientious. She never speeds, at least to my knowledge. What I'm trying to say is, she's one of those people who lives by the book. At least, that's how I perceive her."

"Which means what?"

"I want to understand. I *need* to understand."

"Just tell me what it is you want me to do, and I'll do it," Sela said. She flicked her cigarette in the air and watched a shower of sparks cascade downward. Brie walked over and crushed it out. She picked up the butt and dropped it in the milk box.

"Do you remember," Sela said softly, "how when we used to sleep over, Pearl would let us play out here till nine-thirty or so? We played hide-and-seek or red light, green light. Bode always caught us. We'd dig for worms with that old lantern for light, catch the fireflies, hide in the barn, and romp in the straw. Everything smelled so wonderful back then, kind of the way it smells tonight. It's funny, isn't it, Brie, that we're standing here and the two people who really belong here aren't with us. I wonder if that means something?"

"It means we're having a nostalgia attack of the 'do you remembers,' " Brie said quietly.

"We sort of belong. God, I want so bad to belong. Pearl makes it seem like we do. Is that wrong of me?"

"No, of course not. I feel the same way. This is the place we come back to. Everyone needs a place, Sela. Those crummy apartments we lived in were just walls and floors. This was like home. It still feels that way."

"If Wyn deeds this place back to Callie and something happens to Callie, will this place go to the state?" Sela asked.

"I think so, unless Callie made a will. She never mentioned making one. Did she ever say anything to you?"

"No. God, we have to do something!" Sela said, wringing her hands. "Brie, do you ever . . . I know this is going to sound, well, not right . . . but do you ever think of this place as *ours?* I don't mean owning it, just belonging to it. I think it would kill me if Callie lost it. I'm trying to say something here and it isn't coming out right."

"You really are hooked on this place, aren't you?" Brie said.

"Do you think that's wrong of me?"

"I don't know, Sela, but I think you have to let go to a certain extent. Didn't we just have this conversation a little while ago? Why are we going over it again?"

"Because I'm afraid it's going to be lost to us."

"We'll survive." Brie was brisk.

"Pearl won't," Sela said, snapping a blossom off the crepe myrtle. She snapped a second and third. "I feel like crying, Brie."

"Then cry. It helps relieve a lot of tension. I'd cry myself, but I'm too damn mad to do so. This is one of those senseless things that never should have happened. I don't know how to deal with it. For me, crying won't help. All I want to do is hit the sack. I really need some quiet time to come to terms with the possibility that Callie may never regain consciousness and that I may never see Bode again. Both of them, like you, are a part of my life. I have to face up to it. You can have the room, and I'll sleep on the sofa, okay?"

"Sure," Sela said.

They walked back to the house in silence. In the kitchen, Brie watched Sela fill a bowl with water, then add an aspirin to it from her purse, before dropping the delicate blossoms, one by one, into the water.

"Guess I'll say good night," Brie said.

"Okay. I think I'm going to sit here for a little while and think about my past sins."

"You do that. *I* don't have any sins to contemplate," Brie said spitefully.

"Me-*ow,*" Sela rejoined, pouting.

Brie stopped in the bathroom to wash her hands as well as her feet before she settled herself on the ancient couch in the living room.

Stretched out with her hands behind her head, Brie let loose with a loud sigh. She wasn't tired at all. If anything, she was wired for action. It was the same kind of feeling she got right before a stakeout. She did some deep breathing exercises and felt better almost immediately. Her head felt clearer now.

There were so many things she wanted to think about. Sela was something of an airhead. Callie was docile, most of the time. A friend. Callie was never a mover and a shaker. She had no desire to make inroads, to be the first, the best, in anything. She was content to live her life quietly, taking it a day at a time. Brie had always wanted to be Callie's *best* friend, apart from Bode, but that spot was reserved for Sela. Brie had accepted it early on and was content to be in third place. Bode said it was because Callie admired Sela's flamboyant ways and her recklessness. Not that Callie ever wanted to *do* what Sela did, but she liked to *hear* about it and fantasize.

What was life going to be like without Callie?

Maybe she was feeling this way because in the space of one day she had lost two of her best friends. Bode had gone away. He wouldn't stay in touch; that much she knew. Bode was her own personal haven. He was like a warm fuzzy, someone you could always count on to be there for you when you needed him most. Callie was always there for her, too, but in a different kind of way. Sela . . . Sela was Sela. Oh, she listened, she offered cockamamy advice and then started to talk about the most important person in her life: herself.

Tonight had been an eye-opener in many ways. Brie had had no idea that Sela was so obsessed with Parker Manor. There was no doubt in her mind that Sela would take her real-estate course and then move back here and settle in with Pearl. She would happily drive Pearl back and forth to the hospital for the privilege of living in Parker Manor, in Callie's room. She'd move Pearl out of the apartment, visit Callie, take flowers, drive Pearl to church.

"I need to talk to Bode," she muttered. Sleep was out of the question. She was wide-awake, raring to go, as her police partner said, before they drove off for the day. Even if she had a phone number to call Bode, she couldn't do so because she'd agreed with Pearl and Sela not to get in touch with him. She'd never, ever, go back on her word. She knew she could find Bode in a heartbeat if she really wanted to. She was a cop, for God's sake! All she had to do was say he was a suspect in something or other and put out an APB on him. Santa Fe wasn't *that* far from San Diego. Bode wouldn't kick up a fuss if he was hauled in for questioning. Not when he understood why she'd done it.

Get in the car and drive, her inner voice urged. *Go somewhere and make the call. There are phone booths all over the place. Don't do it here. If you do that, your word is worthless: it means you can't be trusted. Sela probably doesn't realize she's trying to take Callie's place. Sela never thinks things through to a conclusion. This is just your suspicious cop's mind, Brie Canfield.* She argued with herself for another fifteen minutes before she crept off the couch and tiptoed to the bathroom, where she dressed with only the aid of a small nightlight.

Before she left the house, she checked on Sela, who was sleeping peacefully. Sela always slept peacefully when she was at Parker Manor. Pearl was snoring lustily. Satisfied that neither woman would wake, Brie left the house and backed the rental car out to the main road without using the head-lights. Like Sela, she knew every inch of the grounds.

She drove with the windows wide-open, the radio blaring. Johnny Mathis was singing "Three Times a Lady." How could you be three times a lady? Sela would probably know. She turned off the music, and the quiet night surrounded her. *Where was she going?* She was on Trolley Road. It would only take her as far as Dorchester Road and then she would either make a left or a right. Or she'd turn around and go back to the manor house. She passed the South Carolina National Bank. Callie banked with them; so did Bode. Once, she herself had a small account at the same bank. They called you by name, asked about your family, and never made mistakes in your account. Her bank in San Diego made mistakes every month. Once, the machine ate her ATM card. No one knew her name. No one asked how she was. No one even smiled at her. She couldn't even remember the name of the damn bank. Bill O. Duke, that was the name of the man at the bank in town. She wondered what the O. stood for. Callie would know; so would Bode. Maybe Bode had transferred his account and Bill O. Duke would know the name of his new bank. Bode and Duke were probably classmates. Tomorrow she'd go in and ask. But did Callie bank at this branch or the one in town? Bode probably used the one in town. That's where she would go.

The light changed and she was on Dorchester Road.

She passed the Remax building, spotting the phone booth straight ahead. The shoulder on the road looked too skimpy to park so she pulled into the parking lot of the Children's Nook Daycare Center. A sensor light flashed on. She saw colorful wooden balloons nailed to the wall next to the front window. How pretty they looked. She felt her eyes begin to mist. Mothers brought their children here to be cared for.

There had been no place like this when she was growing up. Parker Manor and Pearl were her daycare center.

Brie eyed the phone booth. Who was she going to call? Wyn? Her precinct? Her gaze swiveled to the building with the bright balloons. Would an alarm go off if she walked up to it? Could she look in the window? Why? Did the children who came here play the games she'd played at Parker Manor? Did they have pets—hamsters, rabbits? Did they have jumping frogs for the boys? Were there trees in the back that the children could climb? Was there a brook for wading? Did these children know how to tie a wiggly worm on the end of a fishing line? Did they catch fireflies? Did they have picnics outside? Pearl always made picnics such fun. She'd draw funny faces on the shells of the hard-boiled eggs. She even tied colored ribbons around the fried chicken legs. There was always a shiny apple and a fat sugar cookie with M&M candies baked into it. She thought she liked the old wicker picnic basket the best. It had silver and real cloth napkins that had red-and-white checks to match the tablecloth. It was Bode's job to lay out the tablecloth, Sela's job to put out the silver if they had fruit salad or potato salad, and Callie's job to lay out the napkins and plates. Brie's job was to pack it all up after the picnic. She always folded the napkins just so, and the tablecloth into its proper creases. The used silver went into a little cloth bag, the plates into a bigger cloth bag. Bode always carried the basket. "I hope all the children who come here are as happy as we were," she whispered.

She was standing next to the phone booth, a pile of change in her pocket. Who was she going to call? Nobody. This whole nocturnal trip was nothing more than an exercise in futility.

She was back in the car. She crossed the divider and headed back the way she'd come. Before she knew it, she was almost to town. She passed the Eggroll Express, the Flowertown

Restaurant and then was on Highway 78. Highway 78 led to the hospital.

A long time later, she walked into the ICU unit. Like churches, hospitals seemed to have a different kind of quietness. They were places where miracles happened. A miracle was what Callie needed.

Wyn saw Brie before she spotted him. His heart started to hammer in his chest. What the hell was she doing here? Did she suspect anything? Was she going to do or say something that would bring it all out in the open? He cursed Kallum under his breath. The violent urge to grab Brie by the arm and take her outside was so strong he jammed his hands into his pockets. He wanted to tell her everything, right now, this very second. Christ, why was she here?

"Brie, did you come all the way here to keep me company?"

"I couldn't sleep. I drove for a while, and then I ended up here. Has there been any change?"

"No. They let me see her for five minutes on the hour. It's not much, but better than being told she's the same. This way I can see for myself. You can go in the next time. You haven't seen her yet. It's going to break your heart, so be prepared." Brie nodded. "Did the rain cool things off?"

"A little. We made it home just as it started to come down. We had dinner and . . . Sela and Pearl went to bed. As I said, I couldn't sleep. Did you eat?"

"I had a sandwich earlier. It tasted like sawdust, glue, and mayonnaise. My insides are starting to rebel with all the black coffee I've had. It's been a long day," he said wearily.

"Yes, it has," Brie said, looking at her watch.

"How's Pearl?"

"Pearl is Pearl. She's hopeful like the rest of us. You are hopeful, aren't you, Wyn?"

"Yes, I'm optimistic. Even if the specialists tell me there is no hope, I don't think I'll believe them. I know Pearl won't."

"Probably not. I cannot believe this has happened. Callie was . . . is . . ."

"She's alive. We're going through the worst right now. It can only get better," Wyn said quietly.

"For who, Wyn?"

"Callie. All of us. It's almost time to go in. It's your turn. I'll go outside and smoke. Meet me there, okay?"

"Sure," Brie said.

Brie closed her eyes before she opened the door to the ICU unit. She formed a picture in her mind. Expect the worst. Be prepared. Hot tears pushed at her eyelids. Callie was so still. She touched her friend's arm. It felt warm. That had to be good.

"Callie, it's me, Brie," she murmured. "I hope you can hear me, Callie. Tomorrow, more specialists are coming. Wyn is going to do everything he can. He's taking this very hard. All night I've been thinking about when we were children and how happy we all were. They are such wonderful memories. Pearl told us a secret tonight. She really and truly does have a three-holed button. Sela and I didn't know that. We played secrets. Mine was that I'm going to be accepted into the FBI. Sela's secret is she won three thousand dollars on a horse bet. She's going to give half of it to Pearl. It's so generous of her." Brie wiped at her eyes. "My time is up, Callie. I'll be back. In my heart I don't know if you . . . if you'd want us to call Bode or not. We agreed not to call him. If you could just give me some kind of sign, squeeze my hand, flicker your eyelids, something to . . . Try, Callie, try and do something." When there was no response, Brie bent over the bed and kissed her friend on the cheek. She stumbled from the room, her sneakers squeaking on the shiny floor.

"How was she?" Wyn asked as he handed over a cigarette.

"Very still. Her eyelids didn't even flutter. She's hooked up to so many things. What will happen if all that stuff is taken away? Who decides something like that? Do you think she's in pain?"

"I don't know, Brie," Wyn said, lighting another cigarette.

"It's a new day," Brie said.

"So it is," he replied. "Are you going to call Bode?" There was an edge in his voice.

"Not yet. We want to hear what the specialists you're bringing in have to say. You don't want him here, do you?"

"The truth? No. Bode is hotheaded. He'll blame me for this. God only knows what he's capable of doing. He'll react, he won't stop to think. Look, you know as well as I do that Bode Jessup is in love with Callie. Everyone knows it, for Christ's sake! Callie knew it, too, even though she said it was a stupid assumption on my part. She liked Bode spinning his wheels over her."

"That's a terrible thing for you to say, Wyn Archer. I hate you for saying that," Brie said tightly.

"For saying what? That a piece of no-account trash is in love with my fiancée?"

Brie was faster than a lightning streak. Her knee came up, smack with Wyn's groin, while her right hand shot out to grab his arm and twist it behind him, slamming him against the front end of a Ford Mustang parked beyond the entrance to the hospital. His cry of pain only made her twist his arm tighter.

"Say it again, Wyn, and I'll break your fucking arm. Maybe I'll break the other arm, too. Don't you ever, *ever,* call Bode a piece of trash again!" She was riled now, words tumbling out of her mouth. "Your fiancée was going to give you your walking papers that night. She was calling off the wedding. She told Pearl at the Judge's. She told you in the car, didn't she?"

"You're lying!" Wyn yelped, his face contorted in pain.

"Look at my face. Do I look like I'm lying?" Brie shoved her face within inches of Wyn's. She could smell his coffee breath, knew he'd been smoking too many cigarettes. She stepped back; gave his arm another vicious twist. "Apologize. Now!"

"All right, all right. You're a bitch. You're worse than that goddamn black bitch Pearl."

"That's it! That's it!" Brie screeched as she rummaged in her shoulder purse for her handcuffs. In a blink of an eye she had dragged him to the driver's side of the Mustang and handcuffed him to the steering wheel through the open window.

"Cut me loose, damn you!"

"In your dreams. You can stay here till the owner of this car comes out and calls the police. What Callie ever saw in you is beyond me. How dare you! How dare you talk about Pearl and Bode like that! You're a fucking bigot, a monster. Callie must have finally seen through you. Somehow, some way, I'm going to find out what happened last night, and then . . . then I'm going to turn Bode loose on you. Here's something else for you to chew on, *Mister* Archer. In six weeks I'm going to be an FBI agent. I just bet you've broken all kinds of federal laws. Guess what? I'm going to check you out with a finetooth comb, *Mister* Archer. Thanks for giving me your turn in there," Brie said, jerking her head backwards.

"You aren't going to leave me here like this!" Wyn bellowed. "Goddamn it, Brie, take these cuffs off me!"

"Have a nice night," Brie said, walking away.

In the rental car, she collapsed against the steering wheel. God in heaven, she didn't just do what she did? She didn't say all those things—did she? She pinched her arm and winced. No, she wasn't dreaming. She drove away, her right leg shaking so badly she had to use her left foot to feed the gas.

Wyn Archer bellowed for over an hour before someone heard him.

Dawn was breaking when the local police cut him loose from the Mustang. "I don't know who it was," he blustered. "Two kids out for kicks. I never saw them before."

11

"Pearl, it's almost six. You told me to wake you," Sela whispered.

"*Cain't*. I have a hag on me."

Sela's mind raced. She had to remember what it was she was supposed to do. "I got it. Don't move, Pearl, I'll get the colander."

"Sweet chile, you remembered," Pearl sighed.

"You bet." Sela grinned. "I put the colander under the bed and the hag starts to count the holes and won't sit on your head. Did I do it right?" She shoved a bright green colander under Pearl's bed.

"I'll be needing a few minutes for the hag to see it there. Ah, she spotted it. Now she's going to forgit to sit on my head. I can git up now," Pearl said, struggling to heave her ample body up off the bed.

In spite of herself, Sela smiled. Pearl had a headache, pure and simple. But if the idea of a colander under her bed made the headache go away, it was all right with her.

She was soon back in the kitchen, bustling about as though she was the lady of the manor. When she looked at the kitchen clock again it was time to wake Brie.

"Hey, sleepyhead, wake up," Sela said, shaking Brie gently.

"Smell that coffee. Pearl ground it fresh just for you. She let me squeeze the oranges. You have just enough time to brush your teeth before you tie on your bib."

"I hate people who are smilingly cheerful so early in the morning. What time is it anyway?"

"Ten minutes to seven. Pearl and I have been up for an hour."

Pearl and I have been up for an hour. Brie wanted to slap Sela's smiling face. Instead she got up and shuffled to the bathroom. *Pearl and I.*

She hadn't really slept when she returned from the hospital. She'd tossed and turned on the narrow, scratchy couch, angry with herself for losing her temper. She was going to tell Pearl and Sela what she'd done. She knew better than to let her emotions crowd out her own good sense, but she'd done it anyway. Defending Bode. If Bode was standing right here he'd say he didn't need defending from Wynfield Archer or anyone else. She'd try and defend herself, and he'd look at her with those steely eyes of his and say, sotto voce: "I'm disappointed in you, Brie." At which point, she'd blubber like a kid. Well, goddammit, Bode wasn't here, and it was a matter of honor with her. She didn't feel one bit better when she took her place at the table.

"You look terrible, chile. Didn't you sleep well last night?"

"I think I only slept for twenty minutes before Miss Cheerful woke me up. Look, I might as well tell you right now. I went to the hospital last night because I couldn't sleep." She concentrated on Pearl's unhappy face as she told them both the tale.

"You left Wyn handcuffed to some stranger's car and drove away. You just drove away!" Sela gasped.

"I'd like to hear what you would have done, Sela," Brie snapped. "Are you saying you would have let that . . . that *cretin* call Bode trash?"

"Of course not; but there are other ways of handling

things. You are simply too physical. I guess I would have kicked him in the shins. That's physical, but it isn't the same as—God!"

"What did Mr. Wyn say when you told him my baby was going to call off the wedding?" Pearl asked, her eyes brimming with tears.

"He said he didn't believe me. That man doesn't like any of us. He tolerated us. I'll bet you five bucks that somehow, some way, inside of six months, he'd have had Callie saying, 'Brie who, Sela who, Bode who?' He would have found a way to pension Pearl off and make it look like it was Callie's idea."

"I thought you liked Wyn," Sela said.

"I did and I didn't. I truly believe he loves Callie. Right now, that's the only plus I can give him. I'll tell you one thing for certain though. He's scared out of his wits that we're going to call Bode. Now, why is that? An accident is an accident."

"My boy wouldn't do nothing to Mr. Wyn, 'lessen he did something wrong," Pearl said quietly. "My boy is honorable."

"You are damn unbelievable," Sela said, holding out her cup to Brie for more coffee.

"Why don't you get up and fetch it yourself," Brie snapped, and Sela had the grace to look embarrassed. *That's it, Sela, start paving the way for Pearl to wait on you hand and foot. Miss Sela Carron, stand-in for Callie Parker. Miss Sela Carron Bronson of Parker Manor.* She pushed her plate away and Pearl pushed it back, a frown on her face. Brie picked up her fork. All it took was one look from Pearl, and it was instant obedience on her part. It didn't matter that she was over thirty and out on her own.

"Are you upset with me, Pearl?" Brie murmured.

"No, chile. You did what you thought was right at the

time. I don't think Mr. Wyn will hold it against you. What he called my boy, that don't make no never mind. He has to live with hisself. The man has a good heart. He loves my baby."

"How are you going to face Wyn?" Sela asked.

"I won't have any trouble at all. Don't expect me to apologize."

Sela shrugged. "Pearl, is all this okay with you?"

"Everything is fine with me. All I want is to be near my baby."

Brie finished everything on her plate. She felt bloated, cranky, and miserable when she showered. It wasn't going to be a good day; she could feel the tension between her shoulder blades. "What I should do," she muttered as she plugged in her blow-dryer, "is call Bode. I've screwed up, so what's one more thing?" *That one more thing,* her conscience pricked, *is the look you'll see in Pearl's eyes.*

Brie was standing in the kitchen, next to the phone, waiting for her friend Mona to come on the line. She watched Sela and Pearl through the kitchen window. She blinked several times. Just for one second, she thought she was seeing Callie help Pearl into the car. "You're spooking yourself, Brie," she mumbled.

"Hi, Brie, how's things in South Carolina? Bet you're all set to come back and think about getting a boyfriend so you can be married, too."

"In your dreams. Any important mail?"

"Just the usual Occupant stuff and your Visa bill."

"Okay. Listen, I'm staying on an extra week." She gave her friend a quick rundown on the situation. "So, if anything comes in the mail, call me here in the evening, okay?"

"You bet. Hope your friend is okay."

"Me too. I'll see you when I get back."

Brie made herself a fresh pot of coffee. She didn't want to wake the Judge. She'd heard that the Judge liked to sleep till nine, putz around till ten, arrive in the office at ten-thirty, look over his mail and then head out for lunch. It was just eight-thirty now. Time to drink most of the coffee and review her sins of yesterday. She listened to the coffee perk. She could have sworn the sounds said, *"Bode, Bode, Bode."*

The telephone was so close, she could reach behind her and take the receiver off the hook. If she called, she'd have to tell him about Callie, and then she'd be breaking her promise.

You're losing it, Brie, she berated herself. *You can't call him.* Her shoulders slumped. She wanted to cry and wasn't sure why.

It was a grim assembly of people sitting in the rest area in the hallway outside of the ICU unit. All eyes were on the specialists speaking with Wyn. Why are they saying the same thing over and over? Brie wondered. Do they think we're stupid—that we don't understand the meaning of the word *hopeless?* Wyn was shaking his head as was Pearl. She heard words that made her cringe. Blood gases . . . whatever they were . . . danger of pneumonia . . . weeks of antibiotics . . . brainstem activity . . . a pulmonary specialist was on call . . . chances are one in a million . . . CAT scan . . . Sometimes when the machines are disconnected the patient can breathe on his or her own. What usually happens is the patient is then dependent . . . what that means is the patient can't take care of his or her own bodily functions. That will probably happen . . . We're going to run a few more tests. For now, what we're doing is this: we've ordered splints to be put on her hands, wrists, feet, and ankles to prevent contractures. We don't want her joints to be stiff and contracted so they become useless. I want someone to bring in a pair of high-top sneakers so we can put them on her feet so they don't drop. We need support for her feet. I know this doesn't sound like much to you, but for now, it's all that can be done . . .

The trauma specialist had the grace to look embarrassed when he concluded, "This is a costly procedure where there is little visual evidence of . . ." He let the rest of what he was about to say trail into nothingness.

Wyn said, "I don't care. Callie has health insurance and the car insurance, however that works. If need be, I will pay any and all differences. I want everything that can be done to be done. Money is not important right now. I will not agree to having any of the life-support systems disconnected. The Judge, as her guardian, agrees." He swiveled until he was facing the three women. "Pearl?"

"No sir, no sir," Pearl said.

As Wyn walked toward the double doors leading back to the ICU unit, Sela whispered, "Guess he didn't believe what you told him—you know, about Callie calling off the wedding. He's going to help pay the bills."

"Saying it and doing it are two different things," Brie said quietly. "You're wrong though about him not believing me. He did."

Sela shrugged. "What's the weather like outside?"

"Hot and muggy. I think we should leave for a little while and get a bite to eat. I could use some fast food and a lot of grease in my diet about now."

"My baby isn't hopeless, is she, Miz Brie?" Pearl asked, choking on her sobs.

"Maybe right now it looks that way. Doctors just . . . what they do is . . . they look at what's happening right now, this minute, and they say what they see and think. That doesn't mean things won't or can't change tomorrow, next week, or next month. Those men aren't God, Pearl. They're human beings doing their best. We have to be confident, hopeful, that things will improve. I think it's a good sign that Wyn is conferring with you. I spoke to the Judge this morning at great length. I told him Callie had planned to call off the wedding. He didn't seem at all surprised. He's going to speak with Bill Duke at the bank about Callie's account. The Judge was adamant about not pulling the plugs. I'm glad he's Callie's guardian and not Wyn."

"Why?"

"Don't pretend to be stupid, Sela. If he had a mind to, he could tell the hospital not to let Pearl in to see Callie. He can tell us to take a hike, meaning he could keep us away from her. That's what a guardianship is all about."

"Oh."

"We don't have to worry about that. Are you okay with this, Pearl?"

"Yes'm," Pearl said.

"Sela?"

"You have my vote."

"Then it's settled. Tell me about the apartment."

"It's not really an apartment. It's rather like an efficiency. A large room, small kitchen area. The refrigerator and stove are small. The furniture is real nice, kind of modern. The main reason I took it was because it had a washer and a dryer and I know Pearl will be doing Callie's laundry. You know, all her nightgowns and stuff. There's a small market close by and it's a quarter of a mile from the hospital. The rent is three hundred dollars. I snapped it up. We can pretty it up for her if you want. I thought we'd stock her up on groceries before we leave. What do you think, Brie?" Sela asked anxiously.

"Everything sounds good. It's the walking part that bothers me."

"I don't know how to get around that," Sela said. "When the weather is nice it won't be so bad."

"It sounds jest fine, Miz Sela, and I need to be thanking you for all the trouble you're going to."

"It was no trouble, Pearl, I was glad to do it. We want to make things as easy for you as we can. We'll move you in before we leave so you don't have to tote your things a little at a time." Sela smiled.

"The Judge said he'd drop by once a week and give Pearl money from the account. He'll monitor it."

"What's Wyn's attitude?" Sela whispered. "You got here before I did. He seems kind of . . . pissy to me."

"He said hello, that was it. He just sits here like Pearl. They take turns going in to see Callie. He's being a gentleman about it. He hasn't said anything directly to me though."

"Under the circumstances it's understandable," Sela said. "Pearl, do you want to come with us for a bite to eat or would you like us to bring you something?"

"I'm not much hungry, Miz Sela. You could be bringing me an apple if you have a mind to. It's my turn to go in to see my baby soon."

Wyn was back in the waiting room, a cup of coffee in one hand, the morning paper in the other. In a dead-sounding voice, he asked Brie, "Were you telling me the truth last night? If you were, you just stripped me of my last reason for living. I've asked myself all night long, why you would say such a thing to me unless it was true. I apologize for my remarks last night. I was way out of line. If I could take back those hateful words, I would."

Out of the corner of her eye, Brie watched Pearl struggle to her feet. It was time to see the patient. She didn't look at any of them as she opened the huge double doors, the string bag clutched firmly in her hand.

"Callie confided in Pearl in the Judge's garden. She said she was going to tell you when you went to drop off the keys at your client's house. I wouldn't have said anything to you, knowing how badly you're hurting right now, if you hadn't made those awful remarks about Bode and Pearl. Your apology . . . what good is it, Wyn, if you think of them in those terms? Sorry is just a word. If you're looking for absolution, you're going to have to get it somewhere else."

"Knowing what you know now, is that going to make a difference in helping Callie?" Sela asked.

"No, of course not. I love Callie. Until she tells me herself that she doesn't love me, nothing will change. You need to know I'm here for the long haul. Callie *will* get better, I'm sure of it. She has to get better, she just has to."

"After we leave, you'll be kind to Pearl, won't you?"

"You really think of me as some kind of monster, don't you?"

"Of course not," Sela said.

"Yes, some kind of monster," Brie said.

"That was a pretty shitful thing you did to me last night, handcuffing me to that old man's car. I could have reported you to the police, but I didn't—you know why? Because you're under as much stress as I am. I could have had you locked up for that little stunt, but I'm willing to forgive and forget."

"You're more generous than I would be under the circumstances, and that makes me wonder all the more about you. I wanted to like you because Callie said she loved you. In a way I did like you. I thought in some ways you were good for her, but she saw something . . . or felt something . . . and she changed her mind. Right now, I'm willing to put aside any and all differences and concentrate on what's best for Callie."

"My sentiments exactly," Wyn said.

"Has there been any change?"

"A bit and it's not for the best. Callie was coming down with her annual summer cold. She's congested, and the doctors are concerned she might get pneumonia. That's not good. I spoke to the chief of staff and asked him if he could shorten the wait between visits from one hour to the half hour. He agreed. I can go in for five minutes on the half hour and Pearl can go in on the hour. They're bending the rules a little for Pearl. The last time she went in they let her stay for ten minutes. That's why she won't leave with you."

"We'll bring her something to eat," Brie said.

Neither woman spoke until they were outside. "He's going to be nice to Pearl because he knows if he isn't, Bode will— Well, I don't know what Bode will do, but he'll do something."

"I'm getting a tad tired of hearing about what Bode will or won't do. Don't tell me you still have a crush on him," Sela said snidely.

"Are we forgetting the mad crush *you* had on him at one time?"

"I outgrew that a long time ago."

"He's a good friend, nothing more."

"If you say so," Sela said slyly.

Brie ignored Sela's comment.

"What do we do now?" Sela asked. "I mean after we eat?"

"We wait."

12

The day before Brie was to leave for San Diego, the resident doctor on staff drew her aside, and said quietly, "Miss Parker has pneumonia, but I guess you know that. The antibiotics we've been giving her don't seem to be working. We're going to start a new dose today. The treatment will take six weeks." Brie stared at him. He seemed to be waiting for her to say something.

Brie struggled with her tongue. "Let me be sure I understand what you're saying here. This pneumonia, the emphysema, the cardiac arrest of the other day and maybe some other complications . . . those are rather small things to consider if what all the specialists said earlier is true and Callie isn't going to come out of this. Now you're saying you're going to switch the antibiotics and even if it cures the pneumonia, doesn't that put it all back to square one?"

The doctor nodded.

"Did you speak to Mr. Archer or Pearl?" she asked.

"Yesterday. They're very discouraged."

"Well, guess what, Doctor, I'm discouraged, too. If my opinion counts, this seems like an exercise in futility, but I say go ahead. Will Callie breathe easier?"

"Yes. It will be a medical resolution of sorts."

"Well, whoopee! I'm sorry, Doctor, I'm just tired. You see, I have to leave tomorrow and San Diego isn't around the corner. I can't get back here whenever I feel like it. I was hoping I could leave knowing something more positive."

"It doesn't look good, Miss Canfield."

"I know that. I remember reading about a young girl up North who was in a coma for ten or more years. Her name was Karen something—Quinlan, that's it. She lived in a coma after they removed the respirator. She never regained consciousness. That could happen to Callie, couldn't it?"

"Yes, but it's unlikely. Patients can breathe on their own sometimes when the respirator is removed. If your question is do they die right away when the plug is removed, the answer is no."

"I wasn't going to ask you any such thing, Doctor," Brie said huffily. "You see, I'm one of the people who believe that Callie will come out of this." *The only one,* she thought.

"Would you like to have dinner with me?" the young man said suddenly. "It will have to be in the cafeteria though."

Brie was stunned. She shook her head. "I'm engaged, sorry."

"Okay," the doctor said agreeably. "Anyone I know?" he called over his shoulder.

"Bode Jessup," Brie lied.

"So, old Bode finally went and did it. Say Stone Meyers said hello. You got the best, Miss Canfield."

"Yeah, I know," Brie murmured. Now, where did *that* come from?

She was back in the waiting room outside ICU. She knew every thread in the upholstery, every spot on the carpet. Her eyes were bloodshot from staring at the grainy television set. Wyn looked as if a devil was on his back, Pearl even worse. She knew she herself looked like something the cat had dragged in and refused to take back out. They weren't eating, and they were drinking too much black coffee and smoking too many cigarettes. She had to do something.

"Listen, this is my last night," she said. "Let's go out somewhere for a bite to eat, my treat. How about Oscar's?"

"I'm not really hungry, Brie, but thanks," Wyn muttered. Pearl just shook her head.

"I insist," Brie said. "I mean it, I insist. Look, there's been no real change for the better. I was just speaking to the doctor, and he said Callie's pneumonia is worse so you're only going in five minutes on the hour. What good will either one of you be to Callie if you wear down? She needs you hale and hearty. Get your purse, Pearl. Get it together, Wyn," Brie said not unkindly.

They didn't eat much and they barely spoke to one another. But they were away from the hospital, among people who smiled, laughed, and talked.

"I'll call every night, eight o'clock your time, to the pay phone in the waiting room. I want one of you to promise me you'll answer it." Pearl and Wyn nodded.

Brie paid the check. They went back to the hospital for one more visit before Brie drove Pearl back to the house. Tomorrow, before she left, she would take the last of Pearl's personal belongings to the new apartment. Wyn had promised to pick Pearl up every morning on his way to the hospital. He would drop her off, too, if she was agreeable to the suggestion—which she wasn't. Brie could only shake her head in dismay. She'd long ago given up any idea of changing Pearl's mind about anything. All she could do now was hope for the best.

At the hospital, she held out her hand to Wyn, who took it gratefully. "No hard feelings, Wyn."

"It's not important, Brie," he said wearily. "Pearl and I will do what we can from here. I expect a miracle. Pearl expects one too." His voice said he didn't believe his own words. "One of us will take your call every night. Good luck with the FBI. I think you'll make a hell of an agent. I mean that, Brie. Will we be able to get in touch if . . . you know? Six weeks at the FBI Academy is a long time."

"Yeah, I think you will," Brie said softly. "I'll call you, I think that's best."

The night nurse in ICU, a kindly older woman, gave Brie permission to visit Callie after Pearl did her five minutes.

Tears blinded Brie's eyes at the sight of her friend fighting so desperately for her life. Was fighting the right word? The machines were making all the effort. "Oh Callie," she wept aloud. "I am so sorry this happened. I've been doing everything I can think of. Pearl is taken care of. Sela went back to New York. She calls every day. She'll be moving back here as soon as she finishes her course. She'll take care of Pearl until . . . until you're well enough to do it. I'm leaving in the morning. I'm going to call every day. I know you can hear me, Callie, I know it. We didn't call Bode because Pearl doesn't want us to. We always listen to Pearl, you know that. He'll never forgive us when he finds out. I dread the day. I think you love Bode. I think that's what took you right down to the wire with Wyn. In the end you realized it and couldn't go through with it. I have something to say though. Wyn has been here every waking moment. He's doing everything he can think of. We're not giving up on you, Callie. I guess what I'm trying to say is that time won't stand still for any of us. The nurse is motioning to me that I have to leave. I don't want to leave, but I have to. I'm gonna pray for you, too. That's a hoot, isn't it, me praying?" Brie choked back a sob. "They're going to take care of you, Callie. Pearl won't let anything happen to you. I'll be here so fast if . . . if you need me. You can take that to the bank, Callie Parker."

"You shouldn't be crying, Miz Brie. Tomorrow when you get on that airplane your eyes are going to look like pee holes in a snowbank. You come along and take old Pearl home."

The following day Brie found herself blubbering again. Pearl held her close, stroking her hair and murmuring soft words of comfort.

"I don't want to go, Pearl, but I have to. The FBI won't wait for me or give me a second chance."

"There's nothing for you to do, chile. There's nothing for me to do either, but sit with my baby."

"Pearl, I want you to do something. I know right now you're only permitted a few minutes each hour with Callie, but if she improves and I think she will, they'll extend the visiting time. I read all those pamphlets the doctors gave me. I went down to the medical library and read as much as I could about Callie's condition. One of the books said coma patients could hear. What that means, Pearl, is that I want you to talk to Callie all the time you're with her. Don't just hold her hand and cry. Talk to her. Go back from the beginning, when she was born, and talk about all your memories. Touch her, ask her questions. She isn't going to answer, but ask anyway. Will you do it, Pearl?"

"Of course I'll do it, chile. If they told me to walk on my head because it would help my little girl, I'd do it."

"All right, Pearl, I have to go now. You take care of yourself, you hear me? Wyn will be here by ten to pick you up. I'm going to drop your things off at the apartment. I'll call every chance I get. Oh, I'm going to miss you, Pearl."

"Shhhh, chile," Pearl said as she tried to comfort Brie.

"You love me, don't you, Pearl? Not as much as Callie and Bode, but you care about me, don't you?" Brie whimpered.

"I love all my children the same, Miz Brie, and you should be knowing that."

Brie dabbed at her eyes and then blew her nose. "Pearl, did I ever thank you—I mean *really* thank you—for being so good to me when I was little, and even when we grew up? Did I ever say the words to you?"

"You tried to, too many times, and I had to shush you up. When you be loving someone you don't need to be getting thanks from that person. Now, you mind old Pearl and get on with you."

Brie burst into tears and ran to the car. She honked the horn and waved wildly as she careened down the old brick road.

"Lord, this is Pearl. I'd be most happy if You'd look after that chile. She be hurting something fierce. And don't You be forgetting about my baby. This is Pearl from Parker Manor asking for this special favor. I'll be saying some extra prayers today."

Wyn was so weary, so mentally exhausted, he began to doze off to the hum of the floor-waxing machine. When he started to slide off the chair, he jerked upright to wakefulness and found himself staring into accusing jet eyes. Pearl. He gave himself a mental shake. How in the hell did the old woman do it? She spent twelve hours a day here at the hospital just the way he did, and she looked like she could spend another twenty-four and still do whatever she did when she went home. He knew the thought didn't make sense; twenty-four hours was twenty-four hours and that didn't leave even a minute, which all went to prove he wasn't thinking clearly. He wasn't eating properly, he wasn't sleeping, and he was drinking and smoking too much. He'd dropped fourteen pounds in the four weeks Callie had been in the hospital. It all showed on his face. Even though he was freshly shaven, he looked gaunt and hollow-eyed. He needed a haircut and he needed to go to the dentist.

He wanted to stare Pearl down, but he'd given up on that weeks ago. In his gut he knew she had put a hex on him, and today was the day he was going to ask her to remove it. It had to be a hex. Just sitting in the hospital couldn't make him feel the way he'd been feeling. Maybe it was worse than a hex; maybe it was a *curse*. He started to tremble. That's what the old hag wanted—for him to beg her so she would get some satisfaction. Jesus, he'd tried to be nice. He'd offered to drive her back and forth to the hospital, but she walked when the weather was decent. Other times she arrived in an ancient pickup that was loaded with peat moss and manure in the back end. He'd even brought her fresh fruit and a sandwich from the cafeteria, not to mention coffee. She never touched any of it.

Wyn wished now, for the ten thousandth time, that he had confessed to driving the car the day of the accident. His nightmares, when he did sleep, were full of policemen, insurance agents, and insurance investigators. He had lied to all of them. Kallum hadn't been able to buffer any of them. He'd told the same story so many times he was beginning to believe it himself. A suit was being filed against Callie by the Seagreave family for a hundred million dollars. Who could blame the family? They'd lost a son, a daughter-in-law, their only grandchild, and a second grandchild who never got to be born. There wasn't enough money in the world to pay for something like that.

How many more days can I take this? he agonized. *I have to pull myself together and get on with life.*

"You put a curse on me, didn't you, old woman?" Wyn blurted out. "Don't stare at me like that. Admit it. Take it off. I mean it, Pearl. Whatever you did . . . reverse it. Please," he begged. Pearl stared at him for a long minute before she turned away. "What do you want me to do—beg?" he continued. "How long can this go on? Answer me, damn you!" His voice was out of control. Pearl ignored him, staring straight ahead, her big hands wrapped around her string bag. "Goddamn it, what do you want from me?"

Pearl turned her head slowly. "The truth about my baby. That's all I want, Mr. Wyn."

"I told you the truth," Wyn blustered. His words sounded like the lie they were to his own ears. Obviously Pearl thought so too. "Are you going to take off the spell? Is it a curse?" There was fear in Wyn's heart at what he was seeing in Pearl's eyes.

"I give you pain and sorrow like my baby is feelin'. *Cain't* take it away. Only the Lord can take it away, but first you have to tell the truth. If you don't, you will have pain and sorrow for the rest of your days."

Wyn believed her. Already his joints were aching, and in his life he'd never felt such sorrow. He was stuck with his lie. Pain and sorrow versus ten years on some chain gang was no contest. He wouldn't do well with a pick and shovel with his feet manacled. He would buy aspirin by the barrel.

Wyn's eyes went to the clock. It was his turn to go into the room. Actually it was a tiny cubicle filled with so many machines he had to inch his way to the side of the bed. He felt annoyed the way he did every time he came into the room. How was it possible Callie hadn't moved, twitched, blinked? Her nails seemed to be longer. He wondered why Pearl hadn't filed them. Her hair was neat and tidy. It had been brushed. She looked like a tiny wax doll in the frilly nightgown that Pearl changed every day, sometimes twice. He wanted to look under the pillows to see if there were any of Pearl's charms, but he was afraid to disturb them.

He touched her hand, her cheek. It was warm, but then she had had a fever for weeks. So thin. This wasn't the Callie he knew, the woman he had been going to marry. Who had been intending to jilt him. He was never going to believe that, not in a million years. Sorrow. Pain.

He wanted to say something to Callie, something meaningful, something so profound she would open her eyes, and say, "Oh Wyn, everything is going to be just the way we planned." Yeah, sure.

The sound of the respirator, the coolness of the room, the still form on the bed made the fine hairs on the back of his neck stand at attention. "I love you, Callie, I will always love you. I want you to know if I could get yesterday back, I would do anything. *Anything.*"

Wyn looked around. So many machines, so many little red lights. Bile rose in his throat. He forced it back down by taking a deep breath then wished he hadn't. The smell of the room was overpowering. Disinfectant, alcohol, and impending death. Death had its own smell. Someone had told him that once, but he couldn't remember who it was. Why wasn't he smelling powder or . . . laundry detergent? Pearl was always dousing Callie with something from that damn string bag of hers. He sniffed again, felt himself grow light-headed. He shook his head to clear it, his eyes glued to the blue bags being fed intravenously to Callie. God, what *was* all that stuff? Would her veins explode at some point? The awful purplish bruises on her arms bothered him. It must have something to do with the needles or the tubes or . . . or something.

Then because he couldn't see through his tears, he left, not knowing if his five minutes were up or not.

Pearl was standing by the door when he pushed his way into the hall. He blinked and watched a moment through the glass. He saw Pearl's lips move; she seemed to be talking ninety miles to the minute. What the hell was she saying?

What *could* she say? Whatever it was, her words were having no effect on Callie. He was almost glad.

Wyn walked over to the nurses' station. "Has there been any change at all? Are the antibiotics working?"

"Miss Parker's fever dropped to a hundred degrees last night. The doctors are satisfied with the antibiotic treatment. I'm sorry the news isn't better, Mr. Archer."

"Should Pearl be massaging Callie's legs?" God, how hostile his voice sounded. Evidently the nurse thought so, too.

"It can't hurt. One of the doctors showed her how to do it. Sometimes treatment of the patient means treatment for those who wait—meaning Miss Pearl. It's good for both of them. Surely you understand, Mr. Archer?"

He muttered something he couldn't remember later. "I'm leaving; I won't be back anymore today. If there's any change—any change, even if she blinks—promise me you'll call?"

"Of course, Mr. Archer."

It was another month before the hospital relaxed the rules in regard to Callie Parker. Visiting times were extended to an hour. An hour that Pearl spent talking to her baby. The morning hour was for Pearl and the evening hour was for Wyn. Pearl stayed until ten o'clock when the nurse relented and allowed her another ten minutes.

Devotion such as Pearl's deserved to be rewarded, the hospital administrator said kindly.

It was a beautiful November day, just three days before Thanksgiving, when Pearl marched into the hospital, her string bag bulging. Today she was going to talk about Callie's first Hallowe'en party under the oaks in the backyard.

Today was a good day. Brie had called the night before just when she was crawling into bed. And this morning Sela had called.

As she rode to the fourth floor in the elevator, Pearl thought about the pain she'd been having of late. She wasn't sure if she should pay attention to it or not. Maybe she just needed a good poop and some of that white, thick stuff that made her tongue white and tasted like chalk. Maybe she needed a little taste of Lazarus's wine. Tonight before she got into bed she'd take a little sip.

There was a chair in Callie's cubicle now. An orderly had brought it a few weeks ago. She had been so grateful. She was even more grateful today when she lowered her heavy bulk into it. In the beginning she'd had to squeeze herself into the chair. Yesterday and today she had felt herself slide right into it. She was losing weight. Her friend Arquette had mentioned it earlier this morning during the ride to the hospital. She'd waved the words away as if they had no meaning. If she started to worry about herself, she wouldn't have time to worry about Callie and Mr. Wyn, who now only came to the hospital every other day.

She was pleased with Mr. Wyn's thinness, pleased that his eyes seemed sunk in his head, pleased that he didn't look so dapper anymore. Pleased that he was experiencing pain and sorrow like her baby love. If Callie opened her eyes this minute she would be like a chicken with wet feathers if she knew she'd given Mr. Wyn pain and sorrow. She'd sputter and mutter and tell her to give him happiness and laughter. "Well, I *cain't* do that, even for my baby love," Pearl said. "A spell is forever. I could, if I had a mind to, mix the pain and sorrow with happiness and laughter—*if* I want to. But I don't want to. Maybe tomorrow, maybe next week, I'll think about it. If I'm not too busy thinking about other things."

Pearl settled herself on the chair, took a deep breath, and relaxed. "You look real pretty today, Miz Callie. This morning we're going to talk about your first Hallowe'en party. I know it's way past Hallowe'en and it's almost Thanksgiving. Just three more days. Arquette is bringing me a turkey. He got it hisself at the Turkey Shoot on Dorchester Road. He's bringing me everything I need to make a dinner for my girls. Miz Brie is coming because she has some days off. She said she's finished with FBI school. Now ain't that something, Miz Callie? Then this morning Miz Sela said she's driving here tomorrow. She said she passed her test and got her license. We're going to move back to the house. Mr. Wyn said we could stay in it as long as we want. Miz Sela promised we'd pay him some small rent. They fixed the leak in the kitchen and mowed the grass and trimmed the bushes. They're real good to me, Miz Callie.

"Nobody heard from Bode yet. Guess he's really busy doing what he has to do to get ready to be a judge. I don't rightly know how that works. Miz Brie said he'll send us a card for Christmas. My boy always loved Christmas. He used to give us such fine presents. I'd like to buy him something special this year in return for those fine, fine dresses he got for me. That boy, he jest don't know how to accept a present for hisself. I 'spect you will be outta that there bed by Christmas. I'm praying to the Lord for that. Lord have mercy, this room is chilly. I see they gave you another blanket. That's good, they're taking good care of you when Pearl isn't here.

"Today, your breathing seems much better, Miz Callie. I wish I knew if you can hear me. Miz Brie says you can. She told me never to stop talking to you. So I have to mind her and do as she says, 'lessen my voice gives out on me.

"I said I was going to talk 'bout your first Hallowe'en party. Remember how Bode said the costumes had to be a secret? Yours was so secret you wouldn't even tell old Pearl. You dressed up like Bode, in his clothes. You shamed Bode that day, but he didn't let you see his shame. He thought you was funnin' him. He cried to me when I took him to bed. I had to tell him you didn't mean it, you wanted to be jest like him. He believed old Pearl because he knowed I never lied to him.

"Bode cut all the punkins and put the candles in them and made a big circle around that old oak. When you girls seen that old skeleton hanging from that tree you all liked to die. You all run screaming to Pearl. Bode hid in the bushes and made all those awful wailin' sounds that scared you girls even more. He scared old Pearl, too.

"Do you remember how you dunked for apples and Miz Sela got the most? Bode had this dish with peeled grapes in it and he said y'all had to wear a blindfold and touch what was in the dish. He told you it was vampire brains. Such squealing and yelling I never heard. You ate those little cakes Miz Brie made and Miz Sela decorated, that looked like little punkins. Bode made ice cream, turning that old crank till his arm 'most fell out of his socket. You set the table so pretty, Miz Callie, you made the colored napkins from crêpe paper and used your allowance to buy orange paper plates. You made paper leaves and put them in that old milk jug. It was the prettiest party table I ever seen. That was the night Miz Brie and Miz Sela's mamas forgot to pick them up. You asked me how they could forget their daughters. You wanted to know if their mamas loved them. After that Hallowe'en, their mamas forgot to pick them up too many times. Old Pearl didn't care. I loved having all you children in my kitchen. It gave me great pleasure to tuck you all into bed at night and old Pearl was always real proud when Bode told you all a story that made you hide in the covers.

"I be missing that boy so much these days. I hope Miz Brie is right when she says he's going to be sending mail at Christmas. Maybe presents, too. Bode never forgets us.

"It's time for me to take off those godawful shoes the doctor said you needed. I'm rubbing your feet and legs for a bit. We need your blood to keep moving up your legs, leastaway that's what that woman sitting behind the desk said. She said I do it real good. It would be real nice for Pearl if you'd wiggle your toes for me. I brought clean socks for you, Miz Callie. Powder too. My special powder. Arquette fetched it for me this morning. He promised to bring me a frizzly chicken, maybe two. Soon as I get my frizzly chicken I'll be bringing one of his feathers to rub under your nose. This abomination will end: Arquette said so. I say so, too," Pearl declared, as her fingers worked on Callie's thin feet and legs. "Them frizzlies will scratch up any tobies or conjures. We all will be safe. From Mr. Wyn," she said under her breath.

"Miz Sela asked me if I'd fix some hoppin' John and 'pone for Thanksgiving. I said I'd make it for my girls. We're going to be cooking all day and give thanks to the Lord that you didn't go to the place God takes us to. It jest ain't your time, chile. I seen the signs.

"Now, Miz Callie, don't your feet be feeling better?" Pearl's voice dropped to a hushed whisper. "I sprinkled the powder inside your socks, Miz Callie. It's a mite smelly, but I 'spect no one will notice, and if they do they'll think it's the red onion they're smelling what hangs behind your bed.

"I'm plumb wore out today, Miz Callie. My spirits need to riz up a bit . . . 'Spect they will when my girls git here."

Pearl was back in her chair, Callie's hand in her own. "It ain't right, you lying here like this. It breaks my heart to see you, chile. I want to be doing more, something to make you get up in that bed. If I knowed what to do, I'd do it faster than it takes this old heart to beat. Maybe tomorrow I'll be telling you about Mr. Wyn and what he said to me. Maybe the next day. Pearl ain't sure if she should talk about it."

Pearl felt a slight stirring of the air around her. Her eyes grew big and then rolled back in her head. *A spirit.* Callie's mama's spirit checking on her child. Maybe her daddy's spirit. "Doncha be worrying none; Pearl is doing what she can for Miz Callie," she whispered.

"They're restless, Miz Callie. They're worried about you. You need to be giving us some sign. They want something, but I don't know what it is. I 'spect they be worried a butterfly will fly hisself in this room. *Cain't* happen, Miz Callie. They don't keep the windows open." The air stirred again. Pearl smelled the onion behind the bed. She heaved herself upright, reached behind the bed for the red onion, and stuffed it in the string bag. It was wilted. Tomorrow she would replace it.

Pearl's inner clock made her look toward the ICU window where the nurse was motioning to her and then pointing at the clock. She nodded to show she understood. She heaved herself to her feet. "Miz Callie, I love you more than anything in this whole world except Bode. Come back to us so we can see that beautiful smile. I want to feel you hug me. I want to see you happy. Don't go away from me, chile. I need to be leaving now, Miz Callie."

Pearl bent over and kissed Callie on the cheek. Her rough worn hand smoothed the hair back from Callie's forehead. "I love you, chile," she said again, tears dropping on Callie's thin cotton gown.

Pearl trundled from the room, the string bag clutched in her hands. To the nurse, she said, "I won't be coming back today, ma'am."

"Is there anything wrong, Pearl? Is there anything I can do?"

"No, ma'am." She didn't want to tell this woman with the kind face that she needed to go home to see what she could do about making herself feel better. She wanted to feel good when Miz Brie and Miz Sela arrived.

"Do you want me to call a taxi for you, Pearl?"

"I'd be obliged, ma'am, if you'd do that for me."

The charge nurse's eyebrows shot upward. This was the first time in months that Pearl had taken her up on the offer to call a cab. It was also the first time she'd left at this time of day. Maybe later she'd speak to Dr. Quinto about giving Pearl a checkup—providing Pearl permitted it. If nothing else, she could at least suggest vitamins, probably something the old woman had never heard of.

"Pearl, wait a minute," she called out. "I'm going to give you a bottle of vitamins. I have a feeling you're under the weather. They are good for you. Will you take them?"

"Will they make me feel good?" Pearl asked anxiously. "How much are they?"

"They don't cost anything," the nurse lied. "We'd give them to Callie, but she can't swallow. No sense letting them go to waste. You take two every day for the first week and then one every day after that. There's a hundred in the bottle. When they run out, tell me and I'll give you another bottle. You have to eat first. There's a lot of iron in them, and if you take them on an empty stomach you'll get a bellyache."

"Yes'm. Pearl thanks you." She wondered if the vitamins would help her poop.

"In the beginning, when you first start to take them they might make you go to the bathroom. Once your system gets regulated it will be fine. I'll call the cab now. He'll pull right up to the front door. If there's any change, I'll call you, Pearl."

"Thank you," Pearl said, stuffing the huge bottle into her string bag.

In the coffee shop Pearl bought a bag of licorice. Everyone

knew licorice made you poop. Just in case the vitamins didn't work. She chomped and chewed her way through the whole bag on the ride back to her apartment. She paid the driver and gave him a twenty-five-cent tip.

In her apartment she ate two cheese sandwiches and two of the vitamins. Then she lay down and took a nap, something she'd never done in the whole of her life. She slept until eleven o'clock that night and only woke when she heard someone knock on the door.

"Miz Sela, Pearl is so happy to see you," she said, wrapping the young woman in her arms.

"Pearl, you've lost weight! Is anything wrong? You aren't eating, are you? You spend all your time at the hospital. I bet you aren't sleeping right either. Well, we're going to change that, starting right now. What should we do first?"

"Leave."

"For where?"

"You said we would go back to the manor house."

"Well, sure. We can do that tomorrow. We have to pack up your things first."

"I want to go now. Can we go now, Miz Sela?"

"If that's what you want, Pearl. Sure, get your bag. We can come back here tomorrow and pick up your things. Brie is coming in on the red-eye. She'll get here when the roosters are crowing."

"Arquette is bringing me a frizzly chicken, maybe two."

"Wow! That's great, Pearl." Sela racked her brains trying to remember what it was a frizzly chicken was good for. The only thing she could remember with any clarity was the toadstool business and being called the devil's snuffbox. If she remembered correctly, imps were supposed to come out at night and break off the heads of the toadstools and scatter them about. Then the snuff was made into powder, the main ingredient of a conjer-bag. What it was used for, she couldn't recall. Maybe Brie would remember.

"Pearl, do you think Arquette and some of his friends can fix up one of the rooms at the manor house for me? I have a little extra money for repairs."

"Yes'm. We can stop on the way home."

"You hate this place, don't you, Pearl? Are you sorry we moved you here?"

"Yes'm, Miz Sela. I need to be sleeping in my own bed and cooking on my own stove."

"I'm sorry, Pearl. We thought this would make it easier for you. I guess we made a mistake. We meant well, Pearl."

"I know that, Miz Sela. Can we go now?"

"Right this minute. I'm glad I didn't carry up my bags," Sela laughed.

At one o'clock in the morning, Pearl was busy washing down the kitchen while Sela made up a bed for herself and Brie. At two o'clock they were cleaning both bathrooms.

"This is silly business," Pearl grumbled. "You can sleep in Miz Callie's room."

"No, no, Pearl, I can't do that. That's Callie's room, and when she comes home I want her to walk into it and find it just the way she left it. I wish there was some change, some little thing that would give us hope. I was so hoping you'd have something good to tell me. What is Wyn saying?"

"He wants me to take my spell off him. I might and I might not."

"Uh-huh?" was all Sela said.

"Mr. Wyn don't go to the hospital every day no more. I heard him tell the nurse it hurts him too much. He just stares at Miz Callie, just stands there and stares at her. Sometimes I see tears puddling in his eyes. Sometimes I don't see nothing but . . ."

Sela looked up from stuffing an extra pillow into its cover. "What do you see?"

"Nothing."

"I think you're fibbing to me, Pearl," Sela said gently. "You know what? I'm starving. I say let's go in the kitchen, and I'll make us some eggs and bacon. I'm glad you had the good sense to stop at that all-night market on the way here. Brie will come in here chewing on the doorknob. I'll make us some fresh coffee and we'll sit and talk like old times. You can tell me every little thing about what's been going on since I left."

The dishes were still on the table when Brie climbed from the taxi at six-thirty in the morning. She hugged Pearl, noticed her weight loss, but said nothing. She stared at Sela, ever-fashionable. "For some reason I expected to see a tattoo on your arm or something." She giggled. "Tell me, how's Callie? Has anyone heard from Bode? I haven't. And how's Wyn?"

They told her while Sela made fresh coffee.

"I'll have bacon and eggs, three eggs and six slices of bacon. Four slices of toast. It was a good thing you called the airport and left a message for me that you were here. I'd be sitting by the door of the apartment all day waiting for you."

"Doesn't sound like a smart FBI agent to me," Sela said, laying bacon in the frying pan.

"I'm going to be based in Atlanta," Brie told them. "That's only a few hours from here. I can drive up on weekends."

"Really," was all Sela said.

"That's good, Miz Brie," Pearl said.

"You here for good, Sela?"

"Yes. I feel better already. There's something so right about coming back home. I don't mean this is home, I mean coming

back to South Carolina. It feels *soooo* right. I sent out query
letters to six commercial real-estate firms and got back two
very positive responses. I called Wyn one evening to ask
about Callie. You know, his point of view, and he said he'd
be glad to give me a glowing reference. I don't have a doubt
in my mind that I'll get a job. What I worry about is selling
property. I might even go speak with the Judge. Yep, I'm here
to stay."

"Where are you sleeping, Sela?"

"In that room across the hall from Callie's room. Arquette
is coming today, and he is going to fix it as best he can. I have
a little extra money and I thought this would be putting it to
good use. What do you think, Brie? Maybe we could fix up
that little room off the bathroom for you when you come on
weekends. If I have any money left, I'd be more than glad to
ask Arquette to do it."

"Sounds good, but I can pay for myself as long as Pearl
doesn't mind."

"Makes me no never mind, girls. This ain't Miz Callie's
house no more. You be fixin' Mr. Wyn's house for him."

"That's not the way I see it," Brie mumbled. "This is Callie's house." She directed her question to Sela. "You said you
talked to Wyn. Did he say anything about giving this back to
Callie?"

"Not a word. I didn't ask either. He's an honorable man,
Brie. Everyone in town knows about the trust deed. He won't
keep it."

"How can he deed it back to someone who's in a coma?"
Brie bristled. "I'm telling both of you, there's something
funny about that accident. I'm going to figure it out, too; you
wait and see if I don't. Pearl agrees with me."

"Do you, Pearl?" Sela asked carefully.

"Yes'm," Pearl said quietly.

"I guess that means I'm the only stupid one here then. The police were satisfied. Obviously the insurance companies are satisfied. Wyn did say they paid up on the car. I know the Seagreave family is suing, and that's going to take years. The insurance company is representing Callie. To me that means everyone is satisfied. Why do you keep saying things like this, Brie?" Sela asked irritably.

"Call it my cop instinct. Call it whatever you want. I'm just not satisfied—that's the bottom line. Don't fret about it, Sela. I'll figure it out, then you can apologize. I don't understand why your mind is so closed on this."

"It's *not* closed. Everyone can't be wrong. I'll tell you what, if you can prove Wyn was at fault, I'll dance a jig, in the buff, at Five Points. Howzat?"

"You're on, Miss Sela Carron. You heard her, Pearl? Buck naked. Sunday at high noon when everyone is coming home from church. I'll shoot bullets at your feet to see how high you can jump. Now, *that* I'd love to see."

In spite of herself, Sela laughed. "Listen, if you can prove it, that makes Mr. Archer lower than a snake's belly. God, Brie, how could something like that ever be made right?"

"I can tell you one thing, the press would try it in the papers. Callie got a lot of bad press for a few months. But there's no point in speculating now. Time enough for that later. These eggs are really good, Sela, and the bacon is just right. I thought you were a lousy cook?"

"I am. This is about the only thing I make that actually tastes like what it is. I'm going to learn though. Pearl doesn't have time to do much cooking anymore. Oh look, here comes Arquette. Brie, you'll do the dishes, okay?" To Pearl, she said, "Is it okay if I take a nap in Callie's room? I'll sleep on top of the covers."

"You can sleep on my bed, Miz Sela. I'll be going back to the hospital with Miz Brie."

"I'll be out later. I drove for fourteen hours yesterday and then stayed up all night helping Pearl," Sela said importantly.

"I see no one cares if I slept or not."

"You always sleep on the red-eye," Sela said, following Arquette to the room he was going to work in.

"Does that mean I have to unpack your car? Up yours, Sela. Do it yourself."

"Maybe Arquette will let you use his truck. I'm too pooped."

"Get that skinny ass of yours out here, Sela. I'll help you, but I'm not doing it all, and Pearl isn't doing anything. How *do* you wipe your ass with those fingernails?" Brie said sourly.

"Ha, ha. Very carefully, not that it's any of your business."

"I thought you said you didn't have anything. What do you call all this?" Brie demanded after her ninth trip.

"Stuff. You're ungrateful. I'm letting you use my car and all you do is bitch and complain."

"I was born that way, just the way you were born a bitch," Brie snarled. "And for your information, I did not sleep on the red-eye last night."

"Don't blame me for that. That's the last of it. Now you can do the dishes. I'm just going to sleep for a few hours. Wait a damn minute! If you take my car, how am I going to get there?"

"Do what you told us to do—drive Arquette's truck."

"He's got two frizzly chickens in the back."

"You're kidding!"

"No, I'm not kidding."

"Guess you'll have to take them out, won't you?"

"Shut up, Brie, just shut up," Sela said, flouncing off.

What the hell is frizzly chicken? Brie wondered as she stripped down to take a shower.

* * *

He looked awful, was Brie's first thought. No, he looked as if he was dead and didn't have enough sense to lie down. "Wyn, it's nice to see you again," she said in a neutral-sounding voice.

"You too," Wyn said.

"Any change?"

"No. She's still on the respirator. God, I hate that sound. I hate all those machines, those bags of stuff going into her veins. There's nothing more to do. Callie didn't have the best health policy," he went on. "It runs out next month. It's been paying half benefits for the past month. The doctor . . . I've been paying the difference. Then it's Medicaid."

He's whining, Brie thought. "What did the doctor say?"

"Well, as you know, none of the specialists are holding out any hope that Callie will come out of this. He suggested we— no, that's wrong, he mentioned turning off the machines and moving her to a nursing home. They're frightfully expensive, too. Almost three thousand dollars a month and the patient only gets custodial care. She would still be getting the intravenous nutrients."

It was Brie's turn to speak carefully. "Won't she die if you do that? Since the Judge is Callie's legal guardian, is he prepared to make that kind of decision?"

"I don't know."

"What would be more expensive, moving to a nursing home or to stay in a four-bed room?"

"In the end it's the same. They really aren't doing anything medically for her. She came out of the pneumonia. I thought that was a good sign, but the doctors weren't impressed. It's been over three months, and there's no change. I don't know what to do."

"Can you afford the care, Wyn?"

"For now."

"But now that you know Callie was going to call off the wedding, you aren't sure you want to pay out all this money. Hey, it's understandable. I'd probably feel the same way if I was in your place."

"I never said any such thing, Brie Canfield. Don't put words in my mouth that you want to hear. You asked me, and I'm telling you the way it is."

"What if we move her back to the manor house and get a health aide to come in days? Would that help?"

"That means taking her off life-support measures. I don't think the Judge will agree to that. I know I can't."

"What if someone else made the decision?"

"Like who?"

"Bode. Pearl."

Brie didn't think it was possible for Wyn's face to get any whiter, but it did.

"No, the Judge is the only one who can make the decision. I'm going to suggest she stay where she is for the time being. It's not as though they need the room or anything. I'll pay the bill. They . . . the doctor just spoke to me two days ago. I need time to think, to take it all in. They bend over backward for Pearl, did you know that?"

"I'm glad. This is very hard for her. She's lost a lot of weight, but then so have you. You don't look well, Wyn."

"I find it difficult to eat and sleep."

"Why is that? I'd think you'd be tired with your vigil and all," Brie said coolly.

"I can't turn it off. It's all I think about. Why did this have to happen? Why to us? We're good people."

"What about the Seagreaves? That whole little family was wiped out in a single hour," Brie said callously. "Do you think about them?"

"All the time."

Liar, Brie thought. "I heard about the lawsuit. A hundred million dollars is a lot of money. Did Callie carry anything extra besides the ordinary insurance?"

"She had an umbrella policy tacked on to her auto insurance, but she carried the minimum on her auto policy. The umbrella was a million—three hundred thousand on each occurrence or something like that. Add that up and you're down to ninety-eight million. I've been hesitating on deeding the manor back because the insurance company will snatch it. At some point it might be needed. If Callie comes out of this, I'd like to have it intact for her. I don't mean that the way it sounds. The Seagreave family deserves all they can get, but Callie deserves something, too. Two million dollars is a lot of money. The families are all older people. They won't be able to spend it all before they die," Wyn said desperately.

"Wyn!"

"I know how it sounds. It serves you right, Brie. You asked me why I wasn't eating or sleeping. Now you know why. Be glad you aren't walking in my shoes," Wyn said, his voice blistering.

She didn't feel the least bit sorry for him. "I guess my next question should be, if you don't mind me asking, how long are you prepared to pay Callie's bills? It could be a very long time before she . . . you know."

"I guess my answer would have to be, a little while longer. I'm comfortable, maybe more than comfortable, but I'm not rich in the true sense of being rich. Land rich might be a good way to explain it."

"It was your decision, Wyn." God, she hated this conversation, hated talking about money when Callie wasn't "of this earth" as Pearl put it.

"They've relaxed the rules a lot here. Callie was moved into the back unit since she is no longer listed as critical. I've been afraid to ask how she's listed. I guess if you don't move, you're just there. You can go in if you want."

Tears stung Brie's eyes when she leaned over Callie's bed. She looked exactly the same, thinner though. The machines were the same, whirring and beeping from time to time. The bags looked to be the same. Nutrients, glucose, and something she couldn't pronounce.

"I think you can hear me, Callie. At least I hope so. I have a few days off and decided I wanted to spend it with my family. You guys are my family. As far as I'm concerned, my only family. I have good news. I'm an official FBI agent. I'm going to be based in Atlanta and then I can come here weekends and help out.

"Sela's here. We'll be spending Thanksgiving together. Of course it won't be the same without you and Bode. Maybe by Christmas we'll all be sitting down to dinner and opening gifts together like we used to do.

"Callie, do you remember that scraggly tree Pearl let Bode chop down? We were ten or so, I think. It was one of those tall pines and didn't have enough branches so Bode cut some extra ones and tied them on to the trunk. That was the most god-awful, ugly, yet beautiful tree I ever saw in my life. We spent hours decorating it with our homemade decorations. Bode held you on the chair so you could put the paper angel on the top with a safety pin. It was a big old diaper pin, as I recall. Pearl made us hot chocolate with those tiny marshmallows. Then she prepared us those delicious thick bacon sandwiches spread with butter and ketchup—Bode's favorite. I remember you ate two. Then Sela's mother came to fetch her and Sela said no, she wasn't going home with her. Remember how we all ran to Pearl and hung on to her apron? Sela had guts, even then. I trenched in and wouldn't go either. We all slept in your bed. That night Pearl said Bode could sleep on the blankets on the floor, so Santa Claus would know we were together. You got such grand presents. I know Pearl divided them up for all of us. In later years I often wondered if you minded. That was the best Christmas. This year could be even better than that one if you'd wake up.

"Bode still doesn't know you're here, Callie. I think we should tell him, but Pearl says no. I'm hoping, praying actually, that Bode either comes home for Christmas, calls, or writes. Somehow, I don't think he will. If there was a way to dummy up a card or a call, I'd do it in a heartbeat. If it looks like it's coming down to the wire, I might just fly out to Sante Fe and mail one myself. I know that sounds extreme. Maybe I won't do that at all, maybe something else will come to me. It's just that Christmas is so special to all of us. It's that child part of us we never lose.

"Wait till you hear this. Arquette brought Pearl two frizzly chickens. I've racked my brain to remember what they mean, but can't come up with the answer. I'm afraid to tell Pearl I can't remember. She sets such store by her rituals and whatever else it is she does, I don't want her to know I forgot. Maybe I'll ask Arquette.

"Callie, wake up! Damn you, *open your eyes!* You have to come out of this. Pearl is losing weight. Wyn looks like a cadaver. Try, Callie, move your fingers, blink, do something. You better listen to me, Callie. Your best friend and my friend, too, is going to try and take your place with Pearl. Probably Wyn, too. You can't let that happen. I can't stop her. She's fixing one of the rooms up for herself. She's here for the long haul, Callie. I don't even know if she realizes what it is she's doing, but *I* realize it, and now I've told you. Damn you, Callie, wake up! I don't understand. Even your eyeballs don't move. Where are you, Callie Parker?" Brie demanded, her face tormented.

"You know what else? I know you weren't driving that car. I *know* it! You're being sued for a hundred million dollars. Your insurance is going to run out. Please, Callie, *wake up.*"

Her shoulders slumping, Brie left the room. She nodded to Wyn, who said he would only be a few minutes. His own shoulders drooped when he left the room ten minutes later.

"My whole day is shot to hell when I come early. Usually I come in the evening and allow Pearl the daytime. I have a supper meeting today that will run late, so I wanted to be sure I got here early."

He's whining again, Brie thought.

"Are you going to be here all day?" He sounded like he didn't care one way or another.

"No, I'm leaving. Sela will want to come out. I didn't rent a car this trip."

"What's on your agenda? Just hang out?"

"I thought I'd check out the accident scene again. Something about it bothers me. It's the cop in me," she said airily.

"Good luck," Wyn said just as airily. "If there's anything you want to ask me, just call. It's as fresh in my mind as if it happened yesterday. Unfortunately."

"I think Bode is coming home for Christmas," Brie lied. *Why are you doing this, Brie Canfield? Why are you tormenting this man? Can't you see he's near the breaking point? That's part of it. Some of the hard edges should have dulled by now. He didn't go through the process; it goes in stages. I need to know why that is.*

"Oh, by the way, I'm official now. I'm an FBI agent."

"Congratulations!" Wyn said in a strangled voice.

"Thanks, Wyn," Brie said breezily.

"If I don't see you again before you leave, have a safe trip," Wyn muttered.

Brie nodded. She walked back to Callie's unit, opened the

door, and whispered, "I'm leaving now, Pearl. Sela will bring you back, okay? Wyn left, and said he wouldn't be back today."

"Yes'm, Miz Brie."

When Brie returned to Parker Manor she found Sela grinning from ear to ear. "Just listen, Brie. Doesn't it sound wonderful? Noise. The house is getting a few repairs. If only I was rich, I'd have the whole thing done over from top to bottom."

"You'd do all that for Wyn Archer?" Brie said.

"No, silly. For Pearl, you, and me. Callie, too, if she comes out of her coma, and Bode because we're family. Wyn will give it back. Listen, I won't be here for dinner. Do you think you'll need the car?"

"I can rent one. I guess I should have. Do me a favor, Sela, stop in town and ask them to bring one out. I don't like being without a car. Are you going to bring Pearl back here? I told her you would. I can fetch her if it's going to be a problem. Where are you going that you won't be here for dinner?"

"No, no, I'll bring her home. Wyn arranged a dinner meeting with the owner of this agency he thinks will hire me. I have to get a job as soon as I can. Wyn has a lot of clout around here. I can see you don't approve. Why is that, Brie?" Sela's tone was cool.

"I more or less think of him as the enemy. I'm not sure why that is, Sela. If it was anyone but Wyn Archer, I'd say go for it. That's my opinion. You asked."

"So I did. It was my mistake. Any preference as to the kind of car you want?"

"Anything is okay as long as it has four wheels. Ask them to bring it out as soon as they can. You look nice, Sela. Cranberry looks good on you. I wish I could wear a jumpsuit, but I'm too short." *It fits her like a second skin,* Brie thought nastily.

Brie paced around the kitchen to the sound of Arquette's hammerblows. She had nothing to do, nowhere to go until the rental car arrived. She knew Arquette would lend her his truck, but the frizzly chickens were still in the back, and she wasn't about to move them.

Call Bode, call Bode, call Bode. Why not? She could say she called to wish him a Happy Thanksgiving. She'd done that other years, why not now? She wouldn't say anything unless he asked. "And of course you know he'll ask," she whispered to herself. "You'll be breaking your promise to Pearl if you tell him."

Because she had nothing else to do, Brie called the main post office and asked how she could have mail sent to South Carolina from Santa Fe, New Mexico. It was simple, she was told. You addressed your letter, and put it inside an envelope with a note to the postmaster asking him to post the letter. She felt confident that she could scrawl Bode's signature as well as Bode scrawled it. Since Pearl couldn't read, it would be Sela she had to fool. "I can do it," Brie muttered. If she wanted to she could even buy some silly presents, wrap them, box them up, and have the postmaster mail them, too. Of course there would have to be one for Callie.

Brie fixed herself a bologna-and-cheese sandwich and two for Arquette. She poured huge glasses of iced tea and invited Arquette out to the back porch.

Arquette was a tall, thin man. Stringy, actually. He had the kindest eyes, the sweetest smile she'd ever seen. He was good to Pearl. She made a mental note to buy something nice for Arquette and his family. Maybe money would be better, but Pearl's friend was so very proud, he probably wouldn't take it.

"If you could have anything, Arquette, what would you wish for?" Brie asked lightly. "I'd ask for a moonbeam."

"Anything, Miz Brie?"

"Yep, anything."

"Then I'd be wishing for a wash machine for Coletta. With lots and lots of soap. That woman purely loves to wash clothes. Everything that has the least little speck on it gets washed. I been lookin' at some down at Mortenson's, but they cost too much money. A fortune," he said, his eyes rolling back in his head.

Sears, here I come, Brie thought happily. She'd just paid off her Visa card so she could charge up a storm if she wanted.

"What else, Arquette? Two wishes. My second wish would be for my very own star. What's yours?"

"Maybe a clothes dryer. A e-leck-tric one. I swear Coletta would think she died and went to heaven. Do you think they have wash machines and dry machines in heaven?"

"I bet they do." Brie laughed.

"Bet they have moonbeams and stars in heaven, too." Arquette smiled.

"Pearl's sick, isn't she, Arquette?" Brie said suddenly.

"She be sick over Miz Callie. Seemed right perky to me when you girls got here. I fetched her two frizzly chickens. She be missing Lazarus, too."

"But is *she* sick? I swear I won't tell, Arquette. If she is sick, then we have to do something for her."

"Pearl don't like it when you mess with her business. You best be lettin' that alone, Miz Brie. Miz Sela say she be staying on. It will be good for Pearl. She was pinin' for this here place. I did my best, coming out here, tellin' her what I was doin'. She be real happy today. She home now."

Brie smiled and bent over to hug Arquette. "You're a good friend, Arquette."

"I wish Bode be home," Arquette said, getting up. "Thanks for the lunch, Miz Brie."

"It was my pleasure. I wish Bode was here, too. Maybe he'll come home for Christmas."

"Maybe. Bode is a kind man. He done a lot for us. Done a lot for lots of people. Never talks about what he done. A good man."

"I know, Arquette."

An hour later, Brie's car arrived. She signed the papers and stuck them in her purse.

She had a mission now. She headed out to the highway and the closest Sears store where she picked out a washer and dryer and four fifty-pound boxes of soap powder. She rattled off Arquette's address, which she had copied down from his insurance card in the glove compartment of the truck. She asked to have the appliances delivered on Christmas Eve and to make sure there was a big red ribbon on both machines and the soap powder. The card was to say, *Merry Christmas* and signed *Bode Jessup.*

When Brie exited the store she felt like the cat who not only fell into the cream bowl, but drank it all, too.

From Sears she went to the Bi-Lo and filled the car with groceries. It took her an hour to put everything away.

It was almost dusk when she set out in the car again. She brought all her defensive driving skills into play when she traced the route Wyn and Callie had taken the night of the accident. As she approached the killer curve her heart started to pound in her chest. It sounded to her ears like Arquette's hammerblows. She was crazy to try and pull a stunt like this, but the conditions were exactly right. She was going at forty-five miles an hour, the same speed Wyn had said Callie was going. She felt in control as she approached the curve, her eyes on the car at the stop sign to her left. She almost squeezed her eyes shut at the last second before she crossed the curve dead center with Carroll Court. The vehicle at the stop sign was moving as he let loose with a long blast of his horn. She roared across the curve, her breathing ragged. She was shaking so badly she could hardly get her cigarette to her lips. It hung between her lips because she couldn't steady the lighter.

What in the hell had she just proved, if anything? That the car at the stop sign missed her by a hair. If she'd been hit broadside, that had to mean she was crossing the curve. If she was continuing on Route 17, she would have been hit in the rear of the driver's side. At which point, either way, the car should have spun out of control and done what? Hit the angel oak? Which side? At what point was Callie propelled out of the car? When the Bronco hit the Cadillac, or on impact with the oak?

Brie climbed out of the car, the cigarette dangling between her lips. With her headlights on she could see the damage to the oak. She walked around a bit before she located the exact place Wyn said Callie had landed. Landed. What a terrible word. Did doors on fancy Cadillacs that were almost new just pop open on the driver's side? Why didn't the seat belt work on the passenger side? Wyn should have been the one who was thrown out. Callie should have remained in the car and maybe suffered some injuries.

She was back in the car. She fired up her cigarette from the car lighter. Her hands still trembled. She hadn't really proved anything by the harebrained stunt she'd just pulled. She could have killed herself and maybe the people in the car that blew their horn at her. God!

Brie turned on the engine and drove down the gravel road till she found a place to turn around. Minutes later she was back on 17 and headed toward Parker Manor.

Callie wasn't driving the car. She could sense it, smell it, feel it. "I will never, ever believe Callie Parker was driving

Wyn Archer's Cadillac on the night of the accident," she muttered.

Proving it was another matter.

*Brie Canfield, you are an irresponsible cop. Nobody in her
right mind would do what you just did. That makes you a
fool. If I'd proved my case would I still be irresponsible,
would I still be a fool? Yes, yes, yes.*

If she had had a tail, it would have been between her legs
when she let herself into the kitchen.

Pearl was standing by the stove stirring a pan full of peppers and onions. Sausage and peppers for dinner, her favorite. She'd meant to return earlier and cook herself. Instead
she'd been out playing cop, and Pearl was doing dinner. She
ran to her and blurted out what she'd just done.

Pearl cradled her in her arms while she murmured soothing words of comfort. "It's all right, Miz Brie. You didn't
cause no harm and you was only trying to do good for my
baby. The Lord won't hold that agin you. You listen to Pearl
now. I'm fixing your favorite supper. You wash up and go
look at what Arquette done for Miz Sela."

Brie blew her nose in a paper napkin that Pearl handed
her. "He was driving that car, Pearl. I know it."

"I knowed it, too, Miz Brie. That's why I gave him pain
and sorrow."

"You know what, Pearl? You need to give him another
dose," Brie cried.

Sela risked a look at her watch. It was after nine. For some
reason she thought the quick bite Wyn had suggested would
have been over by eight and she'd be back at the manor
house by eight-thirty. Now it was nine-thirty and Wyn was
suggesting they go over to the hotel for a nightcap. She really
didn't want a nightcap. What she wanted to do was rush

home to Pearl and Brie and tell them she had got the job and would be starting in two days. She wanted to see Pearl beam her pleasure and have Brie clap her on the back. But Wyn looked so sad, so woebegone, she didn't have the heart to tell him no, she wanted to go home.

"It will have to be a quick one, Wyn. I've only had a few hours' sleep in three days, and don't forget I spent over fourteen hours on the road yesterday. I'm not as young as I used to be," she trilled.

"I understand. Tonight was pleasant. I enjoyed your company. I knew Stan and his partner would take you on in a minute once they saw you. It's just that I hate going back to the motel. I've been thinking of going home to Beaufort. What do you think, Sela?"

"I think that first part sounded like a sexist remark. Are you saying I got hired because of the way I look? If Brie was here, she'd punch your lights out for a remark like that. Yes, I think you should go back to Beaufort. Motels aren't meant to be lived in. It's foolish for you and even Pearl, to sit at the hospital twelve and fourteen hours a day. You look terrible, Wyn. I think you need to fall back and regroup."

Wyn snorted his disdain as he held the door of his brand-new Cadillac for Sela to get in. "Buckle up," he ordered curtly. Settled behind the wheel, he said, "Isn't that why you wore that outfit? It looks to me like someone poured you into it. I'm not saying it's unbecoming. Men like to look . . . What they like to see is . . ."

"Sexy women." Sela chuckled. "And since I'm going to be selling commercial real estate I will be dealing mostly with men. Whatever it takes, Wyn. That's how I look at it."

"It's going to be interesting to see you tramping fields in spike-heeled shoes and tight pants." Wyn smiled.

In the hotel, he guided Sela to the bar and ordered Perrier

for himself. "The same," Sela said. "I'm driving. I can't believe we're both drinking water."

"There's a lot of things I can't believe lately." Wyn sounded morose.

"Things will get better—because they can't get any worse," Sela said cheerfully.

"Of course they can get worse. Callie could die," Wyn said flatly.

"That's a possibility, but surely it helps if you think positively. Everything happens for a reason, Wyn. So, you think it was wrong of me to wear this jumpsuit, huh?"

"Maybe inappropriate is the word."

"You said we were going to Shoney's. Casual attire is okay there. Then you switched up on me, and it was too late to go home and change. I got the job, so what's the difference? Oh, I get it. You're comparing me to Callie. Let me put it this way. Callie was prim and proper—*is* prim and proper. She likes little round collars and dimity. Peter Pan–ish look. Brie is sporty. She likes comfort. I prefer elegance and style. That's why we're different people. There's nothing wrong with any of us. It helps to make us who we are. Like Bode. I don't think he even owns a suit. Maybe a sport jacket. Sometimes clothes make the man and sometimes they don't. You take Kallum now. I've never seen that man look anything but perfect. I often wonder how he does it. You always look nice, Wyn," she added as an afterthought. "Listen, I'd like to finish this drink, but you need to take me back to pick up my car. I told you I should have followed you. Now we both have to go out of our way."

"I don't have anything else to do," Wyn said.

"I feel bad about that, Wyn. Life goes on. Try and make the effort."

"I will. Thanks for coming with me. Listen, would it be out of line for me to take you to dinner over the weekend?"

"I don't see why it would be. We're friends. We'll probably spend the whole evening talking about Callie or playing, Do You Remember? I have to tell you, sometimes I hate that game."

"Me too. Pearl and Brie might have something to say about our meeting."

"Then I won't tell them. I'm my own person, Wyn. Remember that."

It was ten minutes past eleven when Sela walked into the kitchen. Her eyes narrowed at what she saw. Brie was chopping celery and onions and Pearl was cubing bread for the stuffing that would go into the turkey. They were both laughing as Brie wiped at her eyes. Sela looked around to see if there was something she could do. She asked.

"Pearl and I have it under control," Brie told her, still giggling. "Why don't you sit down and watch—you do that best. Or you could go and see what Arquette did to *your* room. It's not finished—and guess what: you're going to have to sleep on that scratchy couch because there's Sheetrock dust all over your room. Where the hell have you been?"

"Now, *that's* the Brie I know and love, nasty and mean. I got the job. I start in two days—Saturday!"

"That's nice, Miz Sela."

"Congratulations," Brie said. "I hope you make a lot of money."

"I expect to. Commissions are higher on commercial real estate."

"Better buy a pair of snake boots. You'll probably be able to write them off. You know how you hate snakes."

"They're on my list," Sela snapped. "Listen, I'm going to put on my pajamas and help."

"Where were you, Sela?" Brie asked again.

"Oscar's. Then I stopped at the hotel with Wyn and had a drink. Don't look at me like that, we both had Perrier. Wyn didn't want to go back to the motel. I told him I thought it was time for him to return to Beaufort to get on with his life. I thought . . . it would be good for Pearl if she didn't have to see him so much. He does need to get on with life. We all do," Sela said defensively. "Go on, say it. You think I screwed up."

"I told you how I feel about Wyn. You know how Pearl feels. You eat with him and drink with him. Should I consider that betrayal, Sela?"

"You're full of it, Brie. He helped me get this job, that is all. I didn't see anyone else pounding on the door. No one else offered."

"You get off it. He's the only one you asked. Now, why is that, Sela?"

"He's the one with the most clout," Sela snapped.

"If you'd gone to the Judge and told him Bode sent you, he'd have had something lined up in an hour. Bet you didn't think about that, huh?"

"As a matter of fact, I didn't. Look, I'm only going to say this one more time. Until you can *prove* Wyn was responsible for Callie's accident, I'm going to keep an open mind."

"That's your problem, Sela, your mind is so open, nothing can stay in it. And don't you worry one little bit—I *am* going to prove Wyn had something to do with that accident. Another thing I don't want you to forget is that I'm an FBI agent and what that means to you, Sela, is that I will have the best minds, the best techniques, the best of everything, at my disposal. One last thing," Brie hissed. "If I ever find out you talk to him about us, meaning Pearl and me and Bode, I will personally slice off your silicone tits. Remember that."

"You girls stop fussing now and get on with your slicing, and I mean celery and onions," Pearl said.

Sela flounced off down the hall. Brie winked at Pearl, who turned her head so her grin wouldn't be seen.

"He's a dickweed," Brie mumbled.

Pearl frowned, rolled the word over her tongue. "What is that, Miz Brie?"

"It's sort of like a jerk only a hundred times worse," Brie muttered.

"It don't sound to me like a proper word. Shame on you, Miz Brie. Dickweed."

"Who's a dickweed?" came Sela's voice from the doorway.

Instead of answering her, Brie said, "I didn't know they still made satin pajamas. Where'd you get them? Wait, let me guess. They're Hugh Hefner's castoffs."

"Stuff it, Brie. What do you want me to do?"

"Peel the sweet potatoes and let them soak in cold water. Pick through the cranberries and wash them. But first, why don't you make us some coffee?"

"Look, I'm sorry, okay? I can see your point. Be fair and look at my point. I'm not a cop, Brie. I don't think like you. I go by what I see and hear. Let's start over, okay?"

"Sure. Sela, please don't tell Wyn what we talk about."

"I won't. Don't look at me like that, Brie. If I say I won't do something, I won't do it. Can't you trust me?"

"Yeah, yeah, I'm sorry, Sela. We need to stop snapping at each other. We're a family here. We're all we have. I've said my last thing to you, Sela. You know where I stand and how I feel. You know how Pearl feels. We pretty much know how you feel. What I'm trying to say is let's not spoil what we have."

"Hear, hear!" Sela said, holding the coffeepot aloft. "Thanks, Brie. I mean that."

"How about you taking a crack at these onions? My tear ducts are about wiped out."

"My pleasure. I just love stuffing. I can make a meal on it alone as long as I have gravy to pour over it. All the other stuff is good, too. I'm going to pig out and then I'll watch what I eat afterward," Sela said happily.

"I wish Bode was here. Callie, too, of course. It's not going to be the same," Brie mourned.

"We need to be giving thanks that things ain't worse than they are," Pearl said.

"Amen," Sela trilled.

"I think we should call Bode and wish him a Happy Thanksgiving. I do it every year. In fact, I've never missed a year. I always called Callie, too. So did you, Sela. Pearl, don't you think we should call?"

"No, chile, I don't. Bode will most prob'ly come for Christmas."

Brie crossed her fingers. "Maybe he will, Pearl. Let's count on it."

"Bode knows how much we love Christmas. He'll come," Sela said breezily. "He won't disappoint us."

Bode proved them all wrong.

13

"I didn't know you owned blue jeans," Brie said at breakfast. "Boots too. Hmmmn. And a shearling jacket. Isn't that a waste of money down here? We only get a few really cold days during the winter. I'm making breakfast—what will you have?"

"Just coffee. I have a breakfast meeting. Listen, I won't be home until late. I'm going up to Columbia, and I might get held up, so don't wait supper for me. This jacket, smartypants, is from New York. I used to wear it all the time in the winter. In case you haven't checked, it's damn cold out today. Forty degrees when I looked." Sela yawned and peered out of the window.

"Hey, check out the camellias," she went on. "I swear every single one is in bloom. Do you want me to pick a bouquet before I leave? They might brighten up Callie's room. God, I can't believe how beautiful this place is when they flower. When you tell people up North that camellias bloom here in cold weather, they look at you like you're from another planet. Oh, one last thing—a photographer called and wanted to know if he could come out here and take some pictures of the garden for the Sunday paper. I said it was okay. Don't get spooked if you see someone strange. Thanks for the coffee, it was good," Sela said, backing out of the door. A moment later she stuck her head in again, and asked, "Did you have any luck with Pearl? Will she see a doctor? Are we going to call Bode?"

"No to everything, so far, but today's another day. Pearl isn't up yet. That worries me. She's always up with the chickens."

"Maybe she has a hag on her head this morning. You know what to do—just get the colander and put it under her bed. Gotta run."

Wyn was waiting in a booth when Sela walked into Shoney's. She waved airily, removing her jacket at the same time. The cashmere sweater, another holdover from her New York marriage when her husband paid the bills, was form-fitting, outlining her breasts. Every man in the restaurant turned to look at her skintight jeans. Wyn grinned when she slipped into the seat opposite him.

"So, Wynfield Archer, what are your plans for the day?" she asked nonchalantly.

"I have a mind to play hookey today. Like you, I'm wearing casual clothes. I can do anything—look at property, find an ice-skating rink, or climb a tree. I even have a tie in my pocket in case I find a fancy restaurant that requires one. I have a yen to get in the car and just drive. We could get on the highway and head up to Myrtle Beach if you like the idea. Didn't you say you had a client interested in property for a golf course? There's lots of golfing in Myrtle Beach. What do you say—want to play hookey with me?"

"I'd be delighted. I've been working my tail off, and I need a break. Providing the whole damn town doesn't hear about it. It wouldn't surprise me a bit to learn that they know all about our . . . meeting. I didn't tell Brie or Pearl I was contemplating this. Their minds are pretty closed when it comes to you."

"They won't hear it from me," Wyn said. "Tell you what,

when we leave here let's drive separately to the Holiday Inn and you can leave your car there. We've done it before so there's no problem."

"Sounds good to me. I'm starved." To the hovering waitress Sela said, "Two scrambled eggs, extra crisp bacon, two buckwheat pancakes on a separate plate. Warm the syrup, please. Two slices of whole-wheat toast. A large orange juice and coffee now."

"I'll have the same," Wyn said, his eyebrows shooting upward. "Do you eat like this all the time?"

"Only when someone else is paying the bill. I either eat lunch or breakfast; I never eat both. So, Wyn, how's it all going?"

"Will everything I say find its way back to Parker Manor? Do I have to weigh each word? If so, this little foray is going to be a real downer."

"You don't have to worry about me, Wyn. I know when to open my mouth and when to keep it closed. Let's talk, over breakfast, about all the stuff we won't talk about today, okay?"

"Sure. What do you want to ask me?"

"Nothing really. Well, maybe a few things. Have you seen Callie since you . . . put her in that awful place. It *is* awful, Wyn."

"I stopped in to see her late last night. The place is not picture pretty, but it's not dirty. They have plenty of help. Callie is being seen to. Her room sparkles, and I know that's thanks to Pearl. Nothing has changed. Actually, it's rather cheerful. I was told Pearl's friend Arquette took over a comfortable chair for Pearl. There were flowers on the windowsill, and Arquette's wife sent over a braided rug. The bedspread on the bed is all kinds of colors. The room doesn't look like a room in a convalescent home."

"What will happen if, say, Pearl can't take care of Callie anymore? She's getting old, Wyn."

"It's one of those situations where we have to wait and see. I'll do my best for Callie. I can't help it if you don't approve.

"Was Callie canceling the wedding because of Bode?" Wyn asked quietly.

"I don't know, Wyn. What I do know is she was very upset that you didn't tell her about Bode's going-away luncheon. The Judge was offended with her for not attending. Then there was Bode himself, who wasn't going to be at the reception and the wedding. The job he promised her didn't materialize. Maybe it was a lot of things. It was possible she needed time to think things through. Callie was never one to take any kind of change without making a fuss. She liked everything to stay the same—no surprises. God, how she hated going North to college. We talked so much, over the phone, in the beginning. Callie never wanted to hang up, and she always cried when we said goodbye. I know she spent her whole allowance on her phone bill."

"Callie was so fragile, so loving, so loyal," Wyn said sadly.

"She was all those things, I agree. Sometimes she acted impulsively, but when that happened she worked doubly hard to make up for whatever she thought she did wrong. It was a surprise to me, Wyn, when Pearl told us Callie was canceling the wedding. Apparently her mind was made up. She wasn't just mouthing words."

"I think it was because of Bode," he said.

"You really hate him, don't you?"

"Hate is a very strong word. I don't like him. Now that I think back, all Callie did was talk about Bode. It was Bode said this or we had to do it Bode's way. He was the best at everything. Callie said everyone loved Bode. It appears to be true. Judge Summers thinks Bode Jessup is a one-of-a-kind saint. I believe he stays in touch with Bode."

Sela felt the fine hairs on the back of her neck stand on end. "What makes you say that?" she asked, chewing on her bacon.

"It was an impression, nothing specific. Miss Nela babbles a lot from time to time. Bode made for good table conversation. Both the Judge and Miss Nela were very good to me while Callie was in the hospital."

"They're very kind people," Sela nodded. "I know for a fact that Bode absolutely adored Judge Summers. I believe the feeling was reciprocated. It made for a good relationship. Bode is a good man, Wyn. I would never, ever, say one bad word against Bode Jessup." She was stunned at how fierce her voice sounded.

"I don't get it. He's black. As children I could see that not mattering. But now you're grown, there's a difference."

"To whom? That's about as racist as you can get. I'm ashamed of you, Wyn. I mean it. People are people. Why does it have to matter what color they are? I love Bode as much as if he were my brother. I love Pearl more than life itself. I never, I swear, *ever* thought of them as different. They're my family, and don't you forget it."

"I was raised one way, and you were raised another," Wyn said defensively. *"Those people* have their place, and I have mine."

"Thank God the rest of the world doesn't think like you," Sela snapped. "Nobody should be relegated to *a place*. This is just my opinion, but I think you cannot bear the thought that Callie preferred a black man over you. That's what you can't come to terms with. That's what you *think*, but none of us can prove it for a fact. Even if it's true, so what? Does this mean our hookey playing is canceled?"

"Only if you want it to be."

Sela studied the man across from her. "I guess it takes all kinds of people to make up the world. You know how I feel, and I know how you feel. I'm not going to change. How about you?"

"I can try."

"Do you mean that?"

"Yes. I can't make you a promise that I'm going to fall in love with Bode Jessup overnight. I've got years of . . . whatever it is I have to get through before I can reach where you and Brie are. I will try, though, you have my word."

"Brie doesn't think much of your word; neither does Pearl. I can't speak for Bode, but I can imagine what he thinks."

"Then why are you here?" Wyn asked sourly.

"I don't honestly know. I'm my own person. I'm pretty upfront, Wyn. Until someone can prove to me you were responsible for that accident, I'm prepared to take you at your word."

"Doesn't that cause a rift in your relationship with the others?"

"At times we get testy with one another, sure, but we accept one another for who and what we are. That's why our friendship has lasted all these years. We'll always be close, like a family should be close. I think we've talked this to death, don't you?"

"Pretty much so. You were Callie's best friend. She spoke about you a lot. Oh, she loved Brie, too; but you were special to her. She said you had guts and spunk and weren't afraid to experience life. She told me once you could climb a tree faster than the others."

"That's because Brie and I didn't mind getting scabs on our knees. Bode showed us how to shinny up a tree. Callie was afraid to go above the second branch. She never had bumps or bruises. When I look back now I think of Brie and myself as the two black-and-blue kids. Bode always wore jeans so he didn't get scraped like we did. Pearl used to put Mercurochrome on us. Iodine sometimes, too. We were always half-orange from something or other. I remember once she painted us with this purple stuff. Whatever it was, it fixed us up real good." Sela gurgled. "Pearl always knew what to do to make things better. Bode did, too."

"Are you ready?"

"Guess so. I want to stop in the ladies' room while you pay the check. I'll meet you back at the Holiday Inn, okay?"

"Sure."

It was a fun day even though it was cold and raw. They laughed and told jokes, held hands as they ran along the beach, and giggled like youngsters when Wyn bought a pound of peanut-butter fudge and two hot chocolates. They devoured all of it, moaning and groaning about waistlines.

"Listen, we can either go out to dinner or we can go over to a condo I have on the beach. I keep a fairly well stocked freezer there, and I can cook a little. We can light a fire, have some wine and we'll be back in Summerville by eleven. Your call, Sela."

"Right now, this minute, I'll do anything to get warm. Let's go to the condo. Callie didn't say anything about you having a place here."

"She didn't much care for it. She said it was like something out of a magazine and didn't feel comfortable in it. I had a decorator do it, and I think she got carried away. I always take my shoes off by the door. Yellow carpet." He winced.

"Let's dirty it up." Sela grinned. "My boots are full of mud. Do you have satin bedspreads and drapes that match the carpet, and furniture that looks like it's not to be sat on?"

"Unfortunately, yes." Sela hooted with laughter.

"What are you going to cook for us?" This is nice, she thought, being with a man who's a friend, enjoying each other's company. Wyn was fun when he forgot to be serious. They'd hardly talked about Callie at all since breakfast.

"Probably steak. You can put a frozen steak under the broiler. I have a grill on the deck, too, if you prefer a charcoal flavor. I also have some frozen vegetables. I used to go there after work on a Friday night when I first bought it, and cook when I got there. When Callie said she felt uncomfortable I stopped coming. Someone goes in once a month or so and airs it out and dusts it up. I've been thinking of selling it."

"Beachfront property should bring a pretty penny," Sela said.

"Spoken like a true real-estate agent. Do you know anyone who might be interested?"

"I might."

"Then the commission is all yours. We're here. What do you think?" Wyn asked as he steered the car into the carport.

"It looks nice from the outside. When you said condo I thought you meant high-rise. These are just two floors. I think I like this better. Which floor is yours?"

"Both."

"Then that makes it a town house, not a condo."

"My papers refer to it as a condo," Wyn said tartly.

"Okay, okay. How many square feet?"

"Eighteen hundred, I think. Three bathrooms."

"Ooohhh, this is *nice*," Sela said. "I like this tile in the foyer. I didn't know there were foyers in condos. Guess you can do whatever you want if you're willing to pay for it, right?"

"Look around. I'll turn up the heat and make a fire. If you're really cold you can take a shower. Callie has some clothes here. I don't know if you—"

"No, thanks. I'll get warm once the heat comes up. A glass of wine would be nice. In front of the fire."

Wyn was right, the place looked like no one had ever lived in it. There were no knickknacks, nothing personal on any of the tables. The prints on the wall were standard ocean scenes and dunes. Everything seemed to be a mix of green and yellow or "Florida colors" as she called them. The furniture was excellent-quality white wicker. The tables, and there were many, all had glass tops with lamps to match the green-and-yellow furnishings. The bedroom was done in satin. Satin bedspread, satin drapes, satin coverings on the chaise longues. The television was white. She frowned. She'd never seen a white television set before.

Sela peeked into the bathroom. Yellow sink, tub, and toilet. A green-and-yellow shower curtain with a harlequin design almost blinded her when she noticed it matched the patterned towels and carpet on the floor.

This was definitely not a man's condo. Then again, maybe it was. She remembered the hideous bridesmaids' dresses Wyn had chosen. "No taste," she muttered.

When she returned to the living room, Wyn was holding two wine flutes. The fire was blazing, and the lamps had been turned on. She kicked off her boots and watched them sail across the room. "This carpet is to die for. It must be six inches thick—almost as good as a mattress," she giggled as she accepted her wine. "What should we drink to?"

"Whatever you like."

"How about me selling this condo for you?"

"Fine. How do you like your steak?"

"Walking. Bloody rare."

"I like mine that way, too. Callie liked hers charred—so well done you couldn't tell what kind of meat it was."

"What *did* you two have in common?" Sela asked.

"I really don't feel like talking about Callie. Let's talk about you. What is it you're looking for out of life?"

"A good life, I guess. One where I don't have to bust my ass twenty-four hours a day. Eventually I'd like to get married again to someone I'm compatible with. I'm not sure about children—I don't know if I'm mother material. Of course, that might change if I find a man I can't live without. How about you, Wyn?"

"How about me?" He grimaced. "I don't see myself getting

married now. I plan to go into politics at some point, perhaps next year. What was your marriage like?" he asked.

"A nightmare. I was too young, too inexperienced to get married. Half of it was my fault. I get depressed when I think about it."

"How about Brie?"

"She's been in a few relationships that didn't work. Brie is . . . I'm not sure. I always kind of thought she was in love with Bode, and no one else could measure up. She'd never do anything about it, though—you know, act on it, because we both thought Bode was in love with Callie. Now, Wyn, that doesn't mean Callie was in love with Bode. Callie would never cross over that racial line. Never."

"Would you? Would Brie?"

"I don't know. Why are we talking about this?"

Wyn shrugged. "Conversation, I guess."

"Well, let's talk about something else. Did you find out about that property adjoining Callie's?"

"Yes, I asked the Judge yesterday. He told me one of the heirs lives in the outback in Australia and is not interested in selling. Seems you aren't the first agent to try and sell that property. Guess you're going to have to find another parcel for your golf course."

"That's the problem. There are no other parcels except for Callie's. I found one over on Highway 61, but Heywood said he didn't like it. Actually what he said was it wasn't suitable. He pretty much told me I could name my price if I came up with the right property. He's willing to go as high as a hundred and fifty thousand dollars an acre. Maybe more if the squeeze is put on him. Do you know what that would mean to me personally? Megabucks," she said, her eyes sparkling. "God, what I couldn't do with money like that."

"Money's important to you, isn't it?"

"Since I never had any, yes. I wasn't born with a silver spoon in my mouth like some people."

Sela was on her fifth glass of wine when she said, "What will you do with Callie's property if . . . if she doesn't come out of her coma?"

"I don't know. I haven't thought about it. That's a damn ghoulish question to ask me."

"It's a realistic question, Wyn," Sela said from her cocoon in front of the fireplace. "Whatever possessed you to get brocade cushions? They scratch. Did you and Callie make love here in front of the fireplace?"

"I don't think that's any of your business, Sela," Wyn said tightly.

"C'mon, sure it is. That's why you suggested we come here. You want to have sex with me. Guess what, I want to have sex with you, too," Sela said, slurring her words.

"I'll leave the decision up to you and you're wrong, that's not why I came here. I just don't want to go home, and you are good company."

"Does that mean you don't want to have sex with me?"

"I didn't say that . . . You've had too much to drink, and that's my fault. I'm going to make some coffee and then we're heading back home. Give me the glass, Sela."

"Come and get it," Sela trilled as she rolled away from him, the pinkish wine spilling and beading up on the yellow carpet. "Oh shit," she muttered.

Wyn reached down to take the glass from her hand. One minute he was on his two feet, the next he was on top of Sela. "Bet you didn't think I was that strong, huh?" she said, removing her hand from his waist. "Sorry about that wine flute. Don't you get good luck if you smash a wineglass into the fireplace?"

"That's only in the movies," Wyn said hoarsely.

"Shhh," Sela said, placing her finger over his quivering lips.

Everything happened at once. Her finger came away from his lips, then the tight cashmere sweater was lying next to him on the floor, along with a lacy bra. He stared as she leaned over him balanced on one hand, the other working the jeans down over her hips. He watched, mesmerized, as her flowered panties followed. He felt a tickle of delight when he realized she wasn't going to remove the thick, red wool socks. And then he was breathing so hard he thought he'd come in his Jockeys.

Moments later he was undressed, wearing only *his* socks. He had one brief second to wonder if there was something symbolic about wearing socks if you were going to have sex.

"There's nothing I like better than a hard man under me," Sela said lazily. "Hmmmn, that feels *sooo* good." She giggled then and said something she probably never would have said if she'd been sober. "I had no idea you had such a big dick. Give it to me, Wyn, every inch of it. Now!"

"How do you want it?" Wyn hissed in her ear as he flipped her over onto her back. "Talk dirty to me."

"Faster than a speeding bullet and don't stop for anything, and if you can get your balls in there, that's fine, too. Oh God," she moaned. "You have the biggest damn cock in Summerville. What about my tits? My tits, damn you. Don't you know how to do it? You fuck me and suck my tits at the same time. Just do it," she groaned, undulating under him.

They were a pretzel, contortionists, her fingers sluicing around his balls, his mouth trying to cover her nipples.

"Oooohhh, faster, quick, faster, faster. Oh God, oh God, I'm exploding!"

"*Jesus Christ!*" Wyn bellowed at the top of his lungs.

"Was that good or what!" Sela demanded, her breathing ragged.

"Where did you learn to do *that?*"

"You mean that part where I—"

"Yeah, yeah, that's the part."

"I listen to other people. I read a lot. You liked it, didn't you?" Sela grinned. "Bet Callie never did that. She was straight missionary, right?"

He ignored the question and bent over until her dusky nipple was in his mouth again. His hand moved down to the flat of her stomach. "Tell me what you want," he whispered.

"What I want is for you to fill me with the essence of your body. I want to feel you slide in and out of me. I want you to drive me to the brink, return and do it again and again until I cry for mercy. Then you fuck me, hard and fast like before. What do you want me to do to you?" she whispered.

"Everything. Suck me until my cock falls off. Let me lick you till my tongue is raw. I want you to get on top of me and fuck my brains out."

"Then let's get started," Sela drawled. "Shall I begin?"

"Jesus, yes," Wyn said, lying back against the pillows.

"You got it, big juggernaut. Close your eyes and let Sela work some magic."

"It's not necessary to be *that* gentle," Wyn whispered.

"I'll keep it in mind."

It was ten minutes to midnight when Wyn hobbled out to the car, Sela hobbling behind him.

"I'll never be the same," Wyn muttered. "How about you?"

"Women bounce back real easy." Sela laughed. "I think I can truly say I've never been fucked with such . . . precision, such vitality, such . . . abandon. I loved every minute of it. Of course, we aren't going to do this ever again, right?" she said, buckling her seat belt.

"Right," Wyn said.

"We're such liars." Sela grinned. "How about Saturday evening? I can drive to Beaufort or I can meet you at the Holiday Inn. Give the servants the night off if it's Beaufort. You tend to get a bit rowdy."

Wyn doubled over laughing. "You got it, Miss Hotpants. Were you serious about my dick being the biggest one you'd ever seen?"

"Yep." No need to tell him she'd only ever seen three of any importance in her life and the first guy couldn't really get it up so his didn't count. The second guy's was a thin stick that didn't do a thing for her. The third was her husband, who didn't know what he was supposed to do with it except jerk off before it got to the good part. The babies in high school simply didn't count.

"I'll count the hours," Wyn said.

"Me too."

"I could do this every day," Wyn said.

"Me too."

"Then let's do it. Tomorrow. Let's not wait for Saturday."

"Okay. Call me with the time and the place." Sela laughed.

14

Bode Jessup scrawled his signature in five different places. "Congratulations, Bode, you are now a homeowner. You get to mow the lawn, fix the drains, clean the gutters, and polish your own windows. No one around here does windows. How's it feel?" Hatch cackled.

"Overwhelming. Just tell me why I need a four-thousand-square-foot house. Who in the hell is going to clean it? How'd I let you talk me into this?" Bode said, accepting a ring of keys.

"It's a good tax write-off. You need some new roots, and you can't put down roots in a condo or apartment. You need walking-around room. We have great star-spangled nights. Think about yourself sitting outside in your hot tub with a cold frosty beer, looking up at the stars. You might get married someday, and you want to be able to offer your bride comfort. Women love houses and fireplaces. Kitchens too. Bet you didn't know that. They also like bathrooms. They match the towels to the tile and stuff like that. They put artificial flowers in little baskets behind the toilet. I saw that in a decorating book." Hatch guffawed. Bode offered up his middle finger. Hatch threw back his head and laughed again.

"Did you call the girls or Mama Pearl to tell them?" Hatch asked slyly.

"No. I'm going to call tonight. From my new house using my new phone while my new television is turned to mute."

"Why don't you go home for Thanksgiving, Bode? We're pretty slow around the end of November, and December is nothing more than clients dropping by with grateful gifts. You should plan now on going back for the holidays. Have you given it any thought?"

"Some," Bode said, bouncing the keys from one hand to the other. "I have an arbitration hearing the Monday after Thanksgiving. I need to prepare. Maybe next year."

"Guess that means you haven't talked to your family, huh?"

"They're never home. I haven't figured out yet why that is."

"You ever hear of the postal system? They deliver mail. Usually it takes three days and then you get a letter back. Great system—I use it all the time. When's your housewarming? I want to mark it on my calendar. You get all kinds of shitty gifts you have to hide and pull out every time you entertain. It's an experience."

"I'll let you know." Bode grinned in spite of himself. "What kind of gift do you usually give?"

"Me? Yellow fuzzy blankets. The big, thick kind you snuggle in. Two. I always give two. Tell me the truth, Bode, are you all right with this house thing?"

"Yeah, sure. I'm on my way. Guess I need to stop by the market and get some food. My first dinner in my new house."

Hatch snorted. "What kind of *schlock* outfit do you think this is? Your fridge is stocked, your dinner is in the oven. The wine is chilling. Get the hell out of here before it burns," he said, clapping him on the back.

Twenty minutes later Bode walked into his four-thousand-square-foot house. The last time he'd been there it was empty. Now, thanks to Hatch and an interior decorator, it was in his face, so to speak. His mouth open, he walked around, peering, staring, gawking. Mama Pearl would probably swoon if she saw this pad. He found himself grinning as he imagined holding Pearl's hand and walking her through the door. "Lordy, Lordy, Bode, this is so grand. Do all the judges live like this?" And then when he told her it had nothing to do with being a judge she'd gather him close and whisper, "I am so very proud of you, chile. Pearl's old heart jest wants to bust right out of her chest with proudness." Her eyes would water, she'd give him a smacking kiss that he would return, and they'd walk arm in arm all over the house. The only problem was, it wasn't going to happen. Pearl was with Callie. She'd never been outside of the state of South Carolina. Hell, she'd never been outside of Dorchester County so the chances of her coming to New Mexico had to be one in about ninety trillion.

Bode sat down on a monster couch at least eight feet long. Hatch must have picked it out and measured it with his own body. It was soft, sucking him into the depths. A curl-in-the-corner, swallow-me-into-sleep couch. It was beige with dark chocolate threads running through it. A man's couch. What else? After all, this was a bachelor pad.

And what would Brie say? Bode kicked off his sneakers, watched them sail out and land in front of his fireplace. She'd say, "You have the fireplace, I'll bring the popcorn." They'd snuggle in this big couch and laugh at some zany show on television. The screen was so big it felt like he was in the movies, even with its blank face staring at him. He reached over for the remote and pressed the power button. Jenny Craig in her white suit was saying something about weight loss. He got up, turned his back on the room, and started to explore.

The house had everything: stereo throughout, wet bars,

concealed refrigerators and one that hung on a wall, a slim-line of some sort. It was all so homey, so earthy and yet cheerful at the same time. He wondered how that could be with just him living in the house. The dining room was large, the furniture heavy and masculine-looking. The decorator had gone easy on the flowers and plants, thank God. The kitchen was state of the art with every appliance known to man. Copper gleamed; herbs nestled in little clay pots dotted around the windowsills. A fireplace that backed into the dining room went all the way up through the raised ceiling. He could roast a whole pig in it if he wanted to. A laundry room as big as two bedrooms beckoned him. It wasn't that he was into washers, dryers, ironing boards, and double sinks; it was the noise he heard from the corner where the hot-water heater stood.

He saw it then, Hatch's housewarming gift. He dropped to his haunches and grinned from ear to ear. "Heyyyy, little guy, what's your name?" The bow on the golden retriever was bigger than he was and bright red. A gift card was tied to the end of the ribbon.

His name is Harry. He looked like a Harry to me. Of course, you can change it if you want. By now he's probably hungry. Medusa mixed up a special concoction for him. It's in the green bowl in the fridge. I personally guarantee, old buddy, that this little creature will love you unconditionally, sleep on your bed, be your best friend in the whole world, and before the week is out he'll piss in your sneakers. It will be his way of claiming you. He just left his mother, he's six weeks old today. Medusa has written you instructions if he doesn't eat the mess she fixed. The old rubber-glove teat, if you know what I mean. Remember to warm everything in your brand-new microwave. The card was signed *Hatch.*

Bode picked up the little dog, who was shaking so badly that he opened his shirt and placed him next to his heart. The animal calmed almost immediately. "So, Harry, let's see what we can find for you to eat."

An hour later Bode sat back on his butt to survey his new kitchen. The dog's food was everywhere because Harry had stepped in his bowl and tracked it all over the tile as he looked for his mother and siblings. His water dish was flowing to the four corners of the room. His whiskers were full of glop that he wiped on Bode's pants, but he was game, he kept going back to the dish hoping for a nipple. Unsure of how much his new dog really ate, Bode poked his finger into the pablumlike food and let the dog suck off it. Stepping in the mess, he rinsed the dog off in the sink, then wrapped him in a burnt orange hand towel. He opened his shirt again, and within minutes the little animal was asleep. Bode moved carefully as he mopped and cleaned, trying not to disturb his pet. He could hardly wait to finish so he could call the girls and Mama Pearl. Brie would scream in delight. Sela would say, "Who's going to clean up after it?" and Mama Pearl would tell him, "You treat that animal good, Bode Jessup, because he's one of God's special creatures." Callie would say, "Oh, Bode, better to give it back. How are you going to take care of a dog if you work all day? They make such messes, and they get fleas and ticks. Take it back."

Well, Harry wasn't going anywhere. Harry was his. His first, very own dog. A gift from the nicest guy in the whole world. He'd have to think about putting up a fence in the backyard so Harry could run. Maybe Hatch would let him take him to the office in the beginning. He'd have to paper-train him for a while.

How he'd hungered for a dog when he was growing up. If he'd been given the choice of a new bike, a new car, anything, he'd have picked a dog. But it never happened. Maybe because he'd never expressed, aloud, his desire for one. Even if he had, who was going to get it for him? Brie maybe. No one else.

Brie.

Bode returned to the living room, sitting down gingerly so as not to wake Harry. He turned off the television and picked up the portable phone. He called Brie in San Diego first. He listened to the recording. When he heard the beep he spoke. "It's Bode, Brie. I just called to wish you a Happy Thanksgiving and to tell you I got a dog. He's a golden retriever and his name is Harry. He looks like a Harry. He's just six weeks old and I'm going to let him sleep with me. He doesn't have the hang of eating yet and I guess he's going to mess all over everything. Isn't it great? Hope you're well. I'll call again. I think about you all the time. Take care of yourself."

Next, Bode called Sela, but the operator told him the line was disconnected. He frowned. Sela must have moved. Brie would know where she was, so he wasn't going to worry about Sela.

He reached down and pulled his yellow pad from his brief-case. He dialed the number for the operator and placed a call to Beaufort person-to-person for Mama Pearl. He listened to the same voice he'd heard a few months ago tell the operator that Pearl didn't live at Archer Hall. The phone felt hot in Bode's hand. He dropped it into the cradle and shivered as he wiped his hands on his pants. "What the hell . . ."

Harry stirred, probably because he was aware of Bode's fast-beating heart. Bode took a deep breath and let it out slowly. He watched as Harry's sleepy eyes closed.

The phone at Parker Manor rang twenty-three times without anyone picking it up. Why was it still connected? Where was Mama Pearl? He dialed the operator again and made a person-to-person call to Callie, but hung up before the call could go through. Wyn and Callie probably took Pearl and went off somewhere for Thanksgiving. Pearl wouldn't be a party to going away unless Callie whined and cried and threw a temper tantrum. Even then he wasn't sure Pearl would go. He called the operator again and placed his call person-to-person. The same voice that answered before spoke and said Callie Parker Archer didn't live there. "What the hell . . ."

Harry woke fully this time, wiggling to be free of Bode's shirt. Bode bounded off the sofa and raced to the kitchen, where he sat the wiggling puppy on a pad of newspapers. "That's it, that's it, you got it," Bode said, clapping his hands enthusiastically. "Good boy, Harry." A moment later the little dog was snug again inside his shirt.

Bode watched the six o'clock news, the six-thirty news, and the seven o'clock news. At eight o'clock he put Harry down on the paper again, ate the dried-out dinner in the oven, showered and returned to the sofa where he again dialed Brie's number, left a second message, and then called Parker Manor and let the phone ring thirty-three times. At ten-thirty he gave up, wrapped a hand towel around Harry's bottom, and crawled into bed with the little animal nestled on the pillow next to him. The silky ball of fur licked at his cheek before settling down for the night. Bode's eyes burned as he did his best to free his mind for sleep. Man and dog slept.

15

It wasn't going to be a good day. Brie could feel something in the air, something she used to be able to tune in to, but not anymore. She thought about the spirit world Pearl believed in, the rituals, the hexes and curses. She thought about Callie and Wyn, about Bode and how hard Sela was working. And what was she doing? Cleaning house, cooking, visiting Callie, and driving Pearl to church when she was up to attending services.

She was on her third cup of coffee, her eye on the clock over the doorway. Sela had been gone since six-forty-five. It was now almost nine, and Pearl hadn't stirred from her room. She emptied her cup and made a fresh pot of coffee before she tentatively knocked on Pearl's door. When there was no response she opened the door a crack. "Pearl," she whispered, "it's almost nine o'clock. Is everything all right?" The fear in her voice alarmed her. "Pearl, are you awake?"

"Yes'm, Miz Brie. I'm awake with a bad bellyache."

"Can I get you anything? I'll make you some tea and some Pepto—you know, that pink stuff. You haven't been taking care of yourself, have you?" She fussed about the bed straightening the covers, feeling Pearl's forehead the way the old woman had felt hers when she was unwell as a child. To her immense relief, Pearl's forehead was cool. She bent over to kiss her, tears forming in her eyes. Was this the beginning of Pearl's downhill slide? This wasn't supposed to happen. Pearl was supposed to live forever. Pearl was supposed to be healthy and happy forever and ever, fussing over her children.

Brie dug deep and brought her voice full of tenderness and excitement to the surface. "I have a wonderful idea, Pearl. Today you are going to stay in bed, and I am going to wait on you. I'm going to make some chicken soup and all the things that are good for bellyaches. I'm going to fuss over you the way you always fussed over me. Payback time, Pearl. I can help you to the bathroom if you want."

"I don't want no help. I can get there myself. You make the tea, and Pearl will let you fuss all you want. After, you take the clean nightgowns to Miz Callie. Fetch the soiled ones back so I can be washing them tomorrow. Put the pretty one on her, the one with the pink bows and the ruffle. Will you be doing that for Pearl, Miz Brie?"

"Sure. But first I'm going to get you comfortable in here. Listen, how about if I bring the phone and the answering machine here, too, in case Bode calls. I can fetch that little hall table in here and set it up."

"Bless your heart, Miz Brie."

Once again tears burned Brie's eyes. "Pearl, if your bellyache doesn't go away, will you let me take you to a doctor?"

"We'll see in a few days. You could be fetching me some licorice from the drugstore if it ain't too much trouble."

"A whole sackful. Black, right?"

"Yes'm."

"I'll bring in the little television that's in the kitchen and set it on the dresser."

"No need to be doing that, Miz Brie. Pearl is no invalid."

"I know that. Just for today. It makes the time go faster if you have something to watch. I'll worry about you here by yourself while I'm with Callie. Or would you rather I call Coletta to stay with you?"

"Don't you be doing that. All's wrong with me is I have a bellyache."

"Okay, you're the boss," Brie said lightly.

"You best be remembering that, Miz Brie."

In the kitchen Brie's shoulders slumped. Now what? Pearl's bellyache was more than a little gas in her stomach, she was sure of that. She was also certain Pearl was as frightened as she herself was.

Brie prepared perfect golden toast lathered with soft butter and wild blackberry jam that Pearl made every summer. She set it on the little table next to the bed. "Try and eat it all. I'm going to take a shower. The tea's good, that mint kind you really like."

"Yes'm, Miz Brie," Pearl said. The minute she heard the shower she struggled from the bed and flushed the toast and tea down the toilet. Twice she almost toppled over on her way back to bed. When she fell back against the pillows she wondered if she was getting ready to die. For a week now she'd heard the screech owls, which meant somebody was going to die soon. "Now, Lord, why would You be wanting this worthless old black woman? She ain't no good for nothing 'cept taking care of that sick chile. If You take me, who is going to look after her? I ask respectfully that You wait a small bit, if You have a mind to be doing it now. Jest a little bit longer, Lord. I need to be talking to my boy. This is Pearl, Lord, from Parker Manor." She was asleep a moment later.

Before she left the house, Brie carried the dishes out to the sink, pleased that Pearl had eaten the toast and drunk all of the mint tea. Pearl didn't wake when she plugged in the phone in the hallway and dragged the cords to the night table. The television set was on the dresser, the small remote next to the phone.

It was eleven o'clock when Brie left the house, the chicken soup simmering on the stove. When she got back she'd make a chocolate cake, Pearl's favorite.

She made two stops, one at the drugstore in town, where she purchased three bags of black licorice and two bottles of Pepto-Bismol. From the drugstore she backtracked, turned right on West Fifth Street, and headed for the Judge's house, where she knocked on the door and waited patiently for someone to open it. The Judge himself peered through the curtains before he opened the door.

"Well, if you aren't a sight for these old eyes. What are you doing here, Brie?"

She told him. "The real reason I stopped was to ask if you'd give me a little extra time paying off the balance of my school loan. And to ask you if you could recommend a doctor who will come out to the manor house to look at Pearl. I know it's more than a bellyache she's suffering from. I'm scared out of my wits. Another thing, I just started with the FBI. I could very well lose my job if I extend my leave. I feel like I'm between that rock and a hard place Bode always talked about. Sela and I want to call him, but Pearl says no. At what point, and *is* there a point, when we can do what we think is best?"

"It's a moral dilemma, Brie. As long as Pearl is clear-thinking, she has the right to expect you to obey her wishes. I would feel the same way. Perhaps this is wishful thinking on my part, but maybe Bode is considering a trip back home. I wouldn't be a bit surprised if he didn't show up at the door one of these fine days. He did love to see the camellias in bloom. He was always bringing Miss Nela a bouquet when he was a youngster."

"So, what you're saying is we shouldn't get in touch with him. And it's okay for me to stall on the last seven hundred dollars I owe you."

"Yes, my dear, that's exactly what I'm saying. Now, tell me, how is Callie doing? Has there been any change?"

"No, I'm sorry to say. I don't know what to think. Pearl says she's in the Lord's hands, and I guess she's right. I'm on my way there now. Get back to me after you talk to the doctor. No, no, don't call the house. I'll call you or else you can call Sela at the office and leave a message."

"One way or another, I'll get back to you."

"Judge, have you heard from Bode?"

"No, I haven't. I think about him almost every day. I'm sorry I retired. I truly miss the spirited discussions Bode and I used to have."

"Wyn?"

A veil seemed to drop over the Judge's eyes. "I understand he's considering politics. I've been asked in a roundabout way if I'd endorse him next year."

"Will you?"

"Don't rightly know at this time. A lot can happen in a year. Miss Nela told me that Anna down at the beauty shop told Helen at St. Paul's that Sela had breakfast two days in a row with Wyn at Shoney's," the Judge said slyly.

"Two days!" Brie blurted out. "I only knew about one. You old fox, what else have you heard?"

"That she parks her car at the Holiday Inn and gets in his car," the Judge said, a devilish light in his eyes.

"And who told you that?"

"One of the maids at the motel told Harly Mahew's housekeeper, who told our housekeeper. Didn't know Sela liked Wynfield."

"I didn't know that either, Judge. Well, they're both over

twenty-one and can do as they please. I imagine both of them are lonely. I'm sure it's nothing more than a dinner or luncheon. Or breakfast," she said lamely.

"I expect so," Judge Summers said. "Nela and I are going up to Columbia for a few days. She wants to see her sister— can't imagine why. She's a harpy if there ever was one. I can give you the phone number in case you might need me. I can come right back here the moment you call." *He sounds,* Brie thought, *like he wants me to call so he can come back and do whatever he does to pass the time.*

"I'll try not to call unless it's an emergency. How are your memoirs coming along?"

"The memoirs are going slowly. Nela keeps reading over my shoulder telling me I can't put things in because other people will take offense. If I listen to her, all I'll have in the end is my name on the first page."

Brie pocketed the phone number, kissed the Judge, and left the house, knowing her life had been enriched because of the weary old man watching her from the doorway. "I wish people didn't have to get old and die. I wish I could have yesterday back," Brie muttered as she started the car's engine.

At the convalescent home, Brie busied herself by putting Callie's clean laundry away, adjusting the shades in the room, fingering the new curtains Arquette's wife had hung several days earlier. She wiped down the dresser and the bathroom sink with Lysol. The camellias were dying, their petals wilted on the windowsill. She threw them out, washed the vase, and added the ones she'd picked before leaving Parker Manor. These were pink, delicate, almost translucent, like the young woman lying in the bed.

Brie settled herself, reached for Callie's hand. "It's Brie, Callie. I'll be sitting with you today. Pearl is under the weather, and she's staying in bed. Actually, I think Pearl is ill. She doesn't want you to know. She doesn't want Bode to know either. I wonder, Callie, if you'd wake up if you heard Bode's voice. I want to call him, so does Sela, but Pearl won't permit it. I don't have the guts to defy her; neither does Sela.

"I stopped by to see the Judge this morning. He's upset because he has to go with Miss Nela up to Columbia. Poor dear, he's lost since he retired. He's getting old, Callie, just the way Pearl is getting old. It breaks my heart. I wish I could do something, stop the clock, make time stand still. I want yesterday so bad I can taste it.

"I don't know if you want to know this or not, but I'm going to tell you anyway. You did tell Pearl you were calling the marriage off, so I guess you won't mind. The Judge told me Sela has been seeing Wyn. I think she finally found her niche. She's got the personality to be a real-estate agent, and the fact that she's selling commercial real estate and dealing mostly with men is something she thrives on. I don't mean she's loose as a goose or anything like that. Both of us know Sela is a big flirt, but for the most part that's all she does. I don't know how I'm going to feel about Sela if what the Judge said is true. I mean, she has a right to see whomever she wants. I know she's lonely and she is working very hard. She hasn't said anything to me, and I can't very well say anything to her. She knows how I feel about Wyn; Pearl too. Guess that's why she's keeping quiet.

"I said a prayer last night that Bode would call. I think about Bode a lot—more than I should. It's almost as if Bode has all the answers and only he can make things right. How did it happen that we all felt like that? I still feel that way so that doesn't say much for me.

"Do you remember that time we were playing dress-up? It was raining, and Pearl said we could play in the attic. All your grandmother's wonderful dresses were up there. There was even an old Confederate uniform Bode put on. We made a fort under the eaves and called it Fort Parker. Bode was going to defend us to the death if the damn Yankees came for us. Remember how Pearl brought us up some of those cinnamon cakes and she let Bode tie her onto the chair? God, I can't believe she let us do that. I think you were supposed to be a shrinking violet and Sela and I were the servants. You had an attack of the vapors. Bode was out scouting the terrain on the other side of the attic and just when those damn Yankees were about to set foot on Parker land he was going to shoot all of them with the broom. He swore to us he wouldn't let them take the womenfolk. I can't remember why we tied Pearl up though. Damn, now that's going to bother me all day. You did the perfect faint, crinoline and all. Bode was all fouled up; should he go after the soldiers or see to you in your faint? I knew he would see to you first and they'd capture him. We, the servants, outwitted those damn Yankees and saved your butt; Bode's too. You got mad at us that day and told me and Sela to go home. Pearl smacked your bottom and sent you to your room. Sometimes you were a real snot, Callie. We knew it was because of Bode. You wanted him to like you best, and he did. Sela and I knew that. You had so much then—Pearl, Bode, the Judge, all those fine people who looked after you when your father died.

"It's going to be Valentine's Day soon. I bet Bode sends you a Valentine. He never forgets. One of these days I'm going to send him a real mushy one just for the fun of it. No, I'm not going to do any such thing. I don't even know why I brought that up. To have something to say. I know I have to keep talking. I know you can hear me. It's been so long, Callie. None of us knows what to do for you anymore. We come here, we change your nightgown, we watch that stuff drip into your arms, we brush your hair, put a ribbon in it, change your socks, rub your legs. It isn't helping. Please open your eyes. Look at me and say, 'Hi, Brie. How's it going?' I would love to hear you say that, Callie, more than anything in the world. Do it. Damn you, Callie, do it! Move your fingers, roll your eyes, open your mouth. Do *something!* Do you hear me, Callie?

"You need to think about Wyn and Sela. What if they decide to get married? I know that sounds kind of far-fetched, but it could happen. Sela's a free spirit. What that means is, Wyn got away with it all, and I know he was driving that car, Callie. I know it as sure as I'm sitting here. They'd have Parker Manor and all the land, and you're here refusing to wake up. Are you going to let that happen? Well—are you? I know Sela, she doesn't think she's doing anything wrong. In a way she isn't.

"Callie, I've said this before, and I'm going to keep saying it every day that I come here. You're on Medicaid. You're a ward of the state. You have zip. You were sued for a hundred million dollars. If you wake up, you can set things straight. Do it, Callie. For me, for Bode, for Pearl. What's going to happen to you if Pearl is really sick and she dies? Sela is going to be with Wyn, I feel it in my bones. I'm going to have to go back to Atlanta. Bode's gone. You're going to be alone. You've never been alone, Callie. You can't get by on your own. You need Pearl and the rest of us. I hate to say this, but you're draining our life's blood. Callie, wake up! Please. I'm not going to say another word. I'm going to sit here and stare at you and *will* you to wake up. So there."

She meant to sit there and stare at her friend, but she was so exhausted she drifted off to sleep.

Bode Jessup looked up from his legal pad to stare out the window. The camellias back home would be in full bloom. The ache in his chest was so alive he felt like he was going to choke. He threw the pencil he was holding across the room, then picked up the phone and called Parker Manor. He felt giddy, light-headed when he heard Mama Pearl's voice. For a moment he couldn't get his tongue to work. "It's Bode, Mama Pearl."

"I knowed you was going to call me today, Bode. Are you calling to tell me you're to be a judge, Bode?"

"Not yet, Mama Pearl. I have a long way to go before that ever happens. How are you?"

"Jest fine, Bode, now that you called me. I worry about you, honey."

"Mama Pearl, what are you doing at Parker Manor? I've been calling off and on for some time now and there's never an answer. In Beaufort they say you don't live there. Then when I call this number you don't reply. Is something going on I should know about?" There was such fear in Bode's voice that Pearl rushed to reassure her boy.

"Miz Callie didn't want to live in Beaufort," she explained. "Miz Sela came back here to live. Arquette had fixed up one of the rooms for her. Sela has a job as a real-estate agent and she is helping me around the house. I couldn't sleep in another bed 'cepting my own and you know that, chile," Pearl explained in her familiar, comforting voice. "Miz Brie is leaving soon to go back to her FBI work. It's just a visit, Bode. I don't want you to worry about Pearl."

"I'm the one who is supposed to worry, not you. Is everyone okay?"

"Everything be jest fine, Bode. I need to be thanking you for them fine Christmas presents you sent to me and to Arquette and Coletta. That washing machine and that clothes-dry machine made them so happy. And all that soap . . . my, oh my, Coletta was so happy she didn't quite know what to do. That purse you sent me and that new string bag, they jest made my old eyes fill up. You're such a good boy, Bode. There was no need for you to be spending all your money on us. We didn't know where to send a present to you. Miz Brie, she say we should jest put your presents on the shelf and wait till you come home and then we can give them to you. She's a big help to me; Miz Sela, too. Will you be coming home soon, Bode?"

"I'll try, Mama Pearl. Are the camellias blooming?" he asked wistfully.

"They be so pretty this year, they fair take your breath away. Every day I pick some. The pink ones are the prettiest this year. I know you like the red ones the best. I put some in your room. It pretties it up some. I know you don't live here no more, but it makes me remember when you did. I feel my eyes puddling up, chile."

"Don't cry over me, Mama Pearl," Bode said, with a catch in his voice. "Is Arquette watching over you?"

"Lord, yes. Everybody watches over Pearl. I *cain't* get used to all this fussing. The Judge, he comes by, gives me money, Miz Sela cooks a fair amount and Miz Brie she takes real good care of me. She say it's her turn now. Pearl's jest fine, chile."

"I love you, Mama Pearl," Bode said gruffly.

"I know that. And I love you as much as I love the Lord. You be a good boy now, you hear Pearl?"

"I hear you, Mama Pearl," Bode whispered into the phone. "Take care of yourself. Say hello to the girls for me."

"You can be sure Pearl will send along your best regards."

Bode was staring out the window, his hands jammed into his hip pockets as he rocked back and forth on his heels. His eyes were misty with unshed tears. He'd been standing here for long time. Too long.

"Bode?"

"Yeah, Hatch," Bode said, without turning around.

"I have something for you."

"Hatch, I'm full up. I couldn't squeeze in another case if it was the Queen Mother."

"This is better than the Queen Mother."

Bode turned. He knew what it was before Hatch handed it to him.

"Your plane leaves in an hour. I called your housekeeper and she brought over your bag; it's waiting by the front door. She said it was all packed, like you were maybe expecting to leave on a moment's notice. I clocked you standing by that window. I can see you from my window. I knew it was time."

Bode stared down at the files on his desk. "Hatch, I can't. It's a nice, wonderful gesture, but I can't just up and leave. Do you really think I'm that irresponsible?"

"No, but I am. Hey, I own this firm. Watch this!" A moment later the stack of files were in the air, papers fluttering every which way. "See, now you can't possibly make sense of all of this. Your only alternative is to let me do it, so I'd get shaking if I were you. Listen, Bode, this office will always be here. The offer is forever. Your call, old buddy. You aren't going to goddamn blubber now, are you? I hate it when you get mushy on me. Go on, get the hell out of here before I change my mind."

"Hatch . . ."

"Yeah, I know, I'm salt of the earth, your best friend, and you aren't ever going to find one better . . . One thing, Bode."

"Yeah?"

"Let me know how it's going. If you need anything, just ask. I'm a phone call away." Bode nodded. "You're getting all sloppy-eyed—I can see it from here. Harry's waiting in his new carrier by your bag, and he'll probably have destroyed it by now."

"Look at yourself in the mirror, you big dumb Indian, and tell me who's sloppy-eyed. I'll see you, Hatch."

"Damn right you will. Time is money, Bode, so get moving."

Hatch watched from Bode's window until the cab he'd

called was out of sight. He felt like a mother hen whose chick came home to check on the barnyard.

Hatch bellowed to Bode's secretary. "Clean up this mess," he requested. "Get me two paralegals and have them and these files in my office by three this afternoon. I have no idea what got into that crazy guy," he said, strolling out of the office.

16

❧

"Just drop me off here," Bode told the cab driver. "I'll walk the rest of the way."

It was chilly and he shivered, but not with cold, with apprehension. Where to go first? The Judge's house, of course. He needed to do some man-to-man talking before he headed for Parker Manor.

His backpack secure on his shoulders, Bode loped ahead at a half run, half jog, Harry in his arms, his sneakers slapping on the asphalt road. Three times people stopped to offer him a ride. He declined, not because he didn't know the people, who were just being friendly, but because he wanted to savor the feeling of being home again. It was home, it would always be home, but in a different way now.

Thanks to Hatch Littletree, he had a new life now. He was going to prosper whether he liked it or not. For the first time in his life he owned something besides his bicycle and old car. And he had Harry. He had a pension fund, health insurance, a more than satisfactory bank account, and in his pocket was the last payment to Judge Avery. He was rich beyond his wildest dreams. He didn't think anything could top that until last week when he heard Hatch tell one of the senior partners that he, Bowdey Malcolm Jessup, was the best goddamn lawyer ever to enter a courtroom, next to himself. He remembered how his chest had puffed out.

Rich because he had four people who believed in him so totally, so completely, that he thanked God for it every night. Mama Pearl, the Judge, Hatch and, of course, Brie Canfield. Good old Brie. If he needed a dollar and she had only fifty cents she'd borrow the other fifty cents to give him. That wasn't to say Callie or Sela wouldn't help him; they would, but it wasn't the same with them.

He wondered how Callie and Wyn were doing and if they had a baby on the way yet. What kind of mother would Callie make? He wasn't sure. She had a selfish streak in her. He thought about all the unintentional hurts she'd laid on him in childhood. At least, he was almost certain they were unintentional. Of course, she always apologized with tears in her eyes. And he accepted because she was Callie Parker and because of Clemson Parker he had Mama Pearl and a good life.

For a while, he had thought he loved Callie Parker and then for a little space in time, he had thought he loved Sela. One day he thought he was sure about his feelings for tomboy Brie, who looked into his eyes with such steady intensity; the next day he was unsure. He cringed when he remembered her graduation. He called himself every kind of fool in the world. What would have happened if he'd taken her up on her offer? Would his life have changed? Would hers?

Wind rushed at him, driving him backward. Overhead the trees, dark skeletons in the night, waved their angry, wicked-looking arms. It felt like Hallowe'en for some reason.

Everything about this place was a memory. Everything.

Callie. He'd left here because of her. Left because he couldn't bear to see her married to another man. It had been a mistake to offer her a job. He hadn't thought it through, what it would mean working side by side with her. If he'd been more certain of his feelings, he wouldn't have botched things up and then run like a jackrabbit. The only time he felt he had to stay *in his place* was when he was with Callie. For so long it had hurt, and that hurt had started to fester and boil over.

But finally he was free of Callie Parker's hold on him. He'd paid his debt a hundred times over—with Brie's help. It was funny, he thought. He'd never felt like he owed Brie. Why was that? Because Brie was special.

That day she'd barreled into the airport had given him nightmares for weeks afterward. She'd needed to get the edge that day; the gun just made it possible. They both knew that, too. She must be one hell of a cop. She always gave one hundred and ten percent to everything she did. Good old Brie.

The coach light at the end of the walkway was burning. The porch light, too. Maybe the Judge was expecting company. Maybe he was in tune with him in some way, and knew he was about to have a visitor. Maybe a lot of things. He rang the doorbell.

Judge Avery was in his bathrobe, his pajama collar standing up around his neck. A cigar that had gone out a long time ago was clutched between his teeth; his spectacles were halfway down his nose. *He looks,* Bode thought, *like Colonel Sanders in the Kentucky Fried Chicken ads.*

There were no immediate greetings. The Judge yanked him into the house and closed the door. He put his fingers to his lips and motioned Bode to follow him to the back of the house to his office. Inside, with the door safely closed, he put his arm around Bode and smacked him on the back, waking Harry, who let out a small bark and wriggled his tiny head out through Bode's jacket. "Howdy, little fella," the Judge said, surprised, then he looked Bode full in the face.

"I had a feeling you'd be showing up," he said gruffly. "I've been stalling Nela, hoping I was right. She wants to go visit that fool sister of hers in Columbia again. You look mighty fine Bode. Mighty fine. I spent a lot of time thinking about you these past few months. Can't say I approve of the way you did things, but it isn't my place to criticize. I might have done the same thing if I was in your place. Sit down, son. Sit, sit. I'm going to fetch us some nice cold beer and we're going to talk."

"No need, Avery," Miss Nela said, opening the door on them. "You just sit there with your guest and drink these beers. I fetched some chips, too, because I know Bode dearly loves them. It's good to see you, honey." Miss Nela favored Bode with one of her wet kisses. "I'll put an extra blanket on the bed for you. Guess you aren't used to these cold days. Does it get cold in Santa Fe? Oh well, I'll put the blanket on anyway. You can't keep a secret from me, Avery, and we both know it. I knew Bode was here the moment the doorbell rang. That's why you didn't want to go to my sister's; you knew Bode was coming. All you had to say was 'Bode's coming,' and I wouldn't have pestered you. You don't think, Avery. What would you do without me? Good night, Bode. Help yourself to anything you need for that little dog of yours. Good night, Avery. Don't you be bending this boy's ears until the wee morning hours. Do you hear me, Avery?"

"Yes, Nela, I hear you," the Judge sighed.

When the door closed, the Judge clapped his hands and cackled. "Now we can talk and drink to our hearts' content. She doesn't like me to drink beer, says I stink up the bedroom. Guess she's going to sleep in the spare room. Fine woman, Miss Nela. I love her, but I wish she'd leave me alone for about a week."

"What would you do if she did?" Bode grinned.

"Well, I'd probably . . . What I'd do is . . . Hell, Bode, I don't know! Probably sleep all week. Now, tell me, what brings you back here?"

Bode shrugged. "A feeling that something's not right. A feeling I can't shake off." His heart almost pounded itself out of his chest when he saw the Judge look everywhere but at him.

"Start at the beginning, from the moment I left here. Judge, don't leave anything out."

"Son, I'd rather take a whipping than tell you what's been going on. You should have called, Bode. I wish you'd called."

"Well, I didn't. Obviously I'm going to wish I had. Cut to the chase, Judge, and don't spare my feelings."

"Light a cigarette, then, Bode, and drink your beer. You need to have something in your hands because you aren't going to like any of this."

He told him all of it, right up to Brie's visit and the call he'd put in to the doctor to visit Pearl. "I know you, Bode. You're going to start blaming yourself, but none of this is your fault. It would have happened even if you'd been here. There was nothing you could have done; there's nothing you can do now. Everything is out of our hands. Nela and I go to see Callie every Sunday afternoon. We take fresh flowers and sit and talk for a few hours. Nela cries all evening when we come home. Brie came back because of Pearl. Sela is doing all she can. She even pays the taxes. The part that breaks my heart is that the child is on Medicaid. Her father was a proud man. He must be spinning in his grave.

"I know exactly what you're thinking, Bode. You want to borrow Miss Nela's bicycle and you want to pedal out to Parker Manor. Well, I'm not going to allow you to do that. You need some thinking time. Morning will be soon enough. Pearl will be sleeping, and so will the girls. Morning is good. Breakfast and Pearl's fine coffee will give you something to look forward to. You mind me, Bode."

"You're right, Judge. I can't believe this. I should have known, had some kind of second sense. Is it only women who have instincts about things like this?"

The Judge snorted. "According to Miss Nela, yes. According to me, no. It all happened. We can't change anything. You have to go on and work at it now—tomorrow. Tomorrow will be soon enough, Bode. Now, away with doom and gloom. Tell me all about you and what's been going on in your life."

Bode talked for an hour. When he had finished, he withdrew a check for the balance of his debt. "I'm sorry it's taken me so long to pay this all off."

"I wanted to cancel Brie's remaining seven hundred dollars, but she wouldn't hear of it. She asked for an extension of time and of course I gave it to her. Bode, I'd like you to pay it for her. Now."

"Sure, Judge, that's no problem," Bode said, fishing his checkbook out of his backpack. He scribbled off the amount and handed it over. His eyebrows shot upward when the Judge smacked his hands gleefully and cackled like a rooster.

"Bet you thought I was being a greedy old man. You should know better, son. Now, I can give you this. I have a feeling, especially after what Brie told me, that this is more important than either one of us knows. It'll just take me a minute to get what I need out of the safe. Have another beer. You're going to need it. You'll have to fetch it, I guess. Go on, go on, this will take just a minute."

Bode returned to the Judge's study with four Budweisers under his arm. He sat down, uncapped two, and held one out to the Judge who waved it aside.

"This belongs to you and Brie. It's been recorded and it's damn official. How you both handle it is up to you. You and Brie paid for this with the sweat off your backs." He held out the deed to fifty acres of Parker land to Bode. "Brie doesn't know about this, so you'll have to tell her. She'll take it better from you."

"I don't understand," Bode said, scanning the deed.

"What don't you understand?" the Judge fretted.

"I didn't buy this property."

"I bought it for you. You and Brie paid me back. You were being so damnably noble, saying you had to pay for Callie to go to college and law school. There was your tuition to pay and Brie's, too. The only way that could happen was to sell off a piece of Parker land. I presented the idea to Callie, and she balked at first. Pearl had to take matters in hand. It was time for Callie to find out she wasn't a rich little girl. I bought the land for a fair price and paid for all of you to go to school. You and Brie repaid it all. The two of you paid for Callie, too. Now that the debt is cleared, the fifty acres is yours. Deservedly so."

"I can't take this," Bode mumbled.

"And why the hell not? You paid for it," the Judge shouted.

"Well, that may be, but . . . it doesn't seem right."

"You wouldn't have gone to college or law school, Bode, none of you would have. Sela was fortunate—she had loans, but you three didn't have a chance. I don't want to hear another word. If you're thinking about giving it back, I'd rethink that thought. You'd be giving it to Wynfield Archer. Brie won't stand still for that. I told you what her feelings are and where Sela stands in regard to Wynfield. I'm not saying Wynfield isn't a decent man, he is. Can't take that away from him. He's shouldered all the bills, and he did what he could. Now, you finish that beer and go on to bed. It's tomorrow already. Time is going too fast, Bode. It seems to be catching up to me of late. I'm going to be seventy-nine soon. I was just saying to Miss Nela, I wish for yesterday. Every day I wish for yesterday. Miss Nela says I'm wishing my life away. You do that when you get old. Do you wish for yesterday, Bode?"

"All the time," Bode said softly. "You've been a good friend to me, Judge. I'll never forget your kindnesses over the years. I don't know if I could have made it without you."

"One way or another I suspect you would have. I just

made it a tad easier—and believe me when I say it gave me as much pleasure as it gave you. It's funny, Brie and I had this same exact conversation. Fine girl. You have to be special to work for the FBI. Mighty fine girl. Don't know any finer," the Judge said slyly. "Be a pity if she left here for good."

"I'm not *that* dumb, Judge," Bode said wryly.

"Sometimes you are, especially where women are concerned. You backed the wrong horse, son. You realize it now, don't you?"

"I realized it a long time ago, Judge. Thanks, though, for bringing it to my attention again."

"I'd like it if you'd stay here. That way I won't have to go to Columbia."

"Judge, why don't you tell Miss Nela you don't want to go, instead of beating around the bush?"

"Just like that—*tell* her?"

"Just like that. I even know what she's going to say. She's going to say: 'Well, Avery, if that's how you feel about it, we won't go.' You're off the hook. Trust me."

"You're sure?"

"Yes."

"How'd you get so smart?"

"You were my teacher, Judge. You go along to bed. I'm going to sit here and finish this beer. Like you said, I need some thinking time."

"Good night, Bode. I'll see you in the morning."

"Good night, Judge."

Bode reached into the Judge's humidor for one of his cigars. When the tip was glowing he sat back in the chair to try and appreciate the buzz he was feeling. Did he really have a buzz, or was he feeling this way because of all the things the Judge had told him?

Guilt was a terrible thing. It worked on your emotions and reduced you to a quivering mass of nothingness.

Callie in a coma. How was he going to live with that? Callie had decided to call off her wedding just hours after he left Summerville.

Pearl sick, maybe seriously so.

Sela and Pearl living at Parker Manor.

Sela hanging around with Wynfield Archer.

His and Brie's ownership of fifty acres of Parker land.

Jesus Christ.

How was he supposed to deal with all this? "Very carefully, Bode," he answered himself. He wished he could shrivel up like the last summer peach and disintegrate into dust.

Had he subconsciously prepared himself for something like this when he accepted Hatch's offer? Always honest with himself, he thought he probably had, but it hadn't worked. No matter how hard he tried, no matter what he did, the little family he'd taken responsibility for, for so long, was always with him. He'd read somewhere that a person always yearned to return to their roots.

Callie in a coma. Inconceivable. Mama Pearl would expect him to work some kind of a miracle where Callie was concerned, and he was going to disappoint her. She was holding on, waiting for him to get here. How . . . *what* had made the decision for him? Not Hatch and the airline ticket. Something had grabbed at his soul when he was staring out of his office window. There had been one brief second when he knew totally, absolutely, that something was wrong. Hatch must have felt it, too. From what he'd said, he'd called the travel agent on the first floor of the building and asked for an open, first-class ticket. It was in his hand in ten minutes. Hatch could always read him and often boasted that he knew what Bode was thinking before Bode knew it himself. It had to be some Indian thing that enabled him to do so. Bode cuddled the sleeping Harry closer against his chest and felt the small animal's heart beating against his own, slower rhythm.

If Sela was living at Parker Manor, it was because of Pearl. If Brie had taken a leave of absence, it was serious. Special Agent Canfield, FBI. The thought made him light-headed. Later, after he talked with Brie, he'd think about her suspicions. He could see Sela and Wynfield together. In his gut he'd known Callie and Wyn weren't meant for each other. And now, the biggie—his and Brie's ownership of fifty acres of Parker land. Brie didn't even know about it. When he told her—and he was going to tell her—she'd say: "I don't want it. Give it back!" If it was Sela, she'd swoon and figure out a way to make it work for her.

The awful, sick feeling he had in the pit of his stomach, the same kind of apprehension he'd experienced when he was little and something was really wrong, was going to consume him any minute now. He took deep breaths, put his head between his knees. Harry protested by jumping off his lap and peeing on the Judge's carpet.

He had to get out of there—immediately. He scribbled off a note to the Judge and placed it in the center of the green blotter on his desk. He was going to borrow Miss Nela's ancient bicycle, the one she rode up and down the driveway to slim her hips, the bicycle that had the brakes on the pedals and a basket behind the seat for her water bottle. Harry would love the basket and fit snugly inside it.

Outside in the brisk, cold air, Bode straddled Miss Nela's bicycle and thought about Callie Parker. He didn't love her the way a man is supposed to love a woman. Had he been obsessed with Callie? Brie said he was. Brie said it was that coming-from-the-wrong-side-of-the-tracks thing, the social barriers making Callie seem more desirable than she was. She'd called him a fool, a sap, a jerk, and told him to grow up and *get real*. Brie was always too verbal, so much so she sometimes gave him nightmares. "Come to grips with it, Bode," he told himself desperately. "Admit either that you love her, or you don't." Now she was going to tell him and already he knew the words, could hear them ricocheting around his head: "Callie is in a coma, probably won't recover, and you're off the hook. You need never come to terms with your feelings for her now. Good for you, Bode. You're an asshole."

She was right. Brie was always right. He squirmed on the seat of the bicycle. "Declare your emotions and live with it. Overcome any and all obstacles. Speak up and out, stop dancing around. Do you or don't you?" When Callie had said, "Let's . . ." what had he done? Turned her down flat and walked away. In control. Was it that he had just needed to hear her say the words? "I don't want to deal with this now," he muttered. "That's your problem," Brie's voice mocked him. "You're a coward, Bode Jessup. You do have a flaw, you aren't perfect after all. Now I know your Achilles' heel. So there, Bode Jessup." "Shut up, Brie! Just shut the hell up," Bode grated. Her laughter followed him all the way to Parker Manor. It wasn't taunting laughter; it was sad and vulnerable-sounding.

He wanted to cry then because in the whole of his life he'd never allowed himself the luxury of tears. Pearl said that boys weren't supposed to cry. Colored boys *never* cried, she said. "Well, that's goddamn bullshit," he snarled. But he didn't cry.

Brie climbed out of bed and snuggled into her worn, frayed robe that was so old it felt like the finest satin. In the kitchen she struck a match to the fire in the fireplace, plugged in the coffeepot, and tiptoed down the hall to the bathroom, where she washed her face and brushed her teeth. She finished just as the coffee made its last plop-plop sound.

She liked this part of morning best, when it was just turning light and she sat in Pearl's old rocker by the fire and drank the first cup of coffee of the day. She'd prepared cinnamon buns before she went to bed. They'd go into the oven the moment she heard Sela and Pearl stir. She wondered if the temperature would rise. Last night it had been only thirty-seven degrees when Sela came home. She walked over to the back door to check the thermometer on the side of the house.

She saw him then, hunched up on the porch steps, a tiny dog on his lap, his arms wrapped around his knees, huddled into himself. She sucked in her breath and leaned against the doorframe for support. She should run in and tell Pearl, but she was afraid to open Pearl's door.

Anger, hot and scorching, ripped through her. *Now he comes home! Now, when it's too late!* She opened the door. "Get your ass in here, Bode Jessup, before I push you down those steps."

"And a good morning to you, too, Special Agent Canfield. I see you're your usual charming self," Bode said, getting up and tucking Harry under his arm. "What, no kiss, no hug?"

"Don't tempt me to kick your butt, Bode. What are you doing here?"

"I had this hankering to come home so I acted on it. I got in last night. I stopped by the Judge's house and then borrowed Miss Nela's bicycle and pedaled my way out here. This is Harry, by the way. How's Mama Pearl, Brie?"

"I don't know." Brie's composure broke. "The Judge said he's sending the doctor out today. Pearl doesn't know—she'll probably send him packing. Maybe not now that you're here. How the hell do you do it? You always know what to say, have the right words, show up in the nick of time. I hate you, Bode. Come here, Harry," she said gently, scooping up the tiny bundle. "I love him already."

"I hate it when you hate me. Are you going to hate me just for today, or is it a forever hate? I need to know, Brie, so I'll know how to act toward you. Hey, you look real ugly in the morning," he said. "That's my dog, so don't try to worm your way into his affections."

"Up yours, Bode."

"I love it when you talk dirty," he teased. "Sit down, Brie, and talk to me. I want to hear everything. The Judge ran it through for me, and I have to admit I was in shock. I don't think my fine legal mind took it all in."

"Shouldn't you go in to see Pearl first?"

"Not yet. Talk to me, Brie."

She did. When she had finished, she drained her coffee and watched as Bode got off his chair, looking neither to the right nor the left, and walked over to Pearl's door. He opened it and closed it behind him. She ran down the hall to Sela's room and jumped on the bed. "Sela, wake up and be quiet. Bode's home! He's with Pearl."

Sela shook her head. "Bode's home?"

"That's what I just said. Get up. He was sitting on the back steps when I got up. He arrived last night and went to the Judge's house and then came out here." She looks frightened, Brie thought.

"Listen, Sela, he knows you've been seeing Wyn so don't . . . you know, lie about it. I know all about it, the whole town knows, so you really don't have to sneak around anymore. It's your business, and I'm not going to say anything. Just don't lie to Bode, okay?"

"Okay," Sela said. "You know what, Brie?" she added, around the toothpaste in her mouth. "This kind of ticks me off. He shows up now! We were doing just fine, which goes to prove Bode Jessup doesn't have all the answers. He can't do any more than we've been doing, can he?" she asked nervously.

"I don't know, Sela."

"Did you make coffee?"

"Yes, but we drank it all. I'm making some more. Do you want anything else?"

"Are you kidding? I'd choke if I tried to eat now. How long has he been in there?"

"Fifteen minutes or so. Sela, I was afraid to open Pearl's door this morning. I heard the screech owls last night, and the night before, and the night before that."

"I know, I heard them, too. That's only folklore, Brie. Just because they screech doesn't mean someone is going to die. I stopped believing that a long time ago. I'm surprised at you."

"They screeched for a week before Lazarus died. Pearl said so," Brie reminded her.

"They probably would have screeched anyway. Don't spook me, Brie, I'm antsy enough without all that nonsense. It was different when we were kids. God, when is that coffee going to be ready?"

"Right now," Brie said, filling her cup.

"Brie?"

"Yeah."

"Are we jealous of Bode?"

"I think so. I feel like I should pack and leave now that he's here. It's like, what can *I* possibly do?"

"That's funny, that's exactly how I feel. He'll get Pearl to agree to see a doctor, he'll give her something to clear up whatever it is she has, build her up, and then Callie will come out of her coma and everything will be wonderful. Why do we think like this? Do we have self-esteem problems? Does Bode have an ego? Maybe I should think about going back to New York. Who died and appointed him God anyway?"

"Could you really walk away, Sela?"

Sela dabbed at the tears in her eyes. "It would break my heart, but yes, I could do it. I wouldn't look back. How about you?"

"Me too."

Sela leaned over and whispered, "You love Bode, don't you? It's okay, Brie. It really is. I won't ever say anything.

You need to get it through your head that it's okay. Don't you ever, ever be ashamed of your feelings."

"What about Wyn?"

"Look, it happened. At first I thought it was just a fun thing. Then I got to know him better . . . I didn't mean for it to happen, neither did Wyn. I can walk away from that, too, Brie. *If* I have to. Do I? Or is this one of those things we have to wait and see how Bode reacts to?"

"Not as far as I'm concerned, Sela. I don't want to see you get hurt. I wish someone could tell me if broken hearts heal, and if they do, how long it takes."

"What *is* he doing in there?"

"I'm going to make some breakfast," Brie said, jumping up from the chair. "You're going to eat whether you like it or not, Sela. I have to do something."

"Okay, okay, bacon and eggs. Are you going to make some for Bode?"

"No, I'm not. Let him make his own. Those days are gone, my friend."

"Listen, why don't I make the breakfast and you go fix yourself. Your hair looks like a haystack. Surely you have a better-looking robe?"

"What are you trying to say?"

"I'm not *trying*. I'm telling you that you look like shit."

"Tough," Brie said, slapping bacon into the frying pan.

She was draining the bacon when Bode walked into the kitchen. He kissed Sela lightly on the cheek.

"Well?" Brie snapped.

"Mama Pearl is sleeping. I didn't want to wake her. I was just sitting by her bed. She doesn't look good to me. She must have lost about fifty pounds."

"Sixty-five. We weighed her at the hospital one day. She eats very little, and her stamina is gone," Sela said.

"What time is the doctor coming?"

"Ten," Brie said. She sat down with her plate.

"Where's mine?" Bode asked politely.

"Where mine was. What that means, Bode, is—cook it yourself."

"Do I sense a rebellion of some kind?" Bode inquired.

"How come you aren't at the nursing home?" Sela asked him. "I thought that's the first place you would go. Or have you been there already?"

"I came here first," Bode said quietly. He filched a slice of bacon from Brie's plate.

"Just like that. We don't hear from you for months and suddenly you show up and now the world is going to stop. You really burn me up, Bode," Sela said, wolfing down the eggs she didn't want so that Bode wouldn't eat them. She swallowed some coffee. "We're all grown-up now. As you can see, we've been managing pretty well. What does that tell you?"

"That you don't need me anymore," Bode said. "Look, I came back here because I had a feeling something was wrong with Mama Pearl. I didn't know about Callie. You girls haven't needed me for a long time. I was simply a . . . nudge, to get you to where you are now. I wouldn't have it any other way. Look at you, I'm so damn proud of the two of you I could bust. If I had some small part in helping you along the way, it was my pleasure. My hat's off to the two of you."

As one, the two young women screeched, "I hate you, Bode Jessup," and ran down the hall to Sela's room where they threw themselves on the bed and wailed in each other's arms. "I told you he always says just the right thing at the right time," Brie sobbed. "See, he made us feel bad and grateful at the same time. The worst thing is, he meant every word he said!"

"I guess you know we acted pretty asinine out there. I re-

call having more sense when I was ten years old." Sela blubbered.

"It's this place," Brie said. "We have to let go. I think, Sela,
we should stay long enough to see Pearl through this and
then I say we get on with our lives. How about coming to Atlanta?"

"Would you really like me to, Brie?"

"Sure, we could be roommates. Atlanta is a fast-moving
place. Or, I could ask for a transfer and we would go wherever that place turns out to be. You'd love California. Let's
agree to think about it, okay?"

"Okay." The relief on Sela's face was almost comic. Brie
felt better than she had in days.

It was almost nine o'clock when they walked back to the
kitchen, showered, and dressed for the day. Bode had washed
and dried the dishes. A fresh pot of coffee was on the table
along with clean cups and saucers.

"He's sucking up," Sela said.

"I see that." Brie nodded.

"I'm being considerate and nice," Bode said. "Do you still
hate me?" He sounded genuinely sad, like he really cared.
Harry ran to Brie and leaped into her arms. Sela squealed in
delight. Harry barked and barked as he licked Brie's face.

"No," they said in unison.

Bode smiled and reached for their hands. "Smile for me."
They did, because they could deny him nothing. He was that
rare person they called friend.

"If Pearl is still sleeping, we should wake her as the doctor
is coming at ten. She'll want to fuss a bit. Go ahead, Bode,
you wake her. She won't want you to help her, we'll do that,"
Brie said.

Bode nodded. He entered the dim room and called softly,
"Mama Pearl, it's Bode. Time to get up."

"Chile, is it really you? I dreamed you called on the telephone, and now you're here. Bless you, Bode. I've been feeling poorly these past days. I *cain't* believe old Pearl is lying in this here bed. My bones are getting old."

She was in his arms and he was squeezing her close to his chest. Again he wanted to cry at the feel of her. A lump in his throat the size of a walnut choked him, and his chest felt tight. "Everyone needs a lazy day or two, Mama Pearl. You have a lot of days coming to you. Brie has made some breakfast—can I fetch it for you?"

"No, no, my stomach is poorly. Maybe later. I missed church, chile. I *cain't* hardly believe that. What time is it?"

"Almost nine-thirty. Mama Pearl, the doctor is coming at ten. Don't you be fussing now."

"There's money in the Mason jar to pay him, Bode. Pearl is so happy to see her chile again. You best be getting cleaned up and out to the home to see Miz Callie. Poor girl, she jest lies there. I keep her pretty, Bode."

"I know you do, Mama Pearl."

"Miz Brie and Miz Sela, they help me a lot. Pearl has such good children. Will you promise me something, Bode?"

"Whatever you want, Mama Pearl."

"Swear on Lazarus and Miz Callie, Bode."

Oh God, Bode thought, *this is important.* "I swear," he said quietly.

"Fetch Miz Brie and Miz Sela in here, too. Pearl needs to be hearing them promise the same thing."

It's got to be the Queen Mother of all promises, Bode thought as he opened the door and motioned to Brie and Sela. "Pearl wants you to make a promise to her and to swear on Lazarus and Callie."

Brie's eyes rolled back in her head. Sela cleared her throat.

"Say the words," Pearl said.

"I swear on Lazarus and Callie," Brie and Sela repeated

solemnly; then they asked, "What are we promising, Mama Pearl?"

"That you won't let that town doctor put me in no hospital. If Pearl is going to die, she wants to do it right here in her own bed. You made the promise. Don't you shame me now, you hear?"

Sela ran from the room. Brie stood rooted in the doorway. She nodded numbly. Bode stared at the string bag on the bed next to Pearl, too full of emotion to speak. Just then, a small body leaped up onto the bed and, much to Pearl's delight, began to burrow happily into the curve of the sick woman's arm.

While the girls washed Pearl, and prepared her for the doctor's visit, Bode walked through the old manor house, into the dining room that was no longer used, to the living room with the scratchy furniture. He wandered about, reacquainting himself with yesterday, feeling something squeezing his heart.

Dr. Obecoe arrived promptly at ten and was immediately ushered into Pearl's room. The Judge had chosen carefully, for the doctor was African-American, female, and old enough that Pearl would be able to relate to her. Together, Brie, Sela, and Bode paced the kitchen. They were still restlessly pacing, coffee cups in hand, when the doctor emerged from the room at ten past ten.

"I don't know what to say," she began carefully. "Pearl absolutely refuses to go to the hospital. I can come back again tomorrow and do a few tests, but it will be difficult. The indications are that she has an obstruction of some sort—I'd say a tumor. She hasn't moved her bowels in a very long time— that's why she's afraid to eat. She truly does belong in a hospital. If you could just get her there for one day, we could schedule the tests one after the other and she could go home right afterward. But if we find something that requires surgery, what will we do? I suggest you talk to her, try to make her understand what is required."

"If she refuses, then what?" Brie whispered.

The doctor shook her head. "You don't really expect me to answer that, do you?"

"I do," Bode said.

"She'll die," the woman stated curtly. "She's in a great deal of pain. Have these prescriptions filled, and get her to take fluids. If she won't take the fluids, I warned her she'd have to have an IV. I scared her out of her wits. She'll need nutrients and glucose. If she asked me once she asked me half a dozen times how long it would be before she can get out of bed and go visit Miss Parker. I told her it would depend on how well she responded. I hate to say this, but maybe you can sort of blackmail her into following the treatment. I don't know what else to advise. I can bring Dr. Lewison out tomorrow if you want a second opinion. Arquette and Coletta are patients of mine. Perhaps they can talk to Pearl. It's something to think about. Make sure you follow the directions on the painkillers and try to get her to take liquids as much as possible."

When the doctor had gone, they stared at one another for a long time. It was Brie who finally broke the silence. "If you two feel this is something we should vote on, then I would vote to tell Pearl the truth. If it's something we think Bode should do, that's okay with me, too. Sela?"

"The truth," she said, dabbing at her eyes.

"Bode?"

"The truth. But we'll do it together."

Solemnly they followed Bode into Pearl's room. She looked so drawn, so tired, Brie wanted to cry. She bit down on her lower lip. Somehow she found Sela's hand in hers. She squeezed it.

It didn't matter what Bode said, what Brie or Sela said, Pearl was adamant. No hospital. No operation.

"Pearl," Brie pleaded, dropping to her knees by the side of the bed. "You understand what the doctor said, don't you? If you do as she says, before you know it, you'll be up tending Callie like before. You wore yourself out so now you have to get patched up. Think about when I leave and Bode leaves. Who's going to take care of Callie during the day? Sela can go in the evening, but it isn't the same thing. What happens if Sela gets worn out and sick? Then strangers will be taking care of Callie. Mama Pearl, will you at least think about it today?"

"No, chile, Pearl's mind be made up. If the Lord wants me, He's going to take me and Miss Callie, too. I seen it. I didn't know what it was so I asked Arquette and he tole me. The Lord, He be fixing to take Miz Callie, so Pearl is going first. Don't you be shaming me now and acting like little children. The Lord, He means it to be like this."

"What did you see, Mama Pearl?" Bode asked harshly.

"I saw a bag in the closet where the soap and toilet paper is. That's where I keep Miz Callie's special powder and liniment. That bag wasn't there last week. It was new. I seen it," she fretted.

"What was in the bag, Pearl?" Brie asked, her eyes wild. She felt Sela's fierce grip on her hand.

"It was my sweet baby love's shroud. Arquette tole me what it was when I explained to him what it looked like. The Lord is fixing to take my chile. It don't make no never mind about old Pearl. Leave me be now. I have some praying to do. Don't you be bringing no more doctors here—you understand?"

"Yes, ma'am," they said as one.

"Close the door, my praying is my privacy. You can leave this little dog here."

They trooped out to the kitchen. Brie found herself fighting with Sela over the coffeepot. Bode stood by the window, his head bowed.

"I think we should go and kill Arquette," Sela said in a strangled voice. "How could he say such a thing to Pearl?"

"Arquette is a plain, simple man. Mama Pearl asked him a question, and he answered it. He told her the truth," Bode said from his position by the window. His shoulders started to shake.

"Can't we go to the home and take it away—tell Pearl it was put there by mistake? How do you think it found its way there? Is there one to go with each room, or what?" Brie shuddered.

"I guess they have to keep them somewhere. I rather thought they'd be kept in one place, you know, like where they store the bandages and stuff. I don't know," Sela wailed.

"Mama Pearl would never believe anything we came up with. She saw it, and that's the beginning and the end of it," Bode said.

"That means Pearl is willing to die so she can be *there* if Callie . . . if Callie . . . you know. She doesn't care about any of us. If she did she'd want to get well. It was all a lie. I thought she cared about me, about all of us, but the only one she loves is Callie." Sela burst into noisy tears. "My God, I never heard such a thing. All these years . . ."

Brie's hand shot out and slapped her, hard. Stunned, Sela turned and ran out to the car. Tires screeched as she raced away and she was almost to the main road before Brie could gather her wits about her. "She's hysterical," she muttered in a shaky voice. "When she thinks about this she'll calm down."

"No, she won't. Mama Pearl could stand on her head in the middle of Route 17 and profess undying love for Sela and she wouldn't believe her now. To Sela, this is the ultimate betrayal. Nothing could ever cut this deep. I know what I'm talking about. How about you, Brie?" Bode said quietly.

"Well, I always knew Callie was first in Pearl's heart. I wanted to believe she loved us equally, but part of me accepted that it wasn't true. Oh, Pearl loves us, of that I have no doubt. She loves you second best, Bode. It's worse this way, worse than being a middle child, I guess. I wonder if Callie ever knew how very special she was to Pearl? Callie herself loved Pearl with all her heart, and I think that was part of her reason for calling off her wedding at the last minute. She knew Pearl didn't want to go to Beaufort, and she didn't want to give Pearl up. When my heart isn't so sore, I think I'll be able to look at that love and marvel at it. It's wonderful that two people can care about each other that much. Look, Bode, I think you should call the doctor and cancel tomorrow's appointment."

"What are you going to do, Brie?"

"Well, first of all I'm going to make some chicken soup for Pearl. I make chicken soup a lot around here. Then I'll do a little cleaning up, call my boss and see how things are going. Maybe I'll drive into town and see Sela. She'll need me. I'll wait though till Pearl falls asleep. I assume you're going out to see Callie? Let me know when you're ready, and I'll cut some camellias for you to take. Either Sela or I will stop and clean up Callie later on."

"Why—don't they have nurses? What kind of place is it?"

"Of course they have nurses, plenty of them, but Pearl wouldn't hear of them taking care of her sweet baby love. She always did it, and when she wasn't able to, Sela and I took over. Pearl irons her gowns and her hair ribbons, and does her laundry by hand. She used to wash her with special soap and powder her with her special powder. It's an all-day job, Bode. Pearl massaged her arms and legs every day, hour after hour."

Brie gently took his arm and looked him in the eyes.

"Listen, you better go. Pearl has her own inner clock and somehow she always knows when it's time for something to be done for Callie. Bode, the person in that bed isn't the Callie we all knew. You need to be prepared."

But nothing in the world could have prepared Bode for his first sight of Callie Parker. He gasped and choked back a sob. "Oh God, Callie."

17

The past suddenly swirled about Bode, the memories threatening to engulf him. He backed out of the room and bolted outside, where he fumbled for a cigarette. He didn't smoke much, only when he was under mind-boggling stress; like now. The cigarette was stale, the cylinder crumpled, the package itself tattered and torn. It was habit more than anything that made him transfer the cigarettes to his pocket on a daily basis. Sometimes he didn't smoke for weeks, but on days like today he knew he was going to finish the pack and probably buy a second one.

Bode puffed furiously as he tried to come to terms with what he'd just seen in Room 211. That wasn't the Callie he knew. That thin skeletal form was someone else. Never Callie. He looked down at the bunch of camellias in his hands, their stems wet and wrapped in several layers of wax paper. They were beautiful, a deep crimson mixed with pearl white blooms. When Brie cut them she'd gathered an extra bouquet for Pearl's room. There were some in the middle of the kitchen table, too.He remembered thinking that the bushes needed to be pruned and cultivated. Maybe he could do that on the weekend.

He finished his cigarette, stomped on it, picked it up, and carried it to a trash container next to the rusty bus stop. He looked around. He hadn't really paid attention to the nursing home when he first drove up. It was ugly, an end-of-the-line place. The words *dumping ground* skittered around inside his head.

Back in the building, his eyes burned as he made his way past the small group of patients gathered in the central hall, their eyes glued to the front door, hoping that today one of the visitors would be for them. Bode did his best to smile, to pat them on their shoulders as he made his way down the A Wing to Callie's room. He smelled coffee, disinfectant, urine, and death. He squared his shoulders, certain when he entered the room that Callie would be sitting up, and shouting, "Surprise!"

How much did she weigh? Eighty pounds? She'd never topped the scales at more than a hundred. What surprised him more than anything was that her face looked the same, thinner perhaps, but the same. Her hair, though, had a dry and brittle appearance, the pale blue ribbon doing nothing to enhance the thin locks. She'd always been so vain about her hair. She would make them wait ages while she fussed and primped, putting in combs, then removing them, snapping barrettes on the side, taking them out. He itched to pull up her eyelids to see if her eyes were the glorious brown he remembered. When she was sixteen she'd demanded contact lenses, not because she needed to see better, but because she wanted cat green eyes. He couldn't even remember now where and how he'd got the money for that. Suddenly it was important for him to know. He stood still in the middle of the room until he forced his memory to cooperate. He'd worked the night shift at the liquor store stocking shelves, getting by on only a few hours' sleep until they were paid off. Then, because she was careless, he'd go back and work the shift again to pay for the insurance. Had she ever said thank you? How could she? She had no idea he was busting his butt so she could have whatever she wanted. He'd preferred it that way.

Bode changed the water in the vase, discarded the old flowers, and did his best to arrange the ones he'd just brought. Then he sat down and stared at his childhood friend. Brie had said he was to talk, to reminisce. "Just talk, Bode—say anything. That's what we've been doing. Don't worry if it makes sense or not. And you know what else, Bode? It's been very therapeutic for all of us."

But Bode wasn't ready to talk. He needed to think about Mama Pearl and the awful promise he'd made.

A long time later, when he couldn't stand his thoughts and memories any longer, he leaped off the chair and jerked open the closet door. His eyes narrowed as he touched everything on the shelf. Soap bars and liquid containers. Toilet tissue— four rolls, tissues—three boxes. A container of industrial floor cleaner. Two cans of talcum powder and two bottles of body lotion. Next to them, a large Mason jar full of powder. Alongside it, a second jar full of pink cream. Dry shampoo. A box of ribbons. A plastic bag holding four pairs of pink bed socks. The flat black plastic bag with the zipper stared at him like a single eye. His hand was steady when he picked it up. He could see that it had been disturbed. It was hard to fold anything, much less plastic, into the original folds. He stared at it so long he thought his eyeballs were going to bounce out of their sockets.

His feet moved him swiftly out of Callie's room and into the vacant room next door. Inside the closet there he saw a duplicate of what he was holding in his hand. Did this place buy them by the gross? Or did they order them one at a time when a new patient was admitted? When he finally made his way back to Callie's room he decided they bought them by the hundreds, maybe by the thousands. They probably got a discount, too.

He was still holding the shroud in his hands when he walked over to Callie's bed. In a voice he'd often used with her in the past—a stern, don't-give-me-any-crap voice—he said, "Well, Callie, I don't know if this is for you or not, but I think you need to know it's here in *your* closet *waiting* for you. Somehow, I don't think you'll look very good in it. Your hair is going to get mussed and no one will get to see those green eyes. I want you to think about that, Callie. I'm leaving now because I need to be with Mama Pearl. I might come back, and I might not. It's going to depend on you. If you aren't going to crawl out of that place you're in, then what's the point in me coming here to just sit? You know what the Judge always said: 'Time is money.' I was never good at talking just to hear myself. I'm going to put this . . . shroud that has your name on it and I bet you didn't know it had your name on it, well it does, back in the closet where it's going to sit until it's time to put it on you. You're gonna look real ugly in it, Callie. It's black, and we both know black isn't your color. You said it washed out your features. I suppose I could put in an order for one that's electric blue or maybe bright orange, but the people who make these things would just laugh at me. Guess you're stuck with black. Come on, Callie, I know you can hear me. Crawl out of that place you're in and make us all happy. You can do it if you want to. Do you hear me, Callie?"

Winded by this speech, Bode replaced the shroud where he'd found it and left the room.

In the parking area he sat and stared out of the dirty car window. How had the girls and Mama Pearl come here to this place every day and talked for hours on end and then left, only to return to do it all over again? No wonder they looked like they'd been ridden hard and hung up wet. He wasn't at all sure he could do what they'd been doing these past months.

Did all of this go beyond friendship? Was it the sense of family? Of belonging to someone and not wanting that someone to step out of that family circle? He thought about all the sacrifices they'd made for Callie. At the time he'd never begrudged a single one of them. Mama Pearl would do it over again in the time it took her heart to beat just once. In all honesty he didn't think Brie begrudged it either. Sela was another story. The most important question of all was, if it was Brie or Sela or himself dying in that bed, would Callie do for them what they'd done for her? Would she do it for Pearl? The answer that smacked him in the face was *no*. Maybe she'd put forth some effort for Pearl, but he wasn't even a hundred percent sure of that. He wasn't sure about anything anymore.

He felt like a child again, vulnerable and scared, uncertain what was ahead of him. He gritted his teeth the way he had back then, and prayed, "Help me, Lord. Take my hand and show me the way." How many times he'd heard Mama Pearl say the same words! She was the one who'd taught them to him. *"He's always there watching over you, chile. Don't ever be making the Lord shamed of you. You're His chile the same way you're my chile. And when you're doing good, there's no need to talk about it. The Lord, He knows what you've done."* He'd obeyed because it made sense, and he'd lived his life the way Mama Pearl had taught him to.

A lone tear escaped his eye. He swiped at it with the sleeve of his jacket.

" 'Big boys don't cry.' Well, Mama Pearl, for the first time in your life, and my life, too, you told me something that was a fib. I forgive you for the fib. So many times I wanted to cry, to bellow, to wail, but I remembered what you said, and I swallowed my hurts because you said it would get better. I think I need to cry sometimes to cleanse myself, but I'm going to mind you. Maybe I'll cry sometimes when you . . . when you're *up there* . . . but you'll still see me, won't you, Mama Pearl?"

His heart heavy, Bode headed back to the only place that was ever home, to the only mother he'd ever known, to the only true friends in his life.

Home to his family.

The days crawled by, one by one until it was spring in Summerville again. It was the first of April, the beginning of the Azalea Festival that none of them were going to attend.

They had a routine now, that Brie had instituted. Everyone had his or her job. Bode was in charge of the finances they'd pooled together. Sela worked only part-time so that she could take her turn with Pearl, having forgiven the old woman the words that ate at her soul. Bode, with his kind common sense, had made her see that things weren't as dark as they seemed.

They sat in shifts with Pearl, who was now needle-thin and hooked up to IVs. They washed and did laundry three, sometimes four times a day. They took turns cleaning and cooking. Bode worked in the yard when he had time. They spent every available hour they had at the nursing home talking to Callie. Harry now refused to leave Pearl's side.

This life was taking its toll on all of them. "We need to get away from here, from everything, even if it's just for a few hours. I say we splurge and hire someone to come in and sit with Pearl, and someone else to go in and sit with Callie," Brie suggested one day. "Harry will watch over Pearl. Let's pack a picnic lunch and go to Folly Beach or Isle of Palms. I need to talk to you guys," she told them. "My section chief told me I have one more month, and if I don't go back then,

I don't have a job. No more extensions. The last of my money has run out. What do you say?" She looked at them.

"It sounds good to me," Sela said wearily. "I think Arquette and Coletta would come and sit, if we asked. We really don't have the money to pay sitters, Bode?"

"I'll go over and ask. Will tomorrow be soon enough?"

"Yes, oh yes," Brie said. "I'll make everything Pearl used to make for us. Pickled eggs, fried chicken, potato salad, those little rolls, the ones we used to call one-biters. There's some pickles in the storehouse. Sela makes real good brownies out of a box that taste just as good as Pearl's. Well, almost. We can take some beer or wine or root beer. Remember the time Pearl let us help her make root beer and the bottles kept exploding all winter long? Gee, that was good root beer." She grinned.

"Pearl knew me this morning," Bode said.

"What did she say?" Brie demanded.

"She wanted to know how Callie was. She asked me if I made her wake up yet. Then she asked me to get her a frizzly chicken."

"Oh," Brie said.

"She calls me Callie," Sela whimpered.

"Me too," Brie echoed sadly.

"What's the schedule for today, Brie?" Bode asked, clearing his throat.

"It's my turn to take care of Pearl this morning. Sela is cooking. Your turn to visit Callie. Stop at the Bi-Lo and get some daisies. Ask them to put some fern in the bouquet and some baby's breath. When you come back after lunch I'll go, and you sit with Pearl. Sela sits with her this evening. I'll shop after I visit with Callie. We're low on everything. I'm going to need some money, Bode." She hated to hold out her hand for the cash, but she'd given up on her pride two months before.

"I have a closing tomorrow," Sela told them. "It will take three days for my check to clear. Do we have enough till then?"

"We have enough," Bode said. "The money is my problem, so don't worry about it. I'm going to leave now before the humidity sets in. Callie's room is like an oven when the sun hits it around noon."

"I don't think it matters, Bode," Sela said.

"I guess it doesn't. I'll see you all later."

"Sela, let's have a fifth cup of coffee." Brie yawned. "I'll make it."

"I don't think I've ever been this tired, Brie."

"Me too. Pearl always said dying was harder on the people left behind, and she was right. Look at us, we look like grunge people. I haven't fixed my hair for weeks. I have on my last clean pair of underwear. The washer is always going and when it finally stops I'm too tired to wash my own things."

"Bring them out, Brie. I have to wash some of my own stuff today. I'll do yours with mine. I heard Bode washing at two-thirty this morning. How much weight have you lost, Brie?"

"Nine, maybe ten pounds. How about you?"

"Twelve. In all the wrong places, too."

They sat in silence listening to the coffee perk.

"Brie?"

"Yes."

"Wyn said he had a discussion with Callie's doctor about taking her off the IVs. With the nutrients and glucose she could stay like that for years. It's up to Judge Parker."

"Did you tell that to Bode?" Brie asked wearily.

"Not yet."

"Pearl is failing rapidly, Sela."

"I know."

"When she's gone, are you going to come back to Atlanta with me or are you going to stay here?"

"I'm going with you."

"I'm glad. Do you think God will punish us if we leave Callie?" Brie asked.

"Probably. It will be interesting to see if Bode stays or if he goes back to Santa Fe. What do you think?"

"I think he's dumb enough to stay," Brie said.

"I think so too. I'm making meat loaf."

"Meat loaf again." Suddenly Brie laughed.

Sela giggled. "I can switch up and make meatballs—same stuff goes in it. Or, I could fry it up loose, cook up some grits, fix some string beans."

"Do whatever is easiest. You haven't heard me or Bode complain. We'll eat anything as long as it's cooked."

"Loose it is, then. I wish it would rain. For some damn reason I always feel clean and refreshed when it rains. Do you feel like that?"

"Yep. Sela, why didn't we ever teach Pearl to read and write? She can a little, or else she pretends."

"She didn't want to learn. She said she wanted her children to be smarter than she was."

"I thought so, but I wasn't sure. I'll fetch my laundry. Thanks for offering to do it."

"Sure."

Later on, Brie was dozing in the chair by Pearl's bed, her hand in the sick woman's hot grasp, when Pearl jerked her forward and woke her up. "Miz Brie, I jest seen Lazarus," she said agitatedly. "He said I *cain't* meet him till I make things right. Pearl needs to clear her soul." Harry's head reared backward. Little as he was, he let loose with a heart-rending howl.

"*Selaaaaaa!*" Brie cried. "You were just dreaming, Pearl," she comforted her.

"No, no, Pearl wasn't dreaming. I seen him clear as I'm seeing you and Miz Sela. Do you listen to Pearl?"

"We always listen to you, Pearl." Brie choked out the words.

"It's about my sweet baby love."

"Now, why did I know she was going to say that?" Sela whispered.

"Miz Parker, she was a fine lady, but sickly. Her mama told me she was barren. Mistah Parker, he didn't know that when he married her. When he found out, he took up with a fine lady in town, Miz Genevieve Harrold. Yes, she was a real fine lady, and Mistah Parker, he would sing when he walked through Pearl's kitchen. Lazarus told me all this so I knowed it was gospel. Miz Genevieve found herself in the family way. Her mama took her out of Summerville." Pearl paused, and immediately fell asleep, her eyes shut, her breathing deep and regular.

"She fell asleep!" Brie hissed. "Oh God, Sela, I don't think I'm going to like this." They waited at Pearl's bedside, hardly daring to breathe. When she awoke fifteen minutes later, she continued to talk as though there had been no interruption.

"Miz Genevieve died when she gave birth to her baby. Her mammy took the child and placed it with a black family to be cared for. Later, Bode was given to the preacher when them people had too many children of their own to keep and feed. They never did tell Mistah Parker, Lazarus say. He didn't find out until the boy was six years old. Then he fetched him home. That child is Bode, you hear me? I have his paper in my string bag. Lazarus give it to me to keep safe. Mistah Parker made me promise not to tell. If I did, he said, Miz Parker would surely die of shame. Bode's real name is Michael Clemson Harrold Parker. Lazarus say that's the name on Bode's paper. He be Mistah Parker's son. Bode is a white boy."

"Oh Pearl," Brie cried. "Why didn't you ever tell him?"

"The devil would have cut out my tongue. Pearl made a promise. Lazarus say I should tell when the time is right. He say the time is right now."

"Pearl, why are you telling us? You should be telling Bode."

"*Cain't*. I shamed my boy. *Cain't* bear to see him look at me with shame. When I'm gone you is to tell him. There be more things to tell . . ." Her voice trailed away, and she was deeply asleep again. Harry howled again before he threw himself across Pearl's chest.

"My God," Sela said, covering her face with her hands. "Oh my God!"

"She said there was more. What else could there be?" Brie asked shakily.

"I bet it'll be even worse," Sela decided, sitting down on the chest at the foot of Pearl's bed. "Why do you suppose she's so lucid this morning?" she added. "Do you think she really did see Lazarus? Does that mean her . . . time is almost here?"

"I don't know what to think. What I do know is I wish she hadn't told us," Brie said. She blew her nose lustily. "I always hated other people's secrets."

They waited for an hour before Pearl woke again. As before, she picked up where she'd left off.

"Miz Parker, she wanted a baby so bad," she crooned. "She thought Mistah Parker would love her more—but it don't make him no never mind. He drank too much because of Miz Genevieve dying. So Pearl goes to shantytown because Lazarus told me there be a lady there who has a baby that is right fair-looking. He said for fifty dollars I can take the baby home. My people, they come up with the money. Lazarus give me five whole dollars. I buyed the baby for Miz Parker. Miz Callie be three weeks old when I brung her to Miz Parker."

"Did they adopt Callie?" Brie whispered.

"No. Miz Callie's real mother wouldn't sign no papers. She's colored like me. Miz Callie's real papa, he's white, but poor. He's a good man."

Sela swayed on the chest. Brie reached out to steady her. She felt so light-headed herself she knew she was a heartbeat away from fainting.

Harry wriggled against Pearl's neck, his little pink tongue licking her cheek.

"Are they still alive?" Brie squeaked.

"Yes'm. They belong to my church. They seen Miz Callie every time I took her with me."

"Do they know about Callie now?" Sela managed to croak.

"They be knowing."

"What should we do, Pearl?" Brie whispered again.

"Lazarus say Pearl has to make it right or she *cain't* get in the Pearly Gates. He say they stand guard. Promise me, Miz Brie."

"I'll do my best."

"Miz Sela?"

"I'll do my best, too, Pearl." Sela sobbed.

"Take the paper out of my bag now. Keep it safe for Pearl."

Blinded by tears, Brie stuck her hand into the string bag until she felt a folded piece of paper. She handed it to Sela. "Is this it?"

"It's Bode's birth certificate," Sela gasped.

"Pearl? *Pearl?*"

"Shhh, chile, Lazarus be talkin' to me. He say I need to sleep. Leave me be now."

Satisfied that Pearl was indeed sleeping, the girls left the room. Harry refused to leave Pearl's side when Brie tried to coax him away.

"I have to make the meat loaf," Sela said in a strangled voice.

"I thought you were going to do it loose?"

"Did I say that?"

"I think you did," Brie said. "Maybe I should iron Callie's nightgowns while Pearl is sleeping. Or maybe I should go see the Judge and hear what he has to say. What do you think, Sela?"

"Oh God, Brie, don't ask me. All these years and she never told! It's understandable, but it's also unconscionable. Callie colored . . . dear God!"

"Should I go? Can you keep checking on Pearl? I won't be long."

"Go—I can handle things. I forget, was it going to be loose or a meat loaf?"

"Let's have scrambled eggs," Brie said gently, and fled.

Sela sat down at the table, her hands wrapped around her cold cup of coffee. What was this going to do to Wyn's deal to sell off Callie's property? Whatever, it was none of her business. Earlier she'd made a commitment to Brie to go back to Atlanta with her. Wynfield Archer wasn't the man for her. She had realized that a month ago, and since then had been weaning herself away from him. He still called and said he'd make sure she got the commission check since she'd turned him over to Heywood Mudson. As if she cared about that. She realized she didn't care, not one little bit. Maybe it was time to jerk Wyn's strings a little. And why the hell not? Everything seemed to be happening all at once. This might be just the right time to test Wyn, to prove Brie's theory. Maybe she shouldn't do it on her own though. Maybe she should have Brie at her side. Maybe they should go to Beaufort and confront him. Maybe a lot of things.

Sela dropped her head and sobbed. Was she ever going to be happy? Was there anyone out there who was right for her, someone with whom she could make a life? For a little while she'd loved Wyn, or thought she did. She adored the little presents he gave her, loved their wild lovemaking, the secrecy, the lacy underwear she'd bought because it gave him such pleasure. What she couldn't handle was the look in Brie's and Pearl's eyes. They thought she was a twit, a loose goose. They sucked up her shame because they thought she was too stupid to do it herself. She really opened her eyes the day he told her he was going to sell Callie's property. Thank God she'd had enough sense to sign off on the deal, telling him she wanted no part of something so underhanded. She'd walked away, her head high. She hadn't said anything to Pearl or Brie, but they knew.

"It's all going to work out just fine." Her eyes closed, and she slept, her head in the cradle of her hands, on the kitchen table.

"Then what you're telling me is all true," Brie said quietly. She was sitting in Judge Avery's study.

"All true. I'm a lawyer, Brie. You know about attorney-client privilege."

"I don't care. How could you do that to Bode? How could you?" she demanded, outrage turning her face a deep purplish red. "You let him bust his ass, mine too, when he didn't have to, and you let Callie Parker reap the benefits. I'm so disappointed in you, Judge. You are not the man I thought you were. My God, all these years . . . What's Bode supposed to do now? Answer me that! Ah, I see you don't have any answer. I feel like everything in my life up until now has been a lie. I always grumble and complain about Sela. I fight with her on a regular basis, but you know what? When it counts she's there, and she'll always do the right thing. I'll make sure you're the first person I pay when I start drawing a salary again. Whatever else I may feel at the moment, I do appreciate your helping me when I needed it."

"Your bill was paid. Bode settled it with me the night he got here. Didn't he tell you about the land?"

"Bode didn't tell me anything. What land? Why would Bode pay off my bill?"

He told her.

Brie listened, digested the information. "You took a lot upon yourself, Judge," she said coolly. "I don't want the land. Take my name off the deed. It belongs to Bode. Not Callie, Bode. Now that we all know, how are you going to get it back from Wynfield Archer? Before he decides to sell it, that is."

"Brie, wait! You have to understand."

"I understand, Judge, more than I want to. I can never forgive you for what you did. I don't even know if I can forgive Pearl. The sad thing is, Bode is probably going to let it all slide and do nothing. Now, that's a hoot. Don't you think?"

"Brie, I understand your anger is for Bode. Why don't we wait and see how he responds? I have a small fortune in trust for him that can't be touched until he reaches the age of forty. I had to fight tooth and nail for it with Genevieve's parents, or the boy would have got nothing. Parker Manor is his now. He's the blood heir. Don't forget, Clemson Parker appointed me Bode's and Callie's legal guardian."

"Well, Judge, I hope you can make him see that. I think you're going to have your work cut out for you. No one should ever attempt to play God with other people's lives. You have a nice day now, Judge," Brie said, stomping out of the room.

"And she's still fighting Bode's battles," the Judge muttered as he lit his third cigar of the day. He cringed when he thought about the meeting he would inevitably have with Bode. Maybe he should think about going to Columbia with

Miss Nela. For a month or two. Maybe even three. Maybe he wouldn't come back until it was time to bring the firewood indoors.

Avery Summers sat back in his chair and thought about Brie's words. Yes, he had played God—but at Clemson's request. Didn't the end justify the means? Would Bode and Brie be the upstanding citizens they were today if he hadn't taken the matter in hand? What had he really robbed them of? Their lives, came the silent accusation.

"Nela—I'm ready to go up to Columbia!" he shouted hoarsely.

The hours dragged for Brie and Sela as they waited for Bode to return. Brie hovered over Sela as she stirred and mashed something cooking on the stove. What the concoction was, Brie had no idea.

"What are we going to do, Sela?" she burst out. "When should we tell Bode? Before, or . . . after?"

Sela scattered dried parsley into the mixture she was stirring. "I don't know. If you need an immediate answer, then I'd say after. That doesn't mean it's the right answer. Pearl's passing will be hard enough for Bode to handle. It's only my opinion." She poured a cup of water into the pot and peered at the contents before she stirred it. "What do you think?"

"I guess so. What *is* that?"

"You said loose chop meat."

"I thought we agreed on eggs?"

"Oh." Sela lifted the pot and threw the contents down the sink. Brie turned on the switch for the garbage disposal.

"Is it going to rain, do you think?"

"Looks like it," Brie said.

"I'm in the mood for a good angry storm, with lots of thunder and lightning. Even if it rains, I doubt if it will cool things off. Do you like it when steam or whatever it is comes off the ground after a hard rain?"

"I never thought about it." Brie shrugged.

"Brie, Wyn is going to sell Callie's property."

"What? He can't do that! Fifty acres of this land belong to Bode and me." She repeated what the Judge had told her. "I told him to take my name off it. Can you imagine? I couldn't believe it when he told me. At first I wasn't going to say anything to you because I had nothing to do with it. I've never kept anything from you, Sela. If the property had a clear title, you'd make a bundle on the sale."

"No. I signed off when I found out. It was the hardest thing I ever did, but it was the right thing. We're a family, and families don't knife one another. I'd rather pick shit with the chickens than be a party to that sale. Wyn also asked me to marry him. I want you to know I gave it some serious thought. It was what it was for a time. I needed him, and maybe he needed me. The sex was super, but there's more to life than sex. I wanted to talk to you about him a lot, but I knew your feelings so I . . . held it in. I wish now I'd confided. Everything seems to be crumbling apart right around us. Isn't it funny how we thought if Bode came back, everything would just fall into place and wow, we'd all live happily ever after? What a crock!" Sela snorted.

"You got that right," Brie agreed. "You want some lemonade?"

"If you put some sugar in it—I need a boost. Not that artificial stuff. God, I hate the taste it leaves in your mouth. You fix it, and I'll check on Pearl. Where's Bode? He's late."

"Maybe he stopped for gas or something. I'll fix him a glass. I'm going to leave as soon as he gets here. I need to sit with Callie where it's quiet and I can think. Are you okay with all of this, Sela?"

Sela shrugged. "As okay as you are."

They finished their lemonade out on the porch just as Bode drove up. "I think you need a tune-up, Sela," Bode said, getting out of the car.

"So what else is new? I put a lot of miles on it when I was showing my property. My big dream was a company car. Oh well." She sighed.

"How's Mama Pearl?"

"She knew us. We . . . spoke for a while. What she said was that she's been talking to . . . Lazarus," Sela said as she looked everywhere but at Bode. "Harry refuses to leave Pearl. You should take him out before his bladder bursts."

"How's Callie?" Brie asked.

"The same. It's so hot in that room, Brie. Maybe you want to put on a sundress or something."

"It doesn't matter—the heat doesn't bother me. I don't plan on staying too long. We're having eggs for supper," she added, to have something to say.

"I thought we were having meat loaf."

"I thought I was frying it loose," Sela said, getting up from the swing. "Now I find out we're having eggs!"

"What's wrong with her?" Bode asked.

"I guess she's tired like the rest of us. I'll see you later."

"Is there anything I need to do for Mama Pearl?"

"Hold her hand, talk to her, fluff her pillows. If you think it will help, you can take the air-conditioning unit out of my window and put it in Pearl's window. It's pretty hot in there. If Pearl sleeps through the afternoon, you can help Sela with the laundry," Brie said flatly. She was halfway through the door when she turned, and added, "When were you going to tell me about the deed and the fifty acres, Bode?" She didn't wait for a response but ran across the porch and down the steps and into her car. Before Bode could think of a suitable reply she was roaring down the road.

"What am I missing here?" Bode demanded.

"Why ask me?" Sela mumbled.

"Because Brie tells you everything and you can't keep a secret to save your soul and we both know it."

"First you have to have a secret to keep. It seems to me you're the one with the secret. Brie had a perfect right to ask you that question. When *were* you going to tell her?"

"Probably never. I've been trying to figure out a way to give it back without it going to the state or Wynfield. I didn't know about it, Sela. The Judge shoved the deed at me the night I got back. Maybe I can put it in trust for Callie. I need to read up on it a little; there just hasn't been time. In case you think I've been trying to put something over on Brie, you can get it right out of your head."

"Seems to me you need to get it out of *Brie's* head."

"Listen, did something happen while I was gone?"

Sela busied herself by taking things out of the refrigerator to clean it. "Does it seem like something happened? Look around, Bode, isn't everything the same?"

"Everything *looks* the same, but you and Brie sound different, like you're carrying the weight of the world on your shoulders."

"Guess what? I don't much care what you think. Do you know what I really care about right this minute? I care that I look like shit, feel like shit, and will continue to do so for a long, long time. I know I look like a scrubwoman. My hair refuses to do anything but hang on my neck. All I do is sweat. I can't sleep. I've lost weight, and on top of that I worry about everything. Right now I have no idea why we're having eggs instead of meat loaf. Do you see the place I'm in?"

"Well, tomorrow when we go to the picnic you'll feel better," Bode said, putting his arms around her slim shoulders. "You smell like vanilla."

"I just spilled it on my hands. I guess I forgot to put the cap on tight. Brie said the picnic is off."

Bode threw his hands in the air. "Why?"

"I think Pearl is . . . Her breathing has changed since yesterday. She says she talks to Lazarus and she's *seen* him. I think things like that happen toward . . . the end. I don't want to leave, and neither does Brie. Harry seems to know. He won't leave her side."

"That's fine, Sela. I don't mind. I'm going to sit with Pearl now. If you need me, call."

"Your laundry's in the basket. You can fold it while you're sitting with Pearl."

"Okay. Sela, go for a walk. Get outside or better yet, take my bike and ride around the property. Do something different."

"Maybe later."

Bode entered Pearl's room and, as always, looked around for a moment. It was sparsely furnished, with a bed, a dresser, a rocking chair, a braided rag rug on the floor, and the chest at the foot of her bed. In the past the pine floor had always been clean and polished. Now he could see dust in the corners and on top of the dresser. He knew Brie had cleaned, polished, and dusted the other day so it must be his turn. He'd do it later. Pearl always said cleanliness was next to godliness.

"You can be poor, but there's no need to be dirty," she'd always said. She'd said so many things over the years that had made his life fuller and richer. He reached for her hand and covered it with both of his. "Mama Pearl, it's me, Bode."

"Chile, you best be getting yourself out of that tree before you break your neck," she mumbled. "You best not be skinning your knees and making a hole in them pants, 'cos Pearl don't have no more patches. You listening to me, chile?"

"I hear you, Mama Pearl. I'm coming down."

"You be minding my sweet baby love. Be careful she don't fall into that old cistern. You be watching her real careful, Bode."

"I will, Mama Pearl. I'll be real careful." He sucked in his lower lip and bit down so hard he could taste his own blood.

In all the years he'd lived at Parker Manor the worst thing, the absolute worst thing that sent shivers up his spine and made him weak with fear, was that somehow he would bring shame to Pearl.

"I've always done my best, Mama Pearl," he whispered. "You can meet Lazarus and tell him I'm being a good boy and that I always did what you said. You tell him that for me. I wish you could have had a life with Lazarus, but I under- stand about the name business. Sometimes I wish I knew what my real name was. Other times it doesn't matter. Every- one should have a name. Lazarus didn't care that you were Pearl from Parker Manor. He was Lazarus from Harrold Manor. Sometimes I think you told us all a fib, Mama Pearl. I think you gave up your life for the girls and me. Lazarus thought so, too.

"You worked so hard, Mama Pearl, from sunup to sun- down and when it got dark. I never heard you complain, not once. That pittance Mr. Parker gave you should have shamed him. You spent it all on us. I don't remember if we appreci- ated it or not. I tend to think we did. Brie did, and so did Sela. I'm not sure about Callie. One present was never enough for her. She always wanted two. I remember the day you walked all the way to the drugstore and bought three lit- tle purses for the girls. They had little pearls all over them and the handles. You bought a bigger one for yourself and said you couldn't wait to carry it to church. You loved that purse. You bought me a new roll of fishing twine. I remem- ber the stars in the girls' eyes when you handed over those purses. I can still see the look on Callie's face when she said she wanted yours, too. You handed it right over.

"God, I wish there was something I could do for you, Mama Pearl. I would do *anything* to see you well and sitting up in that bed." Harry's ears stood at attention as he stared at his master. He cuddled next to Pearl.

"I know that, chile," came her voice, faint now yet full of tenderness, "but Lazarus, he says he needs me soon. I'm waiting for his word. You best not be touching my frizzly chickens, Bode. If you do, the devil will git you. You mind Pearl now."

"Yes, Mama Pearl. I won't touch the chickens."

"You're a good boy, Bode. Pearl loves you with all her old heart. So much sometimes it feels like this heart is going to bust right out of my chest. Pearl's biggest happiness is knowing you loved me like I was your real mama."

"You are my real mama, and I love you. Nothing can ever change that." He bowed his head, tears gathering in his eyes. He felt a hand on his shoulder, gentle and comforting, and a tissue dropped in his lap. A moment later Sela was gone, the door closing softly behind her. Suddenly Harry was on his lap, whining as he licked the tears from his master's cheeks. Bode wrapped his arms around the silky dog until Harry woofed softly in protest.

Brie plopped down on the chair in Callie's room and mopped at her face. "You're not going to believe this, Callie, but I'm getting crow's-feet around my eyes. Sela says this hot humid weather is good for us, makes us supple. You know— like the humidity plumps up the wrinkles. Guess you don't care about that. You're just lying there sucking up your nutrients and glucose. I can see you lying there when we're all sitting in rocking chairs. Wake up, damn you. I'm sick of this, Callie. I don't know how much more I can take. I know you hear me, I'm talking loud enough. I bet if I counted up my words I've said over a million. Pearl probably said ten million, Sela the same as me, and now Bode is talking to you. That's so many words you can't pretend you can't hear. You're lazy, Callie. You're too damn lazy to crawl out of that place you're in. You don't want to deal with life the way the rest of us have to. You always expect someone else to do it for you, to pave the way, to make it easier.

"Pearl isn't going to live much longer. God, Callie, if you would wake up and see her one last time. Try. Try for Pearl. You can do it, Callie, I know you can. Don't let Pearl go without saying good-bye.

"You are all Pearl thinks and talks about. She's delirious sometimes and talks about when you and we were little. It's so sad, and there's nothing we can do. If you could just wake up, Callie. If you could just see her this one last time before she goes to meet Lazarus.

"Damn you, Callie Parker, you *owe* her! You're alive, warm and are being fed and someone sees to your personal needs. You take and take and are sucking our life's blood out of us. *Wake up!* Take responsibility for your life. Wynfield Archer is going to sell Parker Manor. Does that mean anything to you? Don't you give a damn? They'll knock the house down and build a pro shop and golf course. If you wake up, you can stop it."

Brie bolted off the chair, her bare feet sticking to the floor as she made her way to Callie's bed, her hands clenched into two tight fists at her sides. "I know you can hear me, I know it! You need to say good-bye to Pearl. You need to stop Wyn from selling Pearl's home. I should push you out of that bed, but you'd just lie there and wait for someone to put you back and pretty you up.

"Listen, Callie. Sela and I are going back to Atlanta. Maybe Bode will stay on; he hasn't said. We'll forget about you after a while. That's what happens when people move away. There will only be strangers around you. You aren't going to like that. Open your eyes, Callie. Move, do something." She took Callie's hand in hers, squeezed it, and let it drop. Deflated, she went back to the chair and mopped at her face and neck.

She tried another tack. "I know a secret," she singsonged. "Sela knows it, and so does Bode. You don't know it though. Pearl's sick so she can't make us tell you. It was Pearl who told us the secret. You don't know it and we aren't going to tell you. We know a secret, a really big secret." She kept up the singsong words for forty minutes before she gave up and picked up her purse to leave.

She turned, and said, "I think Wyn is getting ready to ask the Judge to pull the plug on your nutrients. That means you'll die. He has to get a court order to do it, so I don't think the Judge is going to have any trouble. You better start listening to me and get ready to wake up. Bye, Callie."

So there.

Three days passed. Sela was the first one up on Sunday morning. It was her turn to go to town to pick up the Sunday paper and donuts. She peeked in at Pearl, saw Bode asleep in the chair. He looked haggard. She listened to the strange new sounds assaulting her ears. Strangling, rasping sounds, gurgling sounds, sounds she'd never heard before. She shook Bode's shoulders before she ran down the hall to wake Brie.

"Should we call the doctor?" Bode asked.

"I think we should call Pearl's preacher and Arquette," Brie said. "I'll do it."

"Call the Judge, too," Bode said.

"You want to contact the Judge, Bode, do it yourself," Brie shouted over her shoulder.

They came, one by one, dressed in their finest, to pay their last respects to one of their own. Pearl, struggling to breathe, was unaware of the devotion of her congregation. Arquette and his wife cried openly, as did many of the others.

The preacher, a stately gray-haired gentleman, leaned over the bed and whispered words none of the others could hear. His eyes were wet when he made his way out to the kitchen. "If the Lord placed saints on this earth, then Pearl was a saint. She never said a bad word about anyone. When help was needed Pearl was the first one in line to offer that help. She was a fine, good woman, and the Lord knows that; that's why He's taking her. Her heart was big and full of love for everyone. She'll be sorely missed, and no one will take her seat at services. Bless you all for taking such good care of her. The Lord will reward you. We pray daily for Miss Callie."

"Thank you, Reverend." Brie's eyes burned unbearably when she led the preacher to the back porch and said, "Which ones are Callie's parents?"

"The lady in the blue dress, and her father is the gentleman standing next to her. Speak to them—they're good people. Are you going to church, Brie?"

"No, I'm sorry to say. I will, Reverend, I promise."

"Promise the Lord, not me. Thank you for calling me. We'll pray all today for Pearl. I must be going now, service starts in twenty minutes."

"I appreciate you coming, Reverend."

Brie nodded, kissed the old gentleman on the cheek and watched him drive off.

Callie's parents were sweet, gentle people. Both of them had tears in their eyes when Brie offered them coffee in the kitchen. She didn't know what to say, how to bring up Callie's name. They knew she knew—she could read it in their expressions.

"Pearl was a wonderful mother to Bode and Callie," Callie's mother said. "There was no other way, Miss Canfield. We knew it was best for Callie. We always knew what was going on. Pearl talked to us at church and then when she started to bring the child it was something that made us both very happy. We visit the nursing home once a week and always take flowers. We talk for a spell, then we leave."

"I know," Brie said in a choked voice.

"We won't interfere. The Lord works in mysterious ways, Miss Canfield. Everything in life has a reason behind it. We were glad to come today and be made so welcome. It pleasures my husband and myself to see the place where Callie grew up. Perhaps we'll see you at services."

When they were gone, Brie realized that she didn't even know their names. She wanted to cry.

Moments later, Harry let loose with an ear-piercing howl that sent them all on the run to Pearl's room. Their arms entwined, they could only stare at the puppy, who was doing his best to straighten Pearl's head on the pillow with his nose. He whimpered as though in pain. He looked up once, and later Bode said his eyes were full of tears. They rushed to the bed, Brie taking one of Pearl's hands, Sela the other, while Bode cradled Pearl's head in his arms. Their sobs of sorrow ricocheted around the room. Harry leaped off the bed and ran around in dizzying circles until he reached the closet, nudged it open and rummaged for one of Pearl's slippers, which he dragged to the middle of the room and promptly peed a flood. He then bounded back onto the bed to give Pearl one last lick to her face, before scampering into Bode's arms. Neither Brie nor Sela could tell which of them was whimpering.

Pearl of Parker Manor joined Lazarus just as the sun began to set. Those left behind, standing sentinel, listened to the last strangled breath and then fell into each other's arms. They sobbed together, comforted each other as they tried to lock themselves together, fearing aloneness would somehow rob them of all their feelings. They loved as one, they cried as one, and they grieved as one.

At the funeral, later that week, as hard as he tried, Bode could not quiet the inner trembling in his body. Mama Pearl was really gone, the minister was saying so in many different ways. *Ashes to ashes* . . . Tears burned his eyes. He wanted to stand up and shout something wonderful, something so meaningful, that the whole congregation would rise up and cheer for Mama Pearl.

Bode turned slightly in the pew and was stunned to see the small church was full to overflowing. People were standing in the back with small children in their arms. They were all here to pay their final respects to Pearl.

Out of the corner of his eye, Bode saw Sela offer him a tissue. He reached for it, saw the tears rolling down her cheeks. He turned then, his gaze traveling to the back of the church when he felt a cool swoosh of air on the back of his neck. His eyebrows shot up as his eyes widened in disbelief. *Lazarus.* Lazarus was there, with a warm, golden glow all around him. Bode gasped. He wiped at his eyes, but the golden glow was still there. Maybe he was supposed to do something, make a sign. Was Mama Pearl with him? He had to know. Bode reached out from his seat at the end of the pew and put his hand on Pearl's casket. At the same moment he turned again to stare at the golden glow, at Lazarus. He watched as Lazarus's hand moved until he saw a jaunty thumbs-up salute. Now, where did Lazarus learn *that?* Bode raised his own hand in a farewell gesture. A moment later the golden glow was gone. He turned back, his attention riveted on the minister when he felt a hand on his shoulder. He reached up to cover that hand, thinking it was Sela, but there was nothing on his shoulder. Sela's hands were folded in her lap. Brie's hands were clutched around her purse. *Mama Pearl.*

A smile as radiant as the glow he'd seen in the back of the

small country church settled on his face. He was stroking his chest, that place which covered his heart, when Brie's hand reached out for his. "She's here, isn't she, Bode? I can feel her," she whispered. Bode nodded. His smile stayed with him. Forever and ever, when Mama Pearl entered his thoughts he would smile.

On the way home from the cemetery, Brie swore she saw Pearl floating overhead, her wings flapping noisily.

"You're drunk," Sela said irritably. "It was the wine the preacher gave you. He said he had four jugs. It was Lazarus's wine. I tried to get you to stop because I remembered how potent it was, but you kept guzzling it like soda pop. Ohhh, I don't want to go home. It won't be the same without Pearl," she wailed.

"We have to go home," Brie said carefully. She didn't think she was drunk, but she did have a buzz. "We have to talk to Bode. I told Callie we had a secret. I wouldn't tell her what it was. I thought it would make her wake up. I screamed and yelled at her something fierce. Pearl would have whipped my bottom if she'd heard me."

"She's gone," Sela blubbered. "Callie is never going to get better. She's going to die, too. We're all that's left."

"We number three," Bode said quietly.

"You're going back to Santa Fe, too, aren't you?"

"Yes, but I don't know when. I'm glad you're going to go to Atlanta with Brie. I won't worry about you both so much if I know you're together."

"You don't need to worry about us at all, Bode. Take a good look at us—we're all grown-up now."

"Are we going to leave Callie behind? How can we do that?" Sela cried.

"We can have her transferred to Atlanta. I'm agreeable if you are, Sela. Bode?"

"We can talk about it tomorrow. Why don't we go home,

put our bathing suits on, and turn the hose on ourselves. It's got to be at least a hundred and ten degrees. We can have a picnic supper," Bode said, swinging the basket of food the preacher had given him.

"There's praline-pecan pie in here. Mama Pearl wouldn't think we were being disrespectful. We can sit out under the angel oak. I'm in no more of a hurry to go into that house than you are."

"I don't want to change my clothes," Brie blustered.

"I don't either," Sela said.

"Okay, we do it in our clothes. I hate this suit anyway," Bode said.

"I didn't know you had a suit with you," Sela said.

"I don't. I borrowed it. Solly Cramer loaned it to me. Said I could keep it. He gained twenty pounds."

"That's tacky," Brie objected. "The least you could have done was buy a suit for Pearl's funeral. Shame on you, Bode Jessup." At Bode's stricken look she relented, and said, "It doesn't matter. All that matters is you were there."

"Why are we snapping and snarling at each other?" Sela demanded. "We need to remember we're all that's left."

Later, when Bode drove off the main road onto the dirt road that led to Parker Manor, Sela said, "It looks the same, but it shouldn't. The life force is gone. How can it look the same, Bode?"

"It's a place, Sela, and places don't change. People do."

"Have you changed, Bode?"

"Yes, Brie, but then so have you and Sela. Change is inevitable. It's up to the individual as to whether it's for the good or bad. This is just my opinion now. Well, let's get to it," he said grimly. He jerked at his tie and threw his jacket over an azalea bush. His face was still grim when he turned on the hose and waved it about menacingly. He expected the girls to squeal and run away. Instead they stood still and let him soak them.

"This is no fun. First of all the water is pissy warm, and Pearl won't be hollering from the porch and she won't yank us in the house and scold us and make us change our clothes. Where's the challenge in that?" Brie walked over and took the hose from Bode's hands then turned it on him, squirting first his head then his entire body. "Did you know that if you wet your shoes and keep them on till they are dry, they conform to your feet?"

"How fascinating. You're right, this is no fun. I'll turn the water off," Bode said.

They sat cross-legged under the angel oak for a long time, none of them speaking, their eyes on the back window of Pearl's room.

"I don't know what to do," Sela said finally. "I feel like I should be bawling my eyes out. Another part of me wants to smash something. Is this where we're supposed to say life goes on or something like that?"

"I guess," Brie said.

"Do you think you'll ever come back here?" Bode asked her.

"No. I'll drive up to see Callie once a month or so, but I'll stay at a hotel. I don't think I could come back here. What about you, Sela?"

"Me neither."

"Bode? Will you?" She had to tell him. When would be the right time? How was he going to take it? Maybe she shouldn't tell him, but then the Judge would make some reference to it, assuming she'd told him, and that would only make matters worse.

"I don't remember any other home. Living with the Reverend was all right, but it wasn't the same as living here. This was home—Mama Pearl made it so. They say you always want to come home. What happens when there's no home to come back to?"

"Home is wherever you hang your hat," Brie said curtly.

"That's your present home. Bode's talking about the home you grew up in," Sela said.

"I'm not stupid, Sela. I know what he's talking about. This will be a memory. I don't feel like arguing. I wish the damn place would burn down. Maybe that way it would be out of our systems. Then for sure we wouldn't want to come back."

"I wonder how much Wyn's going to sell it for?" Sela mused.

"He can't sell it—he doesn't have a clear title. We own fifty acres, and the house sits on our fifty acres. I don't want it. Brie said she doesn't want it. But we're stuck with it. What I suggest is we split it in four and record a new deed. Do you agree with that?"

"That means we have to pay the taxes," Sela said. "You're doing this for Callie, not for us. You want her to have a place to come back to if she wakes up. And, as usual, we're picking up the tab. I say no. I don't want it, so don't put my name on it," she told him firmly.

"I agree with Sela. Take my name off it. You can keep it for yourself and Callie," Brie said bitterly.

Bode frowned, his mouth a tight line in his face. "Exactly what are we talking about here?"

"You know very well what we're talking about. Don't play stupid with me, Bode. Sela and I have had months to do nothing but talk about all this and relive our past. Yeah, it was wonderful the way we tell it now, but we said it so many times we actually started to believe it. It wasn't that wonderful, Bode, not for us and not for you. You sucked up the way we did. And all for the privilege of being allowed into Callie's little circle. She was Cinderella and we two were the Ugly Sisters. You were fucking Prince Charming," she snarled.

"I was the only boy—I had to be the prince," Bode said defensively.

"It wasn't a game, Bode," Sela said.

"We gave and gave and gave. Speaking for myself I was doing it for Pearl—I thought it made her happy—and for you too, Bode. Callie was a damn little snot, and you know it, but she had you mesmerized. You still get a sappy expression on your face when you talk about her. You should be married by now with a family. Instead you dream about Callie. You cut and ran when you thought she was getting married. I'm sick of hearing your excuses," Brie said harshly.

"People always fight when someone dies," Sela said sadly. "Pearl wouldn't like the way we're carrying on. God, I still can't get it through my head that she wanted to die first so she'd be waiting for Callie. I need to stop thinking about it, but I don't know how to. By not coming back here, I guess," she assured herself.

"Do you know what else I'm sick of hearing and thinking, Bode?" Brie hadn't finished with him yet. "I'm sick of you playing the martyr. Pretty soon it's going to be a new millennium. So what if you're black, so what? It never mattered to us. We all know it mattered to Callie though, and you goddamn well sucked that up, too. You climbed into a mold and you stayed there. You're still there. I defy you, Bode, to tell me I'm wrong."

"Old habits are hard to break. This is the South, as you well know."

"What would you do if a fairy godmother suddenly appeared and said, 'Bode Jessup, I now pronounce you white?' What would you do if that same fairy godmother said, 'Bode Jessup, I grant you yesterday'?"

"I'd bust my gut laughing," Bode said.

Brie heard Sela suck in her breath. She rummaged in her

purse and withdrew the paper from Pearl's string bag. "Well, Bowdey Jessup, I'm your fairy godmother, only because there's no one else who cares for the job. I now pronounce you white, and yesterday is yours if you want it."

A long time later Brie said, "I don't hear you laughing, Bowdey Jessup. I want to hear you laugh. So does Sela."

Sela yanked Brie to her feet. "Come on, we have to pack up Pearl's things. I don't think Bode wants us to hear him laugh. We can tell him the second installment when he's finished laughing."

As they ran toward the house Sela said, "I had to get you away from there before you started crying. Don't let him see how badly he's hurt you," she said fiercely. "I swear I'll slap you if you start wailing."

"I handled it all wrong, Sela."

"You did what you had to do. I'm not faulting you one little bit. Come on now, take a deep breath, and let's do what we have to do. Bode won't be able to do it."

Sela stripped Pearl's bed and carried the laundry out to the kitchen. She brought one of the pillowcases to her cheek to try one last time to smell Pearl's scent. Tears scalded her eyes. How worn and patched the sheets were, how soft and silky to the touch. She poured detergent and Clorox into the hot water and closed the lid.

In the pantry she gathered up four cartons that said ketchup on the side and carried them back to Pearl's room.

"I guess we should pack this up and put Callie's name on the box. What do you think, Sela?"

"That sounds good. I'd just like some little thing to . . . to remember her by. If you have no objections, I'd like to take her Bible."

"She carried that Bible every time she went to church, but she couldn't really read or write, just a few words here and there," Brie said sadly. "It's okay for you to take it, Sela."

"She used to touch the pages. Look how tattered it is. Maybe it was her mother's. What are you going to take?"

"Well, the string bag should go to Callie or Bode. Do you think anyone will care if I take the three-holer?"

"It's yours. I said so. I'll slam anyone who says you can't have it," Sela blustered.

Pearl's dresses, underwear, nightdresses, and shoes went into one carton. The string bag minus the three-holer was placed on top with her comb and brush. A jar of glycerin and rosewater was carried to the bathroom and placed on the shelf.

"What do you suppose is in this chest?" Brie asked, rocking back on her heels.

"The secrets of the universe," Sela said, squatting down beside her.

"I feel like a sneak going through it. I don't think even Callie or Bode know what's in here. I'm afraid to open it."

"I'll open it," Bode said quietly, appearing in the doorway. He dropped to his knees, and Sela and Brie inched out of the way. They gasped as Bode lifted the lid. "Mama Pearl's treasures," he said gruffly.

"It's our junk!" Brie exclaimed.

"Look, there's that macaroni box I made for her jewels," Sela said, tears streaming down her face. "All my school pictures!"

"Mine too," Brie cried. "Here's the jar I painted to hold her flower seeds. I wondered why she never planted them."

"Here's the clothes I came here in," Bode said, pulling out a pair of faded cotton knickers, "even my shoes." His shoulders started to shake as great sobs ripped through the room. The girls put their arms around him and held him tight.

"A secret to Pearl was absolutely sacred," Brie comforted him. "She truly believed the devil would get her if she told. You can forgive her because she loved you with all her heart.

What she did was wrong, but what was the alternative? Let it all go, Bode."

"What's the second installment?" he asked a long time later.

They told him.

Bode's head reeled sickeningly. He took a deep breath, and another, until his head cleared.

"Callie's parents came by the other day to pay their respects. They were nice people. I didn't ask them their names. The Reverend knows. Arquette knows. Lazarus knew. The Judge knew; probably Miss Nela, too. The whole damn town knew, Bode. Everyone but you and us," Brie said in a hushed voice.

"Are you saying the whole town knows about Callie?" Bode asked, a stiffness in his voice the girls had never heard before.

"I'm not sure about that, but Pearl's people know. I hate calling Pearl's friends 'her people'—I don't know why I do it."

"You do it because that's what Pearl called them. We always deferred to Pearl," Sela said. "Callie has a right to know her parents."

"Her parents have a right to know Callie, too, and to visit more than once a week if they want to. They're her flesh and blood," Brie said.

"Callie could never handle that," Bode said slowly.

"And you know what? It's your fault, Bode. You can deal with it. Sela and I are leaving."

"Yes, we're leaving you with Princess Callie," Sela said angrily.

"Some friends you are," Bode said, just as angrily. "Are you going to cut me out of your lives?"

"That depends on you. We aren't the ones who disappeared for months. We were here. Just out of curiosity, how does it feel to know you're white?"

"I feel the same way I did when I thought I was black. Nothing has changed. I am who I am."

"No, you're Michael Clemson Harrold Parker," Brie said quietly.

"No, it's you who doesn't understand. That's only a name. I *am* Bowdey Jessup. There is a difference. Whatever I am, I made it myself. I don't need someone else's name."

Brie felt like sending up a cheer. "You're going to inherit the Harrold estate when you're forty. All of this belongs to you, too. That should give you some pleasure."

"Why would you think that, Brie?" Bode asked curiously.

"I don't know. A whole new life. Money in the bank. Staring down people who didn't accept you back then. A whole bunch of things."

"I'm past all that. I don't want or need any of the above."

"I suppose you're going to put it in trust for Callie or something stupid like that," Sela said.

"I refuse to dignify that comment with a response," Bode said.

"Then dignify yourself and carry all this stuff to the attic," Brie said curtly. "I've done all I'm going to do."

"Why are you two so angry with me?" Bode asked.

"Because you're an asshole," Sela shot back. "I hate martyrs."

"Me too," Brie said.

"Is that what you think I am?"

"What makes me the angriest is I loved you. I threw myself at you so I guess I'm angry at myself. I wouldn't take you now if they gift-wrapped you in pure gold. You're not the person I thought you were."

"Brie, I never pretended, never presented myself in any way except the way I am. I've lived my life by my own beliefs and what Pearl taught me."

"And look at what Pearl did," Brie said gently.

"It was all a lie. Look, we're beating a dead horse here. Let's just fold our tents and move on," Sela said.

"I'm going to make some coffee," Brie told them. "We can eat the stuff in the picnic basket for supper. I think we should pack, Sela, and leave tomorrow. We can stop and see Callie and go on from there. What do you say?"

"Sure."

"Bode?"

He shrugged.

In the kitchen Brie asked, "Were we too hard on him?"

"Nope. I didn't know he broke your heart, Brie."

"Well, he did. I don't want to talk about it."

"Okay. I hate men," Sela said.

"I'll drink to that," Brie said, and pulled the remains of Lazarus's wine from the cupboard. "There's enough here to toast Pearl. For the three of us. We promised."

Later, Bode made the toast. "To Mama Pearl, may she rest in peace."

"Amen," Brie and Sela said in unison.

18

～

He felt like a spy in a bad thriller, but he didn't turn away from the living-room window. She was, after all, here to see him so why shouldn't he feast his eyes on her for a few more moments?

She was prettier than the first bloom in summer. He knew her cat green eyes (that she confessed were really contact lenses), were sad and probably full of tears. She'd come here so that he could make the sadness and tears go away.

The little VW Beetle was green like a summer meadow, the old cracked leather top pushed back. A rainbow of flowers filled the space behind the front seats. He frowned when he saw the box of frizzly chickens on the front seat. Where was he supposed to sit?

She tapped the horn, the sound ricocheting upward and through the closed windows. The car had a distinctive horn, a sound he didn't care for: *i-oooga, i-oooga.*

The sound was angry, impatient. They must have a time-table of sorts. He sprinted from the room not wanting to give the beautiful girl one more impatient moment. He smiled, but she didn't smile back. Instead a tear rolled down her cheek. "Shall I follow you, darling? Or would you rather go in my car?" he asked.

"I'll never ride in your car, sweetheart. You almost killed me, don't you remember? You ride with me."

"There's no room. I'll follow you."

"Are you afraid I'll do the same thing to you, my darling? Don't be afraid of me, Wynfield. I would never do anything to hurt you."

"Yes, you would. You told your friends you didn't want to marry me. I wanted to die when I heard it."

"But you didn't die. You left me to die instead. You lied. Your soul is going to go to hell. Bode is going to get you. He'll make you pay for what you did to me. Bode loves me. Bode will make it all right. You just wait and see."

"Why did you come here?" Wyn gasped.

"To see if the spell is working. I'm going to Pearl's funeral, and I need to be able to tell her you have pain and sorrow. You do have pain and sorrow, don't you, Wyn?"

"Ask her to take it away. Please, Callie, ask her to take it away."

She laughed, the sound eerie to his ears. "Pearl is dead; it's too late. She wore herself out taking care of me. All because of you. That's what all these frizzly chickens are for. I'm putting the feathers in her casket so she can continue to give you pain and sorrow till the end of your days. When I wake up I'm going to tell everyone what you did. Bode will come after you. You won't be able to find a place to hide. Bode will kill you because he loves me."

"Do you love Bode? Tell me the truth, Callie. Do you?"

"I'm not going to tell you. Good-bye, Wynfield."

"Don't go, please don't go!" he shouted. He turned and ran because one of the frizzly chickens was chasing him. He ran faster, the frizzly chicken squawking, its wings flapping angrily. He made it inside just as the chicken slammed against the door, its feathers shaking loose. He looked down to see a feather slide under the door. Petrified, he galloped up the stairs, the feather following him in the draft his body created.

Wyn sat up in bed, drenched in his own sweat. The room was ice-cold, the air-conditioning set at sixty degrees. His heart was pounding so hard and fast he could hear it above the sound of the cooling unit. God Almighty, what a nightmare!

The bourbon bottle beckoned. It was less than a quarter full, which meant he'd consumed the rest before falling asleep. He knew he'd become a borderline alcoholic. Maybe he was a full-fledged one and needed help. He snorted as he gulped at the fiery liquid. The only thing that could help him was clearing his conscience.

He was sorry he'd listened to Kallum, sorry he hadn't told the truth and taken his punishment. He was sorry about so many things. Sorry about Sela.

Last week in a fit of guilty remorse he'd pressured the Judge for a court order to discontinue Callie's nutrients. Since that day he'd been drinking and drinking. He'd drink, sleep, wake up, drink some more and fall asleep again. He'd gone on a binge and hadn't showered for three full days. He hadn't shaved either, much less eaten any food. He'd been sick, puking his guts out for hours, but he kept right on drinking.

Everything was hitting him right between the eyes. He really cared for Sela and eventually asked her to marry him. When she didn't say yes he'd tried harder, lavishing expensive gifts on her that she gave back, taking her to costly restaurants in Charleston, planning two-day luxurious getaways. For a while he'd lived, counted the hours until it was time for their lusty lovemaking. Until, like everything else, it all came crashing down around his head. The day he heard of Pearl's illness and Bode's homecoming, he'd gone into a funk that left him an emotional cripple. He'd called a locksmith and had security locks and an alarm system put in. Still fearful, he'd called the same security company and hired security guards to patrol the iron gates that led to his house. When two weeks passed and Bode didn't show up he discharged the guards, but kept the doors locked at all times. He didn't venture out past the electronic gates. He was a prisoner in his own home, thanks to his secret guilt.

Wyn looked at the clock. God, he still had three more hours until the sun came up. Today was Pearl's funeral. Should he go? Would he be welcome? Hardly. Did he dare put himself in the same vicinity as Bode Jessup? Would it make him a hypocrite to attend? Of course it would.

He was on the verge of a nervous collapse, and he knew it. Time to get himself together and get on with his life. The best way he knew how to do that was to go to the police and confess and plead . . . what? Nothing. Only the truth. He'd do that and then he'd wait for the court order and free Callie at the same time. She deserved to die with dignity. He'd take all his punishment, even if it meant going to prison. Maybe he wouldn't have to go to prison if Bode got hold of him before he made it to the police station. "You're the better man, Bode," Wyn said, uncorking a new bottle of bourbon. "Everyone says so, so it must be true."

Wyn held the glass aloft. "To Pearl, may she go straight to hell with all her curses and hexes." He cried and blubbered and then, like the drunk he'd become, he slobbered and crawled back into bed with his nightmares.

The day was bright, the early-morning sun warm and golden. Brie served breakfast on the back porch. A huge breakfast of scrambled eggs, the last of the ham, a small mountain of toast with a scoop of yellow butter and Pearl's wild black-berry jam.

They were on their second pot of coffee and had barely said more than "Pass me the salt, please," to one another.

"What are you going to do, Bode?" Sela asked quietly.

"Take care of the paperwork, help Arquette shore up the front porch, mow the lawn, clean out the barn, have the util-ities taken care of, visit Callie, and then I guess I'll head back to Santa Fe."

"You'll go to the cemetery, won't you?"

"Every day," Bode said.

"Will you cut some flowers and take them? Pearl loves . . . loved flowers," Sela said.

"Absolutely."

"Anyone want more coffee?" Brie asked. They shook their heads. "Then I'm going to wash the dishes and clean up the kitchen. Sela and I packed last night. We'll load our cars up and head out. We're going to stop and see Callie one last time. Why don't you come with us, Bode? It will be the four of us together. We've never all visited at one time. I think it might be nice."

"Okay. I don't know if you want to hear this, but last night I called the Reverend and asked him what Callie's parents' names are. It's Margaret and Edward Davis. They have ten children. Well, Callie would have made ten. Four of the chil-dren went to college, five if you count Callie. They have plans for the others to go, too. Mr. Davis is a plumber. Mrs. Davis cleans houses. I think maybe I'd like to find a way to do something for them—you know, make it possible for the other kids to go to college."

"That's nice," both girls said at the same time.

"I'm seriously thinking about selling this place. Do either one of you have any objections?"

Sela wanted to say, hell yes, she did have objections. When she'd thought maybe, in some way, she could take possession, it was with the idea of the three of them always having a home. Too much had happened, however, to have that dream become a reality now. She shrugged and looked away.

"Everyone's gotta do what they gotta do," Brie said, gathering up the plates. "It's going to be hot today. Bet it rains later on. What will you do with the money if you sell this place?"

"I don't know. If you need an answer right now, I'd probably say I'll set up a bunch of scholarships in Mama Pearl's name for kids that wouldn't otherwise get a chance to go to college."

"African-American kids, right?" Sela said.

"Yeah. I think Mama Pearl would like that. Maybe give some money to the Reverend to enlarge the church. It will be a long time before things can be finalized. The Judge is going to have his hands full making things come out right. I'm not going to help him do it either if that's your next question, Brie. Believe it or not, I feel the same way you do. I should have been told when I was old enough to understand." He'd hoped for a smile from Brie, but none was forthcoming.

There was a desperate sound in his voice when he said, "Listen, I'm open to any and all suggestions. Maybe legally this place is mine. That's on paper. But in here," he said, thumping his chest, "it belongs to all of us, and I'm more than willing to share. If you don't want it sold, I won't sell it. I can sell off some of the land and keep some acreage around the house and use that money to refurbish it. It won't be the same for any of us without Mama Pearl. It's my personal opinion that it's time to let it go. You both have a vote, and I'd like to hear about it."

The air *swooshed* out of Sela's lungs. He was right. She

didn't trust herself to speak, so she bobbed her head up and down.

Sela drew in her breath again as she watched her two best friends eyeball each other warily. Brie was going to say something really stupid and then Bode was going to retaliate and things would go downhill from there. Brie's voice when she spoke was so cool and neutral-sounding that Sela flinched. So did Bode.

"Well, Mr. Jessup, I think that's a commendable decision."

"That's it, commendable?" Bode said.

Brie stalked into the house. Sela hurried after her. Bode threw his hands up in the air. He stormed into the house. "What is it exactly that has your panties in a wad, Brie?"

What is it that's wrong? Why am I acting like this? Because, she answered herself, *I expected him to wrap me in his arms and tell me he loved me when he saw his birth certificate. If he'd just tell me he loved Callie, I could handle that. And now this wonderful magnanimous gesture.*

So what if she was acting childish? So what if she was tormenting Bode? He deserved it.

"Do you really want to know what's bothering me?" she said aloud. "Well, I'm going to tell you. I realized these past weeks that I've been a fool. No child, no girl, no woman wants, ever, to admit she made a fool of herself. I realized I tried to buy your affection and then as I got older I tried to buy your love. I used to work myself to a frazzle for you. But it wasn't for you at all, it was for Callie. Indirectly, at least. I would have prostituted myself for a smile, a pat on the head from you. It was wrong of me to expect something in return. Either you give of yourself with a pure heart or you don't give at all. At the time, because I was too stupid to do it any other way, my heart was pure. I didn't care what color you were, or what your background was. Sela didn't care. *But Callie did care.* Therein lies the difference. You're one stupid, mother-fucking son of a bitch, Bode Jessup. And you know something else? I don't give a shit what your *real* name is: you'll always be Bode Jessup to me."

Bode galloped out of the kitchen.

"God!" Sela said.

"Now dry these dishes, Sela, and let's get out of here."

"Yes, Mother," Sela said, saluting her. "Guess you really told him. God!"

"Pearl's wings must be rustling. Do you think he'll still go with us to say good-bye to Callie?"

"Sure. He'll waltz in here like nothing happened, and we'll go on from there. Are you okay with this house thing?" Sela asked.

"Yeah, I am. I couldn't come back here knowing Pearl wasn't here. Could you?"

"No. He's doing the right thing. In the end all the money will go to pay off Callie's bills. You'll see," Sela muttered.

"You mean the ones before the Medicaid took over?"

Sela nodded. "The ones Wyn didn't pay. Bode will honor them," she said.

"Do we have enough money to get to Atlanta?" Sela asked.

"I have forty-two dollars, and six hundred left in my account at the bank," Brie calculated. "I can borrow some from my friend Myrna until I get back on my feet. I'll share. I know you're tapped out."

"I'll get a job and pay you back right away. Thanks for being my friend, Brie."

"Thank you for being mine. We've been through a lot, Sela, and we're still friends. That has to mean something. Do you think Bode will stay in touch?"

"Nope. We're history after today."

"I don't want to believe that," Brie said.

"We are leaving Mr. Jessup a nice clean kitchen. Pearl's things are put away. We tidied up our rooms. We can go now, Sela."

Sela started to cry. "I never thought I'd have to say good-bye to this place. Do we just walk away? Do we look back and wave?"

"I think we walk out to our cars and drive away. I won't be able to look back. I have an idea. When we drive away, let's sing that ditty Bode taught us when we were learning how to count. You know: One, two, buckle my shoe, three, four, close the door . . ."

"Yeah, yeah, let's do that," Sela said shakily.

"I just have these two cases. I'll lug them out and come back and help you. See? When you really need him, he's never around."

When their cars were packed, Sela shouted for Bode. "We're ready!"

Bode wheeled his old bike out of the barn. It sparkled in the bright sunlight.

"I forgot about this bike. How long did it take us to sand it down and paint it? You paid for the front tire, didn't you?"

"Yep, and you paid for the back one. It looks nice, doesn't it?" Sela said.

"Bet we sank a hundred bucks into that bike with the new seat and the new handle grips. You owe us a hundred bucks for fixing that nightmare," Brie shouted.

"It was worth zip when I left it here," Bode shouted back.

"Yeah? Well it's worth a hundred now," Brie said, sliding into the car. "Send a check."

Sela squeezed into her car. "On the count of three . . ."

"Okay. Turn on your engine," Brie bellowed.

"Engine revving," Sela shrilled. "One, two, three . . ."

"One, two, buckle my shoe, three, four, close the door . . ."

He knew what they were doing. His eyes started to itch as

he pedaled after their cars, his voice as lusty as theirs. "Five, six, pick up sticks . . ."

They didn't look back.

They were sitting on a hard, wooden bench surrounded by colorful pots of flowers outside the hospital when Bode pedaled up to them.

"Forty-five minutes." He beamed.

"In your dreams. We've been sitting here for one hour and twenty minutes. Face it, you're getting old, and your legs are shot. Riding around in a car will do that to you," Brie said.

"Mama Pearl always said when you don't have something good to say to someone you should keep your mouth closed," Bode said.

"Guess I wasn't there the day she said that," Brie said, sticking her tongue out at him. Damn, she was acting childish.

They waited while Bode shackled his bike to the pole of the awning.

"I will never understand, no matter how long I live, how a person can look exactly the same for months on end," Sela said quietly.

During the visit, at first they talked among themselves, doing their respective "do you remember?" routines, until one by one they started carrying on a conversation with Callie.

They were youngsters again, arguing and laughing under the magnificent angel oak. "I know a secret," Brie giggled. "We all know it. If you want to hear it you have to wake up. We promised not to tell. Everyone knows but you, Callie. It's a wonderful secret. Well, part of it is wonderful. No, I'm wrong, both parts are wonderful."

Sela took her cue from Brie. "It's the most wonderful secret in the world. Pearl told it to us. You weren't there so you couldn't hear it. It's a secret, a real secret. A better secret than any of the ones we had when we were little. We're going away today, Callie. I'm moving with Brie to Atlanta. We'll come back and visit when we can. Guess you are never going to hear the big secret, and it *is* big. I think you're just doing this to get attention." Sela made her voice sound childish and whiny. "You always used to do that to get attention, and Bode fell for it every single time. Brie and me were too smart for most of your tricks, but because we wanted to go to Parker Manor, we let you get away with it."

"We never told Mama Pearl when you made us give you half of our Popsicles after you gobbled down your own. She would have fanned your bottom. You were selfish," Brie said. "But we have a secret now. That's better than anything you have. Guess what? We had eggs and ham for breakfast and all you get is that shitty-looking stuff in a bag. You can't even chew anymore. What we have is better than a whole Popsicle. Sela and I are going to buy some when we leave here and we're going to eat them all by ourselves. We won't have to give you even a lick. So there, Callie Parker."

Bode blinked. What the hell were they doing? Sela shrugged. Brie stared him down, defying him to screw up.

"It's time for you to wake up, Callie," he joined in. "We're all leaving, and there won't be anyone here to take care of you but nurses you don't know. I suppose they'll do your laundry, but will they brush your hair and put ribbons in it like Mama Pearl and the girls did? There won't be anyone to bring you flowers. Wake up. Come on, Callie, you have a whole life ahead of you. You told me yourself you were going to make a fine lawyer. Are you really going to let me believe you're a worthless pissant? Wake up. Open your eyes, Callie."

"She's not going to open her eyes," Brie said contemptuously. "She's doing what she's always done, waiting for someone else to open them for her. She is too damn lazy to do anything for herself. She made a tired old woman her personal slave and couldn't be bothered to get up out of that bed to go to her funeral."

"Bode's right. You're worse than a worthless pissant. You know what you are, Callie Parker? You're a taker. That's the worst thing in the world. We're all givers and you know something? Pearl knew that. That's why she told *us* the secret and not you. So there. I can't believe I'm saying these things. I don't think it's doing any good. We've been talking like this for months, and she doesn't move an eyelash," Sela whispered.

"We agreed to do it in two-hour segments. I'm telling you, I read that coma patients can hear you. The trick is not to stop talking. We have to keep it up. We're here. I want to leave knowing I did everything humanly possible," Brie said.

"Okay, we'll keep at it," Bode said.

"Get really mad, get stern with her," Brie said. "Stop being Mr. Nice Guy."

"It's worth a try, Bode," Sela urged him. "Hell, anything is worth a try. Ganging up on her just might do it."

A helpless look on his face, Bode's eyes swiveled first to Brie and then to Sela as he laced into Callie—something he'd never done in the whole of his life. "I knew there was a reason I didn't want to hire you, but you whined so convincingly I agreed to it," he began, scarcely able to say the words. "You're not dependable. Jesus, you couldn't even go through with your own wedding. That doesn't say much for you, Callie. All your education down the tubes. Wasted. All our hard work for nothing just so you can lie here in bed and have people wait on you for twenty-four hours a day. Did you really think we'd stay around forever to make your life comfortable? We're not. We're all going to get on with our lives and we'll have our semiannual and annual reunions and you won't be invited because you can't get to wherever it is we're going to have the reunion," Bode said breathlessly, his eyes rolling from side to side.

"Keep it up, you're doing good," Sela hissed. "Don't stop now."

"We all have such a grand secret. I'm sort of sorry you aren't part of it, but we're all tired of sharing with you. Even if you were here with us you'd probably spoil it. You're never going to know the secret. We're going to leave and take the secret with us."

And on and on it went. When Bode's voice started to lag, Sela picked up and then Brie and then they started all over again.

When Sela gave up her turn, she said, "I'm going out to the machine to get us a soda pop. My mouth is as dry as dust."

Brie looked at her watch. They'd been at it for two hours, and were fifteen minutes into the third hour. They'd finish up and be on their way. She leaned back and listened to Bode's voice drone on and on until she wanted to scream. What was the use? Why were they doing this? It was all so hopeless.

It was a warm, wonderful, scary place she was in. Probably the attic. They were calling her, saying things she didn't want to hear, things she didn't want to think about. They were going away and taking the secret. They weren't going to tell her what it was. They were talking about her like they didn't like her. She could hear them. She should crawl out and tell them she was going to tell Pearl. She wanted to tell them to be quiet; she wasn't interested in their old secret. She tried to move, to wiggle out of her warm cocoon and make them stop saying such terrible things to her. They were her friends, how could they say such things? *Don't go away, don't leave me. This place is dark and I'm afraid to open my eyes.*

"I know you hear me. I know it! Don't pretend you can't,

Callie Parker. We want to say good-bye before we leave. It would be nice if you'd open your eyes and say good-bye to us. We don't know when we're going to be able to come back to see you again. Do it, Callie! Open your eyes and maybe we'll tell you the secret. Maybe, but I'm not promising."

"Okay," she cried silently, *"I'm going to open my eyes."*

If they hadn't been standing right beside her bed, they would have missed the sight of her flickering eyelids. Brie's jaw dropped as did Sela's.

"Jesus, did you see that? She opened her eyes," Bode shouted.

They were so pleased that Callie wanted to laugh. She blinked and blinked again. Were they laughing or crying? She kept right on blinking because they sounded so funny.

"Smile, Callie," Brie said.

Callie smiled.

"Blink your eyes again."

Callie blinked.

"Can you move?"

She tried to lift her hand. It felt funny, heavy and dry. She thought she could feel her skin scratch the warm dark blanket.

"Nod your head, Callie," Bode said. She nodded.

"Say something, Callie."

"Tell me what the secret is."

"She's making noises. It's been so long since she used her voice. I bet she's answering us, we just don't know what she's saying. Try again, Callie, we can't understand what you're saying. You've been in an accident, Callie, and asleep for a very long time. Please try, tell us you understand what we're saying. Blink if you know it's me, Brie, and you understand what I just said."

Callie blinked.

"Can you see us clearly? Blink if you can."

She blinked.

"We need to call the doctor, somebody," Sela said.

Bode was already out of the room in search of the charge nurse. A call was put in to Trident. Bode spoke with the neurosurgeon.

Back in the room he said, "They're sending an ambulance. He really thought I was making this all up. He said this was impossible. Can you believe that? They want to put her in ICU and monitor her. They're going to bring a portable cardiac monitor and defibrillator, called Lifepak-6, to hook up to her for her transfer to the hospital."

"You're going back to the hospital, kiddo," Brie said.

She wasn't going anywhere until they told her what the secret was.

"Secret."

They laughed, then they cried. "This must be that one-in-a-million miracle people always talk about. I can see it now. A book, movie rights, the whole nine yards," Sela grinned.

"Secret."

They babbled as one, saying the first thing that popped into their heads. "I won the lottery," Bode exclaimed, "money to burn."

"I had a baby," Sela shrilled. Bode collapsed against the door.

"I found a white knight, and I'm getting married." Brie giggled.

Callie smiled, her eyelids closing.

"Don't go to sleep," they shouted together.

"Baby," Callie said.

"We have to keep her awake until the doctor gets here. He didn't say that, it's my idea," Bode said. "Let's sing, 'One, two, buckle my shoe, three, four, shut the door . . .' "

Callie smiled. She was still smiling when the doctor, a disbelieving look on his face, entered the room.

What seemed like a long time later the doctor joined them

in the hall, and said, his voice awestruck, "She has intentional activity indicating brain function controlled by the patient, not the involuntary, nonpurposeful eye fluttering or occasional grimace she exhibits when she's turned or moved. I've never seen a patient wake like this. I've heard of them though. I think we're seeing a miracle here. It's going to be a long road back, though. Intensive therapy. Costly. Minute-by-minute monitoring. Private nurses, at least for a while. We'll start testing to evaluate her. We'll take it one step at a time. I still can't believe this," he said again as he walked over to the ambulance attendants.

"Bode, get in there and if she's awake ask her who was driving the car. I don't know if she has a memory, but it's worth a shot. You heard him, this is going to cost a fortune. If Wyn was driving, like I think he was, that means Callie's insurance will pay for this after his company pays them back. For God's sake, get in there, and if she's sleeping, wake her up. Talk to her!"

Bode was back minutes later. "She just kept saying 'baby' over and over. You'd better be able to come up with one." Bode laughed uproariously.

"I say this calls for a drink. You're buying, Bode. We'll meet you at Jason's. Lunch would be good, too."

"Does that mean you're staying?"

Brie looked at Sela and nodded. "For a few days. I say after a drink and lunch we head to Beaufort and scare Wynfield Archer. We don't have to tell him Callie didn't tell us anything. The fact that she's awake might be all he'll need to come up with the truth. Is he going to call her a liar?"

"Whatever it takes," Bode said quietly. "I'll ride with Brie."

"Sounds good to me. God, I dread unpacking this car again," Sela grumbled.

"Just take out what you need. I'm in a daze. You drive, Bode. Do you think it was the three of us ganging up on her?

We should have done that sooner. I mean, we were really pelting her. Maybe she was going to wake up anyway. If she'd done it a few days sooner, she could have seen Pearl one last time."

"Mama Pearl wouldn't have known, Brie," Bode said softly. "Maybe Callie has no memory of . . . before."

"She knew us, at least she seemed to. My advice if she does have a memory is for us not to tell her about Pearl until she's mentally and physically stronger. The Judge is her legal guardian, Bode."

"I know that."

"They say Rusk Institute in New York City is the best place in the world for patients like Callie. You might want to think about that. She is going to need so much care. I can't comprehend any of it. Guess you'll be staying on a bit longer. Don't even think about asking me or Sela to stay longer. We can't, we work for a living. You're self-employed."

"Brie, I think you and I—"

"Don't think, Bode. I don't want to hear whatever it is you want to say. We're beyond that now."

Over frosty bottles of Coors beer, Sela brought up the question Brie wanted to bring up, but couldn't. "Are you going to tell her about her parents, and about yourself?"

"I don't know. Certainly not now. If she improves beyond the way she is now, I'll consider it. How can I zap her with Mama Pearl *and* all that, too?"

"Now why did I know you were going to say that?" Sela said.

"Because you're a pain in the butt, that's why," Bode said.

"Are we really going to go to Beaufort?" Brie asked, digging into her tuna salad.

"I think it's a good idea," Sela said.

"I'll go with the majority."

"If I hadn't suggested it, what would you have done?

Sucked it up, sold off the property and paid all the bills?" Brie snarled.

"I don't do things at the speed of light the way you do," Bode said coolly.

"What's that supposed to mean?"

"Let's not get angry here," Sela pleaded. "Callie's awake, that's all that matters. We're leaving Bode in charge. Why don't we let him handle it since he's done so well over the years? I've been thinking since we sat down. There's nothing for us to do for Callie. We stuck it out, did what we could. I want to believe we were a small part of her waking up. She's in other hands now. We'll only clutter up things if we stay on. I'd like to stick to our original plan and head for Atlanta."

"Okay," Brie said.

"I don't believe this," Bode gasped. "You're leaving *now?*"

"Yep, and we're sticking you with the check. It's only half a mile or so back to the hospital; you know the way. See you around, Bode," Brie said, picking up her handbag.

In the parking lot, Brie said, "Don't read more into this than there is. There is not one thing we can do for Callie. If there was, or if I felt she needed either one of us, I'd say yes, let's stay a few more days. It was a stupid idea of mine to go and see Wyn. The Judge will call him since he's her guardian. Let Bode deal with it."

"I never really believed in miracles. In what I've read they always happen to other people, not people like you and me."

"Maybe that's because we don't need a miracle. Callie needed one. Guess that makes us both believers," Brie said.

"I'm so glad." Sela sighed. "It was wonderful, wasn't it?"

"Yeah, it was. Did you see Bode's face? He looked so . . . Lord, I don't know how to describe how he looked."

"Euphoric." Sela grinned.

"Euphoric is good." Brie laughed. "Okay, let's go. You have the map I made for you in case we get separated?"

"Got it right here on the front seat."

"Then I guess we should be going."

They didn't look back this time either.

Bode watched them from the doorway and felt like they'd taken a part of his life with them. He choked on his tears as he trudged down the road in the boiling sun.

Nothing was forever.

19

Wynfield Archer rolled the ice cube around in his mouth. He was on his fifth drink. He knew it was his fifth because four glasses were lined up on the coffee table. He was watching a rerun of *Cagney and Lacey,* a female cop show. Cagney, the blonde, reminded him of Brie Canfield. Cagney was an instinctive cop, honest, a dog-with-a-bone cop. The kind that never gave up. Every sixty minutes she hauled someone's butt off to jail. She was an alky like he was becoming. He frowned. He'd had this same conversation with himself a day or so ago and he'd pretty much admitted he was one. Or had he negated it? He simply couldn't remember.

The phone at his elbow shrilled. He looked at it and then looked away. He knew it was Kallum. Prissy, stupid Kallum had given him an ultimatum a week or so ago. Maybe it was a month. Straighten up, clean up your act, or I'm out of here. Like he was really going to listen to Kallum. Kallum was the reason he was in this mess.

When Sela told him their affair was over, he'd given up all thought of entering politics. Somehow, some way, some smart-ass reporter would have dug into the accident and just when it was time to go to the polls he'd be hung out to dry. He laughed, a pitiful sound, when he recalled the look on Kallum's face. "Guess you aren't going to be with me in the governor's mansion after all, Kallum. Suck it up like I'm doing. Or get lost. I don't need you. If you'd been a real friend you would have let me go to the police and clean the slate." That's what he'd said—and Kallum had looked at him with such disgust he still cringed when he thought about it.

The phone continued to demand his attention. Maybe it wasn't Kallum, but Sela. He leaned over, lost his balance, and fell on the floor, the phone cord wrapping itself around him. Somehow he managed to bring the receiver to his ear. "Yes?" he said gruffly. Then, as he listened, his eyes rolled back in his head with shock. "Yes, yes, I'll be there as soon as I can," he gibbered. "You're sure there's no mistake? Yes, it is a miracle, a wonderful miracle," and he parroted the doctor's words.

Wyn cursed, using every dirty word he could think of, and when he ran out of the standard curses he made up more. Kallum was Memory 3 on his portable phone. His thumb punched the key.

"Kallum? I thought you might like to hear the latest news. I'm sure it will make the six o'clock bulletin, but I wanted to be the first to tell you," he said, enunciating each word carefully. "Callie Parker woke up this morning. When my ass goes into a sling so does yours, you son of a bitch. I imagine the Bar Association frowns on the kind of advice you gave me. Stop squawking, Kallum. I don't want to hear anything you have to say. I'm going to try and sober myself up and go to the hospital. If I can't do that, then I'm going to hire a car service to drive me. Go to hell, Kallum."

He showered and shaved, nicking himself four times in the process, then dabbing at the cuts with a styptic pencil. He dressed carefully before going downstairs to make a pot of coffee.

In the kitchen he looked around at the mess. Had he fired

his household help, given them a vacation? When was the last time he'd seen anyone in the house? He couldn't remember. He measured out coffee, spilling more grounds on the countertop than he put in the basket.

Callie awake. After all this time. He wanted to die.

Goddammit, he was a good person. At least he used to be. He banged his head against the wall. If the court order had come through and they had taken away the nutrients and the IV solution, he would have been a murderer. "I'm sorry. So very sorry," he muttered over and over.

Callie awake. She'd been asleep for months and suddenly she had awakened. He wished he was more religious, knew more about miracles. If Callie woke up, that had to mean Pearl's spell was over. His pain and sorrow would vanish. He would be his old self again, after he had gone to the police.

Jesus Christ, where is everybody? I need to eat. Making coffee was one thing, cooking for himself was not something he felt he was in any condition to do. He yanked at the refrigerator door. Everything inside it had green-and-blue mold on it.

It was a challenge. He shook his fist in the air. "I will eat, I will drink coffee, I will get to the hospital, and I will be sober when I get there. I swear I will."

Callie awake. Bode Jessup and the girls would be at the hospital. Should he go there first, or to the police station?

He cracked an egg into the frying pan and swirled it around with a fork until it was cooked. He slid the egg onto a plate and wolfed it down. He followed this with an over-ripe banana and the entire pot of coffee. He prepared a second pot, made four trips to the bathroom before he called a car service. He had just finished his second pot of coffee when the driver blew his horn. He made one last trip to the bathroom before stepping into the car.

Callie awake.

Bode Jessup.

Supercop Brie Canfield.

Sela Bronson ex-mistress.

It was going to be a hell of an encounter.

"This, Wynfield Archer, is where they separate the men from the boys."

Uh-huh.

Bode leaned his bike up against a trash container. He walked into the car-rental agency. Twenty minutes later he opened the trunk of the Ford Mustang. The bike fit perfectly.

He turned the radio as high as it would go. He didn't want to think until he settled himself into a safe harbor. Parker Manor. He had to remember to call Hatch.

He was shaking when he pulled the Mustang under the angel oak. His feet slapped at the ground as he ran across the yard, up the steps onto the back porch, and into the house. He didn't stop to wonder where he was going. He knew he was headed for the only place that ever gave him comfort— Mama Pearl's room. He closed the door and wished for a lock. He wrapped himself in a worn, softer-than-silk afghan from the bottom of the bed and settled himself in the rocking chair. The blanket smelled wonderful. It didn't matter that the temperature was almost a hundred degrees, he was chilled to the bone. Harry wriggled and squirmed until he, too, was under the blanket, his heart beating next to Bode's.

He leaned back in Pearl's rocker. In his life he'd never felt this safe, this insulated. Maybe he should plan on staying here for the rest of his life. He stroked Harry's silky ears. The puppy whimpered softly.

Everything was wrong. He'd let Brie get away from him because he didn't have the guts to stand up to society and say, "Fuck you all. This is what I want, it's what she wants, and if any of you can't accept it, then you have a problem, not me."

Now it all made sense. As a child Pearl had allowed him to *do* for Callie, but that was it. How many times had she cautioned him to *stay in his place*. It wasn't him she was worried about though. It was Callie. Surely she knew Callie would grow up and want to get married. Would she have told her the truth then? Obviously not. So she'd done the only thing she could think of—she'd refused to go to Beaufort. How relieved she must have been when Callie called off the wedding. He frowned. She'd encouraged him in subtle little ways to pay attention to Brie and tried to partner him up with the little girl. Once she'd said Brie was right for him. He didn't know what that meant, at the time. She must have known the Judge would tell him at some point. White and white. Never white and black, not in Pearl's eyes anyway.

It was a mess, and it was going to get messier. "Oh, Mama Pearl, you don't know what you did."

He had to call Hatch.

Brie. Brie with the crinkly, smiling eyes. Brie's tart tongue. Brie's smile. Brie's generosity. Brie's genuine devotion to Pearl. Brie.

Brie thought he loved Callie, and he'd allowed her to think so. It was easier because he knew he could never, ever cross that color barrier. Now, when it was too late, when he could cross it if he wanted to, he couldn't. Brie wouldn't allow it. *"You snooze, you lose,"* she'd said. She hadn't cared at all. She loved him for who he was, and color didn't matter to her. She would have had his babies and loved them as much as she loved him. He'd blown any idea of that ever happening now.

Callie. How was he going to tell her she wasn't Callie Parker? How was he going to tell her he owned Parker Manor? Would she believe it? She'd probably say, "Oh pooh, you're a squatter," or something offensive like that. She would expect, demand that he give it back to her. And would he? Brie seemed to think so. Sela did, too.

Suck it up, Bode, like you did all these years. All for the privilege of living at Parker Manor and being Callie's personal *slave.*

The good times weren't good at all, Brie said. We were just too damn stupid to know any better. It wasn't quite true, and Brie knew it. There were good times, many of them. But it was Pearl who made the good times, not Callie.

Bode sat for a long time, watching the sun set from Pearl's window. When it was totally dark in the room he unwrapped the afghan and walked out to the kitchen, Harry trotting behind him. He turned on the light, picked up the phone, and punched out Hatch's number.

"Hatch, it's Bode."

"About time you called me."

"Hatch, I need you."

"I'm on my way. Does that burg have an airport?"

"Charleston."

"If the tail winds are good, I'll set down in three and a half hours. Be there."

"I'll be there."

"See you, Bode."

Bode grinned. He felt better already. Not too many people possessed their own Learjet. Not too many people could fly one. Hatch, as Bode was fond of telling anyone who would listen, could do anything. It occurred to him then that Hatch was the same kind of friend Brie was. Was.

He thought about Sela then. Sela would love Hatch. Hatch would love Sela. Hatch did a lot of real-estate work. At least, his office did.

"Aaaahhh."

* * *

The Learjet sat down neatly. Everything Hatch Littletree did he did perfectly and neatly. Hatch had the uncanny ability to look at a problem, roll it around in his brain, and come up with a solution. As far as Bode knew, he'd never been stymied. He was a loyal, one-of-a-kind friend to all he allowed into his inner circle. Bode knew he was at the top of Hatch's list just the way Hatch was at the top of his list.

He waited now at the jetway until he heard Hatch's clomping steps. He traveled light, a bulging burlap sack thrown over his shoulder.

"Thanks for coming, Hatch."

"My pleasure," the big man said. This had to be serious stuff. Bode wasn't smiling, and in all the time he'd known Bode, Bode had never once asked for a favor of any kind simply because he was too busy doing things for other people. "Where are we going?"

"Parker Manor. Callie woke up this morning."

"As in bright-eyed and bushy-tailed?"

"Not quite. They're going to call in a whole bunch of specialists, the ones who said she was a vegetable, brain-dead, those guys."

"One for the textbooks, huh? Bet there are a lot of strange faces around today."

"What's in the sack? Did anyone ever tell you they make luggage?"

"You should talk; you used to carry your things around in a shopping bag because it had handles."

"Old habits are hard to break."

"Do I sense a double meaning there? To answer your question, I have *stuff* in this sack, and I also have about four sets of luggage that's a pain in the rump. Am I embarrassing you or something?"

"Hell no. You could never do that. I just never saw anyone

get off a plane carrying a burlap sack. We used to get potatoes in sacks like that."

"We used to get corn in them." Hatch grinned. "I can get
you one if you think you'll use it."

"Yeah, sure."

"You know what else? I bet I could get you a sockful of
rubies for about two bucks at Wal-Mart. How many do you
want?"

"Yeah, yeah, that sounds good."

"You aren't even listening to me. They cost four bucks."
He guffawed at his own joke. "Is this your chariot?"

"Until the rental lease runs out. Get in and buckle up."

"So this is the Lowcountry, huh?" Hatch said, peering out
into the darkness.

"It's pretty here. It's real hot right now. It cools off a bit in
September. October is nice. November is nice, too. It's almost
cold for Christmas."

"Thanks for sharing that," Hatch muttered. "I'm thinking
about buying an eighteen-wheeler, what do you think?"

"Great investment. What are you going to do with it?"

"Play with it. I never had one. Send it out to the Reservation and let them play with it. Whatever."

"How's Nightstar?"

"She told me two weeks ago she wasn't interested in getting *really* involved with a damn Indian. She wants to marry
a *white* man."

"I guess that singed you a bit, huh?"

"Nah, she was someone to have dinner with. You gonna
fix me up with Brie?" Hatch asked slyly.

"No, Sela's the one for you. Man, she's going to blow your
socks right off your feet. Sela came into her own this past
year. That's one gal that will give you a run for your money,
Hatch. I personally guarantee when you two set eyes on one

another it is instant . . . whatever the word is they're using these days. Trust me."

"Is she the marrying kind? I want a lot of kids."

"Yeah, yeah she is, Hatch. She'll make a good mother, too."

"So when do I get to meet her?" Hatch asked happily.

"Whenever you can go to Atlanta. They took off today like scalded cats. What that means . . ."

"I know what it means. What the hell did you do—or what *didn't* you do is more like it?"

"A lot of things, I guess," Bode said wearily.

"You got any beer at Parker Manor?"

"I don't think so."

"Then let's stop at the store over there. I have this taste for Australian beer. Do you think they have Foster's here?"

"Jeez, Hatch, I don't know. I'll ask."

They found it at the fourth store they stopped in. Hatch bought all they had and placed an order for more that he said he'd pick up in a few days; Bode just rolled his eyes. "You never mention my second biggest accomplishment in life," Hatch remarked. "Why is that, Bode?"

"Just because you can drink a twelve-pack and hold your urine doesn't mean you should go in the record books, does it?"

"You can't do it?"

"Why would I want to?"

"To see if you can do it. That's what life is all about, Bode. You take yourself too seriously. Lighten up, for God's sake."

Bode sighed. "I'm going to say one thing to you now and then we aren't going to talk until we get home. Promise?"

"Sure."

"My name isn't Bowdey Jessup. My name is Michael Clemson Harrold Parker. *Parker,* Hatch."

Hatch rolled down the window. The air smelled sweet and clean. He lit two cigarettes and handed one to Bode. He continued to stare out at the dark night.

Twenty minutes later Bode said, "We're home. Welcome to Parker Manor, Hatch."

In the kitchen he tossed Hatch an opener. "Are you hungry?"

"I was born hungry, you know that."

"We have fried chicken, cheese, some leftover spaghetti. Anything sound good?"

"Yeah, pop it all in that microwave and I'll get rid of it for you. What's for dessert?"

"A whole, as in *whole,* praline pie. I think there's some ice cream, too."

"That sounds good. Warm up the pie, though. This place must be very old. I like old things. Old things have character, like some people."

Hatch finished the last of the praline pie just as Bode finished his story. "This isn't some textbook case we're studying. We're real people with faces and names you know and recognize."

Hatch lit a cigarette and blew a perfect smoke ring. "I'm giving these hateful things up the first of the year. I think you left out one of the most important parts of your story. Until you can admit, commit, you ain't going nowhere, buddy. And don't insult this old Indian by pretending you don't know what I'm talking about."

"She made it perfectly clear she didn't want to have anything to do with me. She said she wished I could have seen my own face when Callie opened her eyes. She misunderstood what she saw. Over the years she gave me so many chances, and I blew them all."

"Unrequited love must be a terrible thing," Hatch said, blowing a second perfect smoke ring. "You aren't a kid anymore, you're all grown-up, so that means you have to take responsibility for your own actions. If I was standing in Brie's shoes, I can't say I would have done anything differently than she did. How much is she supposed to suck up? She covered your ass for the holidays. That's a biggie. She took a leave of absence to come here and do what she could. She made it possible for you to play the White Knight and be a martyr at the same time. I'd say that covers going that extra mile. How could you be such an asshole, Bode?"

"Looking back, it came easy," Bode said, picking at the crumbs on the pie plate.

"Do you have any idea how hard it is to get into the FBI? For a woman it's even harder. I hope you sent her some roses or candy or something."

"She told me on the phone that she was accepted at the academy. I was so proud of her I wanted to bust. I told her so, but she just passed it off. These past months have been a real learning lesson for all of us. Brie and Sela as kids didn't come out here because of Callie. That's what everyone thought and believed. They came because of Pearl and me. I never knew that, Hatch. I don't think they even like Callie. Yet they knocked themselves out for—"

"Mama Pearl and you. They pulled up your slack. Guess that stings a little bit, huh?"

"It stings a lot, Hatch." He paused. "Callie is going to need a lot of care and support if she's to get well. She'll expect me to be there for her. She's never going to accept who she is. I don't even know if I should tell her. Maybe when she's ready to handle it. What if she doesn't recover fully? What if she always needs care? Am I supposed to turn my back on her? The girls think she called off her wedding to Wynfield Archer because she realized she loved me and because of Mama Pearl. Right now the reason isn't important. She called it off. Knowing Callie as I do, that means to me that she expects something."

"She's an able attorney, you said so yourself. She can work like the rest of us if she recovers. She also has a set of parents, real brothers and sisters. Family is important. If we can take care of this insurance business and do what has to be done, pay her medical bills and if she can be rehabilitated, I don't see what the problem is."

"Her expectations," Bode said quietly.

"Look, I'm not saying you should desert her. I'm saying she has a family who I'm sure have never forgotten her and love her just the way they love their other children. You cannot keep sacrificing your life for this girl. It's not healthy. Brie and Sela saw that—that's why they left. Life goes on, Bode. I'm not being cruel, it's reality. That nobility of yours has to stop somewhere. This is a good starting point. You can work on the rest of it. I pay you enough so you can fly back and forth and if you have a mind to, you can take some flying lessons and fly yourself here. Whatever I have is yours, and that includes the jet."

Bode opened two beers and set one in front of Hatch. "Callie will never accept the fact that she's half-African-American. Mama Pearl did a real good job on her. Callie still has the old beliefs. I don't think she's capable of changing. I know her, Hatch, she'll try to *pass*. I don't know if they still use that term today or not. The old people do," Bode said quietly, his eyes somber.

"That's her problem now, isn't it?"

"One we all unknowingly contributed to."

"Do you think the hospital called Mr. Archer?"

"I'm sure they did. The Judge, too. He's her legal guardian. They'd have to call him."

"I imagine he's sweating a lot right now. If Brie is right and Archer is responsible for the accident, it's all going to bust loose. Why didn't you and Brie ever push it further?"

"The police and the insurance companies were satisfied."

"What happened to the car?"

"I guess it was taken to the junkyard and sold for parts. I never asked. Why?"

"It's the little things, the things people don't pay attention to. I'd like to look at the seat belts. He said he was wearing his and she wasn't. Isn't that what you said Brie told you?"

"It's in the police report. Brie had copies of everything she could get her hands on. Wyn told Sela the names of the insurance companies, and Brie called them all. Everything is a matter of public record. She had a file on the Seagreaves' lawsuit, too. I don't think that's been settled yet. Probably sometime next year."

"Let me see it," Hatch said, swallowing in one gulp half the contents of his beer bottle.

Bode reached into the cabinet and withdrew an accordion-pleated brown envelope. "It's all in here."

"Cops have instincts about cases like this, and women cops have an edge with their female intuition. Bet you weren't aware of that, Bode."

"You don't even know Brie Canfield," Bode mumbled.

"That's where you're wrong, Bode. I listen when you talk. I can tell you more about that young woman than you even remember. Every time you talked about her your voice changed. When you talked about Callie or Sela it was a different voice. I think you *thought* you were in love with Callie Parker. That's why you cut and ran and took me up on my offer. What you felt wasn't even close to love. All you were seeking, all you wanted, was approval and validation from Mama Pearl, and she gave it to you."

"You've had five beers, Hatch. Don't you have to go to the bathroom?"

"Nope," he said, uncapping another bottle. "I just love this Australian beer. Tell me about Mama Pearl's funeral. We need to lay that one to rest."

"It was so spiritual I bawled all the way through it. The

Reverend's eulogy was perfect. Everyone in the parish came, even the children. Arquette said some words. Hatch, I swear by God I saw Lazarus in the back of the church. I looked right . . . *through* him. He . . . you aren't going to believe this and maybe I was overcome with grief, but what he did was . . . he gave me a thumbs-up. I . . . ah . . . I gave him one back and then he winked at me. He honest to God winked at me, Hatch."

"Hey, you're talking to an Indian. We see spirits all the time. Don't go thinking you're one-upping me here. I believe it!"

"I guess he came to escort Mama Pearl, huh?"

"That makes you feel better to think that, right?"

"Yeah, yeah, it does."

"That's how us Indians believe, too." Hatch grinned.

"Anyway, the rest of the service was boisterous. Mama Pearl did love a good funeral. We laid her to rest next to Lazarus. The Reverend and his congregation put out a wonderful spread and he gave me a basket of food to bring home. You just finished it off. I'm going to sell this place."

"Sounds good to me. You got a buyer?"

Bode explained what Sela had told him about Heywood Mudson. "Wyn could never have sold it anyway since Brie and I own fifty acres, smack right in the middle. I can do a lot of good with the money if I sell it, Hatch."

"That you could. Callie?"

"I can pay off any outstanding bills the insurance doesn't cover. I can give her a nest egg. Start her out in her own office. Back her a little financially. Set aside some money for her family. Do some scholarships, help the Reverend. I'd kind of like to get the stonemason to carve two angels for the tops of Mama Pearl's and Lazarus's stones. I think they'd like that. I want Lazarus's angel to be giving the thumbs-up salute. Do you think that's tacky, Hatch?"

"Hell no. You do whatever it takes. That's my philosophy. I think Mama Pearl would like that, Bode."

"Why didn't she tell me, Hatch?" Bode asked with so much sorrow in his voice Hatch wanted to cry for his friend.

"I don't know. If I had to guess, I'd say she knew you could handle it when the time came because you loved her. It goes without saying that she loved you. My own grandmother was like Mama Pearl. A secret was sacred. It didn't matter if it was wrong or not. You have to look at the positive side of things."

"What's positive about Callie's side of things?"

"Mama Pearl did what she thought she had to do. I don't think she was able to see what the ramifications would be down the road. From all you've told me, she thought love and home could make up for everything. She didn't take her secret to the grave with her, so that has to count."

"I wish she had."

"No you don't," Hatch said quietly. "You're doing it again, Bode. You're taking responsibility for Callie. You have to let go. You can help out, but that's it. That's my opinion."

"And as usual, it's a wise one."

"It's going to be light in about twenty minutes. Let's head out to that junkyard and see if Mr. Archer's car is still there."

"Don't you have to go to the bathroom, Hatch?" Bode looked at the eight beer bottles on Hatch's side of the table.

"Nope. Noticed you went three times though." He grinned.

"It was the coffee."

"Whatever," Hatch said, lumbering to his feet.

At fifteen minutes past seven they found Wynfield Archer's car with the aid of the young man on duty. It no longer had doors or tires or windshield wipers. The back panel was missing as well as the trunk lid.

"You'll have to do it, Bode. I'm too big to squeeze past this Jeep Cherokee. All you gotta do is check the seat belts."

"It's been here for months. Take the elements into consideration. Hey, the driver's side works. The passenger side won't catch."

Hatch led the young man away from the cars. "Is there any way we can take out the front seat and the belts without ruining the way they operate?"

"Sure. It'll cost you though."

"How about a hundred bucks?"

"You got it, mister. I'll have to go back and get my tool kit and bring a dolly to carry it back on."

Hatch knew he was paying seventy-five dollars too much, but he didn't care.

"We're taking the whole seat and anything else the kid takes off, Bode."

"And what are we going to do with it?"

"Hold on to it until we see if Callie has her memory back. If not, we can use it as a scare tactic. Being as good a defense attorney as I am, I could punch five holes in this whole thing, but Mr. Archer, if I'm right, is going to be running pretty scared. I say he 'fesses up as soon as he sees the seat."

"If what I suspect is true, I can't even begin to comprehend the emotional strain Wyn is under. I don't think I could have done it. Carrying guilt you can't resolve is like cancer. It kills," Bode said coldly.

"Son, how would you like to make another fifty bucks? I saw a pickup by the entrance. If you can deliver that seat out to Parker Manor I'd be obliged."

"You got it, mister. I can't do it until Mike comes in though. Is that okay?"

"Sure is. Park it on the back porch, okay?" A wad of twenty dollar bills changed hands.

"Now what?" Bode asked.

"Now we eat. It's breakfast time," Hatch said happily.

"Then what?"

"Then it's up to you what we do next. We either go to see Mr. Archer, we call the hospital, or we go to the hospital. I do think though you should notify Callie's parents that she's awake."

"Jesus, Hatch, I never thought of that," Bode said.

"That's why you have me around. I'm the thinker, you're the doer."

"Ha," Bode snorted.

They stopped at the Flowertown Restaurant. While Hatch finally headed for the bathroom, to Bode's relief, he looked up the Davises' address in the phone book.

Bode watched in amazement as Hatch disposed of four eggs, two side orders of bacon, a side order of hash browns, six slices of toast, three glasses of orange juice, and four cups of coffee. He himself had one scrambled egg and a slice of toast and one cup of coffee.

It was nine o'clock when Bode knocked on the door of the Davis house. It was opened almost immediately by Mrs. Davis. At the sight of him, fear shadowed her face, and she called out to her husband. When Bode smiled, she relaxed immediately and opened the screen door. Hatch had to duck his head to get in. Mrs. Davis beamed as she craned her neck to look up at him.

"I know you, Mr. Jessup. We met at Pearl's funeral." Mr. Davis shuffled from one foot to the other, his face puzzled at this early-morning visit.

"We came about Callie. I knew you'd want to know. She woke up yesterday. They've moved her back to the ICU at the hospital. She said a few words, she smiled, and if I asked her a question, she could blink yes or no. They're going to be doing an extensive evaluation on her, and I think there's a good chance they'll be moving her to the Rusk Institute in New York City. It's the best in the world, I'm told. That's all I know for now, but I'll call you if there's any other news.

We'll be going to the hospital later today. This is my friend Hatch Littletree. Sorry about my manners. I just wanted to hurry and tell you about Callie."

"It's very kind of you," Mrs. Davis said with tears in her eyes. Mr. Davis's hands were shaking when he held one out to Hatch.

"Is there anything we can do, Mrs. Davis?" Bode asked.

"No. Is there anything you want to ask me, Mr. Jessup?"

"No, thanks. Although when I go home, I'll probably think of a hundred things."

"Is there anything we can do for you, Mr. Jessup?" Mr. Davis asked.

"Yes, there is. Will you pray for Mama Pearl?"

"We'd be honored to offer up our prayers. Pearl was a fine woman and will be sorely missed," Mrs. Davis said.

"I'll call," Bode said.

"Thank you," both Davises said.

"Nice people," Hatch said. "Hey, Bode, wait a minute. Is that one of the Davis children?" A girl of twelve or so was coming up the walkway.

"Guess so. Why?"

"I want to do something. I gotta do this," Hatch said, sprinting over to the girl. Bode watched as he fished around in his pocket for a bunch of crumpled bills. He held it out. "Go spend all of this on soda pop, candy, and ice cream. Don't spend it on anything else, you hear?"

"Yes, sir, if my mama says I can."

"Now you're gonna take all the fun out of it. Okay, okay," Hatch grumbled. The girl ran into the house. She stopped twice to pick up a bill that she dropped.

In the car Hatch said, "You know, when I was a kid on the Reservation I used to dream that some person would come to me and do what I just did. I can't tell you how many times I dreamed of that actually happening. Every day I changed the list of things I'd buy. One day it was Hershey bars, Mallow Cups, marshmallows, licorice, caramel popcorn, triple-decker ice-cream cones. You name it, I ate it in my dreams. God, it was wonderful. Guess that's why I'm such a junk-food eater today."

"Why this kid? You could have gone back to the Reservation anytime you wanted and done the same thing."

"A lot you know. The elders watch me like a hawk. No way could I do that. My people are big on health food and good strong teeth. I don't think these people have a lot of money to spare for junk. All kids need a certain amount of . . . Oh, shut the hell up, Bode. I wanted to do it, and I did it. Do you think I offended them?" he asked anxiously.

"Nah. All they have to do is look at you and they know you're genuine. How much did you give her?"

"About a hundred and twenty dollars. I know she's going to give it all to her mama and maybe keep ten bucks. That's okay, too. I had to do it, Bode. Now we have to stop at an ATM machine because I'm out of money."

"There's one in the hospital. That's where we're going, right?"

"You're driving," Hatch said. "Whatever you decide is okay with me."

"No, it's too early. Let's go home and think about this a little bit. I imagine specialists will be arriving this morning, and there probably won't be anything to report till later in the day. We can call though."

"Okay, but let's stop at a bank."

They were home by ten-forty-five, just as the young man from the junkyard arrived with the front seat of Wyn's old car.

"I'm going to take a shower while you play with that," Bode said.

"Hmmm," Hatch said as he squatted to inspect the seat

belts. When Bode emerged from the bathroom, Hatch had all the papers from Brie's folder spread out on the back porch alongside the white-leather seat. He leaned back on his haunches. "A lot of money has changed hands here, Bode. There's no telling what a jury will award the heirs of the Seagreave family. Millions, probably. If I was the defense attorney I'd be out for blood."

"Callie didn't have that much insurance," Bode said.

"Sure she did. They'll go after every policy she has. I see an umbrella here, her homeowners' and Wyn's policy hadn't expired or else he didn't cancel it when the car was switched over to Callie's name."

"Money is one thing, Hatch, but what about all the things they're accusing Callie of? They said she was negligent. Everything has been said that can be said. I saw the word *murder* in there someplace. Jesus."

"That's just a word. If Mr. Archer bailed out and left her holding the bag like we think he did, it ain't going to be pretty, Bode. Five bucks says he was skunked when he got behind the wheel."

"That's what Brie said. She had the whole thing worked out. Sela told me she presented the case to her fellow agents in one of her classes."

"What did they come up with?"

"Zip. If you have no undeniable proof, all the theory in the world won't make a difference."

"Why didn't she go for the seat?"

"Why don't you call her and ask her?" Bode said, his heart thumping in his chest. "You can offer Sela that job you're going to create for her."

"Wise-ass," Hatch said, lumbering to his feet. "Ask her to come here, and she can fly back with me. If she's interested, that is. Or I can stop in Atlanta and pick her up. Let's do it," he said, his eyes sparkling.

Brie's voice was sleepy-sounding. The moment she recognized his, her own became cold, frostily efficient.

"I'm sorry if I woke you," Bode began. "I need to ask you a question. It's about Callie's accident." He didn't think her voice could get any frostier, but it did. "Why didn't you go to the junkyard to inspect the car seat and the seat belts?"

"Because I couldn't find the damn car. I tried. I went to three junkyards. They told me to look around. Do you have any idea how many cars are in those junkyards? Well, do you?"

"Hatch and I found it right away," Bode said.

"Are you saying I screwed up?" Brie demanded.

"No. We found it."

"And you called to tell me that. Guess what, Bode, I'm not interested. If that's all, hang up so I can go back to sleep."

"It's almost noon!" Bode squawked.

"It's none of your business how long I sleep. Don't call me again."

"If that's the way you feel about it, I won't," Bode shot back.

"Fine. Good-bye."

"Wait a minute, I want to talk to Sela. I think I have a job offer for her."

"You do, huh? Well, I'm going to tell her to pass on it. Get a life of your own and stop sticking your nose in ours."

"Put Sela on the damn phone, Brie," Bode ordered. He heard the clunk of the receiver falling on the floor. A moment later Sela's wary voice came over the wire. She sounded just as cold and nasty as Brie had.

"Let's hear it, oh mighty leader without a following," Sela snapped. "In case you're interested, Brie just ran into the bathroom crying. I hate you for doing that to her," she hissed into the phone.

"I didn't do anything. All I did was ask her a question."

"You're supposed to have all the answers, Bode. You don't need Brie or me. Tell me what you want."

"Well, I have here in front of me your destiny. This is not a joke, Sela. He also wants to offer you a job. It's Hatch, my friend I talk about all the time. Starting salary is forty grand. Not too shabby, Sela. He needs a good appraiser. I thought about you right away. Of course, it will mean you have to re-locate again. Hefty commissions. You could make a hundred grand a year if you're interested." Bode shrugged when Hatch's eyes rolled back in his head.

"Are you talking about the crazy Indian who hatched an egg between his legs," Sela squawked.

"Yeah, yeah, that's the one. To my knowledge no one has ever hatched an egg that way." Hatch groaned. "So, are you interested? He's prepared to offer you a three-year contract. Can't beat that, Sela. Plus, listen to this, he has his own Lear-jet, a house that has no equal, a small yacht, three Mercedes Benzes, a whole fleet of antique cars, and a Porsche you can tool around in. I'd make that part of the deal if I were you. You definitely want your own Porsche. What color do you prefer?"

"Yellow. Stop it, Bode, I didn't say I—Make it a 560SL."

"Done. What color?"

"Candy-apple red. What else does he have?"

"Big feet. Real big. He can drink a twelve-pack and not go to the bathroom. He's a fashion plate. He travels with a burlap sack though. He said he owns luggage. I'm not sure I believe that. But he does own lots and lots of real estate. He's heeled, Sela."

"You can't sell me, Bode."

"I'm not trying to sell you, I'm trying to interest you in a genuine job that pays very well. You can handle it, Sela, but you do have to move," Bode said seriously. "Why don't you drive up today and have a talk with him. If you decide to take it you'll want to make some plans."

"That means I'll be leaving Brie all alone."

"You aren't joined at the hip, Sela. Everyone has to lead their own life. If you're happy, Brie will be happy. What do you say?"

"I'll think about it."

"No, I need to know now. Will you drive up today?"

"All right. But I'm not staying. You better not be trying to pull a fast one on me, Bode."

"You're getting as suspicious and as feisty as Brie. That's not good, Sela. Wear something fetching, so you can impress my friend."

"Impress a guy that hatched an egg between his balls? You got the wrong girl, Bode. What you see is what you get."

"See, see." Bode cackled. "Hatch says that all the time. I knew this was going to work out, I just knew it. Hang up, Sela, and hit the road. We'll be sitting on the back porch drinking mint juleps."

Bode turned. "She hung up. What's wrong with you, Hatch? You look kind of funny."

"You told her about the egg?" he bellowed.

"A long time ago. Is it my fault she remembered? You want somebody who has a mind like a steel trap, don't you? She never forgets anything. You're really going to love her. She doesn't want a Porsche, she wants a candy-apple red 560SL as part of coming aboard. She wants me to act as her agent. Of course, if you get married I'll withdraw my services."

"You son of a bitch!" Hatch laughed. "Is she really coming?"

"She said she was. I'd say she'll be here around three-thirty, maybe four at the latest. She said she's not staying though, so you better have your presentation all ready."

"What presentation?"

"The one you're going to make up to entice her to go to work for you. It's lunchtime," Bode said airily.

"We just ate," Hatch said.

"That never bothered you before. Ah, I love it. Already smitten, and you haven't even met her."

Hatch stomped off to the bathroom.

Bode sat on the steps and laughed and laughed.

The neurologist, Vernon Streeter, shook hands with Wyn Archer. "I'm glad we're seeing each other under such pleasant circumstances. I know how difficult these past months have been for you. Miracles do happen from time to time and are recognized as such by the medical profession. We're taking a wait-and-see attitude for the moment. She's young. She has a strong heart and strong lungs, thanks to her physical condition before the accident, and the therapy Pearl performed every day. All those things have helped. The fact that she is moving spontaneously and understands what we are saying argues well for her eventual recovery."

"How about her memory?" Wyn asked, hardly daring to breathe.

"It's hard to tell. We aren't rushing anything at this point. She tires easily and nods off. You can see her for a few minutes, but whatever you do, don't upset her. Smile, put the smile in your voice. We'll talk again tomorrow."

Wyn walked into the intensive care unit. He hated this place. The only comfort he felt was that Pearl wasn't sitting in the waiting room. He was instantly ashamed of the thought.

Wyn tiptoed over to the bed. "Callie, it's Wyn. Are you awake? Can you hear me?"

Callie's eyes opened. She smiled wanly.

"My God, you really are awake," Wyn said in amazement.

"It's been a long time. We came every day and talked for hours. Did you hear us?" She smiled.

"Can you speak, say a word—or do you smile and blink? You have a beautiful smile, Callie. Say my name."

"Wyn."

"Do you remember me?" Callie frowned and then smiled.

"Silly question, huh?" Wyn said. Callie smiled again.

"I think you're going to get well very soon. Do you remember much? Do you remember the car accident?"

"Yes." Her eyes blinked rapidly three or four times.

"No, no, don't think about it, Callie. I'm sorry I asked. It's over and done with. When you're well we'll talk about it. I'm really sorry, Callie."

"Baby."

"Baby? I don't know anything about a baby. Is it important?"

Callie blinked again and again. "Baby." She smiled such an endearing smile Wyn felt light-headed.

"I'll find out and when I come back the next time we'll talk about the baby, okay? I have to leave now. I'm glad you're awake, Callie, really glad. I was driving the car the night of the accident." Callie nodded. A moment later she was asleep.

Wyn walked out of the hospital, got in his car, and drove to Judge Summers's house. Forty-five minutes later, the Judge at his side, Wyn entered the police station.

The six o'clock news out of Charleston carried the news live.

It was six-thirty when Bode nudged Hatch. "I hear a car."

"She's late," Hatch mumbled.

"Nah, this is about right. She had to spend two and a half hours arguing with Brie, another thirty minutes were needed for them to cry on one another's shoulders, then she had to repair her makeup. This is when I expected her."

"You really know a lot about women. I don't know anything," Hatch grumbled.

"Pretend. God, don't ever let a female think you don't know what's going on. Never, ever. Now, c'mon, big guy, I want you to meet the woman of your dreams. You owe me now. Big-time."

She looked at him.

He looked at her.

She smiled.

He smiled.

She held out her hand.

Hatch took it and brought it to his lips.

Bode groaned.

"You said something about a job with lots of perks?" Sela prompted, never taking her eyes off the big man.

"It's all yours, perks and all. Anything you want, it's yours," Hatch said, drawing her up the steps.

"I'm easy to please," Sela told him.

"Jeez, me too." Hatch grinned.

"She's a hard worker. Gets the job done." Bode beamed.

"Me too," Hatch said.

"He's generous to a fault." Bode continued to beam. "Like you, Sela."

"What a nice thing to say." Sela smiled.

"Why don't I leave you two alone?" Bode suggested.

"I thought you were never going to leave." Hatch sighed.

"He's like chewing gum, he sticks to your shoes." Sela shrugged.

Bode huffed and puffed his way into the house. He walked into the living room and sat down on the scratchy sofa and turned on the small television set that had been in Pearl's room.

The local seven o'clock news was rehashing the six o'clock news. Bode bellowed for Hatch and Sela, who came on the run. "Listen, listen!" Bode shouted.

"I give him credit, he owned up," Sela said, after they'd sat through the bulletin.

"Yeah—and the only reason he did so was because Callie woke up. God, I wish Mama Pearl was here to see this."

"I think she knows, Bode," Sela said quietly.

"By the way, here's my résumé," she said, holding out a piece of paper.

Hatch stuck it in his pocket. "You're hired. When can you start?"

"Next week."

"Next week? That's a whole week away," Hatch grumbled.

"I have to go back to Atlanta, pack up my car. It's a long ride to New Mexico."

"We can ship your stuff and the car. You can fly back with me."

"I still have to pack everything up. Actually, I don't. I didn't unpack yet. Brie isn't going to like this. We made such wonderful plans. You know, the sisterless sisters doing things together, that kind of scene."

"She'll be happy for you, Sela," Bode said.

"I hope so. Well, now that that's all ironed out I should be on my way."

"I'll take care of everything. I'll call you and you can tell me what time to meet you at the airport, okay?"

Sela nodded. "Bode, am I doing the right thing here?"

"Trust me, it's the right thing."

"Okay. It was nice meeting you, Hatch."

"Same here." Hatch grinned.

"And I'm delighted that I played a very small part in all of this. There's no need to thank me," Bode said.

Sela waved airily, tapped the horn in three zippy notes before she roared out of the driveway.

"Ah, my destiny. You were right, Bode. I'm in love."

"The best part is so is she. I know that girl. She set her eyes
on you and that was it. Congratulations. I mean it, Hatch."

"I know you mean that, Bode. What are you going to do
now that Mr. Archer 'fessed up?"

"Hang around for a bit. Put this property on the market.
Ship Mama Pearl's things to Santa Fe so they'll be with me.
See if there's anything I can do for Callie."

"Take all the time you need, Bode."

"You're a good friend, Hatch."

"So are you, Bode. You'll always be Bode to me."

"I'm keeping my name. I don't know Michael Clemson
Harrold Parker. I don't want to know him either."

"Are you black or white?"

"I'm me, Hatch."

"Sounds good to me. Let's finish off this beer, get a buzz on
and tell dirty stories."

"Okayyyy."

Wynfield Archer settled himself on the sofa, a glass of ice
tea in his hand. As of today his drinking days were over. He'd
signed up at the local AA meeting hall and would attend as
often as needed. He was going to punish himself further and
watch his performance, and it was a performance, on the
eleven o'clock news. He needed to shame himself further, to
grit his teeth and watch the man he never thought he could
be, admit to all his wrongdoing of the past months.

"Whatever they do to you, you will deserve it." He was
going to pay and pay and pay, but that was all right. What
wasn't all right was that he could never, ever, make up for the
Seagreave family's loss. He would remember that to his dying
day. Whatever it took, he was going to do. Getting religion

this late in the game had to mean something—it was a second chance of sorts. What he did with that second chance was going to be up to him. He'd told the police and the Judge, and the various insurance companies that he was going to come forward and admit his guilt even before Callie woke up. He could no longer live with that guilt. All of the authorities looked like they believed him. His ravaged appearance, the Judge said, spoke louder than words.

Jail time, years of community service, restitution, was a start. At some point, if Callie recovered, she would probably file a lawsuit against him in civil court. And well she should. There was no way in the world he could ever make up for Callie Parker's suffering. The manslaughter charge was something he'd live with.

Wyn's face flashed on the screen. He sipped at the ice tea and watched himself with clinical interest. He looked like a caricature of himself. "You have to get down in the ditch before you can climb out," he muttered. He sounded sincere, which he was. His reputation was ruined, and he deserved that, too. He watched as his mouth muttered an apology to the Seagreaves family. It wasn't enough; the monies they'd get from the lawsuit weren't enough either. What else could he do? Maybe he could think of something while he was sitting in jail.

He thought about God because God was all that was left to him. He was sorry now that he'd stopped going to church, sorry for so many things, but sorry was just a word. God needed to see what he was about. "I'm going to do whatever it takes, Lord, I swear I will. I won't ask for anything because I'm weak. I don't deserve to be alive and well. If I falter, help me. That's all I ask."

It was over. He remembered the awesome relief he'd felt when he had said the words aloud. He would also never forget the disgust he had read in the faces around him. He hadn't flinched though. He'd stood tall, told the truth. Finally.

His punishment was going to be a balm to his soul.

He remembered how he'd wished for yesterday. No more. Now he wished for tomorrow. For all the tomorrows yet to come.

The demons of his sleep departed. He slept, deeply and dreamlessly. Tomorrow was the first day of his new life. Yesterday was gone forever.

20

～

"Hatch, where did the time go? It seems like you just got married, and now we're drinking this terrible coffee waiting for your first child to be born. We're getting old. I can't even remember the last year and a half."

"I remember it." Hatch chortled. "I remember everything. The wedding, the honeymoon, the day I knew Sela got pregnant. She knew it, too, the exact moment. Hard to believe, huh? God, I'm going to be a father! Me! You don't think anything will happen to Sela, do you, Bode?"

"Absolutely not. She's in wonderful shape, and she didn't gain too much weight. She took care of herself and exercised moderately and you looked after her. The doctor said she was fine."

"Maybe I should have agreed to go in with her, but she didn't want it, and I didn't think I could handle it. Was that wrong of me, Bode?"

"Nah. Men don't belong in delivery rooms. I couldn't handle it either. Guess we aren't modern men."

"Everything would be just perfect if Brie . . . Sela wanted her here so bad, but she's off on assignment. She hasn't seen her since she left Atlanta. Calling isn't the same and when

Brie does call it's usually on the run. You haven't heard from her, have you?"

"I'm on Brie's zero list. She'll never call me. She did send a Christmas card last year but it had her name printed on it. She didn't send a message or anything," Bode said tightly.

"It would be so perfect for Sela if Callie and Brie were both here. If there was a way for me to make it happen I would."

"Sela knows that, Hatch. Lighten up. You look awful."

"Do you think I'll make a good father?"

"Of course! It's all about the time you spend with your kids. That giving thing, you know, every toy under the sun, that's not what parenthood is all about. It's about sitting up all night, holding your wife's hand and the kid's hand when he or she runs a high fever. It's about a smack on the butt, taking the kid to church, setting good examples, eating together, talking about the day you all had. Teaching right from wrong. It's a hell of a responsibility, Hatch."

"I know—and that's what worries me. What if the kid knows I'm not father material? They sense things like that."

"You gotta bond with him or her. I read that, Hatch. You gotta do that right away. You're gonna be the best father in the whole world. No kid will ever be prouder of their old man than your kid. Trust me on this, okay?"

"Yeah, okay. It's been seven hours, Bode."

"It can go seven more. I read that, too. Do you have your cigars?"

"Hell, yes. Sela made sure. They're in the car. The nursery is ready. Sela didn't want a nanny. She's going to breast feed. What do you think of that, Bode?"

"I never would have believed it. You guys were meant for one another. See what happens when you trust me?"

"Eat shit, Bode. You might be good about fixing other people's problems, but you suck at fixing your own. I cannot believe you haven't called Brie. That stinks. You're probably the reason she won't come out here."

"Not probably. It *is* the reason. She made her own decisions, and they didn't include me. That's the way she wants it. I don't like to talk about it, Hatch."

"Sela wants us all to have Thanksgiving together. She suggested we go to New York. The doctor said the baby will be able to fly. She wants to show him or her off to Callie. It might make Callie feel better, too. Do you think it's a good idea?"

"Sure. Where?"

"Jake Deering has an apartment uptown someplace. I'll check out the address. He told me I could use it anytime I was in New York. I don't know why he keeps it. He said he's never going back. Still, I guess New York apartments are like money in the bank. Just last week I heard Sela ask Brie if she'd be able to make it, and Brie said yes."

"Are you serious?"

"Yes. Ah, I saw your eyes light up. It will give you something to look forward to, Bode. All of you will be together again. A year and a half is a long time, and you ain't gettin' any younger, you know."

"I'll mark it on my calendar."

"You going up this month?"

"Yes. Callie's doing wonderfully. It was tough in the beginning. She took turns in delighting the doctors, then she would disappoint them, provoke them, amaze them and even discourage them when she refused to cooperate on certain days. She's past that now. She's regained most of her memory and she's walking fairly well. She tends to panic at times. When she's discharged she's going to have a physical therapist live in with her until she's certified as A-1."

"Is she going to stay in New York?"

"She says no. She wants to go back to Summerville and live in Parker Manor all by herself. Apparently she's going to use the insurance money to refurbish the house."

"You said you were going to tell her you had sold off the property. You said you were going to tell her everything," Hatch reminded him angrily.

"I was, but the doctors warned me that she wasn't ready to handle any of it. Pearl's death was almost her undoing. She had a terrible setback. Wyn's confession and his eighteen months in the slammer was another setback. I'm her lifeline, and I can't jerk that line."

"Have you given any thought to the possibility that maybe you'll *never* be able to tell her?"

"I think about it on a daily basis," Bode said miserably.

"Have they started construction?"

"Six months ago. The house is gone, so is the barn. There's nothing to go back to. I don't know what she'll do when she finds that out."

"That's not your problem, Bode. You're wrong about her not having a place to go back to. She has parents who would welcome her with wide-open arms, parents who will love her if she allows it."

"She won't. I'm not sure I should even tell her *that.*"

"Well, you're wrong, Bode. She needs to be told. When she's mentally strong."

"That's just it, Hatch. She's fragile."

"Sela says that's a crock, Bode. She said Callie is tough as rawhide, and you were the only one who couldn't see it. Sela says Callie wants you."

"Sela talks too much," Bode said irritably.

"Yeah, that's true, but I love listening to her. Brie says it also, that Callie wants you. Are you saying they're both wrong?" Hatch asked slyly.

"Shut up, Hatch."

"You just lied to me, Bode."

"No, I didn't."

"Yes, you did. You said the house was gone. What you didn't say was you had it moved. It's being refurbished as we speak."

"Damn you, Hatch, you've been spying on me again."

"Someone has to look out for you. I'm not letting you make a mistake."

"I did it for Sela and Brie and myself. When it came time to part with it, I couldn't do it. All I could see was Mama Pearl standing on the back porch with the flyswatter. I don't plan on telling Callie. Does that make you happy?"

"No. Sela swears she's never going back there. Brie said they'd have to drag her kicking and screaming because she's not going back either. That leaves just you. Pretty expensive hobby, if you want my opinion."

"It's okay for Jake Deering to own an expensive apartment in New York that he never lives in or even visits, but it isn't all right for me to refurbish the old house."

"Jake Deering isn't carrying a ton of baggage on his back. I wish you had talked to me first, Bode. It's a mistake, a bad one."

"You're probably right," Bode agreed.

"You still haven't cut her loose. Why is that, Bode?"

"I told you, it's not the right time."

"You are going to do it, aren't you? Your word, Bode."

"I'm going to do it when the time is right. I think Callie is striving for January the first. I know I am. A new year and all that. It's only a few more months."

"Sell off that house. Let Mama Pearl rest in peace, Bode."

"What if I give it to Mr. and Mrs. Davis? What do you think of that?"

"Jesus Christ!"

"If they lived there, Callie might . . . she might accept them."

"And make them Pearl clones. Wake up, Bode!"

"Mr. Littletree?"

"Me, I'm him. I'm Mr. Littletree," Hatch bellowed as he bounded over to the nurse.

"That's him," Bode said, pointing to Hatch.

"Congratulations! You have a beautiful, handsome, nine-pound-four-ounce baby boy. You can see him in a few minutes."

"My wife?"

"She's just fine. You'll be able to see her in a bit."

"A boy! She said it was a boy! I have a son! Bode, I have a son! I'm a goddamn father! Nothing in the world will ever compare with this moment."

Bode led Hatch back to the chair he'd been sitting on. "Don't move, you look kind of shaky. I'll get you some coffee. I saw the nurse put a fresh pot on a little while ago."

Bode was back in a moment. "Have you guys picked out a name?"

"Yeah. If it was a girl we were going to call her Briana Pearl Littletree. We agreed to call a boy Shunpus Bowdey Littletree."

"Are you kidding me, Hatch?"

"Hell, no. If it wasn't for you I wouldn't be sitting here. How do I thank you for introducing me to Sela, Bode?"

"You've done it a thousand different ways, Hatch. Don't sweat the small stuff. Jeez, I can't wait to see him. Nine pounds is a big baby. Bet he looks like he's a couple of months old. Usually seven pounds is normal. He's got an extra two. I read it, Hatch."

"Do you think he'll be all wrinkled and puckered and funny-looking?" Hatch asked, his face a mask of worry.

"Wouldn't surprise me about the funny part. You're pretty

damn ugly. However, Sela is beautiful, so I think he's going to be perfect."

"You're the Godfather, remember that. You have to buy presents. You have to take him to ball games, stand in for me, make sure he gets to church if I can't take him. You gotta come to all his birthday parties and play Santa at Christmas. You're gonna be Uncle Bode and my kid is gonna love you like I love you. You gotta buy him his first bike, all the good stuff."

"It will be my pleasure," Bode said, his chest puffing out. "But, just out of curiosity, when I'm doing all that, what are you going to be doing?"

"Watching and marveling at my own personal miracle. I'm going to be loving him and his mother. Look, look, she's telling us we can see him. We have to put on the gowns and masks. Tie yours tight, I don't want my kid getting any germs."

"Up yours, Hatch. Will you let me hold him?"

"Well, sure. You're his Godfather. You can't squeeze him, though. New babies are delicate. Look, he's got a cap on his head. Do you think something's wrong?"

"Nah, look, they all have them on. Jesus, he's gorgeous, Hatch. A real little person. And he looks like you," Bode said in dismay. "God, will you look at that hair!" he marveled, peeking under the little cap.

"Hey, little fella, I'm your dad," Hatch said, tears dribbling down his cheeks. "This guy here, your Uncle Bode, me and him are going to see that you grow up to be the best you can be. Your mama is going to be so proud of you."

Little Hatch squealed, an ear-piercing sound that made Bode's ears ring. "Great lungs." Bode grinned.

"Your turn," Hatch said, holding out his son.

Bode accepted the small tightly wrapped bundle. His eyes

misted. "You are one lucky little boy," he said huskily. "Look at the character in his face, Hatch."

"That's gas," the nurse said cheerfully. "Hand him over."

In the waiting room Bode announced, "I'm going home, Hatch. Tell Sela I said congratulations and make sure you tell her I said he's a beautiful little boy. If there's anything you need, you call me, okay?"

"I will. Bode, about that house and all . . ."

"I'll deal with it, Hatch. You have to stop worrying about me now."

"Okay. How about doing us a favor by calling Brie and giving her the good news? I don't like to ask, but I got a lot to do and take care of right now. If she isn't home, leave a message."

"Okay."

It was the first thing he did when he got home. His heart pounded in his chest while he waited to see if the receiver would be picked up or not. When he heard the recorded message he bit down on his lip. "It's Bode, Brie. Hatch asked me to call and tell you Sela had a nine-pound-four-ounce baby boy whose name is Shunpus Bowdey Littletree. Sela is fine. Hatch is walking on air. I hope you're well. Take care, Brie."

His next call was to Callie. Her voice was hesitant-sounding when she spoke. She seemed to think, to choose her words carefully before she uttered them.

"Callie, it's Bode. Sela had her baby this afternoon. It's a boy, nine pounds four ounces. They're going to call him Shunpus Bowdey Littletree, but I think he'll be known as Little Hatch. How are you, Callie?"

"I'm fine now that you called. You don't call me often enough."

"I'm pretty busy, Callie. Half the time I don't have enough hours in the day. I have a heavy caseload."

"Friends should come first, Bode," she whined.

"No, Callie, that's wrong. I have responsibilities to Hatch and the firm and my clients. It's wrong of you to think like that."

"All right, Bode. Did you see Sela's baby?"

"He's a handsome little guy. Chubby. He's got a hell of a set of lungs. Wait till you see him."

"Does he look like an Indian baby?"

"Does it make a difference, Callie?"

"I guess it does."

"Like a black baby is different, is that what you mean?"

"I guess that's what I mean. You sound angry. Was that wrong for me to say that?"

"People are people, Callie, and that includes babies. It doesn't make any difference."

"Pearl said it did. She said that."

"It was wrong of Mama Pearl to say that. Mama Pearl refused to go forward with the times. She liked the old ways, the old beliefs. She meant well, but that doesn't make it right."

"I miss Pearl," Callie whimpered.

"I'm sure you do, but I think what you miss most is the way she used to wait on you twenty-four hours a day. You let her do it, Callie. You could have done more, been nicer. She wore herself out taking care of you when you were in the coma."

"You aren't being very nice to me, Bode. I didn't tell her to do all those things. Why are you saying all this? Is anyone taking care of the house?"

"Callie, I'm in New Mexico. I have some work to do so I have to hang up now."

"When are you coming to see me?"

He was supposed to go next week, he even had his ticket. "I'm not sure. Maybe the end of next month if I can get away."

"That's too long, Bode. You need to come now. I miss you. Sela doesn't call, only once in a while, and Brie never calls. Y'all don't want to be with me because of what happened. I'm not the same anymore. That's why, isn't it?"

"You're the same, Callie—just as selfish, just as self-centered as you always were. Brie has a job; Sela was pregnant and was sick a lot of the time. I have clients, court hearings, trials. You have to take care of yourself. You should *want* to do things for yourself instead of depending on other people. I'll call you before I come."

"If I'm so much trouble, don't bother," Callie said pitifully.

"Oh no, you aren't throwing that guilt trip on me, Callie Parker. I have things to do. You probably should do some leg exercises or read a book. A lawbook. Bye, Callie."

Bode packed up his briefcase and set out for his office where he worked close to an hour. When he was done he slipped all the letters into overnight mailing envelopes. Bode had established a trust, entitling Arquette and Coletta to live at the house, which upon their deaths would pass to their children and their children's children. The house could not be sold. As soon as the deed could be recorded, Parker Manor would effectively belong to Arquette and his wife, Coletta. After all, it was Pearl's parents, Arquette's parents and grandparents who had made Parker Manor what it was, and it was only right that it be given to them for the rest of their days.

He called Arquette and told him what he'd done. The old man was so flabbergasted he could barely speak. "I just wanted you to know, Arquette, that tomorrow morning FedEx is going to be bringing you an envelope. You take it to town and give it to Rudd Smith. He'll do what has to be done for you. Pack your duds and move. The trust will pay the taxes, so don't fret about that. Take everyone, Arquette, your children and grandchildren. How are the angels holding up?"

"Mighty fine, Bode. Everyone talks about them. Pearl and Lazarus be mighty proud of them there angels."

"Take care of yourself, Arquette. Give my regards to Coletta."

"I'll do that, Bode. You be a good man. Pearl was so proud of you she like to bust some days. You be a judge yet, Bode?"

"No, not yet. Was she proud of Callie, Arquette?" The silence on the other end of the phone went on so long Bode said, "Forget I asked that question. Enjoy the old house, Arquette."

Done.

No turning back now.

The week before Thanksgiving found Bode in a tizzy of his own making. He looked at his appointment book and saw that he had consultations with Callie's doctor. He also had a trial date looming ahead of him. All scheduled for Thanksgiving week. He'd ask Hatch to get a postponement for the trial and he'd go east ahead of Sela and Hatch. He'd open up Jake's apartment and get it ready for Sela and the baby. He could even take off some of the pressure and do all the grocery shopping for Thanksgiving dinner.

He hadn't told Callie about the dinner and wasn't sure why. Now that the time was almost here he knew he was going to have to tell her. He'd made up his mind that after speaking with the doctors he was going to tell her everything. Either she handled it or she didn't. He hadn't called her, hadn't gone to visit her since the call to tell her about Sela's baby. She'd phoned him many times, though, and on each occasion was more petulant-sounding than the one before.

"Listen, Bode, when you get there, buy all the stuff for the kid," Hatch said. "I swear to God a man could go off to war with less gear than it takes for a baby to survive. Buy one of everything. We'll leave it there; Jake won't mind. Here's the key. Don't worry about the trial. I'll tell the Judge you're going for prostate-testing at Columbia. He's had the same problem so he'll be sympathetic. Sela said to get a big bird, twenty-five pounds. Here's the list. Oh, and get plenty of diapers. See if you can line up a sitter, too. Sela wants to show me New York. Can you handle all this, Bode?"

"Guess I'm gonna have to. Don't worry. You're sending a man to do a man's job and a man is going to do it. I gave the house to Arquette and Coletta, and it will stay in their family forever and ever," he said breathlessly.

"White folk had it long enough?"

"That about sums it up."

"Good luck with all those specialists. We're not sure when Brie is going to get there. She's on a job. She called Sela last night, and I heard them whispering, which means Brie was probably telling her something she wasn't supposed to tell her and Sela was swearing she wouldn't let it go past her. I think she's on that stakeout the FBI has going on with the crazy guy in western Pennsylvania. I don't even know if stakeout is the right word. You know—that mess that's been on television for weeks now."

"Brie's on that case?" Bode thundered.

"Whoa, Bode, hold on there. I said I didn't know. Hey, she's an FBI agent. If she is on it, they wouldn't have sent her if she couldn't handle it. The key word here is *if*. She could be shuffling papers in Savannah for all I know. What she does is none of your business anyway."

Bode stared at Hatch for a long time before he stalked out of the office. Hatch raised his eyes. "Listen, I got big plans for those two over Thanksgiving. I could use a little heavenly help where they're concerned. Amen," Hatch said.

Jake Deering's apartment turned out to be a three-story brownstone on East Seventy-eighth Street that was badly in need of serious repairs. Yet even if it was sold as is, Bode knew it would fetch close to three million, and he felt that was a conservative estimate.

He settled himself on the third floor hoping Little Hatch's lusty, middle-of-the-night yowls wouldn't reach him. And he was far enough away to give Hatch and Sela some privacy.

He did two things immediately. He called Macy's and ordered one of everything Sela had on her list. They promised delivery the following day. His second call was to the Food Emporium. He read off Sela's list. Delivery would be at six o'clock. His third call was to a liquor store on the avenue. He ordered four cases of Foster's beer, five bottles of champagne, a bottle of Chivas and one of Crown Royal, all favorites of Hatch. He also ordered a case of diet soda for Sela and Brie. His last call was to the management company. He asked for a cleaning service that afternoon and agreed to pay double for calling at such short notice.

He killed another hour at a deli before he headed to the hospital to talk to Callie's doctor. In the latter's opinion, Callie was holding back. "She's progressed better than we ever dreamed," the doctor told him. "Lately, though, she appears to be regressing. At least, that's what she'd like us to believe. She's very strong-willed. Let me give you an example. Yesterday she wanted to take a nap and that's okay, she still sleeps a lot. She told the therapist to take off her shoes and ankle braces. The therapist told her to take them off herself because she can do it. Callie refused. The therapist refused. Callie slept with them on. She tries to get away with things like that all the time. We don't give in. She is not gracious at all when she has to do things for herself. She demanded last week that someone iron her clothes. We showed her where the iron and ironing board were. She wears wrinkled clothing.

"When you called and told her about her friend having a baby, she was genuinely excited. Then she went into a tailspin and was out of it, totally, for four days. I don't mind telling you I was about to call in all the specialists that treated her. I tried to talk to her about it, but she said she had nothing to say. As late as last night she was looking forward to joining you and your friends for Thanksgiving. It will be her first real outing without any of us there to watch over her. Her sleep patterns have changed, too, just around the time your friend had her baby. She has terrible nightmares. She tosses and turns. This past week she's been accusing all of us, myself included, of spying on her."

"Can she handle some news she isn't going to like? Before you decide, let me tell you the story, and then I'd like your advice."

The doctor listened, rubbing his chin thoughtfully as Bode talked. When he was finished speaking, the doctor leaned back in his chair and made a steeple of his fingers. "Last week I asked Callie what she was going to do when she left here at the end of December. She said she was going to find herself another Pearl and live like a lady on Mr. Archer's insurance money. She said she was probably going to marry you because you'd always loved her. I say you should tell her. I'll make sure I'm around the corner in case she goes into one of her little spells. It's up to you, Mr. Jessup."

"Is she really well enough to leave in December?"

"She was well enough to leave at the beginning of the month, but she didn't want to go. I thought there was something symbolic for her about Christmas, and that's why I agreed to extend her time. What help she's getting now is what any good qualified therapist can do for her on an outpatient basis."

"I didn't know that," Bode said quietly.

"Your friend Hatch appears to be right. You need to open your eyes, Mr. Jessup. You also need to listen carefully. This is just my opinion, but I don't think Callie is the person you think she is. My colleagues and I have a meeting once a week to discuss Callie, and they all concur with my findings. Miss Parker is well enough to leave here."

"What happens if a patient refuses to leave?"

"She's forced to comply. We have patients who desperately need rehabilitation. We'd simply move her to a mental ward and go from there, after we explain the situation. Some sort of plan will have to be made, someplace for her to go to, of course. We never throw people out. I mean that literally."

Bode thanked the doctor, his head buzzing, and headed for the rehabilitation center to see Callie.

Callie was glad to see him, throwing her arms around him and hugging him so hard he begged for mercy. *Good upper-body strength,* he thought. "I'm so glad to see you, Bode. I thought you were never going to get here. Then I thought maybe you were angry with me for some reason, but then I realized just how silly that was. You're never really angry with me. Listen Bode, I've had so much time to think since I've been here and I know we've never spoken about this and I think it's time. I know you love me and have always adored me. I called off my wedding because of you and Pearl. When I leave here at the end of the year I'd like us to . . . you know . . . get married."

"Why didn't you tell me you could have left already?" Bode said, ignoring her words.

"I didn't want to leave."

"Do you have any idea how much it costs to stay here? Don't you realize there are other patients who need help? You could get the same help you're getting here, at home. It wasn't fair of you, Callie."

"Oh pooh, the insurance company pays for it. I wasn't ready to leave. Doctors don't know everything, Bode."

"They knew enough to get you to this point in time with their help. Money doesn't grow on trees, Callie. You just have no idea, have you?" Bode said wearily.

"I'm looking forward to Thanksgiving and Christmas. It's going to be wonderful this year, isn't it? Will you take me home when it's time for me to leave? Did you get someone to clean the house and take care of me?"

"Callie, sit down. I have to talk to you." Callie sat down obediently. "Now, I want you to listen very carefully. There are a lot of things I have to tell you that you aren't going to like, but I spoke with your doctor, and he said you were mentally and physically able to be told."

"For heaven's sake, Bode, do we have to go through all this? It's all right if you're too busy to fly up here to take me back. I can ask Sela or Brie to do it. They'll find someone to take care of me. I do insist you find someone to clean the house, though."

"Callie, the house is gone. I gave it to Arquette and Coletta."

"That isn't funny, Bode. You can't give my house away. I deeded it to Wyn. He said he gave it back."

"It's not your house, it's mine. *I* gave it away. Clemson Parker was my father. My mother lived in Summerville. I was illegitimate and my mother died when I was born. Her mammy gave me to an African-American family to raise and then when they couldn't take care of me anymore, they gave me to the preacher. That's when Mr. Parker found me and brought me to Pearl. I'm not African-American, Callie—not that it makes one bit of difference. My real name is Michael Clemson Harrold Parker. It says so on my birth certificate. I also inherit on my fortieth birthday—the Harrold holdings, whatever they might be."

"I don't believe you! You gave away my house? Well, you just go and take it back! It's mine—I grew up there. I was born there! Do you hear, Bode? *You get it back!*" Callie screeched.

"You weren't born there. Mama Pearl bought you from Mr. and Mrs. Davis for fifty dollars. They sold you. That doesn't make them bad people. They had too many mouths to feed, and they knew you'd have a good life at Parker Manor. You have parents, Callie, and lots of brothers and sisters. There's no easy way to say this except to just say it. Your mother is African-American, your father is Caucasian, you have brothers and sisters. The color issue isn't what's important. What's important is you have parents who love you. They watched you grow up. They saw you all the time Pearl took you to church. When you were in the coma, they visited you every Sunday. They always brought fresh flowers, and they prayed for you."

"Those awful people who always tried to touch me? That man was a *plumber.*" She made the word sound obscene.

"They're good, kind, nice people, Callie, and they love you."

"I don't believe you."

"It's true. You know I never lied to you. I'm not lying now either. You have to accept it."

"I don't have to do any such thing. I'm an attorney! You get my house back, or I'll sue you! Pearl must be turning over in her grave at the way you're treating me. Now you've ruined everything."

"How can the truth ruin something? I'm showing you that you have a family, Callie. That's the most important thing in the world."

"I don't want *that* family. I can't believe you're doing this to me. I thought you loved me. Now you hate me. I never did anything to you," Callie cried.

"Yes, you did. Time and again you broke Mama Pearl's

heart and when you hurt her you hurt me. She loved you, and she felt guilty that she'd bought you for Mrs. Parker. But, in the end, she couldn't go to meet Lazarus without telling the truth. Sela knows and so does Brie."

"You told everyone!" Callie shrilled.

"Everyone already knew. The Judge knew, so that means all the old people in town knew. They kept the secret, but it isn't a secret anymore. You have to come to terms with it."

"Oh no, I don't. I don't have to do *anything* I don't want to do."

"What are you going to do?"

"Well, I'm not going to share Thanksgiving with people I thought were my friends. Christmas either. I'm going to hire the finest attorney in the world and get my house back from you."

"You can't, Callie. There are too many people who know. All that insurance money you think you're going to get will go to pay for something you can never have. You've been through a lot, Callie, and we were there for you. We're here for you now if you need us, until you can decide what it is you want to do with your life."

"I knew," Callie said spitefully.

"Knew what?"

"All about you. I looked in Pearl's bag one day and saw your birth certificate. I was going to tear it up, but I was afraid Pearl would fan my bottom. I knew about the Davises, too. I heard Pearl talking to her preacher. I was hiding behind the tree. She knew I knew, too, even though I never said anything to her. She felt so guilty at what she did . . . I knew all the time."

"When?"

"When I was about eight. That was the first time I saw the birth certificate. Then I went through her bag again when I was older, and I really understood."

"And you never said anything?"

"Why should I? I liked everything the way it was. If I'd said something, things would have changed. When I woke up and y'all heard me talking about the secret and the baby, I was talking about Pearl's secret and I was the baby. You should leave, Bode. I don't want to marry you after all."

"Callie . . ."

"Go, Bode. Haven't you hurt me enough? I'm glad Pearl isn't here to see the way you're treating me. She'd never forgive you, Bode, never in a million years."

"Mama Pearl told, Callie. It's you she wouldn't forgive. It was an awful secret for her to keep, but in the end she made it come right. I'm leaving you some money. You can use it for a down payment on a house, or, if you're frugal, you can buy a house with it. I'm sorry things worked out like this, I really am."

"No, you're not. You, Sela, and Brie are nothing but white trash. Why Pearl made me play with you is something I'll never understand. I don't want to understand either."

"It would be nice if you went back to Summerville to visit Pearl's grave. I had an angel put on top of her stone and Lazarus's. It would be nice for you to do that."

"Don't hold your breath waiting for me to do it, Bode."

"Good-bye, Callie." Bode laid the envelope on the table by the door. He went out, his stomach churning. Who *was* that person he'd just talked to for over an hour?

Callie paced the room wringing her hands, moaning softly to herself. He said everyone knew. Everyone. That wasn't true. *Everyone didn't know.* She picked up the phone and dialed from memory. When the answering machine clicked on, she began speaking rapidly. "Wyn, this is Callie. I'd like it a lot if you'd come to New York and take me back to South Carolina. The doctors say I can leave anytime I want to. I thought it would be nice to share Thanksgiving with you. I'm not angry with you for what happened; it was an accident.

I'm not going to change my mind about the lawsuit, though. I also wanted to tell you I just had a case of prewedding jitters—that was why I was going to call it off. I need you, Wyn. Swear to me you'll take care of me, that nothing will ever come between us. I'll never mention that you were in jail. Never ever. I'll count the hours until you get here. Of course I love you. I've always loved you—I was going to marry you. Bring me a present, Wyn, something special. Something pretty. Bye, darling."

Callie lay down on the bed. It was time for her afternoon nap. When she woke up she'd forget all the awful things Bode had said. She'd never think about them again.

21

Bode leaped off the chair the moment he heard Little Hatch. Thank God. One more minute of his own company and he would be a basket case. He ran to the door. The baby's wails were music to his ears. Sela gladly handed him over while Hatch dragged in two suitcases. "He's got a poopy diaper." Bode handed him back. Sela grimaced as she dropped to her knees and withdrew, to Bode's amazement, all kinds of paraphernalia.

"He didn't let out a sound during the whole trip. Guess that means he's going to be a good traveler. Want to hold him now?"

"Aaah," Bode murmured as he brought the downy little head against his cheek. "He smells so sweet."

"This place is depressing," Hatch complained, looking around. "I never would have thought this was Jake's style. Bet he inherited it like this. He's a wide-open man, likes skylights, green plants and half-walls. This place will have me nuts in two days. How about a beer, Bode?"

"In the kitchen, down the hall, last room on the right. Fetch me one, too."

"I'll have a Diet Pepsi," Sela said.

"I have everything set up in the dining room for Little Hatch. It gave me something to do."

"Here you go, Uncle Bode, you can feed the little tyke," Hatch said, holding out a baby bottle. "I'll drink your beer. The kid comes first."

Bode watched in amazement as the baby gobbled the contents of the bottle, burped loudly, and immediately dropped off to sleep. Sela took him, crooning softly.

"She was so upset when she couldn't nurse him herself. Not enough milk. He was always fussing. Actually, he was starving. Soon as we put him on the bottle the kid turned into an angel," Hatch whispered. "She thinks it makes her less of a mother."

"Women are like that," Bode said because he didn't know what else to say. He snatched his beer just as Hatch reached for it.

"Did Brie call?" Sela asked as she popped her diet drink. "Is the turkey thawing?"

"She didn't call while I've been here. Yes, the turkey is thawing. I did everything I was supposed to do and some things I probably shouldn't have done."

Hatch's eyebrows shot upward. "Maybe you better tell us about that."

Bode described his visit to the doctor and his conversation with Callie. "If it was the right thing to do, Hatch, then why do I feel so shitty? I just left her there with an envelope of money. I can't believe I did that."

"I can believe it," Sela said. "I guess she's not coming for dinner."

"No, she won't be coming," Bode said. "What's going to happen to her? She was so upset when I told her about the house. I ripped the only home she ever knew right out from under her. It had to be traumatic. She never liked any of us. It was all a game."

"I know," Sela said gently. "But look at us now and look at Callie. Everything happens for a reason, Bode."

"Mama Pearl . . . God, you should have heard her," Bode said miserably.

"You forget, Bode, I did hear her for a lot of years. Like Brie and even you, I buried it. When I would see something I knew wasn't right I looked the other way. We were all sick little puppies. So what if she isn't going to be here for dinner? We'll make a toast to her and offer up our own Thanksgiving to our well-being. Oh, I hope Brie gets here. She promised. Hatch, what if she doesn't make it?"

"If it's humanly possible, she'll be here, honey. You said yourself, she never breaks a promise."

"It will be my fault if she doesn't come," Bode said.

"Don't flatter yourself, Bode," Sela muttered. "I have this feeling I should go to see Callie and—and say good-bye. Does that make sense? It doesn't seem right that . . . you know. What do you think, Hatch? Bode?"

"Whatever feels right, honey," Hatch said.

"Should I take the baby?"

"No," Hatch and Bode said at the same time.

"Bode, what do you think?"

"If it feels right, do it. I don't think she'll be looking any of us up in the future, so if you want to say good-bye, this is the time to do it."

"Bode, did you ever find out how old Pearl was?" Sela asked as she slipped her arms into her coat.

"Arquette said she was born the same time he was, the year the First World War ended. Arquette said it was written in a book Mr. Parker's daddy kept in the big house. I never saw it myself."

"Pearl was that old? Good Lord, I thought she was maybe seventy at the most. The poor thing just wore out, taking care of that little snot," Sela said grimly. She was out the door a moment later.

"I just love it when she gets like that." Hatch grinned. "You didn't tell me she had so much piss and vinegar in her."

"It didn't matter, Hatch. Sela always was and always will be a constant. Sela kept us all on track. She told it like it was, and she stood up for anything she believed in. Wonder what she'll say to Callie."

"I don't think we want to know, and she isn't going to tell us either. You can count on that."

"Why?" Bode asked, puzzled.

"She has to reconcile that part of her life. She'd never be able to walk away from here knowing Callie was a loose end. She likes things tidy. She knows Brie is settled. They'll always be the sisterless sisters. She knows you're okay and she hopes that one of these days you'll get your shit together and go after Brie and settle down. When that happens her nest will be complete. She would have allowed Callie into that nest. You need to know that. Not now though. Guess she's going to tell her that. Two more beers, Mr. Jessup," Hatch said, putting his feet on the coffee table.

"Yes, sir," Bode said, saluting smartly.

"Callie?"

"Sela. What a surprise!" Callie held out her arms expecting Sela to rush into them. Instead she slipped out of her coat and perched on the edge of the bed.

"How are you, Callie?"

"I was fine until Bode got here. He just up and switched up on me, Sela. I never knew he was so ungrateful. After all we did for him. He left me money—do you believe that? And he stole my house. Told me I should go live with that *plumber* and his wife."

"That plumber and his wife are your parents, Callie. How can you turn your back on them?"

"I don't even like them. Pearl let them touch me. I used to shiver when they did that. One time they gave me a piece of candy, and when no one was looking I threw it away."

"Why?"

"Because they'd touched it, that's why."

"That was unforgivable, Callie. Aren't you the least bit interested to know you have brothers and sisters? You can't be one of the sisterless sisters anymore because you have real ones," Sela said carefully.

"That's stupid," Callie said.

"You never really liked Brie and me, did you?" Sela asked quietly.

"Not really. Do you like this ribbon in my hair, Sela? It's all wrinkled. I wish Pearl was here so she could iron my clothes. Look how crumpled everything is."

"Do you know how to iron, Callie?"

"No, do you?"

"Of course. Even Bode, and he's a guy, knows how to iron. My husband knows how to iron, too."

"I can't believe you married an Indian. Does he have a war bonnet?" Callie giggled.

"He's good and kind, Callie. We have the most gorgeous son. Hatch loves him so much, and he loves me with all his heart. If I said I wanted moonbeams, he'd try like the devil to get them for me. I feel the same way about him. We share everything. He's so rich it makes my head spin. Any other guy would have made me sign a prenup, but not Hatch. He couldn't wait to share. He's like Bode. You don't understand a thing I just said, do you?"

"Of course I do. You snagged a rich husband, you have a baby, and you don't ever have to worry about anything again.

He's still an Indian. You look so plain, Sela. I liked you better with all those glitzy clothes and makeup."

"I was trying to hide behind those things. That was never who I was. If you'd really been my friend like Brie is my friend, you would have known that. I don't want to fight, Callie. I just came here to say good-bye. I don't think our paths will cross again."

"We can send Christmas cards. Why didn't Brie come?"

"She's on assignment. We're hoping she gets here in time for dinner tomorrow. I was really looking forward to us all sitting down and offering up thanks. For your recovery, for my son, for all the good things in our lives. I'm sorry you aren't going to be there to share it with us."

"Thanks to Bode. I would have come if he hadn't been so hateful."

"You owe Bode so much, Callie."

"Don't be silly! I don't owe him anything. I liked him better when he thought he was colored. He knew his place then."

"The way Pearl knew her place?"

"Of course."

"Did you know Pearl was over eighty years old? You probably never even thought about it. You thought she was going to live forever and always be your slave. That's all she was to you. Damn you, Callie, I hate you for that."

"She bought me for fifty dollars. She owned me and because she owned me she was responsible for me. It was fair."

"My God, I've never come across anyone as mean and selfish as you. How in the world are you going to live with yourself?" Anger rivered through Sela. "Pearl . . . Pearl wanted to die first so she'd be in heaven waiting for you. If that isn't love, I don't know what is."

Callie ignored Sela's words. "I'm not going to live by myself. Wyn is coming in the morning and taking me back to

Beaufort. We'll probably get married. He's as rich as your Indian."

Sela's jaw dropped as she stared at Callie in pure amazement. "Are you going to tell him about your parents?"

Callie laughed. "Not likely."

"Maybe I should tell him," Sela said.

"Maybe you shouldn't," Callie said coldly.

"Are you ever going to use your education that Bode and Brie broke their backs for? Are you ever going to practice law?"

"No. What *are* you talking about?"

"Where do you think the money came from, for you to go to school? Where do you think the money came from, for all those fancy dresses and shoes, the dance lessons, the riding lessons? Didn't you ever wonder? Surely you weren't stupid enough to believe Pearl picked it off a tree. They worked for it, hustled night and day so you could have all those extras. Bode did it because he thought he had to do it. Brie did it to make things easier for Bode. I can't forgive you for that. You, Callie Parker *Davis,* are a worthless piece of shit. I can't believe I ever thought of you as my friend."

"I never liked you, Sela. Oh, I loved the flashy clothes you wore and all that makeup. I knew you were white trash just like Brie. You had such an unladylike mouth, always saying such shocking things. Brie was no better with her patched overalls. Girls don't wear those awful things. She put electrical tape on the holes in her sneakers. She was white trash and Bode was . . . Bode was . . . he was colored trash. So there!"

Sela's hand shot out. The sound was like a gunshot. "That's for saying Brie and Bode are trash. I don't care what you think of me, but don't you ever call them that again. You aren't good enough to lick their feet.

"I'm glad I came here today, glad I heard you say everything you said. Now I can go back to my real world with real people who love me for who I am. It's real, Callie, not pretend anymore. I wish you well."

When the door closed behind Sela, Callie picked up the book she'd been reading and said, "Oh pooh, who needs her and her trashy friends anyway. Not me, that's for sure."

Sela sailed into the brownstone and immediately rushed at Hatch. "I will give thanks to God every night of my life that I found you. Bode, come here. You are the best friend; I couldn't ask for one better. I love you both so much—you'll never know just how much. Now, who's going to help me make the stuffing for this turkey, and what are we having for dinner—or is it too late for dinner? Lord, it's after nine. How about Chinese? Bode, you can clean up the baby. Go, go," she said, making shooing motions. "Don't forget the fortune cookies, honey."

Hatch's expression said, "See? I told you she wouldn't say a word."

"What time is it, Hatch?" Sela asked for the fifth time.

"It's three o'clock, honey."

"Where is she? I told her we'd try for four o'clock dinner. She promised, Hatch. I have this awful sick feeling in the pit of my stomach. The turkey's going to dry out."

"So what? Bode and I have eaten our share of dried-out food. We can eat Spam for all I care, or peanut butter and jelly. It's being together that counts. The turkey just doesn't matter, honey."

"Come on, let's watch something on television," Bode said.

"There's nothing on. The parade is over and all they're showing is that lunatic in Pennsylvania. Oh my God, did something happen?" Sela cried. "Why are they showing that stuff today? It's Thanksgiving! Switch the channels, Bode, there must be something else on."

"Sorry, Sela, there's no cable here, just the regular channels and it's on all of them," Bode said.

"Look, they're shooting. We're actually watching whatever this is. Isn't modern technology something?" Hatch said. "Wow, look at all those ambulances and helicopters. Do you think it was some kind of standoff? McKees Rocks is the name of the place. Does that ring a bell for you, honey? Is that where Brie is?"

"She wouldn't tell me," Sela cried. "Sometimes she's so damn professional she makes me sick. Is the FBI there?"

"And the ATF, too," Hatch said, straining to see the figures running around on the television set.

"Does Brie wear a bulletproof vest?" Bode asked hoarsely.

"She said she does," Sela fretted.

"Sela, did Brie say she was in Pennsylvania on assignment?" Bode demanded.

Sela nodded. "She didn't say where though. Why?"

"Because," Bode said, "this commentator is saying three FBI agents were killed, two wounded, and one ATF agent was severely wounded and one killed. Why isn't she here?"

"Let's take it easy and not get carried away," Hatch said firmly. "We need to be quiet so we can hear what they're saying. They aren't going to release the names."

"Why?" Sela whimpered.

"Because, honey, they have to notify the next of kin first. It would be awful for some parent to hear something like that on television."

"Brie has me and Bode down as her next of kin. We aren't home to be notified if she's— We aren't home, Hatch! Do they leave messages like that on answering machines?"

"No, honey, they don't," Hatch said.

"One female FBI agent killed, one female FBI agent

wounded. The ATF agent was a guy." Bode repeated the an-
nouncer's words. "Hatch, don't we have some FBI agents as
clients? They're yours, aren't they?" The phone was in Hatch's
hands before Bode stopped speaking.

"Of course I know what time it is. So you're going to go to
the office and open it up and get me some telephone numbers. I said do it now. Call me back at this number." He hung
up. "Everybody's celebrating early," he grumbled to Bode
and Sela. "Did I miss anything?"

Bode shook his head. He looked down to see his hand
gripped in Sela's. "I have that same sick feeling in the pit of
my stomach that you have," he whispered. "They've taken
the wounded to Pittsburgh General Hospital. Maybe we
should call there."

"They won't give out any information," Hatch said. "Just
hold on here. Brad will call me back, and then I'll call the
agents and ask them to check it out. Look, we can be ready
to go in five minutes, if we have to. If."

"Who *is* that guy?"

"Someone who thinks he's God. It must be some kind of
cult or something. How can anyone follow a guy like that
and believe what he spouts?" Hatch demanded. "Twenty-
three of his followers are dead. Jesus!"

Sela squeezed Bode's hand. He squeezed it back. "Do you
love her, Bode?" she whispered.

"I wanted to tell her. I even tried—from the day I counted
her freckles."

"You gotta say the words, Bode; otherwise, it doesn't
mean anything. A look, a pat on the head isn't good enough.
You can't assume, and you can't presume. You need to work
on that pride of yours."

"God, she was so proud of becoming an agent. She's a good
one too. She graduated in the top five percent of her class.
When she was a cop, she once took me to the firing range. She

hit the bull's-eye dead center each time. When she finished, all there was, was one big hole."

"I know she's hurt, I can feel it," Sela moaned. "You know it too, don't you, Bode?" He nodded numbly.

The phone rang. Hatch scribbled. He dialed and waited, said what he had to say, hung up, and told them, "He's going to call me back."

Hatch picked up the phone in mid-ring. He listened, his face betraying nothing. "Sela, dress the baby. Bode, turn off the oven. I have to call the airport and a cab. Figure out what to do with all that food or this place will be crawling with bugs and roaches. She's in critical condition. They don't know if she'll make it. She's being operated on as we speak. Don't just stand there, move!" he bellowed.

"The vest . . ."

"She got it in the gut, Bode. That's the worst kind."

"How . . . ?"

"She was dragging one of her fellow agents out of the way because he'd been shot. That's how she got it. I thought I told you to move."

An hour later they were airborne.

When most people were sitting down to a late Thanksgiving dinner, they were clustered together waiting to speak to the surgeon who operated on Brie.

"Seventy-two hours. It can go either way. We did all we could. I find praying always helps," the surgeon said kindly.

Hatch took the baby from Sela's arms so she could cuddle with Bode. He strode down the hall in search of the hospital administrator. When he found him he got right to the point. "I asked your charge nurse if I could leave my son in the pediatric ward for three days and she said I had to speak with you. We're the family of Special Agent Canfield. Take care of my son with a private duty nurse and I'll build you a new wing on this hospital. We'll call it the Briana Canfield whatever it is you need. Is it a deal?"

"We'll take good care of him," the administrator said, reaching for the baby. "Agent Canfield is in the best possible hands. I spoke to the surgeon as soon as he finished operating."

"Agent Canfield is my son's godmother," Hatch said with a catch in his voice. The administrator nodded. Hatch left the office knowing his son would be well cared for and his wife would be able to wait out the seventy-two hours with Bode and not worry about the baby.

"I hate hospitals," Sela said somberly the following day. "It was such a nightmare when Callie had her accident."

"I'm sorry I wasn't here when it happened."

"It's this waiting. Staring at Brie through that glass . . . it's like she's someone else. She looks so vulnerable. She likes being in control of her own person, and now she has to depend on other people. I wonder if she knows we're out here," Bode said miserably. "I don't want to lose her. I don't think I could handle that."

"Does this mean you are finally admitting you aren't Superman? Does it mean you are finally going to admit you love that girl? If so, then you need to tell her that when they let us see her. Maybe you should go in the men's room now and stare at yourself in the mirror and practice saying the words so when you do say them they sound convincing," Hatch suggested slyly.

"Just say what you feel, Bode," Sela interrupted. "Brie's the smart one, she'll see through anything else. She's going to make it, isn't she, Hatch?"

"Sure, honey."

They were standing outside the ICU unit, their heads and hands pressed against the glass. All their eyes were misty with tears. Sela tapped lightly on the glass hoping Brie would open her eyes. She did. They all waved wildly, mouthing words of love and encouragement they hoped she could see.

"I think she smiled. It looked like a smile," Sela whispered.

"She's too sick to smile. It was probably a painful grimace," Bode said morosely.

"Think positive. I think it was a smile. You're outnumbered, Bode. Let's go get some fresh coffee. Say, did you call the management company and tell them to send someone to clean the food out of the kitchen?"

"Yeah, I did. They locked up the place. You should tell Jake to sell that horror and buy some tax-free bonds or something. I'm going outside for some fresh air."

He walked for a long time, up and down the crowded streets. At some point he became aware of the shoppers carrying brightly colored Christmas shopping bags. The beginning of the Christmas season. Miracles were supposed to happen during the Christmas season.

His hands were jammed in his pockets, his neck burrowed into his heavy jacket as he shouldered his way through the crowds. What if Brie didn't make it? What if God decided He needed her more? What would he do? Attach himself to Hatch and Sela and live his life through them? Join Jake Deering and become a guide in the wilderness?

Why am I so stupid, so stubborn? Because I can't take being hurt anymore. Brie would never hurt you, his other self argued. Brie cut you loose, went on with her life. She never backed down and never went back on her word. She told you, not in so many words, but she told you nonetheless, that she didn't want anything to do with you. What was it she'd said? "You snooze, you lose." Yeah, that was it.

How in the hell could she think he preferred Callie to her? Because she's a woman, and women think things like that, his other self continued to argue. Sela's right, women need to hear the words. Would she believe him if he got the chance to say them? *Please, God, give me the chance to say the words. I swear I'll take care of her for the rest of her life.* She doesn't need you to take care of her, the argument went on. She proved she can do it herself. She just wanted you to love her.

"I can do both," Bode muttered, "if she'll let me."

He thought about Sela and Hatch and how happy they were. Then he thought about Callie and Mama Pearl.

He realized he was cold, freezing really, and God in heaven—were those really snowflakes he was seeing? He retraced his steps. At the hospital he took the elevator to the fourth-floor pediatric unit, where he stared at Little Hatch for a long time.

He turned when he heard Sela say, "I can't believe he's mine. That I carried him and that I gave birth to him. I swear to God, Bode, I never thought I would be who I am today. You know what? I don't wish for yesterday anymore, and I don't look forward to tomorrow either. I live for today. I realized when Brie got shot just how fragile life is, and how we're here for such a short period of time. Do I sound maudlin, Bode?"

"No. Do you think it's too late for me, Sela?"

"Nope. She loves you, always has, always will. You have to tell her how you feel. You wasted so many years, Bode," Sela said sadly.

"I know. I don't want them back though. I don't want yesterday either."

"Callie does. What does that tell you?" Sela grinned. "Wait till you hear this. She called Wynfield Archer and he's coming to get her today, or was it yesterday? He's out of jail. I've lost track of time. They're probably gone already. Anyway, he's taking her back to Beaufort. Wyn will allow her to live in the past because neither one of them can handle the future. She said she wasn't going to tell him about Mr. and Mrs. Davis. Now *that's* the Callie I know!"

"Are you as tired as I am, Sela?"

"Yes. I'm glad Hatch got them to look after the baby. I couldn't have stayed here otherwise."

"Hey, you promise to add a wing to a hospital, you get what you ask for." Bode grinned.

"Did Hatch do that?" Sela asked proudly.

"Yeah, he did. Indirectly he was doing it for you, Sela. You're never going to hurt him, are you?" Bode asked anxiously.

"I promise you if I ever have the urge to kill him, I'll kill you instead. No, I'll never hurt him. I won't promise not to fight with him though."

The hours dragged by, one after the other. They were sound asleep on the hard green plastic chairs when the surgeon and hospital administrator shook their shoulders. The surgeon spoke first. "She's out of danger. Recovery will be slow, but she's young and healthy. You can go in one at a time for five minutes each. Then I suggest you go someplace and clean up."

Bode's heart thumped in his chest. It was time.

"You go first, Bode," Sela said.

"Mr. Littletree, could I see you for a moment? If you'd just sign this paper we can get things under way."

"My pleasure, sir," Hatch said, scribbling his name. "Remember now, it's to be called the Briana Canfield Unit or whatever it is you're going to build."

"It will be part of the agreement, Mr. Littletree."

"Brie, it's Bode. Are you awake?"

"I am now."

"I'm glad you're okay. We've been hanging around for the past three days. Hatch and Sela are here. How could you be so dumb as to get shot? I thought you were one of the best."

"I am the best."

"I was teasing," Bode said.

"I wasn't. Bad luck on my part."

"Will you marry me, Brie?"

"Nope."

"Why?" Bode demanded.

"Don't want you feeling sorry for me."

"I don't feel sorry for you. I'm sorry for all the . . . whatever it was I did that I shouldn't have. I love you. I think I started loving you the day I counted your freckles. Brie Day—do you remember?"

"You said I was special. I believed you."

"Did I ever thank you for all you did for me?" Bode asked gruffly.

"A time or two," Brie said wanly.

"I do love you. I wanted to tell you a thousand times. I have to believe it wasn't our time then. That's what Mama Pearl always said. I was going to drag you away and tell you how I felt and . . . ask you. Before we knew you were shot. I had it all planned. The only thing I didn't know was what your answer would be. So, what is the answer?" Bode asked anxiously.

"Get on your knees. What kind of half-assed proposal is this?"

Bode dropped to his knees. "Will you marry me?"

"Damn right. It took you long enough, Bode Jessup." A second later she was asleep, a smile on her face. He turned in time to see Hatch and Sela's fists shoot upward. "Yeah!" they chorused.

"She said yes, huh?" Hatch said, slamming him on the back.

Bode nodded. His tongue felt fuzzy in his mouth. "She's asleep. Sorry if I took your turn. I told her you were here."

"We're outta here," Hatch said. "I'm gonna get my kid and take my family home. You need anything, call."

"I will."

"Bode, I'm so happy for you. So very, very happy. I wish Pearl was here so she could see how it all turned out. I wish that more than anything."

"I think she knows, Sela."

"You're okay, Bode Jessup." Sela grinned.

"So are you, Mrs. Littletree."

"We might not be flesh and blood, but we're family."

"Forever and ever," Bode said, hugging her.

Inside the ICU unit, Brie opened her eyes and smiled as she watched through the window. "Thank you, God," she whispered.

Six months later, on the first day of June, Brie Canfield and Bode Jessup were married. Nine months later the Jessups were blessed with twin girls, whose names were Pearl and Sela Jessup.

Connect with Us

Visit us online at
KensingtonBooks.com
to read more from your favorite authors, see books
by series, view reading group guides, and more.